An Orphan's Promise

Cathy Sharp is happily married and lives with her husband in a small Cambridgeshire village. They like visiting Spain together and enjoy the benefits of sunshine and pleasant walks, while at home they love their garden and visiting the Norfolk seaside.

Cathy loves writing because it gives pleasure to others, she finds writing an extension of herself and it gives her great satisfaction. Cathy says, 'There is nothing like seeing your book in print, because so much loving care has been given to bringing that book into being.'

Also by Cathy Sharp

The Orphans of Halfpenny Street
The Little Runaways
Christmas for the Halfpenny Orphans
The Boy with the Latch Key
An Orphan's Courage
The Girl in the Ragged Shawl
The Barefoot Child
The Winter Orphan

A Daughter's Sorrow
A Daughter's Dream
A Daughter's Choice

CATHY SHARP

An Orphan's Promise

HarperCollins*Publishers*

HarperCollins*Publishers*
The News Building,
1 London Bridge Street,
London SE1 9GF

A Paperback Original 2020
3

www.harpercollins.co.uk

A catalogue record for this book
is available from the British Library

This novel is entirely a work of fiction.
The names, characters and incidents portrayed in it are
the work of the author's imagination. Any resemblance to
actual persons, living or dead, events or localities is
entirely coincidental.

ISBN: 978-0-00-838761-7

Set in Sabon LT Std 11/14pt by
Palimpsest Book Production Limited, Falkirk, Stirlingshire

Printed and bound in Great Britain by CPI Group (UK) Ltd,
Croydon CR0 4YY

MIX
Paper from
responsible sources
FSC
www.fsc.org
FSC™ C007454

This book is produced from independently certified FSC™ paper
to ensure responsible forest management.

For more information visit: www.harpercollins.co.uk/green

PROLOGUE

'I'm 'ungry,' the child whined, dabbing miserably at her dripping nose. 'I want Ma! I want ter go 'ome!' She coughed harshly and rubbed at her thin chest.

'You know that ain't goin' ter 'appen fer a while,' Charlie said eyeing his sister with a mixture of brotherly affection and concern. Maisie was sickly, though the doctors said she would grow out of it; all she needed was warmth and care, but at the moment he had neither to offer her. 'Ma is in the 'ospital and she's proper bad after what that devil did to her.'

Maisie looked at him, her eyes filling with tears. He saw the fear behind the tears and knew that she was remembering the night when Ronnie the Greek, their mother's pimp, had thrown them out of the house in a temper. Charlie had gone back in to find food for them and a coat for her, because it was chilly and that horrible man had caught him and given him a beating. He'd told Charlie to clear off before he broke his bleedin' neck, but when their mother had protested that her children were cold and hungry, he'd turned on her, hammering at her with his fists until she fell unconscious

1

to the ground and then kicking her in the head. Charlie had gone for him then, kicking, punching and biting until Ronnie had knocked him down and stormed out of the house.

Charlie had tried to wake his mother but she wouldn't open her eyes so he'd run to a neighbour for help and then the police had come and his mother had been taken to the hospital. Charlie and Maisie had hidden behind the scullery door and listened until Ma was taken away in an ambulance and then made their escape with what food they could find in the pantry. The police had asked the neighbours to bring them in as soon as they came home and so they'd stayed clear of the house, hiding in derelict buildings of which there were many in the back alleys near the docks.

Charlie knew that he couldn't look after his sister properly yet. He needed to find work and in these hard times that was easier said than done. Scores of men were standing on the corner of Button Street and the roads nearby, eyes dull, shoulders slumped with the despair of knowing that another day was passing without hope of finding a decent job, many already on the streets because they could not feed their children or keep a roof over their heads. Competition for somewhere to rest was fierce and the children had been chased away from all the places where it was safe to sleep.

'Clear orf! We don't want kids 'ere!' Charlie had been yelled at and cuffed more than once as he tried to find a spot out of the wind and rain.

'Come on,' he told Maisie and took her hand. 'We'll go to the police station and tell them we ain't got anywhere to live.'

'They'll lock us up,' Maisie said fearfully.

'Nah, they'll take us somewhere warm and safe and feed us.'

'I'm frightened, Charlie.' Maisie looked up at him and he took her small hand gently in his. 'I wish Ma was 'ome.'

'So do I, but she ain't,' he said. 'I'm not afraid of anyone or anything, Maisie.' It wasn't quite true but Charlie knew he had to protect his sister because there was no one else that would bother about them. So, it was down to him. 'We'll do what they tell us until I can earn a bit of money and then we'll run away. Don't worry, Maisie. I'll look after yer.'

Maisie looked up at him with the trusting eyes of a little kitten. He smiled because she was his sister and he loved her. Ma had done her best but she'd fallen foul of a brute. That brute was going to pay one day. Charlie wasn't sure how but he would find a way . . .

'Come on then,' he said. 'If we're lucky they will feed us – and I'm 'ungry too!'

'I am concerned,' Lady Rosalie said to the woman sitting opposite her in the parlour of her London house. A modest Georgian terrace, she preferred it to the larger house in the country where she'd lived with Sir George until his death – and to the historic but draughty castle where, as the daughter of an earl, she'd grown up. 'I'm sure you will agree that the Adoption of Children Act of 1926 was done with the best intent, but too many adoptions are being granted to those who are not suitable – and, in some cases, utterly wrong for parenthood.'

'I quite agree with you, my lady,' said Mary Thurston,

Matron of the Lady Rosalie Infirmary – affectionately called 'the Rosie' by the residents of Button Street and the surrounding lanes in the grimy district of Whitechapel in London's East End. It was Lady Rosalie who, as a prominent member of the welfare committee interested in providing safe homes for damaged children, had first badgered the council into setting up the infirmary. They had named it for her, though in her opening speech she had dedicated it to her late husband, whose death had inspired her to fight for the poor of the East End.

Lady Rosalie nodded. 'It was thought that adoption or fostering could only benefit the children, but some unscrupulous persons are misusing it and a new law needs to be brought in to safeguard the children.'

'I fear that to be the case – a sad fact of life, my lady,' Matron replied.

It was now 1936 and the Act that had, in 1926, been intended to help orphaned children was, in many cases, being sadly misused. People applied for the care of orphans only to abuse them, or for the small allowance given, very little of which was then spent on the children it was meant for.

'My dear Mary,' Lady Rosalie said, 'I've told you before, no titles are necessary between us. You are not just Matron to me but a friend I know I can trust – and we are in perfect agreement on what needs to be done.' She smiled at her friend of many years.

'If only you had a free hand, Rosalie . . .' Matron said. 'We could do so much more.'

'I raise funds for the infirmary and because of that my voice is listened to in committee,' Lady Rosalie replied. 'Unfortunately, I have only so much time and influence – and there is so much more I want to do.' Her main work was in the provision of reliable foster parents and this took much time and research.

'Are you speaking with regard to those refugee children you mentioned earlier?'

'Yes – I've learned of a group of orphaned children who are coming in from Spain, escaping from the terrible violence there, and I would appreciate any help you can give me with placing them.'

Mary Thurston had been the senior nurse in the expensive private hospital where Lady Rosalie's husband had died of a crippling illness some eight years earlier. It was during one of their long vigils by his bedside that the two women had bonded. Sister Thurston had confided that she wanted to devote her life to the poor of the East End, who could not always afford medical care, and the grieving widow had campaigned tirelessly to set up the Rosie in memory of her husband. She had one son, now fourteen and at boarding school. During the holidays she devoted her time to his happiness, thoroughly spoiling him, but she had longed for a large family and, to compensate for her lack, she had become active in several charitable institutions and sat on the boards of various committees, the most important set up to monitor foster carers.

'I know you have been lobbying your friends in Parliament again,' Mary replied, nodding her approval. 'What chance is there of an amendment to this act, which would prevent those wicked advertisements in the papers?'

Lady Rosalie tutted, because it was scandalous that some people thought it perfectly acceptable to advertise babies – effectively for sale – through the medium of a newspaper, when fostering had never been intended to be used in that way.

'Very little at the moment! I do not know who is worse – those who sell their own children, those who take the children of the poor and send them off to Australia or give them to unsuitable foster parents, who do it only for what they are paid – or those who have the power to change things and do nothing.'

Mary shook her head. 'I thought, if we could use a part of the children's ward at the infirmary to look after orphans on a temporary basis, particularly if they are sickly, as so many are, you might arrange something more permanent for them?'

'Now that is a very good idea,' Lady Rosalie said. 'I do not have the power to act alone, naturally, but my recommendations go a long way . . .'

Mary Thurston, Matron to her staff and the patients, smiled. Very few would go against Lady Rosalie, a dynamic personality who was far too young to be a retiring widow. Married to a man ten years her senior when she was eighteen, she was now just thirty-five.

'Then I shall implement the idea at once,' Mary said. 'We'll use the small ward as a temporary refuge for orphans who are brought in sick, but we cannot keep them for longer than they need to be perfectly well to go to new homes.'

'Good, we are agreed,' Lady Rosalie said. She stood up as Mary prepared to leave and kissed her on both cheeks. 'I bless the day that you came into my life, Mary. You helped me through a time when I felt I had nothing to live for – and now I have so much . . .'

CHAPTER 1

'Eh, but you're a lovely girl,' Woody Jacobs said, causing Nurse Sarah to turn and look at him as he lay propped up against the pillows of his narrow cot in the infirmary ward for men. At past seventy years, his chest was weak and he'd been with them on and off through most of the winter. 'You'll make someone a fine wife, nurse.'

Sarah walked over to him, smiled and adjusted his pillows, then, as he began wheezing, she offered him a glass of water, holding it patiently as he sipped and pulled a face at the taste of lukewarm water.

'I'd rather have a mug of beer.'

'I expect you would.' Sarah laughed. 'But I'm afraid the infirmary's funds don't run to that sort of treat, Mr Jacobs.'

'Pity, that,' he said, a twinkle in his eye. 'Tell me, why hasn't some fine young man snapped you up yet?'

'I *have* someone special,' Sarah told him. She liked talking to Mr Jacobs and never minded his questions, though Sister Norton would have called some of them impertinent. 'We're saving for a home of our own and a proper wedding.'

7

'Ah, so that's it.' Woody nodded his understanding. 'I thought it was strange you not havin' a ring on your finger – a lovely girl like you.'

'They wouldn't let me nurse you if I was married,' Sarah told him, though she wasn't sure that was strictly true. It was a regulation that nurses must not be married in hospitals run by the council or the state, but the infirmary relaxed these rules, because as Matron and Lady Rosalie agreed, the best nurses were often those that had married and returned to their work later in life. Woody was here, not because he was chronically sick, but because he had no home and, living on the streets in the winter, he contracted lots of colds and coughs making his chest painful for him. Matron said that he would always be admitted to the men's ward, providing that there was a bed for him, and he treated it as a home from home. In the summer they wouldn't see him, but in the winter he turned up regularly, coughing and wheezing.

'Nurse Cartwright!' Sister Norton's tone was sharp. She did not approve of the way the old man came and went as often as he pleased. Had she been in charge he would not have been admitted, unless he really needed to be in the ward for the chronically sick. 'I have a job for you if you've finished chatting.'

The sarcasm in the ward sister's tone made Sarah flinch but she didn't allow her expression to change as she said, 'Yes, Sister, what can I do for you?'

'The police have brought in two children,' Sister Norton said. 'There is only Nurse Anne on duty in the children's ward this evening and I want them checked over. Go along and see if they need isolation or simply a good wash.'

'Yes, Sister Norton.'

Sarah caught Woody's wink and had to smother a laugh. She left him propped up against his pillows with his eyes shut. Sister Norton might intimidate her nurses and the cleaners if she caught them doing something wrong, but Woody took her scolding in his stride. Not for the first time, Sarah wondered what had led the old man to a life on the streets. Had he ever had a family? And if so, what had happened to them?

Walking briskly to the children's ward, Sarah noticed that the smell of disinfectant was still strong. The walls were painted with a dark cream gloss, because that was easier to clean, and once a month the cleaners had to scrub them with a fluid that was so overpowering that it took Sarah's breath. However, it helped to keep down the infection rate – or that was what Matron believed.

Matron was in charge of the day-to-day running of the infirmary. Sister Ruth Linton was her assistant on the critical ward and Nurse Anne was a probationer who had not yet taken her final exams. She spent much of her time looking after the children, some of whom were actually ill, while others were simply orphans brought in by the police if they were unwell, because there was no room for them anywhere else. The orphanages in London were always filled to capacity.

Hearing indignant squeals coming from the large washroom next to the children's ward, Sarah went in and smiled as she saw the young probationer, her sleeves rolled up to the elbows, valiantly trying to cope with two very dirty and clearly rebellious children.

'Hello,' she said, 'may I be of help?'

'Oh yes, please!' Nurse Anne looked relieved. 'This is Charlie and his sister Maisie Howes. Their mother is in hospital and Constable Steve Jones brought them to us to look after until a place can be found at an orphanage—'

'Ain't goin' to no orphanage,' Charlie burst out, looking belligerent. 'And I ain't gettin' in that there thing, neither.'

'I ain't neither,' Maisie said copying her brother, her bottom lip pulled down, tears hovering on her lashes.

'Don't you want a nice ham sandwich and a bun with a cup of orange squash?' Sarah asked and saw Charlie's eyes light up at the mention of food.

'I *am* 'ungry,' Maisie said and the tears spilled over. 'Ain't 'ad nuthin' for three days.'

'You 'ad a bun day afore yesterday,' Charlie said and glared at Sarah. 'Why can't we have the food now? The cops said yer would feed us.'

'And so we will,' Sarah promised with a smile. 'But we need you to be clean so we can pop you into bed and then give you your supper.'

'I have a strip wash regular once a week. Ma puts washing soda in the bowl and sponges us both down.'

'I'm sure she does,' Sarah said, and moved her hand back and forth in the bath, making it splash a bit. 'But the water is lovely and warm and you could have a bit of fun . . .' She splashed a few drops of water at him and he recoiled and then moved closer. He leaned over and put his hand in the water, splashing her back. Sarah nodded. 'Why don't you both get in?' She pointed at the two baths side by side.

'I ain't gettin' naked in front of you!'

'Keep your pants on then,' Sarah said and he hesitated.

'Ain't got nuthin' under me trousers . . .'

'Oh, I see . . .' Sarah looked round for inspiration and then handed him a small towel. 'Hold this over your front, Charlie. I promise not to look.'

Still suspicious, he stripped off his things. Sarah and Nurse Anne turned their backs while he got into the water. Maisie stripped off her dress and a pair of tatty knickers before jumping into the adjoining bath. The pair of them indulged in a lot of splashing around, giggling as the water wetted the floor. It was clearly a new experience and one they enjoyed once they let go of their inhibitions. Neither of them objected when Sarah took a sponge and rubbed soap on it before scrubbing their backs.

Charlie winced a bit and she saw there were several yellowish bruises on his back and arms that were obviously still tender.

'What happened to your back, Charlie?'

'It were just a fight at school,' he said but she sensed he was lying.

'It was the bloke Ma brought 'ome,' Maisie said and tears trickled down her cheeks. 'He beat Charlie 'cos he went in the house to get some food for me when he'd thrown us out – and Charlie cheeked him when he asked what he was doin' – and he beat Ma bad 'cos she stuck up fer us. That's why she's in the 'ospital!'

'Shut up, Maisie,' Charlie warned. 'We don't snitch!'

'If that man hurt your mum he deserves to be snitched on,' Sarah said. 'Sometimes it's best to tell the truth – as long as he isn't around to hit you again.'

'I ain't scared of 'im,' Charlie said. 'I ain't scared of nuthin'.'

'Good,' she told them. 'You can finish washing yourselves and afterwards I'll give your heads a good wash with this stuff, too.'

'It smells awful,' Charlie said sniffing the bottle.

'That's what the nits think – and it makes them hop off,' Sarah said.

He grinned.

'You ain't bad,' he told her. 'You wash Maisie's hair. She's got 'em the worst and I can do me own.'

'Yes, I'm sure you can,' Sarah agreed and nodded at Nurse Anne as she brought a pile of clean clothes for the children. 'How old are you, Charlie?'

'Fourteen,' he declared truculently. 'I ought ter be at work . . .'

'Not quite yet,' Sarah said. She didn't think he could be much more than twelve but didn't contradict him. The police report would hopefully be more accurate and she would read it after she had brought these two their supper. 'Well, you both seem healthy to me, apart from those bruises – just in need of a wash and some food. We might ask Dr Kent to take a look at you when he visits, but there's no need to put you in the isolation ward.'

'Ma looked after us good – leastwise, until she got in with that bloke.' Charlie rubbed at his eyes. 'I don't know what he done to her – but she weren't the same. I think he gives her somefin' – funny stuff what changed 'er. Her eyes go all strange after he's been. He's a bad 'un, miss.'

'Do you know his name?'

Maisie opened her mouth and shut it as her brother gave her a glare.

'Nah,' he said. 'Ma was goin' ter tell us but he told 'er ter shut up and 'it her.'

'Charlie didn't half kick his ankles and when he grabbed 'im he bit his hand,' Maisie said, clearly in awe of her brother's courage. 'He give Charlie a proper pastin' and threw us out – and we hadn't had nuffin' ter eat all day, 'cos we was waitin' for Ma to come 'ome. We sneaked in again, though.'

Sarah nodded. The man who had bullied these children had also used force to subdue their mother, but besides that he might have given her drugs of some kind. Evil substances that changed personalities and made addicts do things they would not normally do. Sarah's boyfriend Jim had told her about the prostitutes he saw when he was working at the pub.

'They come in and they don't know where they are or what they're doin',' he'd said once. 'The pimps give them these foul drugs and then set them to work and after a while they're so mad for the heroin or whatever it is that they do whatever their pimp tells them to . . .'

Hearing the children's story made her angry. These children had suffered because of what had happened to their mother and Sarah would have liked to punish the man who had used the unfortunate woman, but she knew there was nothing she could do. Charlie and Maisie were not the only children to tell similar tales, but the police never seemed to do much about it. They removed the children from their homes, but the men in the shadows got away with their crimes over and over again.

'Thank you so much,' Nurse Anne said when both children were wrapped in warm towels. 'I don't think I could have managed without you.'

Sarah nodded. The young probationer loved children and enjoyed looking after them, but children like Charlie and Maisie needed a firm hand when they first came in.

'Well, if you can pop them into pyjamas and get them to bed, I'll bring their supper. I might even find a little jelly and ice cream as well as that sandwich and bun.'

Sister Ruth Linton was in the kitchen making a pot of tea and setting a tray with cups and saucers.

'Ah, Nurse Cartwright,' she said and smiled. 'Have you got those little tearaways settled then?'

'Yes, we managed it between us,' Sarah said diplomatically. 'They just needed a little persuasion.'

'Bribery, I presume,' the senior nurse said with a twinkle in her eyes. 'I find it is often the best way with these children. Nurse Anne will learn in time.'

Sarah liked Sister Linton. She had a sense of humour and seemed more approachable than Matron, who could be a little stern.

'Nurse Anne is very good with the little children,' Sarah said. 'Charlie is about thirteen going on thirty and he thinks he is the man of the house and can take care of things.'

'I expect that is because his father was lost at sea some years ago,' Sister Ruth Linton said. 'I read the police constable's report. The mother looked after them well and they both attended school fairly regularly until

14

about six months ago . . . but things have gone down-hill since then.'

'I expect it is this man – her pimp, I imagine. He is the reason she's in hospital and Charlie's back is covered in bruises.'

'Should we have the doctor to him?'

'Yes, when he comes but there is no need to call him out tonight,' Sarah said. 'It's happened frequently by the look of the bruises – some old, some new. Still, it may be best to get Dr Kent to look when he comes.'

'I'll make sure he is told,' Sister Linton said and picked up her tray. 'I'm taking this to Matron. She has been sitting with a female patient all night. Sal is not expected to last until morning and Matron will not leave her while she lives.'

'I'm sorry,' Sarah said. She understood Matron's wish to remain with a patient she cared for. The nurses were taught never to become fond of a patient but it happened just the same. When you looked after someone, day in and day out, it was always a wrench when they passed away. 'It is a sad time for her.'

'Sal is a believer and has made her peace with God; she will go to her rest soon,' Ruth Linton said. 'However, she is suffering and Matron is trying to ease her passing. I shall take them both a cup of tea.'

Sarah got on with her sandwich making. In a place like this death was a part of life; despite all the efforts of the nurses and doctors it could not be avoided.

She found some jelly and took two small ice creams from the refrigerator. They were kept for the sick children, but Sarah doubted Charlie and Maisie had ever tasted them before and wanted to give them a real treat.

Returning to the ward, she discovered them sitting in bed, faces shining and clean, like a pair of little angels. They sat forward eagerly as she set the tray on Maisie's bed, handing Charlie his sandwiches and a bun on a plate and placing the dishes of jelly and ice cream on the little cabinet between their beds.

'Enjoy your supper. I have to go back to my own ward, but I'll come and see how you're getting on tomorrow night when I'm on duty.'

'Yeah, all right,' Charlie said, his mouth full of ham sandwich. 'This is smashing, nurse – yer all right.'

'Thanks, I'll take that as a compliment,' Sarah said. On impulse she bent and kissed first his cheek and then Maisie's. 'Look after your sister, Charlie. You're both safe now you're here.'

She left them both eating happily. They were the only two in their part of the ward, which was divided by a screen. Nurse Jenny Brown was on the other side of the screen, attending to a young girl named Dora who had been brought in that day with a cut on her leg. It had been bandaged and she'd been fed and looked after earlier, but she was frightened, complaining that her leg was painful.

The worst thing about it was that her injury had come from the man who had been her foster carer. He and his wife had gone out to get drunk and when they returned he'd hit the child and sent her tumbling down the stairs. The wife had come to her senses quickly and sent for the doctor, who had acted immediately, sending the girl to the infirmary, whereupon, her husband had hit his wife and sent her flying to teach her to keep her mouth shut. She'd told the doctor that the girl had

16

fallen, but he'd reported the incident to the police and they were investigating. However, cases like this often went unresolved, because the children and wives were too frightened to speak against the bullies that hurt them.

'It will be a little sore for a while, Dora,' Jenny told her. 'But there's no need to worry. I'll get you a nice cup of cocoa and that will help you to sleep.'

'I thought you were on the women's ward this evening?' Sarah queried as Jenny left the child to fetch her cocoa. 'Isn't Nurse Anne on duty here?'

'I am on women's, but Dora lives in my street so I thought I'd pop in and see her – her mother is on the women's ward and was worried about her . . .'

'Mother and daughter are in hospital together?' Sarah was surprised.

'Mrs Swan says they fell down the stairs but I know what her husband is like and I've heard he knocked them both about. Of course, Mrs Swan will never report him, though she called the doctor to the girl and *he* did, so maybe this time the police will give him a talking to.' Not that she thought it would do much good! The only way would be to imprison him and that would leave the wife and children without financial support, so it was not a solution.

'These bullied wives never do report it.' The nurses shook their heads over the folly of women who put up with bullying husbands. 'But when a child in their care gets hurt it is time something was done.'

Sarah nodded to Jenny and returned to her own ward. Sister Norton was sitting at the desk but rose as she walked towards her.

'Everyone appears to be sleeping, nurse,' she said. 'Are those children in bed?'

'Yes, eating their supper. They were just hungry and dirty – though Charlie had been beaten over the past few weeks.'

'By the same person as attacked their mother?' Sister Norton's dark eyes narrowed in suspicion. 'Why *will* they get themselves into these predicaments?'

'Her husband died at sea. She was probably just trying to earn a living to feed the kids.'

'Surely there are other ways?'

'For us, but not always for a mother with two growing children,' Sarah said. 'Jim's mother found it very hard to bring up her four children after her husband died in an accident at work – that's why we're saving a nest egg before we marry. He doesn't want it to happen to me.'

'I dare say you would be missed – although Matron might keep you on if you marry. She is a law unto herself . . . a good nurse and caring, but I'm not sure she understands what it is like to live in the real world, and how often married nurses are obliged to take time off.'

Sarah was surprised; it was unusual for Sister to criticize Matron.

Sister Norton bid her good night and left and Sarah walked round her ward, making sure everyone was peaceful. It was easy to think someone was sleeping when they were actually lying awake and in discomfort. Medicine could be given to those it had been prescribed for, but for others a nice cup of tea would often do the trick – and if she knew Woody, he would be hoping she would take him one before the end of her shift. She would check everyone else first and then see if her favourite patient was really asleep or just ignoring Sister Norton.

CHAPTER 2

Jenny left the infirmary at the same time as Sarah Cartwright. They smiled at each other in understanding for both were yawning. It had been a long night and the wind was chilly this March day in 1936, a hint of rain in the air as they hurried for the bus. A shelter had recently been built for waiting passengers and it was a little warmer behind the glass panels.

'I'll be glad when spring finally comes,' Sarah said. 'I don't like the winter.'

'Nor me,' Jenny said and moved a strand of long dark hair out of her eyes. She envied Sarah being blonde and having hair that waved naturally when she let it down from the tight knot she wore at work. Her own hair was straight and shiny and she normally wore it in a neat pleat at the back of her head. 'Have you seen the Charlie Chaplin film that's on at the Gaumont?'

'No. It's ages since Jim took me anywhere but the pub. We're saving hard and we just go for a drink once a week . . . and I'd rather see Douglas Fairbanks Jr than Charlie Chaplin; he's more romantic.'

'Yes, dreamy. Anyway, who needs the cinema when

you've got a chap like yours?' Jenny said with a look of envy. 'When are you gettin' married?'

'When Jim thinks we can afford it,' Sarah said. 'Oh, here's my bus. Yours should be just behind. Probably see you tomorrow, then.'

Sarah leapt on her bus and Jenny craned her neck looking for the one she needed, which usually followed up behind the number forty-five, but this time there was no sign of it and she pulled her coat collar up round her neck.

'Cold, isn't it?' a male voice said from behind her and Jenny turned to see a man in a fawn overcoat and a trilby hat pulled down over his brow. He looked smart, she thought, a bit like a film star with his dark, brooding good looks and she smiled. 'It feels as if it might snow again.'

'Oh, I do hope not,' Jenny said. 'I can't wait for it to be summer again.'

'Winter has its place, if you've got a nice log fire and someone to share it with,' he said. 'I couldn't help overhearing you and your friend just now – I like Chaplin's films. I don't suppose you'd like to come with me one evening?'

Jenny was taken aback by his boldness. She was just considering how she could make him aware that she wasn't the sort of girl who could be picked up just like that when her bus came around the corner. Torn between taking the cheeky stranger down a peg or two and not wanting to miss her chance, she waved frantically at the bus to stop. Then, just as she leapt on, she turned her head and looked at him.

'Maybe – when I know you better!'

'Hey, don't go!' He moved towards the bus as if he would make a flying leap to catch it but it was too quick for him and Jenny laughed to herself as she saw the frustration in his face. Her abrupt departure had done all she'd wanted to, giving him a message she'd been unable to form in words. He was attractive, and Jenny really wanted a boyfriend to take her out and maybe to get serious with, but if he thought she was easy he would have to think again. She'd been brought up decently and her sister Lily would hit the roof if she knew Jenny had been in danger of agreeing to visit the cinema with a stranger.

Sitting in one of the front seats in the bus, Jenny smiled to herself. She'd definitely felt attracted to the handsome stranger who certainly had film star looks, but it wouldn't do to let herself be picked up off the street, even though, for a moment, she'd been tempted.

If the stranger had also been attracted, he would return to the bus stop and introduce himself. Jenny would wait and hope – because she was nearly twenty and she'd never had a proper boyfriend, just friends who'd walked her back from school and sometimes offered a mint humbug.

Jenny's smile vanished as she thought of her home life. She lived with her elder sister Lily and their grandmother, Mabel Brown. Mabel was half blind these days but in her own kitchen she knew exactly where everything was and refused to be made an invalid. The two sisters loved the woman who had brought them up single-handed after their parents died, and did their best to look after her now she wasn't so well. Lily, and then Jenny, had trained to be nurses and they both worked for the Rosie Infirmary. At the moment, Lily worked days and Jenny worked nights and that meant they didn't have to leave Gran alone much, though she was forever telling them to go out and have a good time while they were young.

'I was courtin' by the time I was your age,' she'd told Jenny only a few days earlier. 'We made it to the altar just before your father was born but not by much. I lost my man to the Great War – too old for the army, they said, so they gave him a job on the docks, cleaning the ships – and that's what he was doin' when one of them Zeppelins fell on the docks and killed him. That's sod's law, that is, my girl. If he'd gone to fight same as he wanted, he'd probably 'ave come back.'

Jenny knew Gran would have told her she should have grabbed her chance with the stranger, but Lily would say that no men were to be trusted and certainly not one who tried to pick her up at a bus stop! Jenny wondered if it was Lily's attitude to men that had held her back, making her slow to respond to any overtures from the opposite sex, even the young curate who had come to ask after Gran and spent his time staring at Jenny. Her sister had had her heart broken by a man. Jenny knew that, even though she didn't know the details of Lily's unhappy love affair, which had happened when she was eighteen, and Jenny was still at junior school. If she asked, Lily just turned away and refused to answer. All she would say was that Jenny would be a fool to trust any man.

'We're dedicated nurses,' she was fond of saying. 'What do we want with marriage and a husband?'

'What about children?' Jenny asked once but the look

on Lily's face had made her wish she hadn't spoken and since then she'd not mentioned the subject once. For herself, she knew that being a nurse was only a part of the life she wanted – a husband and children were her dream for the future, though she never mentioned it when Lily was around, because she didn't want to remind her sister of what she'd lost.

As the bus slowed at her stop, Jenny got to her feet and made her way down the interior. She wanted to call in at the little shop on the corner of Little Lane and buy a packet of tea, some biscuits, and a tin of corned beef. She would get a fresh loaf too and then she could make some sandwiches for her and Gran; corned beef and sweet pickle was one of the elderly lady's favourites and they nearly always had it on a Friday when Jenny got paid.

Sarah arrived home and put the kettle on minutes before Jim knocked on their back door. Her mother looked at her, eyebrows raised as she glanced in the mirror, fluffing out her hair before she went to answer it.

'Set the clock by you, lad,' Mrs Cartwright said as Jim entered and pulled her daughter into a loving embrace. 'If my Bob had been as reliable in the mornings, he'd be gang master now instead of standing in line waiting for a job.'

'You can't blame Dad,' Sarah said, even though she knew her father was sometimes the last to join the queue of jobless men waiting on the docks for a chance to earn a few quid. 'With his back he ought to have retired years ago.'

'He would if we could afford it,' Mrs Cartwright

said. 'He keeps sayin' we'll be off to the country when you're wed, my girl. A little cottage, vegetables, fruit, hens and a couple of pigs – that's his dream.'

'It's not yours though, is it, Mum?' Sarah said, leading Jim to the table and cutting him a slice of seed cake. 'Eat that while I make the tea, love.'

'Does it matter what I want?' her mother asked ruefully. 'Your father's needs come first and always have.'

'Don't talk like that, Mum,' Sarah chided. 'He's a lot better than most – just imagine how you'd feel if Dad came home drunk three or four times a week like Sid Harding.'

'I wouldn't put up with it like Ruby does!' Mrs Cartwright spoke of her neighbour in a belligerent tone. 'I told her only yesterday she should put her foot down – did you hear him shouting in their yard the other night? Keeping folk awake!'

'I was at the infirmary,' Sarah said. 'Ruby works hard there, cleaning the wards. She must need her sleep and it can't be easy living with a man like Sid.'

'It's because he can't earn a living wage,' Jim put in frowning. The one thing about living in the close-knit communities of the East End was that everyone knew everyone else in their own street and the roads nearby. Jim often saw Sid Harding propping up the bar of the pub where he worked. The Crown and Anchor was down near the East India Docks and always busy. Jim knew most of the men who frequented the docks well. 'Don't be too hard on him. He thinks the world of his daughter Julia – and Ruby too – but it makes him feel inadequate that he can't keep them properly and his wife has to work as a skivvy at the Rosie. You know what the situation is like at the moment – there's never enough work for all the men.'

'It would be a help if Sid brought what he did earn home,' Mrs Cartwright said. 'Anyway, how are you getting on, lad? Any news on your promotion yet?'

Jim had applied to be the manager of the Crown and Anchor which had just been renovated. He was hoping that he would get the job, because the wages would be better and there would be living accommodation over the pub. If he got his wish, it would mean he and Sarah could bring their marriage forward. He sipped his tea and shook his head.

'I wish they would hurry up and make up their minds. If I don't get the job, I'll have to think about doing something else. Life is running away with us and it's time we were planning our wedding.'

'Couldn't agree more,' Mrs Cartwright said. 'I want to live to see my grandchildren – and Bob wants that cottage in the country.'

'Mum!' Sarah laughed. 'If you don't mind, *I* might have an opinion about all this.'

'You know you adore me and can't wait to be my wife,' Jim said and kissed her on the lips. He winked at his future mother-in-law, with whom he got on like a house on fire. 'I'll give the brewery a ring today and see what they have to say – now I'll go and let Sarah get some sleep. I'll pop in around teatime, love.'

'All right.' Sarah gave him a quick hug and let him go. Working nights meant that the only times they got to see each other on a working day were if Jim popped round a couple of times. When Sarah wasn't at the infirmary, he took a few hours off to be with her and they usually took a walk to a nice pub in the Whitechapel Road or spent some time in Mrs Cartwright's front parlour, talking and kissing and making plans for a future when they had their own home. 'Off you go then, I'm tired.'

Jim kissed her again and left. Mrs Cartwright gave her a plate with a thick slice of toast with butter and marmalade and Sarah smiled, biting into the crunchy treat with pleasure.

'Lovely, Mum. I'll take it up with me if that's OK?'

'He's a good lad, that Jim,' her mother said and smiled. 'Not many would be here on the dot when you get back from work. He works late himself, but he's always here for you.'

Sarah nodded, because she knew what her mother thought: if it had been her, she would have married and lived in a couple of rooms. Sarah and Jim wanted a house of their own but failing that, rooms over a pub would do – and that would make life easier for them both. Sarah wasn't sure how long she would go on nursing when she was married; it depended on how soon the babies came along – and nursing was something she could go back to when they were older. She might not find work at the state hospitals until the rule on married nurses was changed, but she knew there would always be a job for her as long as Matron was in charge of the infirmary.

She wondered if Sister's patient had died during the night and thought it likely. The elderly lady had advanced cancer, which the doctors had pronounced inoperable. With no one to look after her at her rather bleak home, the only place for her during the last few weeks of her life had been the Rosie. Matron took all the hopeless cases and said it was her duty to care for those most in need.

Sarah's thoughts moved on to Ruby Harding as she washed her hands and face and cleaned her teeth before tumbling into bed. Ruby was the mainstay of the cleaning team at the infirmary and had a hard life. Sarah's mother was right when she said Ruby shouldn't put up with Sid's drinking, but she probably felt she had no choice.

CHAPTER 3

'I'm warning you, Sid Harding,' Ruby was saying to her husband at that moment as she put a plate with thick doorsteps of toast spread with dripping in front of him, 'it's no use you moaning about eating rubbish for breakfast. I've just got back from scrubbin' three wards on me 'ands and knees and me back aches something chronic. I've got a second shift at the infirmary this afternoon and even that will hardly pay enough to keep a roof over our heads. If you think you're gettin' a fry-up in the mornings on what you bring 'ome, you can think again!'

'Ah, give over, Ruby love,' Sid moaned and put a hand to his head. 'Me 'ead feels like a thousand hammers is at work.'

'They're workin' 'arder than you ever do then.' Ruby glared at him. 'What did you 'ave left in yer pocket when you got back last night, drunk as a skunk? Two bloody shillings, that's all. And if I hadn't snatched that you'd 'ave spent it down the pub this morning.'

'I only earned six bob yesterday – they give me a job sweeping out a bone lorry and I was lucky ter get that, but the stink was so bad I 'ad to 'ave a pint, love.'

'But one is never enough for you, Sid Harding,' Ruby said. 'Eat up or get out of me way. I've got work to do – unlike you, mine never stops.'

Sid muttered something rude beneath his breath, careful not to let Ruby hear what he said, because she wouldn't stand for swearing. Grabbing his threadbare jacket, he slouched off with a glare at his wife.

Ruby nodded her satisfaction when she saw he'd only eaten one slice of toast and dripping. Sid wasn't one for fatty stuff, but Ruby loved it. She ate the second slice with relish. It just served him right and she'd punished him for coming home drunk yet again. It was time he started looking for work properly and kept what he did earn for her and his daughter.

Julia was a bright girl, really clever. Ruby sometimes wondered where she'd got her brains from, because it certainly wasn't Sid, and Ruby herself wasn't one for book learning. Julia's teachers said that she had a good future in front of her, providing she won a scholarship to the grammar school – but that only paid the tuition fees. The uniform – which included indoor shoes as well as outdoor ones, PE and sports outfits and a tennis racket and a hockey stick – *and* books, all cost a great deal of money and had to be paid for by the parents. Ruby had no idea where the funds were coming from. Her wages were just about keeping them afloat but unless Sid started pulling his weight, Ruby knew she couldn't afford to buy all the things her daughter would need. And that was Sid's fault.

Ruby knew that jobs were scarce at the moment, but she'd managed to find a job and so could Sid if he was willing to take any kind of work. He was just going to have to pull his socks up – and this time she meant it. If he let her down again, she would take Julia and leave him.

Telling herself what she would do was one thing but doing it was another. Sid wasn't the worst of husbands; he didn't hit her or Julia – if he had that really would be the end. The problem was, she still fancied him something rotten and there were times when he smiled and she just melted like an idiot. But Ruby had had enough of his drinking. He was going to have to stop and she would need to be firm, because otherwise he would end up on the scrap heap like so many others who drank to forget the misery of their lives.

Ruby had always wanted more children but after Julia they just hadn't come. She sometimes thought she'd like to foster another child, give an orphan a home where the poor little bugger would be safe, but how could she when Sid spent all his wages and couldn't be trusted?

A picture of the kids in the little room at the end of the children's ward entered Ruby's head. If Sid brought his wages home as he ought, she would have offered to have those kids – that boy's cheeky smile made her laugh to herself and the girl was a poor little mite who needed some love. Ruby just hoped they wouldn't stick them kids in a home . . .

'Of course, they ought to be sent off to an orphanage,' Lady Rosalie said to Mary Thurston that evening, when they spoke over a glass of sherry in Matron's office. 'However, the girl is poorly, and I think we should try to keep them together.'

'Is there any chance of putting them with foster parents?' Mary asked, frowning. 'The children's mother is still alive and they should be returned to her when she's well enough.'

'Perhaps . . .' Lady Rosalie frowned. 'I'm in the middle of moving that little girl in your ward to another set of foster carers. Mrs Swan says she loves Dora and wants to look after her when she's on her feet again – but her husband is a brute when he's drunk. I didn't interview him myself or I should never have allowed him to become a foster carer. If I had my way, he would be locked up, but they tell me the police won't prosecute without sufficient evidence.'

'Dora is certainly afraid of Mr Swan and cannot be allowed to return to them,' Mary agreed. 'So, Dora gets priority and that means Charlie and his sister stay here for the time being?'

'Unfortunately, that is the best I can come up with for the moment,' Lady Rosalie apologized. 'I only have one set of approved parents on my list right now – as you know, I am particular about who I take and that means there is sometimes a shortage, but unlike some others I will not place children in homes that might prove unstable.'

'Indeed,' Mary agreed. 'You only have to look at Dora – she was placed with the Swan family ten months ago when her mother died and she has already been into the infirmary with injuries twice.'

'Well, Mr and Mrs Phillips are decent people. They've been waiting for a long time because they wanted a baby, but I have persuaded them to take Dora – they might take Maisie too but they couldn't manage Charlie as well.'

'Oh, we mustn't split them yet,' Mary said. 'I see plenty of children in my capacity as matron and they have not been treated as badly as some, despite Charlie's bruises. I believe Maisie when she says her mother loves her and looks after her; the problem is this man the mother has taken in.'

'It so often is when the father is dead,' Lady Rosalie said and nodded. 'So, I can take care of Dora for you – but you keep the other two until we see if their mother is likely to recover. After all, Maisie's chest still needs treatment, doesn't it?'

'Yes, she could do with a week or two in bed with my nurses caring for her – he ought to be at school, of course, but perhaps they will send some work in for him to do. I think the pair of them might run off if I tried to split them up.'

'Then we'll leave it at that,' Lady Rosalie agreed and stood up.

'Do yer reckon that Matron is goin' ter put us in an 'ome?' Maisie asked as Charlie drank the hot milk one of the nurses had brought them to help them sleep. 'I don't want ter go in no 'ome . . .' Tears welled in her eyes, running slowly down her cheeks.

'Yer ain't goin' ter,' Charlie said and set his mouth in a grim line. 'I promise yer, Maisie. Whatever 'appens, we ain't goin' in no orphanage and we ain't goin' ter be split up. We'll stop here fer a while until Ma gets better and then we'll go 'ome wiv 'er.'

'Supposin' that bloke is still wiv 'er?' Maisie asked looking fearful.

'We'll make sure we ain't around when 'e's there,'

Charlie said and glared. 'He ain't our dad, Maisie, and I 'ate 'im. We'll go in when 'e's not there and 'ide when 'e comes.'

'Yeah.' Maisie smiled at him adoringly. 'Yer always know what to do, Charlie. You'll look after me always, won't yer?'

'Yer know I will,' Charlie said. 'Me and you – we're family and families look out fer each other.'

'I know,' Maisie said and smiled trustingly. 'I wish Ma would get better soon, Charlie.'

'So do I,' he replied. 'I'll see what I can find out from the nurses here. That nice Nurse Sarah might find out for us if we ask her.'

CHAPTER 4

'These are your new foster carers,' Lady Rosalie said to the little girl standing just behind her and clutching at her skirt. 'This is Mrs and Mr Phillips – and they will take good care of you now.' She reached round and gently pushed Dora forward. 'Say hello to Mr and Mrs Phillips, Dora.'

Dora's greeting was a whisper only the most eager ears could hear, but Mrs Phillips bent down to be on her level and held out her arms to her. 'Hello, Dora,' she said and smiled at her in a way calculated to win over even a child who had been ill-treated by her last carers. 'I'm so glad you've come to live with us!'

Dora looked at her uncertainly and her bottom lip wobbled. 'How long will you keep me?' she asked with tears in her eyes.

'I want to keep you for as long as you want to stay with me – forever and ever,' Helen Phillips said. 'Would you like to call me Mummy or Penny?'

Dora hesitated, then, after looking into the loving eyes of her new carer, she said, 'Mummy, please . . .'

Now the tears were running down Mrs Phillips'

cheeks and she bent down to swoop the child into her arms and kiss her. 'Mummy has a lovely bedroom for you, Dora, darling. There are dollies and a teddy bear waiting for you – would you like to see them?'

'What's a teddy bear?' Dora asked, a look of surprise in her eyes. 'Is it nice?'

'Very nice; you can cuddle him,' Mrs Phillips told her. 'Shall we go upstairs and see?' Her eyes met those of Lady Rosalie, who nodded and Helen Phillips departed carrying the child she had waited so long for.

'I can't thank you enough,' Mr Phillips said after his wife had gone. 'I tried to tell her to accept a small child long ago when we knew we should never have our own – but you persuaded her and it has already made so much difference to our lives. Helen looks happy again . . .' His voice broke with emotion. 'If there is anything I can do to help you, ever . . .'

'I may ask you to take another little girl or boy one day,' Lady Rosalie said with a smile. 'I can already see you are going to be good for Dora and people like you are not easy to find. I'm very glad your wife decided to take a little girl rather than a baby. It is the slightly older children we really need homes for.'

'Give us a few months to get the hang of it,' he said, 'and then we will be pleased to give Dora a playmate.'

'I hoped you would say that!' Lady Rosalie offered him her hand to shake.

'There won't be anything we can't handle,' he took it firmly. 'My wife has a lot of love to give a child and I would to anything to make *her* happy – besides, I've always wanted a family myself.'

'I shall leave you to get to know each other,' Lady Rosalie said and took her leave. 'I just wish I could find another hundred couples like you and Mrs Phillips.'

She nodded to herself as she left the neat little home in the suburbs. She would visit the infirmary on her way back and tell Mary about Dora's new foster parents.

Sarah saw the large car pull up outside the infirmary as she left. She watched the well-dressed woman get out and go inside, pausing for a moment before crossing the busy road. Lady Rosalie was a frequent and well-liked visitor at the Rosie.

On her way down Button Street, Sarah lingered in front of the dress shop and stared at the tartan skirt and the soft wool twinset displayed with it. She could do with a new skirt and she loved that fine knit with fully-fashioned sleeves. They fitted so well and that shade of green would suit her down to the ground. A sigh escaped her, because even though both the skirt and the twinset were reasonably priced at thirty-five shillings, she couldn't afford to pay three pounds and ten shillings for a skirt and twinset. All her spare money went into the fund that would contribute to their new home.

Walking past the tempting window determinedly, Sarah turned into Shilling Street, thinking about the children that the police had brought in a few nights earlier. She'd asked Matron what would become of them and she had looked serious.

'We are told that the mother is very ill,' Matron had said looking sad. 'It is a pity that she wasn't brought to us – at least we could have arranged for her to spend some time with her children. If she dies, they will probably have to be placed in an orphanage. I have spoken to Lady Rosalie about it and she is making inquiries. A temporary foster home would be best, since they are neither of them ill. We are not equipped to care for children who are healthy and being idle will lead them into mischief.'

'Yes, I suppose there is nothing else for them – if their mother dies . . .' Sarah's heart wrenched with pity as she pictured the children's reaction to such an eventuality.

'It might be that the Children's Welfare department feels the mother is not fit to have the care of them, even if she recovers,' Matron said thoughtfully. 'I do not approve of taking children from their mothers unless really necessary – but if she is exposing them to a pimp who is likely to beat them . . .?' Her shoulders moved in resignation, for such a situation could not be allowed to continue.

'Yes, I understand,' Sarah said. 'I wondered if they had any other relatives other than their mother.'

'The police knew of none but it might be an idea to ask the boy. He seems intelligent – though a little inclined to aggression and disobedience.'

'Oh, what has he done?' Sarah was surprised.

'He is restless and impatient and he flicked pieces of bread at one of the other boys in the ward. I was forced to smack his leg hard.'

'Oh dear,' Sarah said. 'It's a shame he had to be punished. I know he thinks he is old enough to work – and if he has nothing to do, he will be bored.'

'Yes, I am aware of that and it is the reason we must get him settled – either with a foster parent or an orphanage.'

'He wouldn't be happy parted from Maisie and I know she is frightened of being put in a home.'

'I dare say, but we cannot keep them here forever.'

'Just a little longer?' Sarah pleaded.

Matron frowned. 'We'll see, nurse; I must get on and you have your duties.'

'Yes, Matron,' Sarah said and left to get on with her own work, feeling upset. She wondered if Lady Rosalie's visit to the infirmary had anything to do with the two children and hoped she wasn't about to send them away to an orphanage.

However, when Sarah called in to see them that evening in the children's ward, taking a bag of sherbet lemons and some comic books, she found that Charlie was full of what he wanted to be when he could take up an apprenticeship.

'I'm going to be a carpenter when I leave school next year, nurse,' he confided. 'I like throwing pots – that's what they call it when you make a wheel turn and shape the clay with your hands like this and I learned at school . . .' He mimed how he'd shaped his pot. 'That was fun, but the best was turning a bit of wood on a lathe and carving too. I've made up me mind.'

'Then, perhaps you will,' Sarah said and smiled at him. 'Maisie is a little better now – and perhaps your mother will be able to come home soon.'

'Is she any better, nurse?' Charlie asked eagerly.

'I telephoned and they said no change but she was

as well as could be expected – so I think that means you just have to be patient,' Sarah said and saw the disappointment in his eyes. 'It's all we can do – wait and see what happens . . .'

CHAPTER 5

'We ought ter be at 'ome,' Charlie said to his sister as they wandered disconsolately about the small garden at the rear of the infirmary. It had a high wall and cherry trees, which were beginning to bud. Matron had sent them out to get some fresh air, but the wind was cool and Charlie was bored. 'I want somethin' ter do 'cos I ain't in school.'

'That nice nurse what looked after us when we come in brought us some books and that jigsaw puzzle,' Maisie said. She looked up to her brother, who was four years her senior and the person she cared for most in the world, even more than Ma because Ma wasn't the same any more and she frightened Maisie. 'I like doin' puzzles and the pictures are nice in the books, though the words are hard.'

'You should ask that nurse who plays with the kids to 'elp wiv yer reading,' Charlie said. 'I ain't got the patience, Maisie. Besides, I should be at work. If I 'ad a proper job I could look after us when Ma ain't right. I have ter find somewhere we can live and someone ter give me a real job instead of just runnin' errands.'

'It's that horrible bloke,' Maisie said and two big tears spilled over and ran down her cheeks. 'Why did yer say we had to pretend we didn't know 'is name? Everybody knows Ronnie the Greek.'

Most folk who lived in the narrow lanes that bordered the docks knew of Ronnie and his associates. Apart from running a few girls, Ronnie was the hard man for Mr Penfold and, though no one dared to whisper it, Mr Penfold was the man behind much of the violent crime that went on in Docklands. His was the shadow that lay over public houses, small cafés, shops and warehouses that struggled to survive and pay protection money to the gangs that ruled this part of the East End of London; they were an underlife, seen but unreported, ruling by fear and acts of terrible violence against those that rebelled. It was hard enough to earn a living these days and the gangs took much of what honest folk struggled to earn.

''Cos, we have ter be careful for Ma's sake,' Charlie told her. He knew Ronnie the Greek would squash Ma and them without blinking. The last time the bully had beaten him Charlie had bitten Ronnie's hand so hard that he'd drawn blood and the bully had yelled and knocked him almost senseless. Charlie knew that the man he hated would as soon break his neck as look at him. He was willing to take his chances, but Charlie loved his little sister and Ma was Ma, whatever she did. Charlie might not approve of the way she went with men for money, but he knew that after his father's ship was lost at sea, Ma had had it hard. She'd tried honest work but the boss wouldn't leave her be and she'd been forced more than once before she decided that, if she was going to be a whore, she would be paid for it.

'I hate 'im,' Maisie said tearfully and wiped her nose on the back of her hand. 'I'm cold. I want ter go back inside.'

'You go,' Charlie told her. 'You don't want ter catch a chill, Maisie. I'm goin' down the docks ter see if I can find some odd jobs.'

'You can't!' Maisie cried, scared now and looking about her. 'They won't let you go and the wall is too high to climb.'

'I'll climb that tree . . .' Charlie pointed to the cherry tree. 'I can get up that and over the wall. I'll be back for tea.'

'Don't go – you'll get in trouble!'

'If they ask where I am, say I went to the lavvy,' Charlie said and grinned at her. 'Don't worry, Maisie, love, I'll be back afore they miss me – and if I earn a bob, I'll bring yer back a penny dip.'

Maisie was silenced. Penny dips, sherbet with either a lollipop or a bit of liquorice to dip in the packet, were her favourite. She watched as Charlie climbed the old tree, balanced on the wall, and then disappeared from view.

Feeling nervous, Maisie returned to the ward and sat on the bed she'd been given. Charlie was so brave. She'd never dare to do the things he did, but he was her big brother and she admired him for his courage. She knew Ma wanted them to go to school but neither of them attended more than they were forced; Charlie because he felt he was old enough to work, and Maisie because she got picked on by some of the other girls if her big brother wasn't around to protect her.

'Hello,' Nurse Anne said, smiling at her. 'I was just coming to find you. Would you like a cup of hot cocoa?'

'Yes, please,' Maisie said. She had taken to the young probationer. Charlie said she wasn't a nurse yet, just training to be, but she had a lovely smile and she was kind. Nurse Anne didn't ask where Charlie was and Maisie didn't tell have to tell her lies, which was good.

She settled down on the bed and looked at the jigsaw puzzle that was set out on an old wooden tray. There were so many pieces and without Charlie's quick eyes, Maisie knew she might not find any of the pieces that fitted. Charlie helped her do most things, but he didn't like reading. Maisie wanted to read better than she could and she decided that she would ask the young nurse to help her as Charlie had suggested.

Sighing, she wished that she was as brave as her brother, because she would have liked to be with him, roaming the streets and looking for work. Work was scarce, even for the men who waited in line on the docks or stood on street corners, but sometimes folk would give a willing boy a small job like cleaning windows or delivering something. Maisie suspected that sometimes Charlie took bets to shops and that what he did wasn't legal, but she never questioned his decisions. Whenever Charlie had a few pennies in his pocket, he spent most of them on her and she wished that the two of them could live somewhere together – somewhere that Ma's men didn't get a chance to hit them or leer at Maisie in a way that made her fear, though she did not know what she feared.

'Nurse Anne is helpin' me wiv my reading,' Maisie told Sarah with a little giggle later that evening. She helped herself to one of the precious sherbet lemons the nurse had given them the previous night. 'How did you know these were my favourites?'

'I told 'er, you like anythin' wiv sherbet,' Charlie said and ruffled her fair curls.

When Maisie was clean, her hair freshly washed, face shining and blue eyes bright with pleasure, she looked like a little angel. Sarah found herself wishing she was in a position to offer these two a home. She wasn't sure why they pulled at her heartstrings, because many children came to the ward.

Sarah smiled at them. 'Charlie – do you have any other relatives besides your mother?'

'Why?' he asked suspiciously. 'Ma ain't dead, is she?'

'No, but she is very ill and you might be placed in an orphanage because we can't keep children who are not sick here for long and Maisie is getting better – but if you had an aunt or uncle, they might look after you until your mother is well again.'

Charlie nodded, taking it in. 'There's Auntie Jeanie,' he said slowly. 'She lives in the country somewhere. Ma said she's a teacher and her name is the same as ours, 'cos the man she loved was killed in the Great War and she wouldn't 'ave no one else.'

'So, she is Miss Jeanie Howes?' Sarah nodded. 'And she lives in the country and is a teacher. Well, that is quite a lot, Charlie. Thank you. I'll tell Matron and perhaps the police might be able to find your aunt.'

'I want ter be with Ma!' Maisie whined, on the verge of tears.

Sarah resisted the temptation to pick her up and cuddle her, knowing it was frowned on to make the children dependent on one particular nurse. 'Yes, of course you do – but you'd rather be with your auntie than in an orphanage, wouldn't you?'

'Yeah,' Charlie said. 'Aunt Jeanie ain't bad. Maisie wouldn't remember – but she came to visit Dad once and she brought me a toy yacht and some sweets.'

Sarah smiled. Charlie was using his brains, working out that they would have more chance of a good life with an aunt than in a home for orphans. Maisie would come round when she saw that her brother was happy with the idea – and unless the aunt was found they might find themselves being taken into care even if their mother lived. Now that it had come to light that she was living with a man who ill-treated her, it was unlikely that she would be allowed to keep the children unless she gave him up . . .

'Well, I'll see what I can do,' Sarah promised. 'I'll come and see you another evening when I'm on duty.'

'I don't want to go in no orphanage,' Maisie moaned when they were alone. 'And I don't want ter live wiv Aunt Jeanie. I want ter be wiv Ma.'

'So do I,' Charlie said and put an arm about her shoulders protectively. 'But Aunt Jeanie ain't bad, Maisie – 'sides, if we don't like livin' wiv 'er we'll run away soon as we're ready. I'll soon learn ter be a carpenter and then I can work and keep us both. I give yer me promise, Maisie – I'll look after yer.'

Maisie's tears dried as if by magic. Her brother was brave and he could do anything. She wanted her ma bad and when she lay in bed at night the tears came, because she missed her so much. It wasn't Ma's fault that she was in the hospital and they'd been brought here, it was that horrible man. Maisie wished she could stick Ma's long hat pins in to his body and make him cry with pain the way he'd done with Ma – and all because she wouldn't do what he told her. Maisie didn't know what the man wanted Ma to do, but Charlie said it was bad and he said that man deserved to be punished. Maisie wished he would die.

'Here, 'ave another sherbet lemon,' Charlie said, 'and stop snuffling. Ma might get better and then she'll come and fetch us.'

'Not if that horrible bloke is wiv 'er,' Maisie muttered. 'He told Ma he didn't want us around no more.'

'And Ma refused what he said she'd got ter do,' Charlie said. 'He wanted her to stick us in the orphanage and that's when she refused and he hit her again and again. I tried to stop him, Maisie, but he just knocked me down and by the time I could think straight, he'd gone and left Ma lyin' there. I reckon he thought she were dead.'

'She must be very ill,' Maisie said, her eyes shadowed with fear. 'What we goin' ter do, Charlie? What will they do to us if Ma dies?'

'If they say we're goin' in an orphanage we'll run away and hide until they stop looking for us. I know lots of places down the docks where we can sleep – and I'll find work. But if Auntie Jeanie comes, we'll go wiv 'er until I can look after you.'

'Could we really do that?' Maisie asked. Charlie was so brave. He would dare anything and she felt safe when he was with her.

'Don't you worry, Maisie,' Charlie told her. 'I'll look after yer. I told yer so.'

CHAPTER 6

'I don't know why it upsets me,' Sarah said when Jim came round for his breakfast the next morning. 'She's such a sweet little thing, looks as if butter wouldn't melt in her mouth, but her brother – he's made of stronger stuff. I should hate to see them put in an orphanage or split up with different foster carers. You know what some of these people are like – they won't take two children, and some don't want boys, because girls are easier. Sometimes they send the girls to one home and the boys to another – they might even send them to Canada or Australia.'

'You say their aunt lives in the country and her name is Jeanie Howes?' Sarah nodded and Jim looked thoughtful. 'Right, I'll ask in the pub. She may live in the country now, but if the children's father was a local man then someone will remember the family and they may know where the sister lives. If we can discover the location then the police can probably find them.'

'You're a lovely man, Jim Rouse,' Sarah said. 'I think I might marry you.'

Jim put his arms around her and hugged her close.

She felt a shiver of passion run through him as he kissed her hard on the mouth and knew that he wanted so much more than the touching and kissing they allowed themselves.

'Now then, no more of that,' Sarah's mother said, coming in from the backyard where she had taken some potato peelings to the hens in the run Jim had made for them. They only had three hens but they were good layers and produced several fresh eggs each week. Most of their neighbours looked with envy at the hens but few had gone to the trouble of building a pen and buying their own. Mrs Cartwright didn't understand why, when times were so hard; the hens ate any leftovers and had cost almost nothing. She'd bought a box of day-old chicks in the market and reared eight of the ten successfully – four had been killed for the pot as pullets but the three hens and one cockerel had survived until this day.

'I was just telling Jim about those children,' Sarah said, her cheeks warm, because she knew her mother's eyes saw all.

'Proper daft she is about them pair,' Mrs Cartwright said and shook her head. 'For two pins I think she'd bring them home to me.'

'Oh, Mum!' Sarah laughed and shook her head. 'I know that's out of the question. We couldn't afford to feed and clothe them – and the Welfare would never let us have them anyway.'

'Time is when I might have thought of offering them a temporary home,' Mrs Cartwright said. 'When your father was working full-time, Sarah, he would have taken on any waif or stray that came his way.'

Sarah nodded. As a child, she'd known her father to bring home children who needed a good meal and a bath. Her mother had fed them, cut down some of her husband's old clothes to fit the lads and taken her own or Sarah's for the girls. When the children's parents were over whatever illness or setback they'd endured, they would go home brighter, healthier and usually cheeky. Sarah believed it was her father's charity that had made her want to be a nurse and take care of those in need.

'I know . . .' Sarah smiled and touched her mother's hand in sympathy.

'I've not spoken,' Mrs Cartwright said suddenly, 'but your father agrees and I will make the offer and then it's for you two to decide – if Jim's job doesn't materialize and you want to marry, you can come here until you've saved enough.'

Sarah saw the denial in Jim's eyes. He wanted a house of their own – and his fear was that if they settled for living in a rented house that wasn't even their own the children would come and their plans would be forgotten. It was his worst nightmare and she knew she had to refuse, even though it might hurt the mother she loved.

'I love you for thinking of us, Mum,' she said and put her arms about her mother, kissing and hugging her. 'But you know our dream – we want to have our own home right from the start.'

'Well, the offer is there, so don't use the lack of somewhere to live as an excuse if you forget yourselves. Your father always holds his head high and so do I, Sarah, so make sure you don't let us down.'

It was the severest warning her mother had ever

given and Sarah knew it was her own fault. Jim couldn't always control his passion, though they hadn't yet gone all the way, even when they sneaked into his lodgings while his landlady was at the Mission Hall, but sometimes Sarah wondered how much longer they could wait. Was having a home they could call their own really so important? If they moved in with Sarah's mother, they could still save but enjoy themselves a little more – and it would save them both being frustrated when the kisses just weren't enough for either of them.

Uncannily, as though he read her thoughts, Jim said, 'Tell you what, Sarah love, you're not on duty for three nights now – I'll take you to the flicks. Reg will stand in for me at the pub and we'll have a special night out. We haven't been anywhere much since your birthday.'

Sarah felt pleased. There were films showing at the Gaumont and the Odeon that she would like to see. She would choose one that Jim would like too and make it special for them both. She would miss seeing the children that evening but the other nurses would look out for them.

Charlie looked for Sarah that evening, feeling disappointed when he saw Nurse Jenny Brown take the day nurse's place. She smiled at him as she made her round of the ward, visiting the sick children first and then coming to sit on his bed.

'How are you this evening, Charlie?'

'I'm all right,' he said. 'Where's Nurse Sarah? She was goin' to find out about me aunt.'

'Sarah has three nights off now,' Nurse Jenny said

and plumped his pillows for him. 'It will take a little time for anyone to trace your aunt, Charlie, but I know Nurse Sarah will do all she can.'

Charlie nodded, and then because he didn't want the nurse to think he didn't like her, he grinned cheekily. 'Nurse Sarah is courtin' – are you courtin', nurse?'

'Cheeky monkey!' Nurse Jenny said and laughed, because she liked him and didn't really mind him asking. 'No, I haven't got anyone special, worse luck.' She sighed, because her hopes that the stranger would return to her bus stop had not materialized. 'Sarah is pretty and lovely-natured. Her boyfriend goes round there all the time. She is lucky to have him.'

'You're not bad yerself,' Charlie said and grinned. 'You should 'ave yer 'air cut and mebbe one of them perms. Ma had a perm, curls all over. She looked grand but when she had it peroxided, the ends broke off and she said she wouldn't have no more perms.'

'Well, I shan't do that then,' Jenny said. 'My hair waves a bit when I let it down. Perhaps if I had it cut it would curl at the ends.' She smiled and ruffled his hair. 'Why don't you read a comic until lights out? I'll bring you a mug of cocoa soon. Do you think Maisie would like one?'

Charlie looked at his sleeping sister and his mouth curved. 'She sleeps sound as a bell once she's away.' He grinned at the nurse. 'To look at her you'd think she'd never said boo to a goose, wouldn't yer?'

'Yes, you would,' Jenny agreed. 'I'll bring you some cocoa later.'

Charlie watched her walk away, checking beds and attending to children who were too sick to sleep. He knew that he and Maisie were lucky compared with many of those brought in here. Ma had done her best by them after his father died and it wasn't her fault she'd got in with a wrong 'un. Charlie thought vengefully of what he'd like to do to the man who had hurt his mother. He wasn't big or strong enough yet to thrash him, though that hadn't stopped him from attacking Ronnie the Greek. He'd gone in with fists and feet but he ought to have used a knife, except the coppers would put him in prison if he killed the bully and then there would be no one to look out for Maisie and Ma. Charlie couldn't help wishing that someone would do it, though. The man was evil and one day someone would do for him!

Charlie went to sleep with his head full of what he'd like to do to the man who had hurt his mum and made them flee their home. Little did he know as he finally lay peacefully asleep, something even worse was about to break his heart and wrench his life apart . . .

CHAPTER 7

Ruby Harding stared at her husband with something that was in that moment close to hatred. He'd come home from work late, drunk and swearing because there was no hot supper waiting on the table.

'Where's my grub, woman?' Sid demanded recklessly. He was too drunk to know what he was saying or doing. 'Is it too much to expect me supper when I get in from a hard day's work?'

'Hard day's work?' Ruby mocked furiously, arms akimbo as she faced him. 'Don't make me laugh, Sid Harding – you ain't done a day's work in years, let alone raised a sweat. I've done two shifts at the infirmary today – scrubbing floors, washing windows and walls – *I* know what hard work is. You've stood on the docks wiv yer hands in yer pockets—'

Ruby's tirade was cut short as he struck out with his fist, catching her a glancing blow on the shoulder as she jerked back to avoid it. Ruby was capable of giving as good as she got but Julia entered the kitchen and ran at her father as he swung his arm back, preparing to hit his long-suffering wife again, and his elbow took her right in the face, making her cry out in pain. The young girl recoiled in dismay as her father whirled on her, his drunken rage robbing him of sensible thought.

'Serves yer right,' he said and raised his arm as if he would hit her on purpose this time, but Ruby's rolling pin hit his arm and made him howl with pain. He stumbled and half fell on to the old sofa, looking dazed and bewildered.

'What was that for?' he asked. Ruby knew he would never do such a thing sober, because he doted on the girl, but his mood had been black and he'd lost his temper.

'You hurt Julia,' Ruby told him sharply. 'And it's the last time you enter this house drunk, Sid Harding. On yer feet! I want yer out right now and yer don't come back until you can show me a wage packet and give me a reason to take yer back.'

Sid's rage had receded and he was now just bemused and weary. All he wanted was to lie down and sleep off the bellyful of beer he'd consumed after another day of humiliation on the docks as he was passed over again and again, all the decent jobs given to others and him forced to take the work others wouldn't do. He'd unloaded slurry from the cesspits and cleaned down the lorry before hosing himself with cold water to rid his nostrils of the foul stink. He was sick of being a failure, sick of never having enough money, and he'd drunk away the few pence he'd earned because of his shame. Once, he'd been a qualified bricklayer and then the war came and his injury had made it difficult for him to keep up with the others. When the pain got too bad in his leg the gaffer laid him off and he'd taken to waiting in line down the docks.

Ruby was pulling at him, forcing him to his feet, and he felt her shoving him towards the kitchen door, which his daughter opened for her. Sid was not a small man and had he used his strength he might have resisted, but the belligerence had gone, replaced by shame, and he allowed her to push him out into the backyard without fighting back. After all, it was what he deserved.

Tears trickled down his face as he lurched off into the lane behind the house. He wasn't fit to lick Ruby's boots. Sid knew how hard she worked to keep the house going, feed and clothe them, and it was all his fault because he couldn't get a decent job and keep his family the way a man should.

Sid's cheeks were wet as he wended his way down towards the docks, past the now darkened windows of the pub where he too often spent his money, and on towards the dark shadows of the cranes, warehouses and barges that clustered on the river, waiting for morning. It was not a cold night but the air was sobering Sid, bringing him to a stinging awareness that he'd let his family down. He'd tried to hit his Ruby and he'd accidentally hit Julia in the face, hurting her – he vaguely recalled raising his hand to hit her again and the remorse was like a knife stabbing his heart. He would die before he hurt his beautiful little girl and he'd done it without meaning to. Julia was the only thing left in this world worth trying for and without her he might as well end it in the river.

His morbid thoughts were suspended by the sound of an unearthly scream. Sid froze as he heard someone sobbing in pain and then his instinct to help took him towards the sound, but he stopped suddenly as he saw three dark figures outlined by the faint illumination from an old-fashioned streetlight. It was some distance away, the only one to survive the kids who wrecked everything they came across when rampaging. Someone ought to give the lads a good hiding but no one seemed interested and the cops hardly ever ventured this far into what was accepted as a really rough area,

As Sid hesitated, unsure of what to do, he heard a man begging for his life and then another scream as a knife was plunged into his stomach. The killer stabbed three times and then his companion laughed.

'That will make a few of them pay up, boss,' he said and Sid recognized the voice of Ronnie the Greek. He was well-known in these streets and could be seen regularly each week on his rounds collecting the protection money he extorted from small businesses in the docklands.

'I shouldn't have to do it,' another voice said coldly and Sid knew that too. It was Mr Penfold. He owned much of the property in the better streets and several clubs, betting shops and brothels, too, though Sid knew it would be impossible for the police to prove it. 'It's your job to keep them in line – see it doesn't happen again or I might decide that you're not up to your job.'

Sid shrank back into the shadows as the two men passed him. If Mr Penfold knew that he'd seen him kill, he would end up with his throat cut. A witness to his crime would never be allowed to live, unless he was already on the payroll and under the boss's thumb.

Sid stood without daring to move for a long time. He was terrified that the two thugs would come back and kill him and he knew that their victim was dead. He could do nothing to help the poor man, whoever it was. If he hadn't got drunk, he might have been at home, eating supper and listening to Henry Hall on the wireless. If only he hadn't seen it! But he wasn't going to tell anyone. He couldn't, because he knew how ruthless those men were. If Sid went to the police with what he knew, it would not be just him who paid the price. His wife and child would also suffer. Sid had to keep his mouth shut and carry on as if nothing had happened.

He made up his mind as he finally began to walk back home to find a corner in the shed in his backyard that from this moment he would make a new start in his personal life. Ruby had told him he had to take her a wage packet and give her a good reason before she let him back in and that's what he would do. He was capable of doing many jobs if he put his mind to it, so in the morning, when Ruby was at work and Julia had gone to school, he would sneak in and have a wash and shave, and then he'd put on his Sunday suit and go looking for a decent job.

He couldn't let his Ruby go scrubbing at the Rosie and not help her by bringing in his own wage. It would just serve him right if she threw him out for good. He'd make sure he found something that paid at least as much as she earned, and when he'd got money in his pocket he'd go home and beg her to take him back.

His Ruby worked hard down that place and he knew they appreciated her. Folk round here couldn't manage without the Rosie and he couldn't manage without his Ruby. He just hoped what he'd witnessed that night didn't come back to haunt him . . . Hesitating for a moment, Sid moved silently to retrace his steps to where the knife lay. It might just come in handy to hide that somewhere only he knew about, just in case . . .

CHAPTER 8

Charlie was sitting by Maisie's bed, looking at her anxiously when the nurse everyone called Matron walked in accompanied by another lady he'd never met. Maisie had been coughing harshly all morning and Matron bent over her, feeling her forehead.

'How long has she been like this?' Matron asked him.

'Most of the morning, miss.' He felt his stomach contract with fear. 'Is she bad?'

'Lady Rosalie wants to talk to you,' Matron replied sternly. 'I'll make sure that your sister gets the attention she needs – it is obvious she isn't going anywhere for a while.' This last was directed at the lady Charlie didn't know and his stomach twisted. She wasn't a nurse and she had a posh look about her, something that warned Charlie he wasn't going to like what she had to tell him.

In Matron's office, Charlie stood like a frozen statue, wishing he was back with his sister and feeling fear prickle at the back of his neck.

'It's Charlie, isn't it?' the lady said and gave him what

was meant to be a kind smile but instead filled him with terror. 'I don't want to upset you, Charlie – and we had intended to keep you together if we could – but a chance has come up that I feel we ought to take, although it means that you will be parted from Maisie for a time—'

'No! I ain't goin' in no orphanage!' Charlie protested, poised to run but tied to the spot because Maisie was still in the ward and sick. 'I ain't goin' ter leave her – she'll die without me!'

'She might die if she went with you,' Lady Rosalie said. 'Maisie will be looked after here, Charlie. I give you my word. The couple who have promised to take you run a little baker's shop only a short bus ride from here. I'm sure you can visit her often – and Mrs Robinson will make sure you go to school and are properly cared for. I know it isn't ideal but it is the best we can do for now – at least you will still be in London and near enough to visit Maisie.'

'Can I visit her as often as I want?' Charlie forced the words out. He recognized authority when he heard it and it was in this woman's voice. He might have wheedled round one of the nurses but this woman wouldn't take no for an answer.

'Yes, certainly. We'll let you visit whenever you can – we will not force you to come at a certain time.'

'I just don't want to leave Maisie . . .' Charlie said throatily. He was close to tears but boys didn't cry just because they couldn't get their own way; they fought back and Charlie's jaw set determinedly. He had to do what this woman said, even though he hated her for taking him from Maisie, but he would find a way to get what Maisie and he both wanted, which was to be together and back with their mother. 'What about me Ma?'

'She is still very ill, Charlie,' the lady said and she looked sad. 'Perhaps Mrs Robinson will take you to see her if you ask her.'

Charlie nodded, seeing one small advantage in what he was being forced to accept. If he could see his mum, he could talk to her – and once she knew what was happening, she would soon get out of that hospital and come home to take care of Maisie and him.

'I don't want to go until Maisie is better,' he said, stubborn to the last.

'Maisie will need a lot of treatment and she may be here weeks, even months.' The lady seemed hesitant but then sighed. 'I don't have a choice, Charlie. We can only keep sick children here. I will promise you that I'll arrange for you to be together as soon as I can – will that content you?'

Charlie looked her in the face. He hated her for what she was doing but he thought she meant to do right and his shoulders sagged. He wasn't old enough or able to look after his sister yet and for the moment had little choice but to do as he was told.

'When do I have to leave?' he asked reluctantly.

'On Monday,' she said and looked relieved. 'Mr Robinson will come for you then – and so you have a few days with your sister.'

'She might be better and able to come with me by then,' Charlie said and felt more cheerful. He liked being at the Rosie because the nurses were kind, fed them well and didn't bother him much; it was like being at home with Mum without the chores he'd always done, a holiday. Still, it might be all right living at a baker's shop, because there was a chance of cake.

'That is doubtful,' Lady Rosalie said. 'I believe your sister will prove to have an illness of the lungs, Charlie, and that means weeks and weeks of treatment, I'm afraid.'

Charlie nodded. It was hard to accept that he had to go to live with people he didn't know and leave Maisie here. She would be upset and he felt guilty, as if he were breaking his promise to her – but he was only thirteen and these people ruled their lives. The alternative was to run now and, in his heart, Charlie knew his sister could not live on the streets as she was now; her illness would get worse and she might be in danger.

Hiding his tears and his anger, Charlie nodded. 'You promise I've got until Monday?'

'Yes, Charlie, I promise you,' the lady said and then in a tone that sounded false to him, 'I'm sure you'll be very happy with Mr and Mrs Robinson . . .'

'Yes, miss,' he said obediently, though he didn't believe it. Charlie didn't want to go to these people and if he didn't like them, he would leave as soon as he got the chance. Maisie might not be able to survive on the streets but he could – and he would find work he could do, search for somewhere for his sister and him to live if Ma didn't come home soon . . .

Maisie was a little better on Sunday afternoon. For a couple of days, she'd been so ill that Charlie had feared she might die; the nurses were always coming to her and they took her somewhere for treatment that she came back from looking like a lifeless doll, but on Sunday, she looked better.

'I'm goin' ter stop wiv someone fer a while,' he told her, throwing it into a conversation about her puzzle as if he were just asking what she wanted for tea. 'It's a baker's shop and I reckon I'll do all right there, Maisie – probably deliver cakes or bread or somethin' when I'm not at school.'

'You'll sleep here with me?' Maisie looked alarmed as he shook his head and tears welled in her eyes. 'No, you can't leave me, Charlie. I'll be frightened 'ere on me own.'

''Course yer won't, Maisie,' he said and grinned at her, though inside he was hurting because she was hurt. 'The nurses are 'ere all the time and they're nice; they'll look after yer.'

'You promised yer would never leave me,' she whimpered, tears on her cheeks. 'It ain't fair – you promised me faithful!'

He had and it wasn't fair and Charlie wanted to hug her and defy those in authority who were making him break his promise.

'It's just until you're better, Maisie,' he told her. 'I'll visit as much as I can and I'll come back for yer – and I shan't break my promise. I'll always look after yer, love. I'm goin' ter tell Ma what they've done and she'll come home and look after us.'

'I want Mum,' Maisie said tearfully.

Charlie wanted his mum too, wanted her so badly that he felt like howling. He considered making a fuss when they came to fetch him but realized it wouldn't help him. He would still be made to go and they would watch him more closely. Brought up on the streets of the East End, Charlie knew enough to think before he committed to anything. He was old before his time, because he'd had to be – Mum would never have managed if he hadn't brought home wood and coal he'd scavenged for the fire and popped a few pennies in her housekeeping pot when she wasn't watching. She'd never known that he did odd jobs for anyone who would take him on and she hadn't asked where the extra came from.

Charlie had washed windows and carted stuff since he was seven. The cart his dad had made him was still in the shed at home and he'd fetch it the moment he could. There was sure to be someone on the docks that would give him work – he looked the fourteen which was what he told anyone who asked and most didn't.

'I'll be bringing yer sweets,' he told Maisie. 'It will be like now but I shan't be in the next bed.' He reached for her hand but she pulled it away, her face sullen. 'It ain't my fault, Maisie – that woman arranged it. I don't 'ave a choice!'

Maisie sniffed and looked at him as if searching for the truth.

'I give yer me word on Dad's memory,' he said and she sniffed harder.

'I 'ate 'er,' she said, still miserable but no longer looking at him through the eyes of betrayal. 'She's rotten, Charlie.'

'No, Maisie, I suppose she's right,' he acknowledged with a sigh. 'I ain't sick and this is an 'ospital. I ain't allowed to stop here no more – but I shall never abandon

68

you and she promised we'll be together again as soon as Ma is better.'

Maisie nodded. She didn't like it but now she was looking with concern at her brother. 'Do yer think they'll be all right wiv yer, Charlie?'

'If they ain't I shan't stay there,' he said. 'I've got plans up 'ere.' He touched the side of his head. 'No matter what they say or do I'll be back fer yer, Maisie, and as soon as yer better I'll have yer out of 'ere – and on me life, I shan't break that promise . . .'

Charlie was summoned to Matron's office after breakfast. He hugged his sister, told her to be good and went reluctantly. He'd had to be brave for Maisie's sake and he wouldn't let anyone see how scared he was but, just as he was wise to the way of the streets, he knew that everyone wasn't kind or to be trusted, even on Button Street, and he was wary of what would happen to him in his new foster home – that was what the lady had called it.

The man standing in Matron's office was of medium height; he didn't look like the kind of men Ma had sometimes brought home and Charlie's stomach settled a bit. Maybe it wouldn't be too bad . . .

'Charlie,' Matron said and something in her voice made him look at her sharply, 'this is Mr Robinson. Mrs Robinson is busy in the shop so your new foster father has come to fetch you – say hello to him.'

Charlie's skin prickled. Matron didn't like Mr Robinson. She wouldn't say so, but he knew it instinctively. Something had made her doubtful and that warned Charlie to be careful.

'Thank you, sir,' he said and held out his hand politely. Mr Robinson nodded, made a sound in his throat and ignored Charlie's hand.

'We need to be goin',' he said gruffly. 'Thank you, Miss Thurston. My wife will take good care of the boy, treat him like a son.'

'So I should hope,' Matron said and she seemed hesitant as she turned to Charlie. 'Remember you're always welcome here, child. We'll look after Maisie for you and you can visit when you like.' She saw the small paper bag he was carrying. 'Do you have all your things?'

'Yes, thank you, Matron,' he said in a small voice. His courage was at a low ebb and he almost flung himself at her and begged her to let him stay but knew he couldn't let this man see how vulnerable he was inside. He had to be strong for Maisie and his mother; they would need him in future and this was just temporary. The thought restored his confidence and he turned to the man waiting. 'I'm ready, sir.'

'You'd better be,' Mr Robinson said in a voice Charlie knew Matron wasn't meant to hear. 'Come along, boy, I have work to do.'

Charlie forced his feet to move, even though they felt like lead. He was screaming inside, begging someone to stop them and say he need not go, but he knew it wouldn't happen. He was going to live in this man's house and his senses told him it wouldn't be what had been promised him; this man might speak politely to Matron but there was cruelty in him and Charlie knew it – had seen it before in the man that had terrorized his mother. He was being delivered to the enemy and there was nothing he could do.

CHAPTER 9

Jenny saw the headlines as she called in to get a paper at the corner shop that morning. A few nights previously a man had been murdered on the docks, knifed in the stomach. The police seemed to think it was a gangland killing, so she read the article as she waited for her bus to come.

'Makes you wonder what things are coming to, doesn't it?' a man's voice said close to her. Jenny tingled as she turned to face him. 'Those thugs want hanging.'

Jenny stared. He looked even more attractive today, and the fact that he'd come back this way when she'd thought he never would, robbed her of the power to think properly.

'It is awful that things like this go on round here. My sister Lily always tells me never to come home late at night alone – but I work nights and it's usually early morning when I finish.'

'Yes, I know,' he said. 'I've seen you catching your bus a few mornings.' He extended his gloved hand. He was wearing black gloves and a light-coloured coat over narrow trousers and black leather shoes. 'My name is

Chris Moore – short for Christophe, my mother's choice – she is German. May I ask yours?'

'I'm Jenny Brown,' she said, blushing a little as he smiled at her. 'I'm a nurse at the Lady Rosalie infirmary and I've been on night duty.'

'I'm pleased to meet you, Jenny,' he said and his hand felt cool as it closed about hers. 'I wonder if you would permit me to take you for coffee one day – or we could meet for afternoon tea, perhaps. I have a car, just a small Morris. I could take you home or fetch you . . .'

He looked so eager at that moment that Jenny's caution was lost and she smiled. 'Do you know, I should love to go for tea with you. We could meet before I go to work at six – if you don't mind me wearing my uniform?'

'I think you look beautiful in your uniform,' he said, his eyes dwelling on her with approval. 'Why don't we meet later today? I could pick you up at home – or meet somewhere?'

'I think we might meet this time . . .' Jenny said and then blushed hotly as she realized that sounded as if she expected to meet often. 'I mean . . . there is a nice little teashop around the corner. It is run by Lavender and Lace . . .' She laughed as his eyebrows rose. 'Two sisters who wear lavender and lace. They're both widows from the last war with Germany and they run the teashop together.'

'Ah, I see,' he nodded. 'I had thought to take you up the West End but it would be easier for your work here – we'll save the high lights for when you have time off, shall we?'

Jenny gave an embarrassed little nod and then

laughed. It was exciting – and she knew she shouldn't let his words go to her head but couldn't help herself. She'd thought about him so often, hoping he would return, and now he had and it was all turning out the way she'd dreamed. She felt like pinching herself to make sure she was awake.

Somehow it was no surprise to her that he got on the bus when it came and sat down next to her. He asked the conductor for a tuppeny fare for them both, as if he already knew where she was going. Jenny's head was whirling; she felt flattered by his smile and the attention he was paying her.

'Did you know that it is hoped that a new German car costing £61 will be produced? Hitler is the inspiration behind it. They were speaking about it on the wireless last night and saying we ought to have something similar here for the working man.'

'I don't have much time for listening to the wireless,' she told him. 'I read the papers for news because I can take them up to my room or skim them on the bus in the mornings.'

'Then you will have seen that the government is blaming the ladies' craze for slimming for the drop in potatoes sales.' His eyes danced with mischief and she knew he was bent on catching her interest. 'And Cambridge won the boat race in twenty-one minutes and six seconds, the slowest winning time since 1925 when the Oxford boat sank . . .'

'I read more important things!' Jenny glared at him.

'When I was last in Germany, they had banned the British film *Catherine the Great* because its star and director are Jewish. Doesn't seem fair to me . . .' He frowned as if he disapproved of something but she wasn't sure if it was of Jews or the banning of the film.

'Do you often travel to Germany?' Jenny asked.

'I travel all over,' he said, 'but my mother still lives there so, yes, quite often.'

'Have you been to America?' She looked at him with interest.

'Yes. I was there last year,' he replied. 'I travelled by sea – it only takes a few days now – but Pan American is developing planes that they believe will carry passengers non-stop from New York to Britain one day.'

'That sounds exciting.' She looked at him curiously. 'Do you travel a lot?'

He nodded and looked thoughtful. 'I travel for my work.'

Jenny wanted to ask more but he was not forthcoming and she didn't want to seem curious. When they arrived at her bus stop, he stood up to let her out into the aisle.

'I shall see you at Lavender and Lace this afternoon,' he said and Jenny smiled.

'Yes, please,' she said and hurried down the bus to get off before the impatient conductor rang his bell again. She turned to wave to Chris from the pavement but he wasn't looking, his head bent as he wrote something in a little black notebook. She felt disappointed that he hadn't looked for her and then dismissed it as foolish.

Lily had the kettle on when she walked into the kitchen of the small terraced house. It had belonged to their father and been left to their mother and then equally to the two sisters. They shared all the expenses and the chores and Jenny would normally have been back too late to see her sister but Lily had the day off.

'Where is Gran?' Jenny asked, looking round.

'In bed,' Lily told her. 'She had a bit of a chill and said she would go up rather than infect us both.'

'I'll pop up and see if she wants a cup of tea before I have mine.'

'I've made you some toast and there's a new pot of marmalade,' Lily said. 'If you're tired, I could bring a tray up for you later?'

'No, I'll eat now,' Jenny said. 'I was tired when I came off duty but I'm not now.' It was the excitement of talking to her new friend – but Jenny wouldn't tell her sister that, because she knew Lily would not approve.

'I'm off today so I'm going shopping when we've eaten,' Lily said. 'I need some new shoes and I'll bring back some food – bread and ham and tomatoes – for tea before you go.'

'That sounds lovely but I shan't be here,' Jenny said, feeling mean as she saw Lily's face fall. 'I have to get in early for a meeting . . .'

The lie came awkwardly and Lily sensed that it wasn't the truth but Jenny seldom lied to anyone and so Lily accepted it despite her instincts. Jenny knew she ought to have told her sister the truth but she hadn't wanted to be subjected to one of Lily's lectures on the dangers of having anything to do with men. She wanted to dwell on the pleasures awaiting her later that day and savour the thought of what might come in the future.

'I'll pop up to Gran,' she said, avoiding her sister's eyes and feeling guilty as she went up to the elderly lady's room. She peeped round the door, looking at her grandmother. 'Would you like a cup of tea?'

'Not yet. I'll have some cocoa when you've had your

tea,' Gran said. 'You look pretty, Jenny. Did you meet someone nice today?'

Jenny blushed and shook her head. 'I'll bring you a cup of cocoa up later . . .'

Gran saw right through her, but she wouldn't tease Jenny and she wouldn't tell Lily. Jenny smiled as she ran down the stairs again. She might tell Gran later that she'd met someone she liked . . .

Jenny wore her uniform but put her best coat on over it and a little red hat with a feather that she knew gave her a mischievous look. She would take her nursing cap with her and put it on at work – though if Sister Norton caught her in uniform without her cap, she would catch the sharp edge of her tongue.

Gran gave her an approving look. 'He'll think he's meetin' a film star,' she said and grinned. 'Get off, love, and have a good time.'

'Will you be all right?'

'Of course, I shall. It's just a little chill.'

Jenny threw her a loving smile and left.

Chris was waiting outside the little teashop when she arrived. His face lit up and he came to meet her with outstretched hands, looking into her eyes and smiling.

'You are beautiful,' he said. 'That colour suits you – but shouldn't you be wearing your cap?'

'I'll put it on when I get to work,' Jenny said. 'This is a special treat for me and I wanted to look decent.'

'You couldn't look anything else,' he told her. 'Please, call me Chris and I'll call you Jenny, if I may?'

'Yes, please,' she said. She looked up at him as he ushered her inside. 'Have you been waiting long?'

'I booked our table earlier but I only arrived a few minutes ago.'

Jenny saw that a table had been set for them with flowers and a fancy cake stand with delicious sandwiches, almond comfits and cream eclairs, and a rich fruit cake was brought out together with a large pot of fragrant tea and two cups. Jenny poured, asking if he took milk and sugar.

'Milk, no sugar,' he said and laughed softly. 'My mother says I'm sweet enough.'

Jenny gave a little giggle. 'I need two lumps in mine. I have a sweet tooth.'

'Good – you will enjoy these, then.' Chris took a small box of Fry's chocolates from his coat pocket and passed them to her. 'I wanted to bring you flowers but I thought you couldn't take them to work . . .'

Jenny thanked him, her cheeks a little flushed. She had never been made such a fuss of before and felt a little overwhelmed. To cover her slight embarrassment, she asked, 'Does your mother like living in Germany – wouldn't she rather live here with you? Mine died when I was only twelve and I live with my sister Lily and Gran.'

He nodded, as if he already knew. 'My mother lives in – or rather near – a forest in Germany, well away from Berlin. Her family were once rather posh but the money ran out years ago. I came to England for my education and lived with my uncle after my father died. He was English. I visit Mama several times a year; it seems to be enough for her.'

Jenny studied his face, noticing the little flicker at his temples as a nerve jumped. Speaking of his mother disturbed him. 'I'm sorry. It was a personal question to ask.'

'Not at all, you must ask what you want to know, Jenny,' he said and she noticed a faint accent that she hadn't particularly observed before, probably because he was disturbed. 'My father's family were wealthy and Mama married him because of the money, but his estate passed to me when I was twenty-one and I was not prepared to waste it all on her family's old schloss that is almost falling down.' He saw her puzzlement and nodded. 'It's a small castle or chateau.'

Jenny nodded, once more in awe. She'd known from the start that there was something different about him. He wasn't from the East End and he'd been reared as a gentleman.

'I'm sorry . . .' she said because it seemed the right thing but he shook his head.

'My father knew she never loved him. He thought marriage to someone of her class would take his family up the social scale to marry into the German aristocracy, but a minor title meant nothing and he was disappointed. He left her and came home to die when he knew he had a terminal illness.'

Jenny nodded, but was not sure what to say. Chris wasn't asking for sympathy. 'So, do you live here or in Germany?'

'I have a nice country house in Hampshire and spend most of my time in England,' he told her. 'I travel when I have to and my father's money enables me to choose what I do. I do not despise where it comes from – which is a factory in Northampton making boots and shoes.'

Chris was telling her all his family history or so it seemed to Jenny. She responded by telling him about her life and her sister and before she knew it, he reminded her that it was twenty minutes to six. Jenny stared at her watch and jumped up in panic.

'I'm sorry, I have to go,' she said. 'It has been lovely – but Sister Norton will murder me if I'm late!'

'Of course, you must go,' he agreed and smiled. 'Tomorrow I shall be away – but will you meet me again on Friday?'

'Yes, please,' Jenny said. 'Thank you so much for my lovely tea and the chocolates. Where shall I see you on Friday?'

'We shall make this our meeting place – until I can take you somewhere special. You must have time off?'

'Yes, I have three days next week.'

'Then next week we shall go somewhere special but on the days you work we shall come here.'

Jenny agreed, smiled, thanked him again and fled.

'Evening, nurse,' Bert Rush, the caretaker said as she passed him on her way to the cloakroom. 'Look out for Sister tonight. She's on the warpath!' He winked at her as she hurried into the nurses' rest room.

Jenny hung up her coat and hat and fixed her cap before walking as quickly as she dared to the children's ward. Sister Norton was making her first round of the evening and looked pointedly at the silver watch she had pinned to her uniform, but since Jenny had made it on time by the skin of her teeth, she did no more than send her a warning look.

Jenny went up to her and was given a report on the admissions that day. A young boy had fallen from a wall he'd been climbing on and broken his wrist and was in a lot of pain.

'Ned will need watching this evening, nurse,' Sister Norton said, 'but otherwise there is nothing out of the ordinary. Unless we have some new admissions brought in, it should be a quiet night.'

CHAPTER 10

Sarah was feeling weary when she got in from work that evening. Maisie had been miserable when she'd popped in to see her and needed reassurance, because Charlie hadn't been.

'He's settling into his new home,' she'd told the little girl, feeling a tug at her heartstrings as she saw her wan face. Sarah hoped he was all right and truthfully, she missed the sight of his cheerful grin.

She'd been kept late by Sister Norton on the ward, missed her bus and had to wait for the next to come along and she was cold and cross. Yet the moment she entered the warm kitchen and saw the terrible look on her mother's face she knew something was badly wrong.

'What is it, Mum?' she asked and her heart started beating too fast, making her breathless. 'Where's Dad?'

'He's in the London Hospital,' her mother said. 'He had a heart attack in the night, Sarah. I ran down to the corner and phoned from the box. Dr Park had him rushed in immediately and I went with him. They told me to go home at about three this morning and I've been sitting here ever since . . .'

Sarah sat down heavily because it was such a shock. Her father suffered with a bad back and they'd all thought he was fine otherwise but this explained why he didn't get on with things these days. He'd been suffering but he hadn't told them, because he didn't want to worry them . . . just as her mother hadn't contacted the infirmary because Sarah was working and she didn't want her upset.

'He will get better,' she began but her mother shook her head.

'No, Sarah. I rang them a few moments ago – and they told me he passed away a few minutes after I left the hospital. They were going to send the police to let us know this morning.'

'Mum – no!' Sarah was stunned. 'He can't be dead just like that!'

'They told me he must have been ill a long time. They seemed to think he knew but he never told us . . .' Now, Mrs Cartwright had tears trickling down her cheeks. 'Why didn't he tell me? I used to tell him off for not fetching in the wood and stuff like that – if I'd known I wouldn't have said a word . . .'

'Oh, Mum,' Sarah sobbed, feeling sick and stunned, 'to think he kept it to himself all this time! Why?'

'I wish I knew,' her mother said and looked angry. 'He should have told me, Sarah. I could have looked after him more, wouldn't have let him go to work. He could have been here with me.' She dashed away her tears. 'I'll never forgive him for doing this to me – never!'

'Dad was just trying to protect us the way he always did,' Sarah said. 'Dad loved us too much to have us worrying about him . . .'

'I know . . .' Sarah's mother bent her head and wept, her body wracked with deep, painful sobs. Sarah knelt and put her arms about her as they both cried out their loss. 'But I loved him too and he didn't know . . .'

'Of course he did, Mum,' Sarah said. 'You moaned a bit but we all do. You were a good wife and he knew it.'

'I can't forgive myself for not knowing,' Mrs Cartwright said, lifting her head to look at Sarah. 'I should have taken more care of him and then he would still be with us.'

Sarah felt guilty too. She was a nurse and should have seen the signs. It was more her fault than her mother's, but they would both feel this guilt because they'd lost the man they loved so much . . .

Sarah stood by her mother in church a week later and listened to the singing. These hymns had been her father's favourite and when she'd been younger, he'd been a regular churchgoer, taking her every Sunday morning. When she'd left school and started work, he'd stopped going to church and Sarah wondered if that was a sign that he'd known he was very ill. Had he lost his faith because it was so unfair? He was only fifty and should have had another twenty years at least.

Sarah had thought she might find peace in the church but she hadn't. As she and her mother placed a rose each in the grave, she found herself asking: why her father? What had he done to deserve this?

'I'm really sorry, Sarah, love.' Ruby Harding came up to her as they walked away from the churchyard.

'Your dad was one of the good ones. If there's anything I can do . . .?'

'Thanks, but no one can do anything,' Sarah said. 'Mum will get a tiny pension he'd paid in for and they had some small savings so we'll manage without her having to work – but that won't make up for him not being around.'

'Nothing makes up for that,' Ruby said. 'It's strange the way the heart just gives out. My brother was working down the docks when he died. One minute they said he looked as right as rain and then he just dropped where he stood – and he was only twenty-three. It broke my mother and she died a few weeks later.'

'I'm so sorry, I didn't know,' Sarah said and her gaze went to her mother, who was looking pale and anxious. 'I'd better look after Mum . . .'

'Yes, you do that,' Ruby said, 'but your ma is made of sterner stuff than mine. She will go on, Sarah, and so must you.'

Sarah turned as Jim touched her arm. 'Are you ready to go, Sarah? Your mother is in need of a cup of tea and a sit down.'

'Yes, I know,' she said. 'You'll come back with us, won't you?'

'I can't, love,' he replied. 'I'm on duty this lunchtime. I took an hour off but I have to get back.'

'All right . . .' Sarah allowed him to kiss her cheek and then hurried after her mother, slipping her arm about her waist. 'We'll soon be home, Mum.'

'Yes.' Mrs Cartwright looked at her. 'I'll be all right now, Sarah. You don't need to worry about me.'

'I love you, Mum,' Sarah said. 'You're special . . .'

She smiled and held the door of the car they'd hired to take them home. 'You're my mum . . .'

Her mother smiled and for the first time in days it reached her eyes. Sarah's throat caught. She'd told her mother how much she loved her but she would never stop wishing that she'd told her father the same thing more often, because perhaps then he would have shared his burden with her.

Shaking her head, Sarah made a determined effort to stop moping. Her father had loved them and if he'd kept his secret it was because he wanted it that way. She'd loved him and he'd loved her, but now she had to look forward to the future. Jim would pop round the next day and they would have a little time together before she went to work and he was taking her out in the evening . . .

On her way home the next evening, Sarah saw Sid Harding at the end of the lane that led to his house and smiled at him. He gave her a half-hearted grin and hesitated, then approached her.

'Ruby ain't in – do yer happen to know where she is?'

'I think she'll still be at work,' Sarah told him. 'She is on late shift today – didn't she say?'

Sid coloured and then mumbled. 'Ruby threw me out the other week. I deserved it, but I've got somethin' for 'er and I'm hopin' she'll take me back.'

Sarah couldn't help giving a little laugh as she saw his hangdog expression. 'I'm sure she will, Mr Harding. We all know Ruby has got a temper but she soon gets over it – and I'm certain she cares about you.'

'I hope yer right – yer won't tell 'er I said anythin'?' He hesitated, then, 'I was right sorry about yer dad. I knew he was under the weather, of course, but he were never one fer makin' a fuss. Nice chap, do anythin' fer anyone.'

'Thank you, Sid, and of course I shan't say anything to Ruby. 'And good luck. I'm sure it will be all right . . .'

He nodded but didn't look convinced and Sarah hid her amusement because it wasn't funny for Sid. He must have been sleeping rough – probably in the shed at the bottom of their garden. It was his own fault for coming home drunk once too often, but she hoped Ruby would relent and let him in. Sid wasn't a bad man, not when you thought about what went on in some of the houses around here. Sarah knew from her work at the infirmary that some men regularly beat their wives on a Friday night. Drinking was the problem – men who had been humiliated all week drank to forget and then took their frustration out on those they were supposed to love and care for.

CHAPTER 11

Maisie was crying when Sarah went in to visit her the next morning and wouldn't stop no matter what anyone said to her. Sarah reached for her, drawing her into her arms and hugging her.

'Please, tell me what is wrong?' she asked and Maisie looked up at her, hiccupping.

'Charlie hasn't been to see me once and he promised faithfully. I think he's sick or dead!' she wailed in despair. 'He *never* breaks his promise 'cepting when they make him, so he must be dead.'

'No, he isn't, because we would have heard,' Sarah said and stroked her face. 'He will come as soon as he can, I'm sure.'

'He promised faithfully and it's years since he came!'

Sarah smiled but then it faded. It was ten days or so since Charlie had been taken to the baker's house and surely he would have come on Sunday if he could? There was no school and he wouldn't be doing chores for the couple every night, and Saturday and Sunday. A frown creased her forehead. She knew that not every foster family was good to the children they took in and something wasn't right.

She kissed Maisie's cheek. 'Try not to worry, love,' she told the little girl. 'I will ask Matron about Charlie – see if she knows why he hasn't been. I'll find out for you, I promise.'

Maisie looked at her and nodded. 'Charlie says you're nice. Please tell him I need to see him – I'm lonely without him.'

'Yes, I know.' Sarah nodded. Maisie's mum was ill in hospital and with her brother gone she had no one to care for her but nurses – and however kind they were it must be upsetting for her. 'I'll try to go round and see if Charlie is all right, darling.'

Maisie gave her a watery smile. 'Thank you – I feel so sad without him.'

Sarah knew that despite her own grief and worry over her father's death, she must find time to visit the people who had taken Charlie.

'Yes, that is a little strange,' Matron said when Sarah asked if she'd heard anything. 'No, I've not been told he is unwell or anything of the kind – but they might not have thought it important.' She hesitated, then, 'Would you like me to inquire about Charlie – or do you wish to yourself?'

'I promised Maisie I would,' Sarah said and sighed. 'It's not easy, because Mum is on her own and things are a bit hard just now.'

'Of course they are,' Matron replied. 'Let me do it this time, Sarah. I think it is my job – after all, I allowed Mr Robinson to take him.' A slight frown touched her forehead. 'I know he received all the back-ground checks but there was . . . something. I thought it was my imagination but – yes, I shall certainly go round this afternoon. And I have the authority. I shall tell them Charlie must visit his sister this weekend.'

'Thank you so much; I feel better now,' Sarah said. 'Maisie is pining for him and she won't start to get better unless her brother comes to see her.'

Mary stood outside the shop and looked in the window. The bread and cakes looked good and she thought she might purchase a Victoria sandwich for herself while she was there. The shop was nearly empty and, as she waited to be served, she heard a cry from out the back; it sounded like a boy's yell of pain and she frowned; Charlie ought to be at school.

'Yes, madam, what can I get you?' the woman behind the counter asked.

'I've called to ask about Charlie Howes,' Mary said. 'He hasn't been to see his sister and she needs to see him – so, now I'm here, I should like to see him.'

'And who are you then?' the woman asked, her tone belligerent all of a sudden. 'What's it to you?'

'I am Matron of the Rosalie Infirmary and I am a friend of Lady Rosalie – one word from me and the Welfare Officer will be here and Charlie will be taken out of your care!'

The woman turned pale. She went to the back of the shop and called out, 'Alfie, – a Welfare woman is 'ere and she wants ter see the boy . . .'

There was a second of silence, whispers that Mary couldn't quite hear and then Charlie emerged from the back shop. He had a black mark on his face and looked at her sullenly, his eyes dull. Mary's heart sank. Something *was* wrong. This wasn't the same boy she'd sent away from the Rosie.

'Miss Thurston . . .' Mr Alfred Robinson followed Charlie into the shop. 'You've come to see the boy. To tell the truth he's had a bit of a cold. I thought it was best he stay off school and not visit his sister – don't want him passin' on his infection, do we?'

The excuse was one she could hardly dispute for Charlie's nose was red and so were his eyes.

'How are you, Charlie – is it all right here?' she asked.

Charlie hesitated, looked towards Mr Robinson and then lifted his head, a glint of pride in his eyes. 'It's all right, Matron,' he said. 'Nuthin' I can't handle.'

Mary felt ice at her nape. She knew without doubt that he'd been bullied into giving her that answer and felt angry, but there was little she could do at this moment. Despite her threats, she did not have the right to take him from his foster home, even though she suspected cruel treatment. However, she wouldn't leave it here now that her doubts were roused.

'I want your promise to visit Maisie on Saturday afternoon,' she told him and her gaze moved to Mr Robinson. 'If you don't come, I shall fetch you myself – and that is a promise!'

Would Charlie understand that she was on his side? Was he sensible enough to know that she wouldn't just walk away and leave things as they were?

'He'll be there,' Mr Robinson said gruffly. 'I'll bring him meself.'

So, he had no intention of letting Charlie visit without him. Mary's instincts told her he was afraid the boy would run or tell his story. There was something dreadfully wrong here. She knew it, but her hands were tied by red tape and the law.

'Very well,' she said and nodded sternly. 'I shall expect you at two sharp – and if you don't come, I'll be round to fetch you.'

She walked out of the shop feeling as if she would burst with anger. Everything was screaming abuse at her but she couldn't prove it. All she could do was to report it and wait for the authorities to move . . .

Mary's first call was to her friend Lady Rosalie, who seemed stunned when she told her she suspected abuse. 'But surely if the boy had a cold . . .?'

'I know he may have done but to me it looked as if he'd been crying,' Mary said. 'I've seen enough abuse in my time to know, Rosalie. I'm as certain as I can be, without actually seeing it, that he's been beaten and bullied into submission. He told me he was all right but I saw the truth in his eyes.'

'Then we made a mistake,' her friend said sounding upset. 'They were entirely convincing and the background checks were thorough . . .'

'And they tell you that Mr Robinson has a good business and his wife looks after the shop and that neither have convictions for any crime – but do they tell you if he is vindictive or why he wants a child to foster? Charlie looked as if he'd been cleaning ovens or something of the sort.'

'Cheap labour,' Lady Rosalie said and her voice

caught with anger. 'I just pray that is all it is, Mary. I'll have someone investigate as soon as possible – a day or so at most.'

'And in the meantime, what happens to Charlie?' Mary asked.

'I can't promise he won't be harmed,' Lady Rosalie said, 'but I will tell them it is a matter of priority.'

'Thank you – I knew you would get something done,' Mary said, but the worry was still there. 'Supposing they can't find evidence – what happens then?'

'We can't do anything without evidence.' Lady Rosalie sounded shaken. 'I trust your instinct, Mary. I am sure if you think there is mistreatment then it will be discovered.' She paused for a moment. 'What made you go there?'

'Nurse Cartwright was concerned for Maisie, who is pining for her brother, and so she asked me for the address and something made me go, and it is as well I did – they would just have sent her away. I forced them to let me see Charlie and I know, Rosalie, I just know that boy has been beaten!'

CHAPTER 12

His bedroom door was locked and the windows had bars on them. Not that you could truly call it a bedroom; it was more of a storeroom with a mattress on the floor. Charlie shivered as he pulled the one blanket up around his neck. He was a prisoner and there was no way out until his master came to let him through into the bakery where he worked. He thought of his foster father as a master, because he'd been treated as an unpaid servant since the moment he'd left the Rosie. Mrs Robinson had a sharp tongue and slapped him every time he was slow to answer or obey her commands. However, she fed him bread and dripping and a bit of stew yesterday that was left over when she and her husband had finished their meal; it had congealed and gone cold by the time he ate with the bent spoon she shoved at him. His hopes of a slice of cake had never been realized, because she sold her cakes until they were so dry that even the birds wouldn't look at them.

Charlie didn't like her, but she didn't frighten him the way her husband did. His master was a brute – and when, in the early moments of realizing what his life would be, Charlie had tried to protest and run, he'd been beaten with hammer fists that knocked him to the ground and left him reeling with pain and dizziness. The big man had stood over him, grim-faced and threatening.

'You're here to work, boy, and that's just what yer'll do,' he'd said coldly. 'Defy me again and yer'll wish yer had never been born.'

Charlie was wise enough not to defy his master openly after that but it hadn't saved him from a blow to the head or a spiteful pinch if he was a bit slow answering or didn't do his work satisfactorily. Boiling with anger inside, Charlie knew he had to use his wits to escape the evil couple who had fooled the folk at the Rosie into thinking them suitable foster parents.

Once he got the chance he would run. He'd been watching everything they did and it wouldn't be easy, because there was always one of them in the shop or the bakery behind it. Only on a Thursday did Mr Robinson leave for any amount of time and that was to go to the warehouse to buy his flours and the other ingredients needed for the cakes and bread he baked. When he went out, he locked the back door, and all the main windows had bars across them to stop anyone breaking in – or an unhappy lad getting out. Charlie had wondered if he was the first to fall prey to their cruelty and then, from various remarks they made to each other, discovered he was the latest in a string of unlucky boys.

'He's worse than the last,' Mrs Robinson had remarked when she thought Charlie was busy eating his tea. 'Too much spirit left in him.'

'I'll soon break that,' her husband grated. 'Anyway,

people are always making a fuss over these bloody brats, but I know what I'm doing and we won't have no bloody coppers sniffing about if I have anything to do with it.' He'd given her such a look that his wife had gone quiet, making Charlie wonder what had happened to the child before him.

That had been before Matron came to see them, making Mr Robinson promise to let Charlie visit his sister and threatening to fetch him if he didn't turn up. It had nearly broken him when he'd heard Matron say Maisie was crying because he hadn't been. The devil that was his master wouldn't even let him out alone in the backyard for a breath of air. The yard was surrounded by a high brick wall and had big wooden gates that were kept bolted from the inside. After Matron's visit he'd been locked in his room for two hours before he was dragged out and told to start scrubbing the bakery floor.

He'd heard the row that was going on while he was locked in.

'I told you it would bring trouble on us!' Mrs Robinson screamed at her husband. 'I warned you not to be too clever but you wouldn't listen!'

'Shut yer mouth or I'll shut if for yer!'

'Threaten me would yer?' There was a scuffling noise and then a yell from Mr Robinson.

'Bitch!' he cried. 'You nearly broke my arm with that thing.'

'You'll get more than the poker, Robinson,' she said furiously. 'Just remember what I know could hang yer, so treat me right or I'll see yer behind bars.'

'I'll take yer down with me!'

'No, they'll believe I was scared of yer,' she retaliated. 'Folk will side with me – and I'm tellin' yer to get rid of that boy. He's too dangerous to keep. Yer want a boy orf the streets no one cares about – that nosy bitch what came 'ere won't let up on yer. She'll make trouble, mark my words.'

'I've got an idea . . .' Her husband lowered his voice and Charlie strained to hear. He could only catch the occasional word but one he did hear sent the chills down his spine. 'The Greek . . . 'e's told people he'll pay money for the little runt.'

Charlie's teeth chattered, as much with fear as with the cold. Why did Ronnie the Greek want him? Perhaps Ronnie was afraid he'd tell the police about what he'd done to Charlie's mother. Or maybe he thought he knew more about his evil ways. Charlie had heard him boasting of various beatings he'd administered to his enemies and those who refused to pay protection money, but he'd never really listened – Ronnie might not know that, though . . .

The next day, both Robinsons kept giving him evil grins which made him shiver inside, and when Mr Robinson went out, Charlie knew that he must be going to find the man who had beaten his mother senseless. They were going to sell him to his enemy and then tell Matron that he'd run away.

Charlie hadn't slept all night because he'd been working out a plan of escape – and he knew this was his chance. Mr Robinson had locked the door that led from the bakery into the shop; the back door was also locked and bolted and he couldn't get out of the windows or the yard. So there was only one way –

through the shop. He went through to the kitchen, his gaze falling on the long iron poker that Mrs Robinson had used against her husband. He picked it up, testing its weight, and then looked for one of her cooking knives. The lock between the two doors was strong, but the wood itself was rotten and Charlie believed he could prise it open and then force the door. He listened for voices and heard several. Good! His master's wife was busy and wouldn't be able to think about what he was doing at first.

Charlie used the sharp knife on the wood that surrounded the lock and, just as he'd thought, it crumbled and fell away when he'd made a big enough hole to insert the heavy poker. It split with a sharp crack and then the door swung open. He moved forward and saw the look of shock on Mrs Robinson's face as he walked into her shop. A woman was about to pay for her purchases from the counter and she stared as Charlie advanced on them.

'Thanks, missus,' he said and snatched up the paper bag from the counter. 'They ain't been feedin' me much – these will come in 'andy!'

'You little varmint!' Mrs Robinson found the use of her tongue and moved towards him, but Charlie brandished his poker at her. 'Just you come back here! It will be the worse fer yer when Mr Robinson gets back.'

'From sellin' me to that crook?' Charlie chirped, his cheeky nature reasserting itself. 'Shan't be around, missus – watch out, lady, I don't want ter hurt yer!'

He ran past the startled customer, who shrank away in fear. No doubt Mrs Robinson would spin her a tale about them having to lock him up because he was dangerous but Charlie didn't care. He was out of that prison and had no intention of being caught again.

To begin with, Charlie just ran blindly. He abandoned the poker a few streets away because it was heavy, but he hung on to the bag of cakes he'd snatched. Mrs Robinson would have to replace them or the customer wouldn't pay and that just served her right. She could have protected him from her husband's bullying and she could have fed him properly, but she hadn't and so she deserved to lose a few cakes – and he was glad he'd threatened her with the poker, even though he wasn't sure he could have used it. However, the threat had been enough, because one lucky blow could have broken her arm or leg.

Charlie was out of breath by the time he reached the docks, where he felt at home. There were lots of places he could hide here and people he knew – good men who had sometimes given him an odd job or even sixpence just because they had done well that day. He found a pile of old ropes behind a stack of crates and sat down to investigate the contents of the bag. Three sticky buns with pink icing – Maisie's favourites!

The thought made Charlie's eyes sting and because it was over a week since he'd eaten sufficient and the bread and dripping had been slightly rancid, he ate two buns rapidly. He eyed the third but decided he would keep it.

It was mid-morning. At the Rosie the nurses would be busy washing sick patients, giving out medicines and replacing dressings. There was a good chance he could sneak in and spend a little time with his sister and leave before anyone saw him. He'd climbed the wall at the back, which was easy to do as outside the wall of the hospital garden there was a pile of rubble that had been placed there at some time and never cleared away. It had made it easy for Charlie to get over the wall, because there were holes in the old bricks that he had used as footholds.

Charlie had considered whether he should go to Matron and tell her about the way he'd been treated – but would she believe him? Even if she did, it was only a matter of time before he was given to another set of foster parents and while they might not be as cruel as the Robinsons, they would make him do as he was told. Charlie had had enough of being told what to do. He reckoned he could manage on his own, earn enough from blokes he knew and trusted – and he'd eat better than he had at that bakery!

No, he wasn't going to tell anyone that he'd run away. He would simply use his way in and out to visit Maisie and take her little treats. He would make her understand that his visits were their secret, because if Ronnie the Greek was after him, Charlie had to be careful. If they thought he'd gone back to the Rosie they would follow him and snatch him so it was best to lie low for the moment.

Charlie grinned. He'd put the wind up that old witch! It was a good feeling to know that he'd escaped despite all they'd done to keep him a prisoner. They'd thought he was stupid, but that was their mistake. Charlie had had to fend for himself for most of his life so he'd learned to think things through. He'd been frightened when he was beaten, thought he might die at that bully's hands, but it had just made him more determined to get away. He would have to keep his wits about him, make sure neither Mr Robinson or Ronnie the Greek nabbed him, but no one knew the docks better than Charlie and he could hide there from those that threatened him – and now he was going to see Maisie . . .

'Susan is over the infection now, but she is still unwell,' Nurse Jenny said as Charlie listened near the door. 'So, try not to make a noise.'

Maisie was used to being told to keep quiet. When her mother brought men home, she was sent out into the garden to play by herself and spent a lot of her time daydreaming. She mostly thought about when she was very little and her daddy had come home from the sea, tossed her into the air and kissed her. He'd always had a small gift for each of them, but then one day he hadn't come back and Charlie told her he'd gone in the sea. At first, she hadn't understood but some of the other kids in the lanes had told her that her daddy was dead and she would never see him again. The tears had come then, until Charlie put his arm about her and told her that their father was watching over them from Heaven.

'You can't see 'im, Maisie,' he'd told her, 'but he can see us and he looks after us as much as he can.'

Maisie was comforted, but since her mother brought that horrible man, Ronnie the Greek home, she had felt that her daddy must have forgotten about them, because surely he wouldn't let them be beaten and sent out without food if he knew?

Charlie stood just outside the door of his sister's room and listened. The nurse had gone but someone was still there. He grinned as he recognized the voice. That was Ruby – he liked her. She wouldn't tell on him even if she guessed he shouldn't be here.

'I bet yer miss yer mum,' Ruby was saying sympathetically. 'Tell yer what – how about yer come to my house fer tea on Saturday next week? Yer can bring Charlie and all. We always 'ave jelly and a bit of strawberry ice cream from the shop on a Saturday.'

'Yes, please,' Maisie said excitedly. 'Where is your house?'

'I'm just round the corner from where yer ma lived,' Ruby said. 'My Julia will come to fetch yer after lunch on Saturday.' She smiled at Maisie. 'I wouldn't mind havin' the pair of yer round whenever yer like – love kids, I do, always 'ave.'

'Thank you . . . I don't know your name, missus . . .'

'It's Mrs Ruby to you, love,' Ruby said and smiled at her. 'Maybe Nurse Sarah will pop in fer a bite too on Saturday.' She winked at Maisie as she piled up her trolley with used plates and dishes and went off down the ward.

Charlie slipped into the room and his sister sat up, a smile of welcome on her face. 'Charlie! You've come at last!'

'I told yer I'd be back, didn't I?' he said and sat on her bed, giving her the bag with the stolen bun inside. 'I got this for yer.'

'My favourite,' she said and smiled at him. 'Why didn't yer come sooner?'

'They wouldn't let me.' Charlie put a finger to his lips. 'I ran away from 'em, Maisie, 'cos they were horrible and made me work 'ard – but you mustn't tell.

It's got to be our secret.' She nodded, looking excited to be sharing a secret. 'Good girl.'

'What did yer 'ave ter do wiv them people?' Maisie asked, curious now.

'Scrubbin' and stuff – the toilets out the back an' all; they didn't 'alf pong.' He grinned at her. 'I'm goin' ter be working fer a mate of mine in future. He's got jobs deliverin' stuff, see – and he wants me ter take bets to the bookie's shop fer 'im. It ain't legal, but I know how to avoid the coppers.'

'You're clever. I wish I was wiv yer . . .' She sighed and coughed and he frowned. She was better but not really well yet.

'I'll buy a present fer yer birthday when Mick pays me.'

'Can I 'ave it when yer come?' she asked, sitting up eagerly.

'Not until yer birthday,' he said and smiled, because he loved his little sister and he'd promised his dad and Ma he would look after her.

'Ruby invited us to tea at her house on Saturday.' She told her brother all about it as she licked pink icing from her finger. 'They have jelly and ice cream on Saturday.'

'She's one of the cleaners,' Charlie said nodding. 'I know her. Yeah, she's all right, so we'll go. I'll meet yer when yer come out wiv her daughter like she said.'

'She said Nurse Sarah might be there too.' She looked at him anxiously. 'You won't forget about me?'

'Yer my sister and I promise I'll look after yer while I've breath in me body.'

Maisie smiled up at him. Charlie saw the love in her

eyes and vowed in his head that, no matter what, he would visit his sister – and as soon as she was well enough he would find them a place to stay and look her after himself.

CHAPTER 13

Sarah's mother was boiling the kettle when she got in. The table was spread with a lavish tea of homemade sausage rolls, jam tarts, slices of fruit cake and sandwiches made of tomatoes and lettuce with a little salt, pepper and vinegar.

'You *have* been busy, Mum,' Sarah said looking at the food in surprise. Her mother seemed almost back to normal but she hadn't expected a special tea. 'It isn't your birthday or mine – so what's the occasion?'

'Jim called in earlier and said he has some news. I invited him for tea and thought I would make it a bit special.' She shrugged. 'It gave me somethin' to do. I don't have much to think about now there's just the two of us . . .' Her sagging shoulders told Sarah that, despite her upbeat mood, she was struggling with her loss.

'Oh Mum,' Sarah said throatily and gave her a quick hug, 'what did I do to deserve you?'

'I'm not sure,' her mother said with a brave smile. 'I dare say I'll think of something . . .'

Mrs Cartwright was back to her normal calm self on the surface but was obviously lonely. Sarah felt anxious about leaving her but she couldn't afford to take too much time off work. Grief was something you had to work through and, as Ruby had said, Sarah's mother was strong. She would work it out for herself.

Sarah unpacked her basket. She'd been to the market to buy vegetables and some other shopping her mother needed before coming home.

'I'll just go up and tidy myself before Jim gets here.'

'Fine,' Mrs Cartwright said and warmed the old brown teapot with boiled water, 'he'll be here any minute . . .'

Sarah brushed her hair. The breeze had blown it all over the place when she'd stopped to talk to a neighbour in the market. They'd heard the sound of a band playing and marching feet in the distance.

'It's them men marchin'' again,' old Mrs Green had grumbled. 'I reckon them fascists are stirring 'em up ter make trouble.'

Sarah had seen articles about Mosley's Blackshirts in the papers and didn't like what she read at all. He'd been calling for a dictatorship in Britain and stirred up men, who were out of work and desperate, to clash with the police, causing riots and unrest – and they were reported to have beaten Jews, smashed their shop-fronts and threatened them with death.

Fortunately, the march passed by and did not enter the market place. Sarah was relieved. Everyone said the Blackshirts weren't from round here and no one wanted them or their master preaching anarchy in their streets.

As Sarah put on a short-sleeved yellow jumper her mother had knitted her, she heard Jim's voice downstairs and smiled. She never tired of his company and was always pleased when he popped round, even if only for a few minutes.

She went down to the kitchen. Jim turned to look at her and his face lit up but then the smile faded and Sarah knew his news wasn't good.

'What happened?'

'The Brewery has appointed a manager from out of town,' Jim said. 'I've given notice and I've been after a new job – trouble is, it's up West.'

'Oh Jim!' Sarah started towards him, her hand reaching out. 'Surely that's good news? It must pay better up there?'

'Yes, it does and it is for an under manager. They seemed to like me – and I've got to go and see them on Monday for my answer. If I'm in, I'll get training and the pay is an extra thirty bob a week.'

'But that's wonderful!'

'If I get the job . . .'

'I'm sure you will,' Sarah said and tucked her arm through his, smiling up at him. She rubbed her face against his cheek lovingly. 'Don't worry, you've done the right thing, love.'

'If I don't get it, I might be out of work for a while.'

'They needed a bit of a jolt,' Sarah's mother said. 'That firm have taken you for granted for too long, Jim. You've been helping run that place for a year or more – and then they give the manager's job to a stranger. It's a damned insult.'

Jim nodded, but his gaze was fixed on Sarah. 'I was angry when I threw my job up – but if I get this, we'll have more money.' He hesitated, then, 'It means we shan't get to see each other like this, though.'

Sarah nodded, understanding that he wouldn't be able to come right across town a couple of times a day. It would be a sacrifice for them both and yet the money would enable them to save for a home quicker.

'I'll miss your visits in the mornings but we will see each other sometimes?'

'Sundays and my day off,' Jim said and Sarah felt a sinking sensation inside. She'd been used to him popping in every day, if only for a few minutes. For a moment she wondered if Jim's dream of having their own home was worth it. They could quite easily live here with her mother or find a couple of rooms.

'That's as much as most couples get,' Sarah's mother said. 'You've been spoiled. Now, you'll probably see sense about making a compromise.'

'I've got to live on the premises,' Jim said. 'It's just a room but it's a part of the contract – and if I succeed, I might get a promotion and the managers get their own flat. We could marry then.'

It was an olive branch, but Sarah wasn't impressed. She felt a surge of anger but there was no point in taking her disappointment out on Jim.

'Sounds lovely,' she said. 'Shall we have tea? Mum got it specially for you.'

'Yes, and it looks delicious,' Jim said. 'I'm really going to miss this, Mrs Cartwright. I'm sorry it wasn't the news we'd all hoped for.'

'Don't apologize, lad,' Sarah's mother said. 'We know it isn't your fault – and no one blames you. Give this job a go but in the meantime keep your eye open for something better, something nearer home.'

Jim nodded and sat down at the table. Mrs Cartwright

had started to pour their tea when the back door opened and Ruby Harding poked her head round.

'I shan't disturb yer long,' she said and came in without needing an invitation. 'Sarah, love, I've invited them pair of kids from the infirmary on Saturday fer tea. You'll come down and 'ave a bit wiv us, won't yer?'

'Yes, of course she will, Ruby,' Sarah's mother answered for her. 'Do you want to share ours with us today? Jim has got a new job so we're celebrating.'

'Not certain yet,' he reminded her.

'You'll get it,' she said and Ruby approached the table, eyeing the food enviously.

'I'll take one of them sausage rolls for my girl,' she said, 'and a jam tart – if that's all right?'

'Yes, of course.' Mrs Cartwright put two of each on a small plate and Ruby grinned at her. 'How is Julia – and Sid?'

'She is lovely as always,' Ruby said. 'As fer Sid – well, the least said the better. I'll see yer on Saturday, Sarah love.'

'Yes, thank you, Ruby.'

Sarah looked at her mother after Ruby had gone, raising her eyebrows. 'You might have let me answer, Mum. Though I do want to go – I've been quite worried about how Charlie is getting on.'

'You couldn't say no – not when she's havin' them kids you're always fussing over,' her mother said and smiled. 'Eat your tea, Sarah – and then you two should take a walk. It may be the last chance you get for a while.'

'Only if you leave the washing-up for me.'

Mrs Cartwright shook her head and offered Jim the sausage rolls. 'There's more in the tin, lad. I made plenty. Ruby has a habit of popping in when she knows I've been baking – not that I mind. When she has anything to share, she's always generous. It's just that doesn't happen often – except on a Saturday. She gives Julia a good tea when she gets her wages but the rest of the week it's likely to be bread and dripping.' She looked at her daughter thoughtfully. 'Ruby was telling me she would like to foster those children if she could be sure of Sid's wage. I hadn't ever thought about it before . . .'

'Ruby is all right,' Sarah said. 'She looks out for young Kathy at work. It is her first job and she wasn't very good when she first started, but Ruby took her under her wing and helped her out. I think Matron might have had to fire her if Ruby hadn't shown her the ropes.'

'You're talking about Kathy Saunders?' Mrs Cartwright nodded. 'I've seen her walking home a few times. She always looks so miserable and it's not surprising. Her mother is a widow and she never stops complaining. Whenever I see her, she always has a tale of woe – and I've heard her get on to that poor girl something terrible. I'd bet she has a hell of a life at home.'

'I didn't realize,' Sarah said. 'Poor girl . . .' She smiled at Jim. 'I'm lucky and I know it – and you did the right thing. It won't be as easy to meet as it was but we'll manage, love.'

'Yes, we will,' he agreed and wiped his mouth on the linen serviette Mrs Cartwright had put out for him. Gwen Cartwright had high standards and they'd never wavered, even in hard times. 'Come on, let's go for a walk down to the docks – and then we'll both do the washing-up when we get back.'

'Get off with you,' Sarah's mother said. 'When I need the washing-up done, I'll ask – now go and enjoy yourselves while you can. Ruby's given me something to think about . . .'

CHAPTER 14

'You're lucky, Sid Harding, and don't yer forget it,' Ruby said to her husband as she looked inside the wage packet. There were five one-pound notes and some shillings. More than he'd brought home in a long time. 'How did you get this, then?'

'I went down the labour exchange and they sent me after a bricklayin' job and they set me on,' Sid said, a smile lurking in his eyes. 'That's two weeks' money; I 'ad ter work two weeks afore they paid me. I ain't forgot how to do it, Ruby. It's just since me accident I thought they wouldn't take me on the site no more.'

'Well, you can't climb scaffolding with your leg,' Ruby reminded him with a frown. 'You might miss yer step and fall and break yer daft neck.'

'The boss knows that – but he wants a brickie who can do foundation work for a large building – and that was always my favourite job, Ruby.'

She nodded, looking thoughtful. 'Yes, I know you were always good with settin' out and layin' the foundations.'

'I promise I won't go back to the drinkin', Ruby. I've learned me lesson.'

Ruby glanced at her daughter. 'Have yer said sorry to Julia, then?'

'She knows I didn't mean to hurt 'er,' Sid said. 'I lost me rag but it won't 'appen no more. I give yer me word, lass.'

'What do you say, Julia – can yer dad stay?'

'Of course, he can, Mum,' Julia said and smiled at them. 'I know it was an accident – and Dad has promised me he won't get drunk again.'

'I'm orf the beer,' Sid said. 'I had a shock the other night – and I don't mean just you throwin' me out, though that was bad enough.'

Ruby waited but he said no more. 'Sit down and have some tea then. These sausage rolls and jam tarts are for Julia – but I'll fry you a bit of liver and onions. I know you like it and I saw yer hangin' about the lane earlier so I nipped down the butcher and bought it.'

Her words told both Sid and Julia that he'd been totally forgiven and he sat in his chair by the fire, watching as Ruby prepared their tea. Julia ate one of the jam tarts and then waited for her mother to sit down at the table, before giving her mother and father the news she'd been dying to tell them.

'I've won that scholarship to the grammar school,' she announced. 'It's a chance for me, Mum – but you know you have to pay for the uniform and all the other stuff I'll need, like books and PE gear and a hockey stick and boots . . .?'

They stared at her with a mixture of awe and dismay.

'Grammar school?' Ruby stared at her in silence for a moment. 'You never 'ave?'

'Yes, Mum,' Julia said and the longing was in her

face for her parents to see. 'It would give me a chance of going to college free too later on – and that's what I need to do if I'm going to be a teacher.'

'A teacher, is it?' Sid looked at her with pride. 'Well, I reckon we'll have to find the money for that uniform and stuff somehow . . .'

Ruby just nodded and ate her tea in silence as Julia told them excitedly how wonderful it would be at the school she longed to go to. It would take more than five pounds in a wage packet, Ruby knew that much – but she didn't want to disappoint her daughter or squash her husband's good intentions. Later, she would ask him if he really meant what he'd said about stopping the drinking and hear what had changed his mind about trying for building work, but for now it was good to see her family happy and together again.

'You'd better tell me, then,' Ruby said later that night as her husband lay by her side in their bed. She'd kissed him and welcomed him home properly, just to remind him of what he'd been missing and what he'd get no more of if he stepped out of line. 'What happened that night – it must 'ave been somethin' bad?'

'Yeah, it were pretty terrifying,' Sid confessed and she could hear a tremor in his voice. It wasn't like Sid to be afraid. He was a large man, could be handy with his fists if he chose, and didn't fear much. 'I heard and saw a murder, Ruby. It were down by that old warehouse near the wood yard. I heard a man screamin' and then beggin' fer his life – but they killed him. I hid out the way 'cos I knew their voices and I saw their faces clear by the light of that old street lamp. It don't throw out much light but they passed underneath it and I see them – I see the one with the bloody knife and I see him throw it in the water . . .' Sid hesitated. 'Only, it weren't in the water. It lodged on one of the barge posts, caught in the ropes.'

'Sid!' Ruby sat up in bed and looked at him. 'You didn't do anythin' daft?'

'I hid and then I walked orf, only me conscience wouldn't let me so I went back and made sure the bloke was dead. He was dead all right, knifed in the stomach, his hands tied behind his back. He'd been beaten and tortured before he was killed . . .' Sid sounded strange. 'I don't know why I did it, Ruby – but I went down after that knife and I wrapped it in me hanky. I suppose I thought it might have his prints – Mr Penfold's prints. He was with that Ronnie the Greek and it were 'im as stuck the knife in the poor bastard's guts.'

'Sid! They didn't see yer fetch that knife?' Ruby clutched at him in fear, because she knew the men he'd spoken of and had heard what they did to anyone who got in their way.

'Nah, they'd gone by the time I got back. I hid it in a place I know where it will be safe.'

'You can't go to the bobbies,' Ruby said. 'Mr Penfold would send his men after yer, Sid, and we'd never be safe. Even if they got Mr Penfold and his guard dog, he'll have others capable of sticking a knife in you.'

'I know,' Sid agreed and she felt his tremor of fear. 'I wish I'd left it there. I still don't understand what made me go back – I knew that poor bugger was dead and I should've left the knife for the police to find.'

'It would have been safer,' Ruby said, 'but who can know? They'd gone and, thinking about it, I'm sure they wouldn't return in case they were seen – so you're in the clear. Just forget it, love.'

'Yeah, yer right,' Sid said and sighed with relief. 'I feel better now I've told you, love. Anyway, it made me realize that if I 'adn't got drunk I'd 'ave been eatin' me supper and then in a warm bed rather than out on a cold night watchin' a murder.'

'Then maybe it was for the best,' Ruby said. 'Just leave that knife where it is and put it out of yer mind. Folk like us can't go up against that sort, whatever we know. Leave it to the police to catch the criminals, Sid. We've got more important things to think of – like how we're goin' to find the money for Julia's uniform.'

'I never told yer,' Sid said and his hand reached for hers in the darkness, 'the boss liked my work and he's got a contract for a big estate. They're clearin' one of the slum areas. The boss thinks things are taking a turn fer the better. He'll take me on full-time if I want and I can do all the groundwork for the estate; in the meantime, I can earn a few quid labouring. We've got to knock them old houses down behind where they used to have a cattle market, years ago.'

'That might cause yer a bit of pain wiv yer leg,' Ruby said.

'If it does, I'll rub some liniment on and get on wiv it,' Sid said determinedly. 'I meant it, Ruby. I'm finished with the booze. I know what our Julia wants and it won't be for lack of tryin' on my part if she don't get it.'

'I'll 'ave ter go down the school and ask where the uniforms and all the rest of it come from and find out how much they are,' Ruby said. 'Like you, I don't want to let Julia down, Sid. She's got more brains in her little finger than the pair of us together – I've no idea how we made her!'

'I reckon there's someone up there has somethin' to do wiv it,' Sid said, and chuckled. 'I promise I shan't let yer down, Ruby love. I'll do me best to bring home a full wage packet every week so we can send our girl to the grammar.'

'Right. Now, there's somethin' else on me mind, Sid. I ain't sayin' I've set me mind to it, 'cos I ain't sure they would take me on the list, but the lady what funds the Rosie is lookin' fer folk to foster kids. I'm thinkin' I might put me name down. They pay a few bob fer the kids' keep – but we'd have ter provide the rest.'

'Yer a daft woman,' Sid said affectionately. 'Thinkin' of takin' on more when yer've got that job of yourn and me and the girl ter look after.'

'Well, as I said, I'm only thinkin' on it,' she said. 'They probably wouldn't look at the likes of us anyway . . .'

Ruby was in a good humour when she got to work the next morning but the smile left her face when she saw young Kathy Saunders come in, looking dreadful. She'd made an attempt to put her hair up, but it was straggling down her neck and her face was patchy, her eyes red from crying.

'What's wrong, lovey?' she asked but her sympathy made Kathy's tears start again and it was a few minutes before the girl could stop sobbing.

'It's Ma,' she said at last when she'd dried her cheeks

with Ruby's clean handkerchief. 'She was so mean to me last night, shouting and calling me names, just because I stopped to talk to a friend from school on me way home from work. Anyone would think I'd been fornicating the way she carried on – shaking me and screaming that I was a slut.'

'Oh no, you poor love.' Ruby was all sympathy. Kathy was a little mouse and the last one she would accuse of going with men. In fact, she was so shy that she hadn't even noticed Bert Rush, their very own caretaker, always smiled like he'd won the pools whenever he saw young Kathy. Some might say he was a bit old for her at thirty-something, because she was no more than eighteen, but he was a decent bloke and Ruby often thought the girl needed someone to look out for her. Bert was the kind of bloke who would do that, Ruby knew. His job as caretaker was steady and paid a small but reliable wage and he had his own house and an allotment he worked, which would provide all the vegetables and soft fruit a family would need.

'I expect yer mum was just worried about you,' Ruby said, trying to comfort her, but Kathy shook her head.

'She hates me,' Kathy said. 'I'm sorry, Ruby. I know I shouldn't be wasting your time. We need to get on or we'll never get done.'

Ruby nodded and gave her a list of jobs that needed doing before the day started for the nurses and patients.

Shaking her head, Ruby got started on the scrubbing. It was the hardest job; she'd given Kathy the easier ones, like washing down sinks and dusting in the nurses' rest room. She couldn't help feeling sorry for the girl with a mother like Mildred Saunders. It must be hell on earth and Ruby counted her lucky stars. Now that Sid had turned a corner, life was looking brighter than it had for a long time; and before she went home she was going to speak to Matron and ask her if she stood a chance of getting on that list Lady Rosalie was making.

CHAPTER 15

'Mrs Wright from the Welfare visited the Robinsons yesterday,' Lady Rosalie said when she called in at the infirmary that Friday evening. 'They told her Charlie Howes had run away – apparently, he was sullen and difficult from the start, and finally he threatened her with a poker and stole some cakes before he went off.'

'Are you certain he wasn't still there but prevented from seeing you?' Mary asked, frowning. She knew what she'd seen but it was only her word against the foster parents'.

'They told her to look and she was shown through the back and upstairs. She was sure he wasn't there – and Mrs Robinson had bruises on her arms she claimed Charlie had inflicted before he ran.'

'I doubt he did that,' Mary said, feeling anxious. 'Have they reported his disappearance to the police?'

'She claimed they were about to – but it may have been a lie. Mrs Wright has, however, so they will be looking for him.'

'Good.' Mary was still worried about Maisie's brother but she'd done what she could and it was up to the police to find him; it shouldn't be that hard. 'So how is Dora?' she asked, changing the subject.

'I'm reliably told that she is like a different child even after just a few weeks with Mr and Mrs Phillips,' Lady Rosalie replied. 'I was certain I'd made a good choice for her and now I know I was right – in fact, they are ready to take on a brother or sister for Dora much sooner than I expected.'

'Do you have a child in mind?' Mary asked with a little frown.

'Well, I was considering Maisie Howes, because I know she is a little better now and you really cannot keep her here indefinitely.'

'Perfectly true,' Mary agreed, 'but I should prefer that you leave her with me for a little longer, because I'm still worried about her chest, even though she is responding well to treatment – so you can take the next suitable child on your list.'

'Well, I do have a little boy who desperately needs a home. His mother died a few weeks back and the father neglected him. If anyone needs a loving family it is Peter.' She sighed. 'He has a club foot which reduces his chances of finding a home.'

'Then I suggest you approach Mr and Mrs Phillips,' Mary said with a smile. 'Maisie is all right with me for a bit longer – and that child you've just told me about needs a home.'

'As usual you are right,' Lady Rosalie said and smiled fondly. 'That is why I come to you when I have a problem. I shall go to see them myself tomorrow and hope their love will extend to a little boy who sorely needs help.'

'And I shall keep praying that Mrs Howes will be able to take her two home one day . . .'

'Don't go down the docks looking fer work today,' Maisie begged her brother when he came into her room at breakfast. She'd taken an extra bit of buttered toast for him from the trolley in case he came and he ate it hungrily, sitting on her bed. 'It's Saturday and we're goin' ter tea wiv Mrs Ruby. If Matron catches you sneaking in, she won't let us go.'

'Don't you worry, Maisie,' Charlie said and grinned. 'We'll get our tea with Ruby and her family. I ain't goin' on the docks but Mick wants me to run some errands. I'll only be gone fer a couple of hours. Just play in the garden and no one will bother yer.' He grinned at her, winked and warned her to keep their secret and then went out through the window of their room into the walled garden.

Charlie climbed the branches of the old cherry tree easily and went over the wall and down the pile of rubble left against it. The whole area was due for demolition, so folk said. One day those crumbling tenements would come down, but for the moment they were homes to dozens of families, the women gossiping on the front steps. One or two waved as he passed, but most just stared balefully as they moaned about everything from the infestation of cockroaches to the way their husbands drank away what little money they earned.

It was one of the worst areas Charlie had seen in his young life. Ma's house had been a king compared to these decrepit homes, cleaner and, at one time, prosperous when Dad was alive. Charlie felt a pang of grief and regret as he thought about his father. He'd been gone since Charlie was seven and things had got harder and harder at home. Men paid his mother money for what went on in the bedroom – the vicar called it fornicating. There were other rude words the men on the docks used, and Charlie had once heard men laughing about his mum. When he'd flown at one of them, they'd laughed and called him a bantam cock.

'Take no notice of him, lad,' Mick had told him and yanked him off. 'He's an ignorant sod but he's right – yer ma *is* a whore. I ain't condemning her and neither should you. Yer father's dead and she's got two kids to bring up – and she keeps the pair of yer clean and fed. I give her credit fer that.'

Charlie liked Mick. He had dark blond hair and blue eyes and he was London bred and born and proud of it. Mick was a trader. Charlie didn't know what he bought and sold but he had a small warehouse and he always seemed to be busy. He asked Charlie to deliver packages to various places, most of them private clubs, restaurants and small commercial hotels. They were never light, but Charlie had a little trolley he could use if they were too heavy for him or there was more than one. He supposed they contained food but he suspected that there was something a little dodgy about Mick's dealings. Perhaps some of the stuff fell off a lorry or got accidentally unloaded at the wrong bay. Charlie didn't know and he didn't ask. He'd promised Mick he would deliver for him this morning and he knew he might be asked to call in at the bookie's and give the man behind the counter an envelope. The envelope would contain money and betting slips and Charlie knew that it wasn't legal for him to do that but Mick paid him well and for a long time before Ronnie the Greek came along, Charlie had been putting food in the pantry at home and Mick had promised him a proper job when he left school.

Charlie hadn't attended school on a regular basis for months before Ronnie the Greek came into their lives. He went just enough to keep the inspector from going after Ma but that only happened if the kids stayed away too long; if you went in a couple of days a week, they thought you'd been off sick and Charlie wrote his own excuses. Sometimes, he went to school first thing – long enough to get his name ticked on the register – and then slipped away during the break. Most of the teachers didn't notice he was gone. The only classes he'd ever enjoyed were the ones Reverend Little had given him in pottery and woodwork; he came into the school two mornings a week to help the boys decide what skills they would need when they were older and Charlie had chosen woodwork, which the Reverend took himself, having been a carpenter before he became a vicar.

'You'll need to learn maths too, if you want to be a carpenter,' the kindly vicar had told him, and Charlie had made him stare when he recited all his times tables without blinking. Numbers came easy to him, they always had. It was one of the reasons he got bored in school. He was ready to do the work in senior class when the rest of his year was still learning by rote.

Charlie had thought he would join Mick as soon as he could get out of school altogether but he was torn by his desire to learn about working with wood. He'd been allowed to turn the leg of a table in his class and it had given him a thrill of sheer joy to see how elegant and perfect it looked. He'd wanted to make the whole table, but the other boys all had to have their turn and Charlie was quickly bored. He needed something to keep his quick mind active, which is why he'd started slipping down to the docks in the first place.

There was always something of interest down here, he thought as he watched the heavy cranes swing out the heavy loads lifted from the boats tied up at the quayside to the dock. From there they would be lowered into lorries or on to wheeled platforms that could be moved into one of the warehouses. Out on the river a tug was hooting its horn and seabirds swooped down low, their cries loud. Charlie wondered why they came inland to the river when they truly belonged to the sea. Sometimes, he fancied that his father's spirit inhabited one of the swirling white birds and he watched for some kind of message but it never came.

'Yer came then,' Mick's voice broke into Charlie's reverie and he smiled. 'Good. I've got two special deliveries today – but first, I want you to take this to the bookie on Flint Street.'

'That's a new one,' Charlie said and grinned. 'Think yer'll change yer luck, do yer?'

'None of yer business,' Mick said and clipped his ear but not hard enough to hurt. 'If yer must know, the last one got raided. Someone grassed and they got caught in the act – cops closed 'em down. Well, temporary. Penfold will start up again somewhere. I reckon he's furious about it – shouldn't wonder if that's why that poor blighter got done in.'

A little shudder went down Charlie's spine. 'Was there a murder?'

'Yeah, a couple of weeks or so back. Didn't yer 'ear about it?'

Charlie shook his head. They hadn't heard any gossip living in the infirmary. At home Ma would have heard and she would have told Charlie. His throat caught because he didn't know how his mother was and he worried about her.

'Well, I've got a big mouth so you didn't 'ear it from me, right?'

'Don't know nuffin',' Charlie said and Mick laughed.

'Yeah, that's right, lad. Plead ignorance and yer can't go wrong.' He brought Charlie's trolley out with three largish parcels and gave him the directions. 'Now, don't forget – the bookie in Flint Street. Will yer know it?'

'Yeah,' Charlie said. He'd never been inside, and outside it claimed to be an import/export firm specializing in sending goods to America, but everyone knew illegal gambling went on in the back rooms. Charlie thought the local police knew too, but they were probably paid to turn a blind eye. A lot of rough types hung around and most cops stayed clear of trouble. Gambling away from a racecourse was illegal but everyone knew it went on. Charlie thought it was daft, all the secrecy and the shifty types that hung around. If the Government were to make it legal it would stop the gangsters making lots of black money – at least, it seemed simple to him.

He reflected on what Mick had said about Mr Penfold being involved with that murder. Ronnie the Greek worked for Mr Penfold and Ma had told Charlie that he was never to mention Mr Penfold's name.

'He's a bad man, Charlie,' she'd warned him. 'I avoid anything to do with him and sometimes I wish . . .' Ma had shaken her head and turned away but not before Charlie saw she was upset. He'd known what she was going to say. She wished that she'd never met Ronnie the Greek. Charlie did too, because then she wouldn't be in the hospital and he wouldn't be stuck in limbo, having to sneak in each time he wanted to see his sister in the Rosie.

Charlie found the betting shop easily enough. Inside there was a lot of men standing around, listening to something that was coming from a loudspeaker. It sounded like a horse race was about to take place – leastways, they were describing the runners and riders. He went up to the glass counter and took the envelope he'd been given from inside his jacket.

'Mick Larsson sent me,' he said and the man behind the counter nodded, taking the envelope and opening it. Inside was a list of something Charlie supposed were horses running in races that afternoon and several notes, both pound notes and two white fivers.

Charlie couldn't help thinking it was too much money to place on a horse. He accepted the betting slips and put them into his jacket pocket and left the shop, dragging his trolley behind him. He dared not leave it in the street in case someone pinched it; the contents might be valuable, though he suspected that the money he'd just handed over the counter was far more than the goods were worth.

He was glad to get out into the fresh air. It had stunk of stale sweat, urine and cigarette smoke in there and some of the men had looked at him in a way that sent shivers down his spine. The old betting shop had had a comfortable atmosphere and Charlie had known most of the customers by sight; here they looked a harder lot and he wouldn't trust any of them further than he could throw them.

A few paces down the street he glanced back – and what he saw sent shivers down his spine. Ronnie the Greek was standing outside the bookies and staring at him, an evil grin on his face. Increasing his pace, Charlie knew he wouldn't feel safe going back there in a hurry now he knew that the man who had beaten both him and his mother hung around there. If Mick had money to waste on gambling, he could put it on himself.

Charlie had always admired the man who gave him odd jobs but now he thought he must either be rich or daft in the head. For the first time he really thought about what he was delivering. Something must be valuable or Mick must be dealing in a lot of knocked-off stuff. It was more than likely the latter, he thought as he continued on his way. The coppers wouldn't suspect a kid of delivering anything important, and a few small parcels would slip through unnoticed, whereas a lorry or a van packed with pinched stuff might attract attention. He grinned. Mick was using him but he didn't care, because Mick was a mate – but he didn't want to be like him. Charlie had made up his mind – he wanted an apprenticeship in carpentry.

He delivered his parcels quickly, was given another four to deliver and then paid ten bob and told he was finished for the day.

'You're a good kid,' Mick said and ruffled his hair. 'See me next week and I'll find yer a few jobs.'

'I'll come when I can,' Charlie told him, 'but I'm learning to be a carpenter; that's me future – and that comes first. I'll see yer.'

He walked off whistling. Mick thought he didn't know he was delivering pinched stuff, but Charlie was pretty sure Mick was a fence. He hadn't tried to discover just what was inside those boxes, but he knew there was more than Mick let on.

One of these days Mick would get caught, just as the bookie had, and Charlie didn't intend to get punished for someone else's crimes. He would work hard at learning a trade as soon as he could find someone to take him on and, in the meantime, earn a few shillings where he was able. He'd seen a couple of cards in shop windows asking for lads to deliver groceries. Charlie reckoned he could do that, even if it didn't pay as much as Mick.

He fingered the ten-bob note in his pocket and smiled, but his smile disappeared as he reached the back wall of the infirmary and saw that most of the pile of rubble had gone; someone must have fetched it away and he wouldn't be able to climb the wall from this side without it. Charlie would look for something he could use to get him over the wall, but in the meantime, he would have to go in the front way and ten to one Matron would see him or someone would tell her. He just hoped she didn't find out about him in time to stop him and Maisie going to Ruby's for tea . . .

Sister Rose Harwell saw Charlie enter the ward that afternoon but she hadn't been told he'd run away from his foster home and just smiled. It wasn't strictly visiting hours, but it didn't matter and it would keep Maisie happy. Like all the nurses she liked both of the children and did what she could for their patient.

Maisie was sitting on the floor of the ward putting pieces of a puzzle together. She looked fed up and Charlie felt sorry for her; it couldn't be much fun here on her own. He squatted down beside her and helped her find a few pieces.

Nurse Lily Brown brought in the lunches on a trolley. She saw Charlie and offered him some sandwiches and he took them gratefully. Anything he got here saved him buying food and he was keeping his money safe for when he and Maisie were back together.

The nurse went off to take trays to the other children on the ward, many of whom were not well. Some of them refused anything but a little jelly and ice cream so no one missed the sandwiches Charlie ate, smiling at his sister as she tucked into hers.

'We're lucky,' she said as they ate ham sandwiches with mustard pickle. 'These are scrumptious. Mum only makes these as a special treat.'

'Yes, they're good,' Charlie said and scoffed his hungrily. 'Before I left, I asked Nurse Sarah if she would find out about Mum for us, Maisie. She ain't said nuthin' to yer?'

'Nah – I wish I could see Mum,' Maisie said wistfully.

Charlie looked at her sadly. 'I could go to the hospital but they wouldn't let me see her and I doubt they would tell me anything.'

'I wish she would get better so we could go home. I don't like being here, Charlie. It's *boring*.'

'You should be at school, Maisie,' he agreed.

'I like colouring and making things,' Maisie said. 'I'm not good at sums or spelling.'

'That's why you need to learn them,' Charlie told her seriously. 'I want to be a carpenter – or a cabinetmaker. Reverend Little said men who make tables and chairs and stuff are cabinetmakers and very skilled.'

'I'd like to cook or sew,' Maisie said. 'Ma used to teach me until . . .' Her face clouded because she didn't want to remember the man who had treated them all so harshly. He'd only hit her a few times, just glancing blows, but she knew what he'd done to her mother and brother.

'Hello – I'm Julia,' a voice said and they looked up to see a girl of about eleven smiling at them. 'I've come to take you to my house. It's early for tea, but there are some swings on the playground behind the infants' school. We can go on them for a while if you'd like.'

'Yes, please,' Maisie said and jumped up at once. 'I'm ready!'

'Get yer coat then,' Charlie instructed. 'It ain't cold really but Sister said Maisie was to wear a coat when we go out.'

'Come on, then.' Julia held out her hand to Maisie and she took it.

Charlie scowled. He wasn't a kid and he wasn't goin' on no swings – but he'd go along with it for Maisie's sake.

Charlie had a go on the swings after all. It looked fun and Maisie was enjoying herself so Charlie tried it out. He made it go higher and higher and then jumped off midway up so that he nearly stumbled and fell, but it made him grin as Maisie squealed and he saw a look of disapproval in Julia's eyes.

It was warm and pleasant on the swings and they stopped for longer than Charlie would have expected, but then Julia told Maisie that she had to come off or they would be late for tea.

Maisie took her hand, smiling up at her in a confiding way. 'It's my birthday on Monday. I'll be eight,' she said. 'Charlie has bought me a present. He always buys me a present for my birthday.'

'He looks after you,' Julia said. 'We have a nice tea on Saturdays so that is a little treat for your birthday too.'

Maisie nodded happily and looked over her shoulder at Charlie, who was following on behind. He nodded to her and looked round with interest. They were in a small cul-de-sac and the houses were better than many in the area. The front steps all looked as if they'd been polished with red wax and shone, and there were crisp white lace curtains at the windows. The curtains twitched at one of the windows and Julia walked past with her head in the air, but Charlie saw a woman with wire curlers in the front of her hair staring out.

Julia looked back at him. 'That's Mrs Morton. She's a widow and both her sons are away in the Merchant Navy. Her husband used to be a foreman down the docks but he died a few years ago. Now she has nothing to do but watch the rest of us. Mum says she complains about everyone behind their backs.'

Charlie nodded but didn't make any comment. He knew that some of the women, who lived in Barrett's Courtyard, where his mum's house was, were much the same, only most of them gossiped about his mother. He'd warmed to Julia a little; she was bossy, but she was looking after Maisie and that meant a lot.

Just before they entered Ruby's house, Charlie looked back. His nape was prickling and he'd felt someone was watching them. A man was standing on the pavement, staring at the house, but when he saw Charlie look at him, he turned and walked off. Maybe he was just one of the many jobless who spent their days wandering around with nothing to do. Charlie hadn't seen him before so he dismissed him as unimportant when he saw the spread Ruby had put on – she'd even got egg and cress sandwiches and, of all things, Charlie loved egg and cress. Ma always made them for his birthday and it made him wish he was home with her and tucking into a special tea to celebrate her homecoming . . .

'Ah, here comes Sarah,' Ruby was saying as the nurse walked in at the back door. 'Now we're all here, let's sit down and enjoy what the good lord gave us this lovely day . . .'

Charlie had bought Maisie a special colouring book and some crayons. He popped in just before breakfast when the nurses were busy and went again quickly. She could colour several sets of clothes and then cut them out and fasten them on the paper dolls that went with the set.

Maisie's face lit up and she'd hugged him and thanked him over and over before he said he had to go and that made her sad, but then Nurse Jenny came on duty and gave Maisie two parcels.

'We've all put together and bought you a present,' Jenny said.

Maisie stared at them in disbelief. She'd never expected anyone else to buy her a gift and she unwrapped them with shaking fingers. One was a new jigsaw puzzle with a scene of puppies and kittens, and the other was a soft wool cardigan in pink.

'Oh, I've never had anything as pretty,' Maisie exclaimed and slipped it on. She smiled at the nurse. 'Thank you so much, Nurse Jenny.'

'They are from all the nurses,' the nurse said and went on her way with a happy smile.

As the day progressed, Maisie was given several pretty cards; one was from Kathy and another was from Ruby and Julia, and there was a pretty handkerchief inside that with flowers on it.

'I've had a lovely birthday,' Maisie said when Charlie popped in at visiting time that night. She'd saved him a sandwich from her tea and he'd brought her a sticky bun. 'I got lots of things – but I like your present best.'

'It didn't cost as much as that cardigan the nurses got fer yer,' Charlie said. 'I couldn't afford that, Maisie.'

'No, but the colouring book is what you knew I liked and it will give me something to do,' she said and smiled in the dim light of the ward as he prepared to slip away again. 'Goodnight, Charlie. I'm glad yer my brother.'

'Night, Maisie,' he said gruffly and put a finger to his lips. Nurse Sarah had asked some tricky questions when he'd seen her at Ruby's, but he'd managed to come up with a plausible lie about how busy he was at the Robinsons'. As yet the nurses who had seen him hadn't questioned what he was doing visiting his sister. He wondered each time if one of them would pounce on him and make him go back to his foster home, but as yet they didn't seem to see anything strange in his frequent visits to Maisie. Not that they were aware of most of them because he sneaked in when they were busy. 'I'm glad too . . .'

CHAPTER 16

'Oh, what have you done to your ears?' Sarah asked Nurse Alice as she met her in the rest room for her break. She was on days for a couple of weeks and it was the first time she'd seen her friend in ages, because they were usually working opposite shifts. 'It looks as if you've got little holes in them.'

'I've had them pierced,' Alice said and blushed. 'Matron doesn't quite approve but it's all the rage in Mayfair. I went up for a shopping spree at the weekend a month ago. My sister was looking for a wedding dress – and we both had them done on the spur of the moment.'

'I think it will look nice when you have pretty earrings in,' Sarah said.

'I have to wear the little hoops that they first put in for work and cover my ears with my hair, because Sister Norton doesn't like jewellery on the wards. I told her I had to wear them for a start, but I forgot them this morning.'

Sarah nodded. She thought small gold earrings would be nice. One reason she never wore earrings herself was because the clips made her lobes sore. Yet she wasn't sure whether she would dare to do it, even if the younger girls were doing it now. Traditionally, it had only been older married women or rich families who had pierced lobes but now the fashion was spreading fast.

'Did Millie find a dress she wanted for her wedding?'

'Yes, it's lovely.' Alice described the creation of satin and lace and both girls sighed over it, suddenly realizing the time as the door opened and Sister Norton entered. She glanced at the little watch pinned to her lapel and both nurses hurried back to their separate wards.

'Millie asked if you would be one of her bridesmaids,' Alice said before they parted. 'Come round one evening and she'll get you measured – she and Mum are making the dresses together.'

'I could come this evening?' Sarah said and Alice smiled and nodded, turning away to the women's ward. Sarah went into the men's ward. Nurse Lily Brown and Kathy Saunders were both standing by Woody's bed and she hurried towards it. 'What happened?'

Woody was lying back with his eyes closed. He had vomit all over him and the bedclothes and Sarah immediately saw that there were some bloodstains.

'Mr Jacobs started coughing and then he was sick,' Kathy answered. 'I helped him to sit up and gave him a little water so he could spit the taste out – and then I fetched Nurse Lily.'

'Thank you, nurse,' Sarah said. 'I'm here now and I can help Kathy get Woody cleaned up'

'If you're sure? I have some dressings to do – an ulcerated leg . . .'

'Sorry to make so much mess.' Woody looked

ashamed and Sarah quickly touched his hand and smiled.

'Nothing to worry about. It happens and you're in the right place, but we'll ask the doctor to take a look at your chest when he comes, Woody.'

'Bless you, nurse,' Woody said. 'It will be just something I ate – maybe that porridge they brought me this morning for breakfast.'

'That is what came up,' Sarah agreed, 'but we need to know why.'

Kathy had gone to fetch clean sheets from the linen cupboard and between them they manoeuvred Woody into the chair beside the bed and stripped and remade it.

'I'm a blinking nuisance,' Woody said as they settled him again. Kathy brought him a fresh glass of water and he took another sip.

'No, you aren't,' Sarah told him with a smile. 'You're here because you're not quite well and this sort of thing happens. Please don't worry about it.'

'Thank you – you make me feel cared for,' Woody said and smiled. He lay back against the pillows and Sarah went to make her rounds of the other patients. She gave medicine to those that needed it and tucked in corners on several beds, knowing that the minute her back was turned the men would kick them out again.

She had just finished her round when Sister Norton entered with Dr Hershaw. He was one of the more approachable and Sarah took the opportunity to explain about Woody Jacobs.

'You're sure there was blood in the vomit, nurse?' he asked, eyes honing in on her intently.

'Yes, not very much but it was definitely there. I managed to reserve a little in the sluice room.'

'Quick thinking, nurse.' He nodded his approval. 'I think I'll see the patient first – just in case we're dealing with an infectious disease.'

Sarah didn't think it was an infection. Woody did not have a temperature, nor had he mentioned aches or pains and she'd seen no signs of fever but she did not venture an opinion. Dr Hershaw was experienced and careful and would give Woody a thorough examination.

He read Woody's notes thoroughly and then sat on the edge of the bed, smiling at the elderly man. 'A bit under the weather this morning so nurse tells me?'

'I'm all right, Doc,' Woody said. 'I just started coughing and then it all came up – I reckon it was the porridge.'

Doctor Hershaw nodded sympathetically. 'Not my favourite at any time, Mr Jacobs. Can you cough for me?' He warmed his stethoscope and moved it over Woody's chest and then his back. 'Well, doesn't seem too bad to me – but we'll do a few tests just the same. Nurse will take some blood and sputum and I'll test the vomit too. You can bring the samples to my office.'

Dr Hershaw caught Sarah just as she was leaving that evening. He called to her as she was about to push the door open and she waited as he came down to her.

'I thought you'd want to know. I've sent those samples off for further tests – my own indicate consumption, and if I'm right, we'll move your patient into the isolation ward as soon as we're sure. He probably isn't too infectious yet. I think it's early stage – that's why I want confirmation. He will need to go to the hospital for X-rays and we'll need another sputum sample. I'm sure it isn't an infection or a vomiting sickness, and with his history and the blood the most likely is TB.'

'I'm not sure Mr Jacobs will want to go for those tests.'

'I'm afraid it isn't just a case of what he wants, nurse. He could be a carrier – and if he is, then he must be isolated from our other patients and he ought to be sent to a special unit for treatment.'

Sarah nodded but she didn't think he would be inclined to go along with what the doctors thought would be best for him.

'I think I'll just pop back and tell him what's happening,' Sarah said. 'It will be better coming from me.'

'I thought you might feel like that – I hope I haven't spoiled your evening?'

Sarah shook her head. He was approachable and always had a good way with patients. In her experience, some of the doctors were impatient and thought too much of their own importance, but even so she knew that Woody would not want a load of doctors and nurses pulling him about – and he certainly wouldn't want to be sent to an isolation unit somewhere he didn't know.

He shook his head when Sarah told him what the doctor had said and muttered something that sounded a bit rude, but it wasn't aimed at her.

'I'll think on it,' he said and smiled at her. 'Don't you worry, lass – get orf and enjoy yer evening.'

Sarah left him lying with his eyes shut. She wished she could save him all the treatment, bother and upset that would result from a positive test and hoped that Dr Hershaw was wrong. Shaking her head, Sarah caught her bus home. Perhaps it was just the porridge and Woody would come back to them . . .

She tried to push the whole thing from her mind. After supper she would go round to Alice's house and talk to her sister about the wedding. It would be fun being a bridesmaid and if the dresses were to be sewn at home, they wouldn't be too expensive. Sarah felt that she needed something to cheer her up. With Jim in his new job she wasn't seeing much of him and she missed him. Visiting friends would help fill the gap that had appeared in her life and it was no good worrying over her patient, even if he was a favourite, because his treatment was out of her hands.

Sarah knew something was wrong the minute she walked in the men's ward the next morning. Sister Norton was checking her list, Ruby was helping Kathy to change beds at the other end of the ward – and Woody's bed was empty.

'Where is Mr Jacobs?' she asked Ruby. 'Has he gone to hospital for tests so early in the morning?'

'He scarpered last night,' Rose said. 'Sister Ruth Linton went off to fetch a drink for 'im and when she got back, he'd gone. At first she thought he'd just gone to the bathroom, but then she saw everythin' 'ad been taken from his locker. He's took himself off on his journeys again. The weather's warmer and he's 'ad enough of lyin' 'ere.'

Sarah nodded. She knew Woody had no intention of being forced to have tests he didn't want and he didn't want to be sent to an isolation hospital for treatment. Mostly, he came for a rest and then went off – but usually with Matron's approval. She would not have given it this time and that was why he'd done a runner.

Sarah felt anxious for him. He was used to life on the streets but he'd seemed frailer this visit than before – and if he did have consumption, then, alone on the streets, he might die. She regretted telling the doctor of the blood in his vomit, though she knew it had been her duty, but now when Woody felt ill, he would have nowhere he could go . . .

But Woody wasn't the only one to be homeless. Her thoughts turned to the children Matron had allowed to stay on the children's ward. Unless their mother was able to take them home soon, they would be passed on to an orphanage or a foster home. Lady Rosalie was looking for parents for them and Sarah had been thinking that perhaps her mother would consider having them for a while . . .

CHAPTER 17

'Here I am again,' Lady Rosalie said when she called in the following week. 'Well, I have good news, Mary. Mr Phillips took to Peter immediately and he's bought him a special pedal car that he can manage. I also understand that either a kitten or a puppy is on the cards soon.'

'What lucky children Dora and Peter are,' Mary said. 'You must be so pleased. I know how hard you've worked to find foster parents you can trust and this is a big success.'

'Unfortunately, I need many more. I had another six children added to my list this week – so that brings me to my reason for visiting you again so soon. You were going to give me some names and addresses?'

'Yes, I have my list ready for you,' Mary said and handed it over. 'There are three couples, all of whom I've helped in the past few years. All of them have brought up families but their children have left home and I believe they would be willing to take in these homeless children you need to place.'

Lady Rosalie smiled. 'Now, tell me, how is Maisie getting on – and have you seen anything of the boy?'

'The girl is an angel,' Mary said. 'I don't know if Charlie has been to see his sister. I've been so busy of late that his situation slipped from first place in my mind. I tried to keep what happened as secret as I could so I haven't told the staff to look out for him as yet.' She looked thoughtful. 'Perhaps I should – the police haven't seen anything of him, I suppose?'

'No, and they are anxious to find him,' Lady Rosalie said. 'An informer told Constable Steve Jones that a known criminal has been making inquiries about the lad.'

'That sounds worrying,' Mary agreed nodding. 'I'll speak to the nurses on Maisie's ward and ask them to tell me if they see him.'

'Should they not ring the police?'

'I don't think so,' Mary said. 'Charlie must be nervous and if we try to apprehend him, we might scare him off completely. If he is seen to visit his sister, I'll alert Constable Jones. He might be able to keep an eye out for him, see if he can persuade him to come in and talk to us. Or perhaps Nurse Sarah could try. I think she got on with him well.'

Charlie went to the grocers where he'd seen the advert for a delivery boy. They wanted someone just on Saturdays and that suited him well. He would get five shillings and sixpence for working five hours, which was about half what Mick would have paid him, but safer. If he got caught doing something illegal he'd be put in some reform house and Maisie would end up in the orphanage.

He'd asked Nurse Sarah if there was any news about

his mother but she said Mrs Howes was still ill and that was all the hospital could tell her.

Charlie was tempted to visit his mother. He knew the nurses wouldn't allow him on the ward, but perhaps he could sneak in and just look at her.

Charlie decided to try his luck. He knew where the London Hospital was and caught a bus there from Poplar. He decided to go straight up to the information desk and ask. The receptionist looked down her nose at him and Charlie knew he didn't look very respectable; even though he was clean, his clothes were threadbare and his trousers were too short and he had no socks on. His things were in need of a wash since he'd left the Rosie too.

'Can you tell me where my mother is?' he asked. 'She was brought in as an emergency some weeks ago . . . her name is Mrs Howes.'

The girl looked at him, frowned and then opened the large register and ran her finger down several columns until she found it. 'Mrs B. Howes?' she asked and Charlie nodded, because that was his father's initial. 'Yes, she is in ward B9 – but I'm afraid you can't see her. Children under fifteen are not allowed.'

'I'm nearly sixteen . . .' Charlie lied, daring her to deny it by staring at her.

'Even then you would need an adult with you,' the girl said. 'Sorry – get your father or someone to bring you in one evening after seven – visiting is for an hour only.'

Charlie glared at her. If he'd got a father he wouldn't need to be here, asking after his mother. He nodded and walked towards the door as if he was leaving, but then, when he saw her talking to an elderly couple, he dodged past and up the stairs towards the wards. At the top of the stairs he noticed arrows pointing one way for B wards and another way for A wards. He turned towards the B wards, counting them until he got to number nine.

There were wood and glass swing doors at the end of the ward. Charlie pressed his face against one, peering inside. Several beds were lined up on each side of the ward and three nurses were on duty. At the infirmary there was rarely more than one on most of the time, but the patients all looked to be quite ill in this ward.

Charlie stared hard through the glass and then he saw her – or he thought it was Ma, though it didn't look much like her, because the woman who lay there was pale and wan. She was in the first bed on the right-hand side and lying with her eyes closed. He thought she looked proper bad, and even when a nurse bent over and took her pulse, she didn't open her eyes.

Charlie waited until the nurse had gone and then slipped into the ward. He bent over his mother and touched her pale hand.

'Ma . . .' Charlie spoke to her even though he sensed she couldn't hear him. 'Ma, we need you to come home and look after us. I'll work and you won't need anyone else . . . please open your eyes . . .'

For a moment, his mother's eyelids flickered and he thought she would open them and look at him but she didn't, even though her fingers moved in his hand as if in distress. Charlie bent down and kissed her cheek.

'Please, Ma – we need you. Maisie needs you . . .'

'Charlie . . .' the whisper was so soft he wouldn't

have heard if he hadn't been bending over her. 'Maisie . . . promise me . . .' A little sigh issued from her lips as if she were distressed.

'Don't worry, Ma, I'll look after Maisie until you're better.'

'Be careful . . .' It was so soft he strained to hear. 'He will hurt you . . . police . . .'

'I love you,' Charlie said and there were tears on his cheeks. 'Get better, Ma – we love you . . .' She didn't answer and he knew it had taken all her strength to say those few words, but what had she meant about the police?

He jumped as a hand descended on his shoulder and looked up at a woman he knew must be a nursing sister by her uniform.

'What are you doing here, young man?' she asked. 'I'm sure you've been told you cannot visit without your father – and then it must be in the evening.'

'I ain't got a father, he's dead,' Charlie said. 'I need to know about Ma – is she goin' ter get better?'

'What is her name?' the sister asked.

'Mrs Howes . . .'

Charlie saw a flicker of concern in her eyes and she frowned. 'I'm afraid your mother is still quite ill. What are you called?'

'I'm Charlie and me sister is Maisie – and we're stayin' at the Rosie in the kids' ward until Ma gets better. We want ter go 'ome and we want Ma.'

'I'm sure you do, Charlie,' the sister said and smiled at him sympathetically. 'I'm afraid I can't let you stay with your mother, because it's against the rules – and she is still not well enough – but I will come to the

149

Rosie another day and bring you news of her. When she is better I will tell her you came looking for her.'

Charlie nodded. 'Thanks, Sister Sonya,' he said, reading her name on the little badge she wore. 'Me and Maisie are worried about her.'

'Of course you are,' she said. 'I promise I will come to see you soon – and perhaps I'll have better news for you.'

Charlie took a last lingering look at his mother.

'I hope that devil gets beat up like he beat my mother,' he said fiercely. 'I'd stick a knife in 'im if I could but he's too strong!'

'You know who hurt your mother?' When Charlie nodded the sister said, 'Then you should tell the police, because he deserves to be punished for what he did. You have told them, haven't you?'

'Nah, she told me not,' Charlie said, although he still wasn't sure what his mother's last words to him meant. Was she saying he should go to the police or that it would bring Ronnie the Greek after him if he did? He looked at the nurse tearfully. 'You promise me you'll tell us if she gets better? Just tell Maisie if I'm not there, please!'

'I will tell one of you myself whatever happens.'

Charlie nodded at her and then ran off. He'd done better than he'd expected and, if Sister Sonya kept her word, she would let Maisie know whatever happened. It was all he could do.

Charlie ran down the stairs, past the reception area and out through the entrance yard to the pavement beyond. In his rush to get away from the stink of disinfectant and sickness, he nearly ran into someone. He looked up as a man grabbed his arms and the apology died on his lips, his hatred rushing up to the surface as he saw the man he hated.

'Got yer!' the man growled. 'Knew I would!'

Charlie felt his hatred boil up inside him, making him reckless.

'You!' Charlie spat the words angrily. 'You're the reason she's in there. I'll get even wiv yer one day – you see if I don't!' He kicked out at Ronnie the Greek's shin and then, when the bully moved his hand towards him, he bit it as hard as he could. The ferocious bite brought a cry of fury and Ronnie recoiled swearing. In that instant, Charlie wriggled free and was off down the street like a greyhound.

'I'll teach yer!'

He heard Ronnie's roar of anger but didn't bother to look back. The street was too crowded for Ronnie to give chase but Charlie knew what that devil would do if he got the chance. He was as bad as that bully Alfie Robinson or worse. Charlie's bruises from the last beating he'd been given had not long healed.

As he ran and then jumped onto a bus just beginning to move from its stop, which would take him back to Poplar, Charlie thought about the man he hated so much. That senior nurse had told him he should have gone to the police, but weeks before she was so ill, after Ronnie had beaten her badly and a neighbour had said she was thinking about reporting him, Ma had expressly told him he was not to give the police the name of the man who had hit her, whatever happened.

'It's only your word, Charlie,' she'd warned him. 'Likely the police wouldn't believe yer – and if they did, they'd think I deserved it for goin' with him in the first place.'

Charlie knew Ma was right. He'd heard what the men said down the docks about women who sold themselves. They scorned the women they used and said they deserved what they got, laughed about it, and that made Charlie mad – and the police would say the same.

'Ronnie would likely murder me and both of you if we split on him,' Ma had warned her son. 'Whatever he does, just get help but don't say you know who did it to me . . .' Yet with her last words she'd spoken of the police – what did she want him to do? He couldn't decide what was best.

Charlie's eyes were stinging with tears he was too proud to shed. He didn't care what that devil did to him; he'd as soon stick a knife in his guts – but he cared about Maisie and his ma. Yet he knew that sister at the hospital was right, he should tell the police all he knew . . .

CHAPTER 18

Lily was tired when she came off duty at the end of a long day at the infirmary. They'd had two deaths that morning and losing patients, despite all the care and treatment they'd been given, was always draining, especially as one of them had reminded her of Gran, now so fragile that she knew they would not have her long. She felt thoroughly miserable, even though the sun was shining and it was a beautiful June day. Life was always the same, work and then home to a house that of late seemed empty since Gran kept to her room and slept much of the day. Added to which Jenny often left for work before Lily got home and she knew something had changed in her sister – she was sure she was hiding something from her.

It was Lily's birthday and she decided that she would visit Lavender and Lace and buy a cream sponge as a treat. If Jenny was still home, they could share it and, if not, she would leave her a piece out for the next day. Jenny had never yet failed to buy her a card and a small gift and she did not think her sister had forgotten the day – Jenny would probably have a nice tea and a gift ready for her when she got home.

Walking round the corner, Lily stopped to buy an evening paper, her eye caught by the headline that the Orient Line was offering a first-class passage to Australia for one hundred and twenty-four and a third class for fifty-seven pounds. And she was counting her money to decide whether she could afford to buy a cream cake for tea!

As she started to cross the road, she saw Jenny get off a bus and rush across just a short distance ahead of her. Lily waved but she didn't notice her and disappeared into the teashop. Smiling, Lily walked more sedately across the road and went inside the shop, which smelled deliciously of baking and a hint of lavender. Almost immediately, she saw Jenny being greeted by a young man, who kissed her cheek and held her hand for a moment before they settled down at their table. A waitress appeared with their tea, smiling at them and chatting in a way that told Lily this was not the first time her sister had met this young man here.

Jenny hadn't seen her and for some reason she didn't understand, Lily didn't want her to. The assistant behind the counter asked what she wanted but she shook her head and went out without buying the cake she'd intended. The bus she needed to get home was just approaching the stop but Lily ignored it and kept walking. She wasn't sure where she was going, but she couldn't face going home to an almost empty house on her birthday and the knowledge that her sister had been lying to her.

She headed towards the shops in a better part of town, though she had no intention of buying anything, but she just had to go somewhere and there was another little teashop where she'd been for tea with friends once, a long time ago. Lily didn't think she would ever want to visit Lavender and Lace again, because it would always remind her of Jenny's deceit.

She wandered around for a long time, staring at things she didn't want to buy, and then realized that Gran would be expecting her home and be worried. She ought to get back for the sake of the elderly lady she loved, even though the hurt was still festering inside her. Jenny had lied to her and she wasn't sure she could forgive her – but life had to go on.

Jenny was in the middle of her shift at the infirmary that evening when she suddenly remembered that it was Lily's birthday. She felt cold all over with the shock of it, because it was the first ever time she'd forgotten to buy her sister a card and a present, and it made her feel awful. Chris had wanted to meet and she'd been so excited, because he'd hinted he had something to tell her, that she hadn't given what day it was a second thought. She would have to take Lily a card and present home in the morning but that meant she would be delayed and her sister might have left for work.

Because she wanted to get home before Lily left the house, Jenny just bought a card and some chocolates from the newsagent on the corner. She wrote the card on the bus and felt guilty because every other year she had bought her sister a personal gift.

Lily was sitting at the breakfast table eating a piece of toast when she got in after being at work all night. Jenny bent to kiss her sister's cheek and placed the gift on the table beside her, but Lily turned her head aside, not wanting to be kissed.

'I'm really sorry I forgot,' Lily said. 'The chocolates are just to say sorry. I'll get you something nice on my day off.'

'It is a matter of indifference to me,' Lily said in a cold voice that Jenny had seldom heard. 'Why should you bother to remember my birthday? You obviously have far more important things to think about, meeting a young man at the teashop.'

Jenny went cold.

'I didn't tell you I was meeting someone because I wasn't sure if it was more than just a casual acquaintance,' Jenny said defensively. 'I wanted to be certain of my feelings – and his – before I asked him here to meet you.'

'What were you going to do? Tell me on the eve of your wedding? It will be one of those register office affairs, I imagine. I just hope you haven't been stupid—'

'What do you mean?' Jenny felt a spurt of anger. Lily had a right to be upset that she'd forgotten her birthday but not to dictate her life. 'If you mean, have I slept with him, the answer is no. We just meet for tea and talk and there's nothing wrong in that, so don't try to ruin it for me.'

'Is that what you think I'm doing?' Lily looked up at her and if Jenny hadn't been so angry, she would have seen the hurt.

'Well, isn't it? Just because you were let down once you think I should never fall in love, marry or have a family – but if Chris asks me, I shall say yes!'

'Jenny – you don't understand. My warnings were only meant to stop you being hurt as I was.'

'Not all men are cruel or cheating so-and-so's,' Jenny

156

said. 'I like Chris and it's fun meeting him – and if you think ill of us, then it's your bad mind, not ours.'

With that she flounced out, ignoring Lily's call to come back and let her explain. Jenny ran upstairs and stripped off her uniform. She crawled into bed, still wearing her underwear, and buried her face in the pillows, but she didn't cry. It hurt to quarrel with Lily but in her heart, Jenny blamed herself. Lily was right to be hurt; she'd forgotten her birthday and she'd kept her secret for some months. If it had been the other way round, Jenny too would have been hurt and angry.

'Jenny . . .' The door of her room opened and she knew her sister was by the bed but kept her face hidden, still torn by a mixture of anger and shame. 'I've never told you what happened with Roger Stainton – and I ought to have done. I was ashamed, because I believed his lies. He told me so many times that he loved me and wanted to marry me. I fell for his charm and I – I let myself down, Jenny. I slept with him a few times . . .'

Jenny sat up and looked at her, because Lily had never admitted anything like this before. 'What happened?' she asked, a little shiver running down her spine as she saw her sister's look of pain.

'You were still at school the day I told Roger that I was pregnant. At first, he said we would marry and it would be all right, but when I explained that the house was left between us and I would always look after you . . .' Lily sighed. 'He wanted you sent away – to a school or an orphanage, and he seemed to think that I should sell the house and let him invest the money for us. When I refused, he accused me of not trusting him – and then he walked out and I never saw him again . . .'

'Oh, Lily – you think he just wanted the money from the house?'

'I know he did,' Lily said. 'A few months later a woman came to see me – she accused me of sleeping with her husband and she showed me her marriage lines . . .' Lily looked pale and unhappy. 'He would have gone through a bigamous marriage to get his hands on whatever we had and then left me in the lurch – as he had her. She told me he'd sold property her father left to her and then deserted her. She had a small boy and he was given to a foster mother because she couldn't afford to keep him.'

'Oh, Lily!' Jenny clutched at her hand. 'I am so sorry. I had no idea. You never told anyone, did you?'

'I couldn't.' Lily's face was frozen. 'I lost the baby soon after Roger deserted me and I was ill for a while. I don't know how we would have managed until you had left school and completed your nursing training if Gran hadn't looked after us.'

'I wish I'd known before . . .'

'Why – would it have made a difference?'

Jenny stared at her. 'Perhaps not. I was afraid to tell you about Chris because I knew you would tell me not to trust him and I didn't want to spoil things . . .'

'You thought I would spoil things for you?'

'No, not exactly – but I knew you would question and I wanted to keep it to myself for a while.'

'I see . . .' Lily nodded. 'Clearly, you thought I was a sour old spinster who would be jealous of my sister's happiness!'

'No, of course not.' Jenny shook her head. 'But we met by accident at a bus stop and I don't know his friends or his family – or where he works. I just know that I enjoy being with him and he says he feels the same.'

'Then bring him home and let me meet him,' Lily said. 'If he is a good man, I'll be happy for you, Jenny. When you marry, we shall come to some arrangement about the house – I could pay rent or we could sell and I'll buy something smaller for me and Gran.'

'Lily, don't!' Jenny cried. 'I know I've hurt you and I didn't mean to. I'm sorry I forgot your birthday and I'm sorry I didn't tell you about Chris – but I wasn't ready. I'm not sure he would want to meet my family yet.'

'Well, I can't dictate to you,' Lily said. 'I came to Lavender and Lace yesterday and saw you greet him. I was going to buy a cream sponge for our tea . . .'

'Bring one home today and I'll be here,' Jenny said. 'I want to make it up, Lily. I care for Chris but you're my sister and I'll always love you.'

'I was feeling depressed. We'd lost two patients and I needed something to cheer me up.' Lily looked at her sadly. 'I was so angry with you, Jenny. I couldn't understand why you'd lied to me.'

'I'm sorry . . .'

'No, I should be the one apologizing,' Lily said. 'I thought I was keeping you safe – but if you felt you couldn't trust me with your happiness . . .'

Jenny stared at her, because there was nothing more she could say.

'We could go somewhere nice together on Saturday – have tea out?'

'I'm working on Saturday,' Lily said. 'I rang up from

the box on the corner and told them I didn't feel like coming in today and exchanged my shift for Saturday.'

'Well, we can have a nice tea today before I go to work if you're home in time. . .'

'I'm not a child, Jenny. You don't have to make up for it because you forgot my birthday. Just don't shut me out in future, please?'

Later, Lily made ham sandwiches with pickle and a buttercream and jam sponge for tea. Jenny ate her share, helped with the washing-up and then left for work. They hadn't talked much and Jenny knew the rift was still there between them. She wasn't sure what she needed to do to heal it and thought perhaps only time could do that.

Sometimes, Chris was hanging around when she got off the bus and they had a quick chat before she went into work, but that evening there was no sign of him. In the infirmary she saw Bert Rush putting a poster up about a dance that was being held in aid of charity.

'Does Matron know you're putting that up here?' she asked and Bert grinned.

'That she does, Nurse Jenny. I asked her permission first. I'm not daft enough to do it without asking – but it looks like a good do. They're havin' a few snacks, drinks, and a draw for a bottle of sparkling wine. You should get yer young man to take you to it.'

'Perhaps I shall,' Jenny said and laughed. Suddenly, the cloud cleared. Other people thought it natural she would have a young man. Lily was making too much of it all. 'Are you taking someone special, Bert?'

'I just might be,' Bert said and winked at her. 'Suffice it to say that I bought two tickets – after all, it is a good cause.'

'Perhaps see you there then.' Jenny smiled and went upstairs to the children's ward. She saw two nurses by one of the beds and the smile left her face. Alice ought to have left by now and Sister Norton looked worried. 'What is wrong?'

'Ah, good, I'm glad you're here, nurse,' Sister Norton said. 'Susan was very sick and she has a rash. I think she may have an infection of some kind. I want blood and urine samples taken, please, and then you can give her a bed bath, because she is much too hot and we need to get her temperature down. I'm going to get a doctor here.' She went off to her office at the end of the ward.

Jenny had just finished giving the little girl a nice cool sponging when the doctor arrived with Sister in tow. He examined the child thoroughly, pulling back her eyelids, checking her chest and back with his stethoscope and looking in her mouth before pronouncing.

'I'm pretty sure it is chickenpox,' he said. 'I thought it might be something worse for a start, but this is bad enough in children already weakened by a previous illness. I don't know where the illness came from – have you noticed anything with any of the others?'

'Nurse Alice said that Maisie Howes was a bit hot earlier and quiet. If she has it, it is probably too late to isolate Susan, because Maisie was sitting on her bed yesterday. She will want watching, nurse. I'm going to spend as much of my time on this ward as possible today – though I shall have to divide it with the women's ward, because Sister Rose is off sick.'

'Let us hope it doesn't spread to the chronically sick ward,' the doctor said and frowned. 'Chickenpox can be something the kids just throw off – but in severe cases it can kill. So, let's be alert here, nurses. If either of you have to visit the chronically sick ward, I want clean gowns, masks and scrubbed hands.'

'Yes, of course, doctor,' Sister Norton said. 'I'm sure you do not need to tell my nurses to take strict precautions when we have infectious diseases on the wards.'

He nodded, gave Jenny more instructions, leaving her to carry them out as he walked off to wash his hands in the basin provided at the end of the ward.

'Well, as if . . .!' Sister Norton said more to herself than to anyone. 'I see no reason why either of us should be called to the chronically sick ward – Matron and Sister Linton run that themselves and seldom ask for extra help.'

'I think there were two deaths on the women's ward yesterday?' Jenny said as she took the used water and towels away.

'Yes, unfortunately that is true. One lady was elderly and seemed to be recovering from the chest infection she was brought in with – and the other was quite young. She was pregnant and she had some kind of infection that she had ignored until she was vomiting all the time. She died badly, I'm afraid, and that upset your sister – she was caring for her at the time, but there was nothing more she could have done. By the time she arrived with us, the poison in her body had done its work and both she and the child were dying.'

'No wonder Lily was upset!' Jenny frowned as she got rid of the dirty water and towels and then went back to her patient. Susan had been given something to ease her fever and she appeared to be sleeping peacefully.

Jenny made a round of the other children. The majority had small injuries – a nasty cut on the leg, a broken ankle – but most of them seemed to be healthy enough, even if they complained of hurting. However, when she reached Maisie, she knew at once that the little girl had the same sickness as Susan. Maisie's face and hands were covered in red spots and she was whimpering.

'You've got the chickenpox,' Jenny told Maisie. 'You need to stay in bed tomorrow and not go out in the garden. And you're infectious, so I don't want you leaving your room except to go to the toilet. You must stay away from the other children until you're over this illness. Is that understood?'

'Yeah . . . Do you think it was me give it to Susan?' Maisie asked anxiously.

'Who knows where it came from?' Jenny said.

'Don't feel well,' Maisie whimpered and Jenny bent over her, placing a hand to her forehead.

'I'll give you a nice cool sponging and then ask Sister for something to help you rest. I know it's horrid, Maisie, but it will go away soon . . .'

Maisie nodded but the tears trickled and she turned her face to the pillow, trying to find a cool spot while Jenny went off to fetch some cool water, a sponge and towel.

It took most of the shift to look after the patients with chickenpox, because they became very hot again and needed sponging and other patients needed drinks and medicine and Jenny had no time to think about her own problems until she was leaving the infirmary.

She went to Lavender and Lace and bought a selection of cream cakes to take home for tea. Lily might still be angry with her but she would not refuse such a treat surely. Besides, it was silly to carry on the quarrel because they were going to have to go on living together – and if the sisters were at loggerheads it would only upset Gran. And neither of them would ever want to do that because they both loved the woman who had always been there for them.

CHAPTER 19

'I have good news for you,' Lady Rosalie said when she entered Matron's office. 'I have manged to find a foster mother for Maisie – for both those children once the boy is found.'

Mary looked at her and sighed. 'Unfortunately, Maisie has gone down with chickenpox,' she said. 'The girl is very poorly. I just couldn't reconcile it with my conscience to pass her on to a foster mother for a few weeks at least. With her delicate chest she could die if she isn't properly looked after – and we ought to find the boy first before we do anything drastic.'

'That is unfortunate,' Lady Rosalie said and shook her head. 'However, I trust your judgement and I have two other children in desperate need of a home. They haven't settled at the orphanage and this carer is an excellent woman; her husband has a steady job and they very much want a boy and a girl. It would have been just the right place for the Howes pair.'

'That is such a pity,' Mary said, feeling disappointed. She hesitated, then, 'I've had one of my cleaners approach me about fostering – she knows that she may not be accepted but she says her husband now has a decent wage coming in and she would be happy to take the children – or any others. Ruby is a good worker but I believe her husband drinks at times . . .'

'Then I'm afraid I couldn't accept him on my list,' Lady Rosalie said. 'I've made it a rule not to accept a man who drinks as a foster father. They are so unreliable.'

'So, she doesn't stand a chance?'

Lady Rosalie shook her head regretfully. 'I'm very sorry, Mary, especially as we're so short of carers – but that is a hard and fast rule as far as I'm concerned and I can't break it for one person.'

'I quite understand,' Mary said and sighed. 'I suppose I knew it but I promised her I would ask you.'

Lady Rosalie pulled on her gloves and stood up. 'I must go now. I have an appointment with some prospective parents and I mustn't be late.'

Mary went down to the kitchen when she knew the staff would be preparing to leave. Ruby was putting her coat on, the last to go as always. It was so hard giving her the news that she would not be acceptable to Lady Rosalie.

Ruby looked at her and her shoulders sagged. 'She's turned me down, ain't she?'

'Yes, Ruby, I'm afraid so,' Mary said regretfully. 'I put in a good word for you, but your husband's history of drinking . . .'

Ruby nodded her head, her expression accepting but sad. 'He's not a bad man, Matron. He's turned a corner and promised me he won't do it again – and I believe

166

him. I warned him I'd throw him out if he does and he knows I mean it.'

Mary hesitated and then made her decision.

'Look, if you can come and tell me in six months' time that your husband hasn't drunk in all that time, I will talk to her again. I know you would make a good foster mother, Ruby, and I think you should have a chance.'

'Thank you,' Ruby said, her face lighting up. 'Will it be all right if them Howes kids come ter tea again?'

'Did you mean both of them?'

Ruby nodded. 'They both came the other week, enjoyed themselves, bless 'em – what made yer ask if it was both?'

'Charlie ran away from his foster home and we're looking for him,' Mary said. 'We're a bit worried about Charlie for various reasons – so if you see him again, can you tell him that I want to help him, please? Say he isn't in trouble and I won't send him back to the Robinsons.'

'Yes, I'll tell him.' Ruby frowned and looked thoughtful. 'I think he visits Maisie a few times a week – but I don't often see him. I know she takes an extra sandwich now at lunch or tea and I doubt she eats them all.'

'That sounds positive – at least he is getting some food.' Mary smiled. Trust Charlie Howes to turn up when the food was going! 'Let her take whatever she wants and don't alarm them – but if you get the chance, tell him we want to help and let me know if you can, please.'

'I'll do that, Matron.' Ruby hesitated, then, 'You won't

forget me if there's even a temporary situation while you find a better place for the children . . .?'

'Yes, of course I'll do what I can and you're welcome to take the children home to tea,' Mary said, happy that she could at least do this for the woman she valued. 'While Maisie is under my care I am in charge of her welfare. I'm happy for you to have her visit for tea – but you will need to wait until Maisie is well enough. This last illness has really affected her badly.'

'Yes, I know, poor little mite. It fair pulls at me 'eart ter see 'er so poorly,' Ruby said. 'Me and Sid are lucky to 'ave our Julia. He thinks the world of 'er and I should've liked more – and I reckon I'd look after an orphan or two as good as a lot what they take on. Some of 'em only do it 'cos they get paid a couple of bob extra. I don't care about the money as long as Sid is bringing in his wage.'

'Well, prove to me that he's been sober for six months and then we'll see.'

'Thank you, Matron,' Ruby said and picked up her shopping bag. 'I'd best get on and see to their tea at home.'

Mary returned to her office feeling saddened. Lady Rosalie was a good woman and did as much as she could to help the poor of London's East End and the orphans needing foster care – but sometimes she made strict rules that didn't always fit and that was part of the reason her list wasn't growing as fast as it could. Ruby would make an excellent foster mother – much better than those wretched people Charlie had been sent to – and if she said her husband had turned a corner then he probably had!

CHAPTER 20

'It's so good to see you,' Sarah said and flung her arms around Jim when he arrived that Sunday morning in time for lunch. 'I've missed you so much!'

'Me too,' Jim said and his kiss was warm and filled with passion. 'I wondered at first if I'd done right taking it, but it's a good job for me, Sarah love. I enjoy the work and I feel as if I'm gettin' somewhere at last.' He looked at her anxiously. 'As long as you can put up with me not comin' round as often?'

'I miss you and I wish you'd got the job you were promised,' Sarah told him frankly. 'But if you're happy – well, we'll just have to wait until we can afford to marry.'

'They wanted a single bloke for this job, because of the hours,' Jim said. 'I do a lot of overtime but I'm paid extra for it and I'm saving more, Sarah. I reckon by next year I'll have proved myself and I'll put in for a manager's job somewhere nearer home. I'll have saved a fair bit by then and we might be able to put down a deposit on a cottage of our own.'

Sarah gave him a hug. She wanted to tell him that

nothing made up for not seeing him every day. If he'd hated his new job, she would have told him to give it up and look closer to home, but Jim seemed to be thriving. Throughout the time he spent with them, he was full of the customers who came and went, some of them famous faces he'd seen in the newspapers.

'We've had sportsmen, actors and even one of the minor royals,' Jim said his eyes glowing with enthusiasm. 'It's a different way of life up there, Sarah love. If you could find work at a hospital near where I work, we might get more time together.'

Sarah didn't answer him, just smiled and let him talk. He was asking her to change her life to suit his and that was too much for her just yet. Her father was hardly cold in his grave and she knew her mother missed him terribly. Sarah would have to find lodgings nearer her new place of work, which would leave her mother alone – and take Sarah from her friends and the people she knew and liked. Sick people were sick people wherever they were and she would adjust to the work, but she'd thought that, when she married, she would be living just round the corner from her mother and could pop in most days. Jim was excited and talking without thinking things through. He would probably begin to see the drawbacks when he'd been in his job a bit longer and go back to his old way of thinking – the friends and neighbours you'd known all your life were the best.

Sarah's mother didn't question Jim or even remark on his plans until after he'd gone. Instead, she watched her daughter's face, waiting for Sarah to speak.

'It's just Jim's enthusiasm for a new job, Mum,' she

said. 'When the gilt wears off the gingerbread, he'll realize it's not all honey.'

'And if he doesn't? Supposing his ambition to be the manager of a big pub – or even a club – clouds his judgement and he asks you to go and live up West? You're not to turn him down. He's always been the one for you, Sarah. I don't want you torn and breaking your heart for my sake. If Jim needs to move on, you have to be ready to go with him, love.'

'But then I'd hardly see you, Mum.'

'I'd miss you, of course I would – but Jim will be your husband and in time you'll have your own family. Besides, it's not that far, Sarah. You can pop on a bus and be here before you know it. Grannies often see their grandchildren just a couple of times a year, because they live at the other side of the country.'

'Yes, I know,' Sarah admitted and bit her lip. 'But I didn't want it to be like that, Mum. If Jim had got that job he should've had . . .'

'You could have lived just round the corner,' her mother said and smiled. 'I'd hoped for it too – but life moves on and we stand still at our peril, Sarah. I would not come between you two for the world. Besides, I'm young and strong enough to look after myself. I might find a little job – or take in a lodger. I've got friends here, good friends. I shan't be entirely alone.'

'I know . . .' Sarah went to hug her. It was just like her mother to put her first. 'You're the best mum in the world. You haven't criticized Jim or tried to hold us back – but that just makes me love you more and want to see you every day.'

'The time is coming when you may have to choose,'

her mother said. 'I'm telling you now, don't refuse Jim's request just for my sake.'

'Won't you be lonely, Mum?' Sarah said. She hesitated and then said, 'I've got an idea but I don't know how you would feel about taking on the responsibility of two youngsters . . . It's only one at the moment but the police are bound to find Charlie soon. Constable Steve Jones told me they've had sightings of him near the docks – at least they think it's Charlie who has been hanging around.'

'You mean the child at the infirmary and her brother who is missing?' Sarah's mother smiled and nodded, because Sarah talked about them all the time. 'Look, I know Maisie isn't well at the moment but when she is feeling better perhaps you could bring her home to tea – her brother too if he turns up – and then we'll see.' A gleam entered her eyes. 'I like the sound of that lad, Charlie, and I don't blame him for running off if they were mistreating him like Matron told you.' She frowned. 'I give him credit for having the gumption to do it.'

Sarah nodded. 'I saw him leaving the ward twice recently but I didn't know they were looking for him until Matron told me and then I spoke to Constable Jones when he came to the infirmary to ask after Maisie.'

'Does he often do that?' her mother asked innocently.

'A couple of times a week,' Sarah said. 'He wants to talk to Charlie about the man who hurt his mother – apparently, they think he may have some information that could help to put him behind bars.'

'Oh, is that the reason?' her mother said and smiled to herself. 'What a caring young man he is, Sarah . . .'

*

172

Charlie didn't get the chickenpox as badly as his sister or poor Susan, who was suffering the worst of any of the children, though he felt a bit rotten one day and when he made one of his secret visits to Maisie, she told him he'd got spots on his face and said he was like her.

'I've got chickenpox,' she told him. 'I ain't been near no chickens but nurse says that's what's wrong wiv me – and you've got it, too.'

'Mick asked me if I felt all right,' Charlie admitted. 'I felt a bit sick and hot in the night but I'm all right.'

Maisie nodded and gave him a piece of bacon and toast she'd saved from her breakfast. It was cold but he ate it with relish and drank some of the orange squash by her bed.

'I'll come and see yer as soon as I can,' he promised and went out of the back window just as the door opened. Maisie was standing by the window when Sister Norton spoke to her. She'd been watching her brother climb the tree and admiring his skill. Charlie could do anything!

'What are you doing by the window – and why is it open?' Sister Norton asked and looked out. She frowned as she saw the young boy clamber over the wall at the back of the garden. 'Has Charlie been to see you again?'

Maisie looked red in the face and didn't answer, because she was a bit afraid of Sister Norton.

'There is no need to be afraid of telling me,' Sister Norton said. 'Neither of you are in trouble, Maisie – but if Charlie comes back please tell him that we want to help him. The police think he might be in some danger out there alone on the streets – and we promise he won't go back to those foster carers. They have been taken off the list and will never be allowed to foster children again.'

'Good! They beat Charlie and didn't feed him much.' Maisie's eyes filled with tears. 'They was goin' ter sell 'im ter that horrid man what beat Ma so he ran away.'

'So *that's* what made him run,' Sister Norton said and nodded. 'Matron will tell the police and they'll go round there – indeed, they should be arrested and punished for such wickedness.'

Maisie smiled through her tears. Suddenly, she wasn't afraid of Sister Norton. 'Thank you – I'll tell Charlie. I like being here. Everyone is kind and we have nice food to eat.'

Sister Norton nodded. 'Your friend Susan is feeling much better this morning. If she continues to get better, she will go home at the weekend. Her mother will come and fetch her.'

'I wish my mum would fetch me,' Maisie said, a little tearful because Susan was now her friend and when she went home, she would be alone.

'Never mind,' Sister Norton told her. 'I'm sure it is only a matter of time now before Matron finds you a new home – either with a foster family or in an orphanage.'

Maisie stared at her, her heart racing. She couldn't speak but she didn't want to be sent to an orphanage or to foster parents.

'I ain't goin' nowhere without Charlie,' she said at last, her face screwing up as the tears came back. 'I want my mum – I want Charlie!'

Sister Norton looked cross. 'Now stop that, child. We can't keep you here forever!'

*

'I dare say you are sick to death of being here, Maisie,' Matron said when she visited a couple of days later. 'It was only meant to be a stay of a week or two while your mother recovered but I'm afraid you've been here more than two months and that is far too long. I've been told your mother is no better and unless I can find a foster parent for you, as soon as you are well, I have no alternative but to place you in an orphanage, which will not be in London.'

'No!' A loud wail issued from Maisie. 'I want to go 'ome. Don't want to go to no orphanage – they lock kids up and beat them – and I shan't see Charlie no more!'

'Has he been to see you again – since Sister Norton saw him run off?' Matron asked but Maisie remembered what her brother had told her and shook her head.

'Maisie, it would be better if you told Charlie to visit me and then I can arrange for you to go to the orphanage together,' Matron said. 'I am quite sure most orphanages are very good places and Lady Rosalie has recommended this one to me. Unfortunately, they do not have an opening for you just yet, but some of their young children have been adopted recently and will be leaving for new homes at the end of the month and so you will go then.'

'Nurse Sarah was goin' ter ask about our aunt,' Maisie said tearfully. 'She promised me!'

'Inquiries have been made,' Matron said sadly, 'but thus far we have had no response from our efforts. Unless we can find foster parents to take both of you, the orphanage seems the best option, because your brother can join you once we find him.'

'Ma wouldn't want us to go away,' Maisie said stubbornly. 'Couldn't I stay 'ere until Ma gets better?'

Matron looked unhappy, then, 'I am not certain that your mother *will* recover. The hospital tells us that she shows little sign of it. I am very sorry. We are here to care for the sick – and although we take in children like you for temporary periods, we cannot give you a permanent home. At the end of the month Lady Rosalie will take you to Essex, where the home is situated. It is a very nice place and you will go to school – and be given work training when the time comes.'

Maisie looked mutinous but said nothing though she wept when Charlie sneaked in to see her later that day and told him what had been said.

'I ain't goin' without you,' she sniffled. 'Come back so we can be together, Charlie.'

'We ain't goin' in no orphanage, Maisie. We've got a few weeks ter plan. I'll start lookin' for somewhere we can live. It won't be comfortable like this, because I shan't be earnin' much fer a start – but yer won't starve . . .'

She stared at him, her eyes wide with fear. Maisie remembered the time they'd spent on the streets when Ronnie the Greek had thrown them out; she'd been cold, hungry and the nits had made her skin crawl. She liked being here, where the nurses looked after her and she could make friends with other children. What she wanted was to live somewhere nice and go to school – but that wouldn't happen unless their ma came home.

'Is Ma goin to die?' she asked her brother tearfully. 'If she ain't gettin' no better – will they make us go to an orphanage?'

Charlie shrugged. He'd promised he would look after her but he knew it wouldn't be easy. Earning a few bob for pocket money and buying Maisie sweets and a gift for her birthday was one thing, but keeping them both warm, fed and clean? Charlie would do his best, but he hadn't forgotten his sister's tears and complaints of hunger before the police had brought them here.

It was all that rotten Ronnie the Greek's fault! Charlie's hatred of the man grew and he vowed that one day he would get even with the brute who had made his mother so ill and ruined their lives.

CHAPTER 21

Sid looked uneasily over his shoulder. For a while now he'd sensed he was being followed but whoever it was had a knack for keeping out of sight. Shaking his head, he walked quickly home. It was Saturday and he'd worked a full week and his wage packet was bursting. He felt proud to give it to his wife and know that he was doing his bit towards getting his little girl to that grammar school of hers. They'd accepted the scholarship and she was due to start in September. Just over two months to find the rest of the money for her uniform and all the other things the school said she would need, like a hockey stick and a tennis racket.

Julia came flying out of the house to greet him as he approached. He swept her up and swung her round, grinning as she chattered excitedly about her shopping trip with Ruby.

'Mum bought my skirts and a blazer today,' she told him. 'The skirts are grey and the blazer is maroon – and there's a special hat to go with it. We're going to buy that next week!'

'Good, that's right, as long as you have all you need

when you go,' Sid said and smiled at her fondly. 'That's my girl . . .'

Julia kissed his cheek and then went running back to the house. He watched her with pride. She was a lovely girl and he loved her to bits. Sid knew that she would use her opportunity at the grammar school to make a good life for herself. Her happiness was worth all the hours of work, the ache it caused in his back – and the thirst for beer that he refused to quench. Drinking would lose him his job and he was lucky to have it. Work was still scarce and Sid knew that there were another twenty men waiting to take his job if he messed up – but he also knew his skill wasn't given to every man. He'd been a fool to let his pain get in the way and take to the drink. No, he certainly wouldn't do it again. He'd learned his lesson the hard way.

He stood for a moment in the sunshine before entering his house and looked about him. Suddenly, he saw a man standing halfway down the street leering at him, his thick lips pulled back in a mocking sneer. Ice ran down Sid's spine.

Why was Ronnie the Greek watching him? Sid shivered, suddenly afraid, though he didn't know what he was afraid of – surely Mr Penfold couldn't know that he'd witnessed that murder?

The newspapers had reported it, speculated that it was a gang murder, and then forgotten it. Sid supposed the police had done the same.

He went inside and shut the door quickly. Ruby called out to him but Sid went upstairs and looked out of the landing window. Ronnie the Greek was still there and he looked up, saw Sid and grinned, then he drew a finger across his throat to signify a cut throat. Sid jumped back as though he'd been stung.

Did they know he had witnessed the murder? Ronnie the Greek's gesture was plain enough; it was a warning. Had someone seen him return and pick up the knife? He was telling Sid to keep quiet or he'd have his throat cut . . .

Sid was shaking as he backed away from the window. They knew where he lived and that meant that it wasn't just his own life that was at risk . . . He cursed himself for the fool he was. So many weeks had passed that Sid had believed he was safe, but now he knew that he wasn't, that Julia and Ruby weren't safe either . . .

What would they do next? Sid's stomach was twisting with nerves as he went down to the kitchen. He knew he couldn't tell Ruby what had just happened. She would blame him for bringing trouble home – and it *was* his fault. She gave him a sharp look as he entered the kitchen but Julia was sitting at the table writing and Ruby didn't need to speak. Sid knew he was in for an interrogation later – and he would just have to think of some excuse that she would believe. It was no use pretending nothing had happened, because his wife knew him too well.

In the end, Ruby got the truth out of him.

'Take the knife to the police,' Ruby said. 'I know I said yer shouldn't – but I didn't think then that they knew you'd got it and now I think they might. They certainly know you saw somethin'. If they come after yer, Sid, they'll hurt yer, even kill yer . . .'

'I daren't,' he said and he could feel beads of sweat

181

on his brow. 'They wouldn't just murder me if I took that knife to the cops, Ruby girl. They would come after you – *and* our Julia.'

'No!' she gasped. 'Get rid of it then – give it to them, or leave it on the street where the police can find it.'

'I'd give it to them, Ruby – but I'm not sure it will stop them. If they've decided I'm for it . . .' A shudder went through him. 'Cor blimey, girl, I've made a bloomin' mess this time.'

'It wasn't your fault,' Ruby said. 'If I hadn't put yer out that night you wouldn't 'ave seen that murder and you wouldn't have hidden the knife.'

'I should 'ave come straight back after,' Sid said. 'I don't know why I went back and got the damned thing . . . I just thought there was a chance the victim might be alive but I should 'ave known.'

'Yer must have been seen when yer went back,' Ruby said and gave him a little hug, because she sensed his fear. 'It were just bad luck.'

Sid agreed but that didn't help him with his problem.

He knew that he should take the knife to the local police station and report what he'd seen that night, but they might not believe him – they might think *he'd* done the murder. Sid was caught between a rock and a hard place and for the life of him he didn't know what to do for the best.

CHAPTER 22

Jenny placed the little parcel by the side of her sister's plate at breakfast that Sunday morning. Both had the day off work and she'd been saving the gift for the right time.

'I saw that and thought you would like it – it's your colours.'

Lily picked the parcel up and opened it, looking at the pretty artificial silk scarf. It was in shades of autumn – browns, oranges and russet – and very attractive. She smiled and looked at her sister.

'Thank you, Jenny, I love it, but there was no need. You've already made up for forgetting my birthday.'

'Perhaps, but I should have told you about Chris.' Jenny looked at her tentatively. 'I asked him to come round for tea this afternoon but he has something important on. He promised to come another day.'

Lily nodded. 'Well, it looks like being a lovely day. Why don't we go up to Regent's Park and have tea there? We might get to listen to a concert if we're lucky.'

'What a good idea.' Jenny smiled. 'You have forgiven me – haven't you?'

'Of course I have. I shouldn't have made so much fuss – but I had a wretched day and then . . .' She sighed. 'It was a shock and it upset me, Jenny, but I know you have a right to your secrets.'

'Yes, I do,' Jenny said, 'but I should have told you I was seeing someone. I thought you would warn me off and I didn't want that – but it was wrong of me to hide it from you.'

'We'll forget all about it,' Lily said. 'Let's get these things cleared away and make a day of it – we can pack a few sandwiches and eat them in the park, and take those sausage rolls I made.' She turned to the elderly lady sitting by the kitchen range that never went out even in high summer. It was nice to see her up for once. 'We're going out for the day, Gran – would you like to come with us?'

'You two go and have a good time.' Gran smiled. 'I'll ask Mary Abbott from next door to come in for a bite to eat. She's often lonely now that her children have gone. Poor lass lost her man in the war and she's had a hard time. We'll have that corned beef with some red beet and roast potatoes.'

'Can I do anything for you before we go?' Jenny asked.

'The day I can't get me own lunch ready I'll go to the old folks' home,' Gran said, a twinkle in her eye. 'Get off, the pair of you, and have a good time. I shall enjoy myself with my friend.'

'All right – are you ready, Jenny?' Lily asked.

'Yes, it all sounds lovely,' Jenny said. 'We'll eat our packed lunch and then have tea somewhere smart before we come home.'

'We could go to Lyons' Corner House,' Lily suggested.

'I love their little cauliflower cakes. Do you remember Dad taking us there for a treat when we were very small? We always had little round ice creams and a plate of cakes.'

'I hardly remember him at all,' Jenny said and Lily nodded sadly.

'I suppose you were only a few months old. It was a birthday treat for Mum and I was so excited but of course you wouldn't remember – you were still a babe in arms.'

Jenny nodded and smiled. She'd had somewhere more exciting in mind, but if Lily wanted to visit Lyons' that was where they would go. She cleared the table and then hurried upstairs to put on a pretty yellow rayon summer dress. It wasn't often they went out together and she wanted it to be a lovely day.

The sun was really warm as they walked in the park, watching ducks on the pond. A mother with a brood of about ten chicks went swimming by and Jenny threw them the remains of their sandwiches. Quite a few people were in the park, walking and laughing together, enjoying the lovely day. Most of the chairs for the concert were taken when Lily and Jenny squeezed in at the end. The band were taking their places when the strident sounds of drums and trumpets blared and they could hear the voices of a crowd shouting and jeering.

'It's a parade through the streets by Mosely's gang,' a man sitting next to Jenny informed her. 'Listen to the yells from the crowd, telling them what they think of them. You'd think they would know they weren't wanted.'

'Oh, I think they're coming into the park,' Jenny said. 'What a nuisance – just as the band was about to start.'

She turned her neck to look at the noisy crowd that had erupted into the park, destroying the peace of the summer's day. Men in black shirts and trousers were waving banners and some of them had loudhailers. One of them was trying to announce a speech by someone but he was shouted down by the hostile crowd who didn't want to hear the propaganda.

'Bloody Fascists!' someone cried out. 'Why don't you take yourself off to Germany or Spain and join that lot of thugs? We don't want your sort here!'

'We have the right of free speech—'

'Not if your lot got into power!' another man yelled. 'It's only 'cos you're in a free country, mate. That so-and-so Franco would soon shut your mouth for you if you disagreed with him!'

Suddenly, someone threw a stone and then there was a hail of missiles being thrown at the marchers and those with the loudspeakers were the ones that were hit. Jenny saw blood pouring down the side of a man's face and then it turned into a free-for-all. All at once the men on both sides were throwing punches, and those in the black shirts were using wooden clubs to hit their opponents. It was a mass of cursing angry men and it lurched towards the bandstand and the people sitting there waiting to be entertained. The women and children scrambled to their feet and ran, trying to avoid being caught up in the fight.

'Come on, Jenny,' Lily said pulling at her arm, but Lily was being swept away by a tide of frightened spectators. Jenny found herself knocked to one side and then she was in the middle of a group of angry men hitting out with their fists. One of them caught her a blow on the cheek and she almost fell. She would have fallen if a hand hadn't grasped her arm and dragged her clear.

Jenny was shaken by the suddenness of the violence and had started to shake. 'It's all right,' a voice said, making her look up sharply. 'You're all right now, Jenny.'

'Chris!' She stared at him in bewilderment. 'What happened? We were waiting for the concert and then – then those men started fighting.'

'It was the thugs paid to disrupt the meeting,' Chris said and sounded angry. 'I think they were communist agitators and someone paid them to cause trouble.'

Jenny was calmer now and she saw that Chris was wearing a black shirt and trousers. He was one of them! One of the Blackshirts who had marched behind Oswald Mosley's banners.

'You – you're one of them,' Jenny said in disbelief. 'You're one of those men that were parading!'

'It was supposed to be a peaceful march,' Chris said, bitterness in his voice. 'Don't judge what you don't understand, Jenny – I have my reasons. Besides, it's the men who start the fights that are to blame for what happened.'

'But – Oswald Mosely is a *fascist*,' Jenny said. 'His followers believe in Hitler – and I've heard people say bad things of him.'

'I know, but it isn't as simple as that,' Chris said. 'Mosley has friends in high places and none of this other stuff can be proved – yet.' The last word was so soft that she wasn't sure she'd heard it right. 'I'll explain one day.'

'I don't understand how you could march with them. Surely you can't believe in his cause?' Jenny was too shocked to think clearly. 'I have to go and find Lily. We got separated.'

The police were blowing whistles and had started to break up the fight between the two gangs of angry men. Jenny had stopped shaking but she was worried for her sister.

'I would have told you when the time was right,' Chris said. 'Don't label me as a troublemaker until you hear what I have to say, Jenny. I'm not a thug, believe me.'

'You can tell me another day. I need to find my sister.'

'Is that her coming now?' Chris asked and Jenny saw a very worried-looking Lily walking towards her.

'Yes, it is.' Jenny hesitated, then, 'Perhaps you would like to meet her?'

'I'd rather leave it for another day – I must go.' He smiled at her. 'I'll try to explain tomorrow – usual place?'

Jenny didn't answer as Chris strode off, back towards a group of men in black who were arguing with the police. Lily came up to her, looking anxious.

'What was that man saying to you, Jenny?'

'Oh, he saved me from getting knocked over,' Jenny replied and forced a smile to stiff lips. 'Come on, let's go to Lyons' and have that cup of tea. We shouldn't let what happened spoil our day.'

'No, we won't,' Lily agreed. 'As long as you're feeling all right, love? You looked pale and upset just now. I thought that man had harmed you.'

'No, I'm fine,' Jenny said. She felt uncomfortable because Chris's refusal to meet her sister had put her in an awkward position again. She didn't want to lie to Lily but couldn't very well say that it was the man she'd been meeting – the man she'd been halfway to falling in love with.

It had shocked her to see Chris dressed like that, though she vaguely recalled his wearing a black shirt under his overcoat previously, but she'd never considered he might be one of Oswald Mosely's followers. She'd thought he was nice – someone she could trust – but now she wasn't sure she wanted to see him again.

Sleep was impossible for Jenny that night, no matter which way she turned. Chris was half German, she'd always known that, but he'd been educated in England and chosen to live here and she'd thought he would have her values and ideals. Jenny knew very little about the Oswald Mosely movement but she knew the newspapers called them a load of thugs and political agitators. They wanted to make Britain more like Hitler's Germany. Jenny knew even less about that but her instincts told her she could not love or marry a man who belonged to such a group.

Unable to sleep, Jenny got up and went downstairs to make a pot of tea. Tears were slipping down her cheeks, because she knew her friendship with the attractive man she'd found so intriguing was over. She could not continue to meet a man who was involved in something she felt instinctively was wrong.

'I knew there was something wrong . . .' Lily's voice from the doorway made her look round. 'It was that man at the park – he was the one you met for tea on my birthday, wasn't he?'

'Yes,' Jenny would not lie to her, 'I had no idea he was one of—'

'Oswald Mosely's fascists?' Lily nodded, sat down and poured herself a cup of tea. 'Yes, I can see why that would shock you, love. It was all rather horrid – and to discover your friend was one of those thugs!'

'Chris said it was communist agitators who stirred the crowd up. He said they intended a peaceful march.'

'That's what they always say. There have been several skirmishes but one of these days people are going to be killed. They're not our sort of people, love. Dad fought in the first war against Germany and he would turn in his grave at the thought of you going out with a man like that . . .'

'Yes, I know.' Jenny was choked with emotion. 'I thought I might be falling in love with him . . .'

'He *is* attractive,' Lily agreed. 'I shan't demand that you give him up, Jenny – that's your decision, but I don't want you to bring him here.'

Jenny bent her head and burst into tears. She'd known from the first moment she realized that Chris was a member of the fascists that it would be either her sister or him. Jenny might have given him the benefit of the doubt, she might even have tried to listen and understand his reasons for belonging to the movement, but Lily wouldn't, even for a moment. She remembered the last war and the men who were gassed – their father included. It was the reason he'd died, coughing up blood.

'Hitler is gearing up for another war,' Lily said. 'The Germans thought they were humiliated after they lost the last one and they can't wait to make us pay for it. Men like Oswald Mosley are trying to cause dissension here in Britain and weaken us. There will be men – influential men – who say we mustn't fight again. They will be all for peace, because Hitler is pretending to be our friend, and perhaps some of what he says is reasonable – but he wants to divide us and make trouble with our allies. Believe me, Jenny, the man you thought you loved won't be fighting for us!'

'Oh, Lily, don't talk about wars,' Jenny begged. 'Surely it can't happen again? The last one was supposed to be the war to end all wars.'

'If only it were!' Lily grimaced. 'I'm sorry, Jenny. I shouldn't try to make up your mind for you – but you don't know this man. I'm only glad you've discovered the truth before it went too far . . .'

Jenny looked into her eyes and then closed hers. Lily was right, of course she was, and Chris couldn't have any possible excuse that would make what he'd done acceptable.

'Yes, I know you're right,' she said at last, 'but it hurts – more than I expected . . .'

'I do understand. You'll break your heart over him, Jenny – but in the end it will mend, I promise you.'

Jenny nodded but said nothing. At the moment she knew two things: one, she was going to avoid meeting Chris in future and two, it was going to be painful.

'Get some sleep,' she said. 'You're on duty at eight . . .'

'It is six thirty now,' Lily said. 'I'll get washed and dressed and have my breakfast, and then I'll get off to work. You should try to get some sleep, love, or you will be tired this evening.'

191

'I'll make breakfast and then I'll go up for a while, see if Gran is all right, but I doubt I shall sleep . . .'

That afternoon Jenny dressed in her uniform, kissed Gran goodbye, left a note for Lily and caught an early bus. When Chris arrived at Lavender and Lace, she was standing outside.

'I don't want tea,' she told him. 'Can we walk for a while? I need to talk to you.'

'Of course . . .' He seemed hesitant. 'I know what kind of a reputation the Blackshirts have but we're not all thugs, Jenny.'

'No, I don't think you're a thug,' she admitted. 'I like you, Chris, and I thought it might be more – but I could never care for someone who behaved in the way those men do.'

'We didn't start that fight!'

'No, perhaps not – but the parade was provocative. Lily says you want to cause dissension and trouble – that you're looking to weaken us, our government and our people, so that Hitler can dominate us all.'

'He has done quite a bit for his country,' Chris said but sounded unconvincing. 'Look, it isn't what it seems – but I can't tell you the truth. I just need you to trust me.'

'That isn't easy,' Jenny said. 'I don't understand how you can march with those awful men.'

'You just have to take what I say on trust, Jenny.' He looked at her and now there was a glint of anger in his eyes.

She took a deep breath, because this had to end. 'My father was in the trenches in the last war and he was

192

gassed. He didn't die immediately, but he died little by little. Lily remembers that and she has asked me not to bring you home.' Jenny took a deep breath. 'I'm sorry, Chris – but I can't see you again.'

'Just because your sister remembers your father dying?'

'She doesn't want to meet you. I have to choose – and I choose Lily.' Jenny looked him in the eyes. 'I trusted you. I thought I might love you – but you lied to me.'

'I have never lied to you, Jenny.' There was a mixture of emotion and anger in his voice. 'Like a lot of people, you're prejudiced when you don't really understand—'

'I know all I want to know,' she said. 'You don't deny that you're a member of that movement and that is unforgivable to Lily. I'm sorry, I can't see you again, ever.'

'Then you're a silly little fool and you will regret it!' Chris stared at her furiously. 'You're not even prepared to listen – so to hell with you! I don't know why I wasted my time.'

Jenny felt the tears sting her eyes. She wouldn't let them fall and give him the satisfaction of seeing her hurt. Despite all Lily had said, she'd hoped there was a good explanation but he couldn't even tell her why he'd become a fascist. If he'd had good reason, perhaps she might have accepted it, but he couldn't – or wouldn't – tell her anything that made sense.

Before she could let herself down, Jenny turned away and walked off towards the infirmary. She thought she heard Chris call her name and there was a note of entreaty in his voice but she wouldn't turn around.

Jenny walked into the infirmary without looking

back. She washed her face in the cloakroom and repaired the damage as best she could, though her eyes still looked red and her nose was blotchy. Too many tears had been shed in the night to hide her distress and Sister Norton had a long look at her as she took her place on the ward.

'Are you quite well, Nurse?'

'Yes, Sister, thank you.'

'If you have a cold you should go home.'

'I've been crying,' Jenny said. 'I don't have a cold.'

Sister Norton nodded. 'If you're fit to be at work, get on with your duties. I shall not interfere with your private life – unless there is something you wish to tell me?'

'No, Sister. Nothing that would interest you or affect my work, I give you my word.'

Jenny went off to check on the patients. A new case had been brought in that morning. A little girl had a broken leg and she was looking and feeling very sorry for herself. Jenny spent some time making her comfortable and then went to see how Maisie was doing. Just as she was about to enter the room, a hand touched her arm.

'Nurse – may I speak to you for a moment please?'

Jenny looked at the woman who had spoken. She was wearing the uniform of a nurse from the London and looked uneasy.

'Yes, of course. How may I help you?'

'I need to speak to Charlie and Maisie Howes. I'm Sister Sonya and I have news about their mother – not good news, I'm afraid . . .'

'Is she worse?' Jenny read the expression in the other woman's eyes and felt chilled. 'Oh no, that is terrible!'

'The boy came to the hospital to see his mother but she was too ill – and I'm afraid she died early this morning. I promised I would visit and tell him myself if there was any change . . .'

'That is going to be a severe blow to them,' Jenny said and her throat caught with emotion. Her own sadness seemed as nothing besides the plight of the children and she took a deep breath. 'Was she in distress?'

'No, she simply went to sleep and didn't wake up – we think it may be for the best. The doctors suspected brain damage. Whoever beat that woman was a wicked devil and he deserves to be punished; he murdered her whether or not he intended it.'

'Do they know who did it?' Jenny asked.

'The police have an idea but they don't have a witness. I think the children may have seen it happen – the boy hinted that he knew. I tried to tell him he should go to the police but I doubt he will . . . they never do.'

'I'm not sure where the boy is, but his sister is here.' Jenny nodded at her. 'I'll come in with you. I know Maisie well and this is going to upset them both a lot. They hoped their mother would come home – now it looks as if they will be sent to an orphanage – Maisie now, Charlie once the police find him.'

'That wretched man took her life but he ruined the children's,' Sister Sonya said. 'Thank you, I'll be glad of your support. It is never easy giving news of this kind . . .'

Jenny led the way to the room Maisie was in and opened the door. Maisie looked immediately anxious and Charlie, who was sitting on the bed, jumped up poised for flight – then saw Sister Sonya and halted.

'Is it Ma?' he asked, his young face white and his eyes darkening with grief as he read the truth in her eyes.

'Yes, Charlie, I'm afraid it is,' she said and a wail of grief escaped him as he sat down on his sister's bed. 'She's gone – peacefully, but she's gone to Heaven . . .'

'Ain't no 'eaven,' he said brokenly. 'Not fer the likes of us . . .'

CHAPTER 23

'I am so very sorry,' Jenny said to the children after Sister Sonya had left. 'I know what this must mean to you, and I know it hurts. I cried all the time for weeks when my mother died and I was older than either of you.'

Maisie was sobbing but Charlie looked at her dry-eyed. She saw what looked to be anger and hatred in his dark eyes and suspected that he was thinking of the man who had murdered their mother and ruined their lives. Jenny was under no illusions that Mrs Howes had been a perfect mother, but her children loved her.

'I don't know what I can do to help . . .' Jenny said hesitantly. She was aware now, like most of the nurses, that he was living on the streets and visiting his sister when he could.

'We want to be there when Ma is buried,' Charlie said firmly. 'She hadn't got much but if her things are sold it might cover the cost of a proper funeral – I don't want her shoved in a pauper's grave. I know about them 'cos it happened to me neighbour.'

'I'll talk to Nurse Sarah and we'll go round to your

house and see what we can do,' Jenny promised, her heart wrung by his pain and his bravery. 'Promise me you will stay here now and let us help you? Matron won't make you leave us until your mother is buried, Charlie. You can talk to her and decide what to do after the funeral – but stay here until then, will you, please?'

'Ain't got no choice if we're goin' ter bury Ma proper . . .' He put his arm about Maisie's shoulders, his expression proud. 'We'll be all right, nurse. You've got things to do . . .'

Jenny agreed, because she'd already spent more time with them than she ought, but their plight tugged at her heartstrings. She wasn't sure what the situation would be with their mother's things, because the house had been empty a long time. It might have been broken in to or the landlord could have helped himself if he hadn't got his rent paid; such an action might not be legal, but landlords in the slum areas did pretty much as they liked.

Smothering a sigh, Jenny put her mind to her work. She wasn't sure how much the cheapest funeral would cost but she and Sarah could organize a whip round if the children's things didn't raise enough to pay for a proper burial.

'Stop crying, Maisie, and listen,' Charlie said once the nurse had left them alone. 'We shan't be sent to that orphanage until after Ma's funeral. When that's over, we'll scarper.'

'Run away?' Maisie's eyes were red where she'd rubbed at them and her pretty face was blotchy. 'I wish Ma was coming home, Charlie. I miss her!'

'So do I,' Charlie said, 'but she's gone, Maisie. We shan't see her again – not until we die. Ma says we go to Heaven when we die so we'll see her then but it will be a long time. You and me – we've got to look out fer ourselves.'

'I'm not sure I c-can,' she said and her bottom lip wavered. 'I'm not as brave as you, Charlie.'

'I ain't brave, I just do what I 'ave ter do,' he said and his chin firmed. 'I'm goin' ter the cops, Maisie. I'm goin' ter tell them what he done to me and what he done to Ma.'

'Ma said he would come after yer,' Maisie reminded him. 'You know she did – he'll beat yer again and this time he might kill yer.'

Charlie nodded, suppressing the shiver of fear her words sent through him. He knew the risk he was running, but he also knew that Ronnie the Greek had it in for him and Maisie whatever he did. Charlie suspected he'd been there at the London to discover whether or not Ma had recovered enough to tell on him. She would never have done it, because she lived in fear of the man who had beat her so many times – but Charlie was going to tell. He wanted that brute to suffer just a bit of what he'd inflicted on Ma and Maisie.

He knew that some folk would think he was a grass – and perhaps he was, but that man deserved to be punished for what he'd done to Ma, and Charlie wasn't going to live in fear of being caught by him. Once he and Maisie were on the streets, they would be more vulnerable – but not if that cruel devil was where he belonged, behind bars.

'If he's in prison he can't hurt us,' Charlie told his sister. 'He *would* kill us if he found us, Maisie. I'm goin' to the cops in the morning and I'm goin' to tell.'

'All right,' she said, though her eyes were wide with fear and her bottom lip trembled. 'I 'ate 'im too, Charlie. I wish 'e was dead!'

'If I was older and stronger, he already would be,' Charlie told her and his eyes glinted with anger. 'If Matron comes lookin' fer me while I'm out just tell her I've gone ter the shop ter get some sweets.'

'I'll do what yer say,' Maisie promised. 'But yer won't leave me behind, Charlie? When yer run away – you won't let them put me in an orphanage, please?'

'Nah, 'course I won't,' he said stoutly. 'I'll always be there fer yer, Maisie. Yer my sister, ain't yer?'

Maisie nodded, sniffed and dried her eyes. She went to sit on her bed and suck her thumb as she studied a book of sums that Nurse Sarah had brought in for her.

Charlie flicked through the comic books that he'd been given as he thought about what he would tell the police . . .

Charlie was surprised that the constable who listened to his story believed him straight off. He'd expected they might think he was making it up, but it was Constable Steve Jones and he was one of those who had dealt with Charlie's mother's case. He'd taken them to the infirmary in the first place and he was all right in Charlie's opinion.

'Why didn't you tell us before?' asked the police sergeant Constable Jones fetched into the interview room to hear Charlie's story. 'We suspected it might be him – and we know he's done a lot worse – but we had no proof.'

'It's only the word of a young lad now,' Constable Jones pointed out. 'Unless we can get a confession, we may not get him for murder – though Charlie here says the nurses at the hospital will testify to the bruises he had when he was taken there – and that's enough to send him away for a short stretch.'

'He killed Ma,' Charlie said. 'He threw me and Maisie out but I sneaked back in to get us food and a coat, 'cos she was cold. I 'eard them 'avin' a row. He beat 'er and beat 'er and then he kicked Ma in the head and I ran at 'im and kicked 'im and bit 'im. He knocked me to the ground and yelled 'e would kill me if I opened me mouth.'

'We know about him running prostitutes,' Constable Jones said. 'Most of them are too scared to complain when he takes their money and beats them – but if we've got enough to arrest him, some of them might come forward.'

'He ought ter be hung fer killing Ma,' Charlie said fiercely. 'But if yer put him away fer long enough 'e won't bother us no more.'

'We'll do our best, lad,' Constable Jones promised. 'I'd like to see that devil hang and maybe if we can get him behind bars that will come.' He smiled at Charlie approvingly. 'You're a brave one. Not many would have come forward. If a few others did the same we could put the whole gang of them behind bars – hang some of them. We suspect Ronnie and his boss of more than one murder, but we need the proof. You'll be at your Ma's funeral?'

'Yes,' Charlie said firmly.

'I'll be there too, but not in uniform. I'll be there to protect you and your sister in case we haven't managed to apprehend Ronnie before then – but with any luck we'll have him. That cocky bastard struts around as though he owns London but he's in for a nasty surprise.'

Two days later, Charlie looked at the collection of coins and notes that Nurse Sarah put on his bed in suspicion. 'We don't want no charity, nurse . . .'

'This is your money from the sale of your mother's things,' Sarah told him. 'The police said they're arranging to pay for the funeral out of general funds – they think you've done them a service, Charlie.'

'Thanks . . .' Charlie picked up the money and thrust it into the pocket of his threadbare jacket. If the police were paying it was for information received so he felt a bit like a copper's nark – but his motive had been revenge rather than greed so it wasn't blood money. Anyway, it was better than charity and the money from Ma's stuff would come in handy for when he and Maisie ran away.

Charlie had already found a place they could go on the docks. He'd used it a couple of times himself. It was a disused watchman's hut and there was a chair and small table in it, as well as a cupboard they could put their stuff in. They didn't have very much, but Maisie wanted to keep the puzzles she'd been given, and Charlie now had the money to buy them some sleeping bags. To Charlie that seemed a sensible way to spend his small fortune. They could put cardboard on the ground to keep out some of the cold, the way the homeless did, and the sleeping bags would keep them warm. He knew the bags were used for camping and that's what he and Maisie were doing, really. He might be able to buy a little paraffin stove like campers used, too, which was better than lighting a fire.

Charlie wondered why Matron had been unable to find his aunt, but perhaps she hadn't tried very hard, believing that Charlie and Maisie would be better off in an orphanage. He decided that if he got a chance at the funeral, he would ask Constable Jones if he could find out where their aunt lived.

CHAPTER 24

Mary stared at the report she was trying to write but instead of the words all she could see was the sad faces of the children she was preparing to send to an orphanage. It wasn't right for them to be sent off to the country to an institution, where they would be separated, but what else could she do? Lady Rosalie's attempts to find their aunt had come to naught and she had no one on her list of foster carers who would take both the children. That bout of chickenpox had come at an unfortunate time.

What they needed was a few good-hearted women locally, Mary reflected, as she studied her hands and considered. It was a pity Ruby had been turned down without even an interview. Perhaps she might speak to some of the nurses, ask if they knew anyone around Button Street or the nearby lanes. If someone was ready to take in the Howes children for a short period then Lady Rosalie might have enough time to find someone who could take them on until they were old enough to cope for themselves . . .

*

The day of the funeral was bright and sunny, which made it better for Charlie and Maisie than if it had been raining. Ma had always loved the sunshine and it seemed fitting that it should shine for her funeral.

Nurse Sarah had volunteered to accompany them to the funeral and Ruby gave their clothes a press and polished their shoes. Neither of them looked particularly smart, but better than they did most days. Maisie was pale and appeared scared, holding tight to Charlie's hand as they were taken in a taxi to the church where the service was to be held and she whimpered and cried all the way through, even though Charlie and Nurse Sarah both held her hands. Only a handful of people were in the church besides Charlie and his sister. Constable Jones and another man stood at the back of the church watching as the others walked in. Matron was there and she had a small bunch of carnations for them to place on their mother's coffin.

'May God give our dear sister Ellen Howes peace,' the vicar intoned at the last and then the coffin was taken out into the sunshine to be lowered into the ground. Charlie was given some earth to sprinkle on the lid and then the vicar smiled at him and Maisie and walked away, followed by Matron and Ruby, who had come out of sympathy for the children.

'You haven't seen anything?' Constable Jones asked, coming to stand by Charlie for a moment.

'No – but I'll keep my eye out,' Charlie promised. 'I wondered if you would do something for me, please?'

'Glad to if I can . . .' The constable raised his eyebrows.

'My aunt is Miss Jeanie Howes and lives in the

countryside somewhere; I think it might be Cambridge-shire but I ain't sure. She's a teacher and I need to let her know about Maisie and me.'

'Yes,' he said, seeming to understand. 'Not much fun in an orphanage. I'll see what I can do, Charlie.'

'Thanks – and if I see that devil I'll come and let yer know.' Charlie had decided this copper was all right and he'd help him all he could.

Constable Jones nodded and walked off to join his colleague. Ruby had lingered until he went and then she came up to him. 'I'm sorry about yer ma, love. I can't take yer in 'cos they wouldn't let me keep yer – but yer can come ter tea any time yer like.'

'Thanks, Mrs Harding,' Charlie said. 'Maisie really enjoyed her tea at yours. I know she likes you and Julia.'

Ruby frowned and said, 'Did I hear Sarah say you went ter the cops and told them who beat yer ma?'

'Yeah, I did,' Charlie said. 'He killed her and he deserves ter die. I hope they 'ang 'im when they get 'im!'

'I hope so too.' Ruby smiled at him. 'You're a brave lad, Charlie. There's many a man that wouldn't dare to do what you did.'

'He put me to shame, Sid,' Ruby said to her husband when she got home that evening. 'He's a brave lad and no mistake. He knows that Ronnie the Greek will kill him if he learns he told on him – but he still went and did it.'

'Are you sayin' I ought ter do the same?' Sid looked at her uncertainly. 'I know it's the right thing to do –

and I should've done it at the start – but I was thinkin' about me family. If that devil got his hands on you or Julia . . .'

'Yeah, I know,' Ruby said anxiously. 'I'm not tellin' you to do it, Sid – but I would stand by you if you did.'

Sid nodded and fidgeted with his cap. The murder he'd seen came back to him in his dreams night after night and he knew it was his conscience telling him he should go to the police. He found his steps taking him towards the local police station next morning, and stood looking up at it for some minutes before walking away. He just couldn't risk his family. Charlie was a child. Perhaps he didn't realize what men like that could do to their victims . . .

Shaking his head, Sid caught a bus that would take him to work. He might be a spineless coward but it wasn't just him. Ronnie the Greek knew where he lived and he'd seen Julia. Sid just couldn't risk anything bad happening to her.

CHAPTER 25

'I've dropped our bundle over the wall,' Charlie told Maisie that evening after tea. 'We 'ave ter go now or they'll 'ave us on our way to the orphanage.'

Maisie nodded. She looked frightened and Charlie knew she wanted a warm home and her own bed to go to, but they no longer had a home or a mother to take care of them. He was thirteen. If he could keep them going for a year, he would be able to find a proper job and a home, though he knew that even when he was old enough to work, the law would say he wasn't adult enough to care for his young sister.

Charlie wondered if Constable Jones would keep his word and try to find his aunt for them. He wished he'd spoken to the police months ago; he and Maisie might have been living in the country with his aunt. Charlie wasn't sure he would like the country but he could be a carpenter anywhere and if Maisie was safe with his aunt and he had an apprenticeship, life could offer nothing more. In the meantime, he had to look after his sister.

'Don't be frightened, Maisie,' he told her stoutly. 'You've got me ter look after yer.'

'Yeah, I know.' Her eyes looked at him trustingly and for a moment Charlie's courage faltered. He didn't want to let her down but if he did nothing they would end up in that orphanage and Maisie would hate that. He took a deep breath.

'Come on, we're leaving,' he said. 'I've found a place no one uses, Maisie. I've got some money to buy what we need – and we'll 'ave chips tonight fer our supper. Tomorrow I'll get something for us to sleep on and a picnic stove so we can make a cup of tea.'

'Can we 'ave cocoa instead?' Maisie asked, taking his hand. Charlie nodded and she smiled up at him as they left the ward.

Nurse Jenny was busy with a patient who had been brought in that afternoon and there was no sign of Sister Norton. The pair walked hand in hand down the stairs to the front hall and then out of the swing door. Maisie saw the caretaker looking at them but she smiled at him and he smiled back, making no attempt to ask where they were going. Like everyone else, Bert Rush was feeling sorry for the children. Charlie often went out to fetch sweets or a comic and Bert saw no reason for alarm in the two of them going out for a while.

Charlie forced himself to walk slowly until they were round the corner and out of sight of the front door. Then he pulled at Maisie's hand, racing to get the bundle containing their bits and pieces that he'd thrown over the wall. He'd worried that a tramp or some youths might find it, but it was lying half hidden by what was left of the huge pile of rubble that had once made his escape and re-entry into the infirmary so easy.

Once he had the bundle over his shoulder, Charlie

headed towards the docks. He had a padlock and key for his shed and he intended to keep it locked whenever he and Maisie left it; that way no one could steal their things and once he'd bought their stove and sleeping gear, he would need to protect them. Charlie had seen the homeless men who slept in doorways and under arches; he knew they roamed the streets the whole day looking for something they could steal and sell, anything that would provide food or, more likely, alcohol to help them through their wretched lives.

Charlie didn't want to be like those men. He wanted good honest work that would enable him to care for his sister. It was in his mind that he might need to ask Mick for work again, but he would avoid that unless he was forced. What he really needed was an apprenticeship to a carpenter but when he'd mentioned it to Matron, she'd said it would cost money. Apprenticeships did not often come free and that might mean Charlie would never realize his dream, but he wouldn't give up yet. There were yards that used wood in their work on the docks and once he'd got their little hut set up and made Maisie comfortable, he would begin his search for a real job.

'When did you notice the children were absent?' Sister Norton asked Nurse Jenny when she reported they were missing.

'Not until I went to ask if they would like cocoa and biscuits for their supper,' Nurse Jenny replied. 'I'm sorry, Sister. I don't understand where they could have gone.'

'They've run away,' Sister Norton said and looked crossly at her. 'Their things are gone and if I know that lad, it must have been his plan to run away once the funeral was over.'

'He knew Matron intended to send them to the orphanage. We all knew they didn't want to go.'

'This is why we should have kept a strict watch on them,' Sister Norton pointed out. 'Now I have to report to Matron that they've gone and she will not be pleased.'

'It's a pity their aunt couldn't be found,' Jenny said. 'I know Sarah asked around and so did I – we spoke to neighbours who might have known Mr Howes' sister but no one remembered where she'd gone.'

'Did anyone ask the police to make inquiries?'

'Matron said she would see to it.'

Sister nodded, because she knew that Matron considered the children would be better off with them than in the care of an unknown woman. It was possible that they had not passed on the nurses' concerns to the police.

'Well, I shall speak to her. I am sure the police will pick them up shortly, because they were hungry and dirty when they first came to us and they will not fare well living on the streets.'

Jenny nodded but, as she told Sarah when she came on duty the next day, 'Charlie has had weeks to plan this. I saw him delivering groceries on a shop bike one Saturday and I wouldn't mind betting that he has it all worked out this time.'

Sarah nodded. 'I asked Mum about giving them a home for a while but she said we couldn't manage to keep them forever and it would only upset them if we had to let them go to the orphanage in the end.' She sighed. 'I hate to think of little Maisie on the streets. With her chest she will start to be ill as soon as the weather changes. Neither of them realize how dangerous it is to sleep in shop doorways or under the arches.'

'I doubt if they'll sleep on the streets. Charlie has more sense,' Jenny said thoughtfully. 'I've seen the way he looks after his sister and I think he has somewhere safe for her to be – whether or not she will like it is another matter. Maisie likes her comforts and Charlie won't find it easy to please her.'

'I wish I'd persuaded Mum to have them for a while. And we could have tried harder to find their aunt. I asked around but I've had other things on my mind . . .'

'Yes, of course you have, losing your dad, and I've been upset too.' Jenny shook her head. 'I thought I'd found someone special, Sarah, but he turned out to be the wrong sort – I wish I had someone like your Jim.'

Sarah looked sad. 'I don't see much of him now. He's busy working. Last Sunday he only paid a flying visit because he had a special party to get ready for the next day and it meant a lot of extra work.' Sarah shook her head. 'I'm so worried about those children, Jenny. I think I'll visit the police station in the morning and tell them what little I know. Someone I spoke to said she thought Jeanie Howes had been married for a short time to someone who worked on the ships. My informant thought he might have been killed and that might make it harder to find her.'

'Yes – unless you know her second name?'

'No, no idea – but if I tell that nice Constable Jones, he might have some idea how to find out.'

Jenny thought about what Sarah had said as she boarded her bus that evening. She'd been brooding over Chris

213

and perhaps because of that she hadn't noticed that Charlie was up to something. Of course, she'd known they were upset over their mother; everyone had sympathized with the two orphans and wished they could do more to help them. Because of their extended stay on the ward, they had become a part of the family that was the nursing staff of the Rosie. Nurse Anne had spent a part of her day playing with the children, particularly Maisie, but that very day she had been sent back to the large teaching hospital, because she was due to complete her studies to become a nurse.

Lily and Gran had cooked a delicious stew and the smell made Jenny very hungry. She told her family what had happened to the children as they ate and Lily frowned.

'They will be all right for a while, because the weather is so pleasant but what happens when the winter comes?'

'Surely the police will spot them before it gets really cold?' Jenny said and felt guilty. She ought to have seen them leaving and questioned them, though in her heart she knew they would have found a way to escape whatever she'd done.

'In my day there were always street kids,' Gran said thoughtfully. 'The orphanages used to take them in if the family couldn't, but some of them have moved out to the country. They say it's better for the kids but I'm not so sure. Anyway, it isn't all your fault, Jenny. Don't look so guilty.'

Her sister nodded. 'From what you've told me, that lad was pretty determined. If he wanted to leave, he would, whatever you or anyone else said or did.'

'Yes, I know,' Jenny said and bit her lip. 'What sort of a day did you have?'

Lily frowned. 'I cleaned and cooked – and that man came here, Jenny. He asked me if I would listen to him and hear his side of the story but I refused.'

'Chris came here looking for me?'

'No – he wanted to talk to me. He said if I would only talk to him you would see that he wasn't a monster.'

'I hope you sent him away with a flea in his ear. I told him it was over.'

'She did!' Gran said and gave a cackle of laughter. 'Your sister has a tongue like a whiplash on her when she likes.'

'You haven't regretted breaking it off?' Lily was looking at Jenny anxiously

'Yes, of course I have,' Jenny said truthfully. 'I liked him a lot, Lily – but he deceived me. He should have told me that he was a member of Oswald Mosely's gang.'

'Some people think they have a certain amount of truth in what they claim,' her sister said fairly.

'You don't and I don't,' Jenny said. 'I do regret that I can't see him, Lily, but I won't change my mind.'

'You won't want this then?' Lily held out a sealed envelope. 'He said he was going away – leaving the country – and he didn't expect to be back for some time. He says this will explain things you didn't give him a chance to tell you.'

'Burn it,' Jenny said. 'I don't want to read lies and excuses.'

'I won't burn it because you might change your mind,' Lily said. 'I shall put it in the dresser drawer and it will stay there until you can think calmly about what you want.'

'You sound as if you've changed your mind about him?'

'About the people he was marching with and what they stand for – never!' Lily said. 'But I do see why you liked him, Jenny. My life has been shadowed because of the man that destroyed me – and I don't want it to happen to you. You have to think calmly about this and at the moment you're too angry.'

Jenny was surprised. She would have expected Lily to destroy the letter and say nothing about Chris's visit. The fact that she'd been so honest made Jenny pause. She watched as her sister placed the letter in the drawer and then started to clear the used dishes. They washed up together and then Jenny washed her sister's hair for her and Lily put some wire curlers in the front so that it would curl a little under her cap the next day. Her hair was much shorter than Jenny's and easier to keep tidy. Jenny usually washed hers on her day off, because it took a long time to dry.

She went up to bed, thinking about Chris's letter. A part of her wanted to go downstairs, retrieve it and read what he had to say, but she was still angry and she knew she wouldn't believe a word he'd written. Lily was right – she needed time to cool down.

Closing her eyes, she forced herself to think about other things and started to wonder how the children were managing. Were they warm enough and had they found something to eat?

CHAPTER 26

Maisie ate all her chips and drank her cocoa. Charlie had found some cardboard lying on the docks and he piled all their clothes on it to make a bed for them in the hut. Because it was a warm night, they wouldn't need more than a coat over them and Maisie had thrown hers off saying she was too warm.

'It's hard on the floor,' she complained as she wriggled one way and then the other.

'I know. It's only fer one night,' Charlie said. 'Tomorrow, I'll buy the camping stuff and it will be better.'

He wished he'd made the effort and bought what he needed sooner. Had he thought in time, he could have stored it in the hut, but he'd been too upset about the funeral. Now that was over, he could think better and he knew what he needed to do. He would keep them on the street for as long as he could and after that they would have to go to the cops or back to the infirmary.

'I don't like it 'ere, Charlie.' Maisie sounded scared and he snuggled up to her, putting his arm about her.

'It ain't so bad, Maisie. Think of it as an adventure.

We can have fun. We'll eat what we like instead of what they give us and, when I'm not working, we can go out and play.'

Soon she was sleeping and Charlie stared into the darkness. It would be better once he'd bought the camping stuff, but Maisie wasn't like him. She was gentle and she needed someone to love her and look after her. Charlie could only do so much and he wished he knew where his aunt lived. He'd only met her once but he remembered how she'd laughed with Dad and told him he'd got a lovely son. Auntie Jeanie was kind and generous; she was like their dad and if he could only find her, she would love Maisie and his sister responded so well to being fussed and loved.

Sighing, Charlie closed his eyes. This business of being the man of the family and looking after others wasn't easy . . . As he drifted into sleep, he found himself thinking of the father who had played football with him on the street the night before he joined his ship for the last time; he'd laughed and talked about what they'd do when he got back on his next leave. Dad had been strong. He would have looked after them if he was here.

'I'll look after Maisie, Dad,' he murmured as he fell into a dreamless sleep at last.

'Of course, yer will, son.' Charlie heard the voice vaguely as he drifted off and it made him smile, comforting him, making him feel stronger. It had been all right at the infirmary, but they'd been going to send them away so Charlie had had no choice . . .

Sarah was on duty when Constable Jones entered the ward the next day. He grinned at Sarah as she approached him. 'I've got a bit of news for the lad,' he said. 'We cornered Ronnie the Greek last night as he left his master's club. He put up a fight but we'd had a tip-off that he would be there and we've got him safely locked away. He knocked a police officer out cold in the fight so we've got him on one charge and we can hold him while we find some more.'

'That is brilliant news,' Sarah said and smiled. She liked the open quality of the young officer. 'Unfortunately, the children aren't here – they ran off yesterday without any of us seeing them go.'

He looked stunned. 'What happened?'

'They were due to be taken to the orphanage this morning and neither of them wanted to go.'

'That would do it. Well, I'll report it down the station and we'll keep an eye out for them – the lad asked me to find his aunt for him. I'd better get my skates on . . .'

'My friend says Jeanie Howes may have married a sailor who died at sea.'

'Right, thanks for that,' he said and wrote the information in his notebook. 'I think some sort of inquiry was made for a Miss Jean Howes – but I'll check the register and see if there's a record of her marriage. If there is, we may have a last known address.' His eyes twinkled. 'I shouldn't worry too much, nurse. I reckon Charlie is capable of looking after them both fine for a while. He won't manage in the winter but if I can't find him by then I don't deserve to be a copper.'

'If you find their aunt or the children – please let us know. We are very fond of those two.'

'Yeah, I imagine they would be easy to like,' he said. 'If I had a young brother, I'd want him to be just like

Charlie. I've got two sisters – both of them still at school and both of them want to be nurses.' He looked at her with interest. 'Should I encourage them? Is it a good job?'

'If you want to do it then you wouldn't want to be anything else,' Sarah said.

'Right, I shan't discourage them then.' He fingered his helmet. 'I'd best get back to work. Thanks for your help.'

Sarah smiled as she watched him leave. He seemed a decent man and he had a nice smile. If anyone could find Charlie's aunt, Sarah thought it would be Constable Jones. She just wished the children were still here, safe and cared for . . .

'Do I have to stay 'ere on me own?' Maisie asked as Charlie prepared to leave her. He'd taken her with him when he went to buy their sleeping bags and the camping stove, but later he'd gone out looking for work on his own. 'It's boring in here – there's nothin' to do.'

'I'll never find work with you trailing behind me,' Charlie told her. 'Read them comic books and you've got the sum book Nurse Sarah gave yer – and yer puzzles. It ain't no different to when you were at the infirmary.'

'You were there some of the time and the nurses used to bring me drinks, and Ruby talked to me when she brought me lunch.'

Charlie's patience was stretched. 'It's 'ere or the orphanage, Maisie.'

Maisie nodded and sighed. She'd got a chair and a little table she could spread the pieces of her puzzle on and it was comfortable enough in the hut, almost too warm in the middle of the day, but there was a window she could open, though Charlie didn't want her to, because it might attract attention and he didn't want anyone to realize they were using the hut.

'I shan't lock you in,' Charlie told her. 'But don't leave our stuff, Maisie. If it gets pinched, we shan't be able to replace them sleeping bags because most of the money has gone. I've got to earn more to pay for the paraffin and the food.'

'All right.' She gave in with a sigh. 'I'll put the table up against the door so no one can open it. Knock and tell me when it's you and I'll let you in.'

Charlie nodded and grinned at her. 'I shan't work every day, Maisie. When we've got enough money for a few days, we'll go to a park and have some fun – buy some ice cream. The schools are on holiday now so no one will think it's odd we ain't in school.'

Maisie smiled at him. She didn't much like being left in the hut, but with Charlie's promise to take her out another day she would put up with it for a while. It was better than being sent to an orphanage and they could never go home to Ma. The thought made her want to cry again but she knew it would only upset her brother and he was trying to look after her.

Charlie was the most important person in Maisie's life; he had been for a long time, even before Ma died. Maisie had loved her mother but Charlie was always the one that looked out for her. He brought her sweets and the one time she'd been to a fair, it was Charlie who had taken her on the swings and bought her a sticky candyfloss.

After he'd gone, she pulled the table up close to the door and put the chair behind it so that she could work on the puzzle. She'd done it several times now, but it was better than sums or Charlie's comics. It seemed a long time since she'd been to school and able to play with other children and the thought brought tears to her eyes. If only Ma hadn't got in with that horrible man! She hoped something bad would happen to him and the thought made her smile. Charlie had been to the police and once they got him, he was sure to go to prison for a long time.

The hours dragged by and Maisie was half-asleep on her bed when she heard someone try to open the door. She almost called out to ask who it was but something stopped her. Charlie would tell her to let him in if it was him so she kept quiet, holding her breath as whoever it was tried to push the door back, and then she heard voices.

'Hey you! What are you doin'?'

Maisie heard the sound of running feet as the would-be intruder ran off. She sat silently, fearing that the second person would come in and see her, but nothing happened and she began to relax. She was hungry and she looked for the remains of a bag of biscuits that Charlie had bought; they were broken so they were cheaper than the good ones but they tasted the same. She crunched one that was nearly whole and then two more pieces but decided to leave the rest for later. If Charlie was lucky, he would find some work and then he would buy them a pie or chips; she didn't mind which, because she liked eating with her fingers and eating out of a paper bag was still new enough to be an adventure.

She knew it was a lovely day outside because the sun penetrated the sacking that Charlie had nailed over the window to stop anyone peering in at them. It also stopped Maisie looking out. She pulled a little bit of it back and peeped out, being careful not to move it enough to be noticed. Several lorries were drawn up outside the big warehouse in front of her and she thought they were unloading goods rather than loading them, because two of them drove off empty. She thought it was curious, because when they'd walked on the docks the previous day, most were unloading from the barges tied up at the wharf and she'd seen a lorry arrive at one of the other warehouses to take a load away – so why had they brought goods to the docks? Perhaps they were going to send them abroad on one of the ships. Yes, that must be it, Maisie thought and then forgot all about the lorries as she heard Charlie's knock and his voice asking to be let in.

'Yer back,' she said joyfully as she let him in and caught the smell of pie and mash with gravy. Charlie had been to the pie stall further up the docks and bought them both a carton of tasty fish pie and mashed potato. 'That smells lovely. I'm glad I didn't eat all the biscuits.'

'I did well this mornin',' Charlie said and grinned. 'Mick gave me a job delivering things and I earned ten bob. That means we can 'ave a day out tomorrow, Maisie.'

He put the parcels of food on the table and Maisie fetched the salt packet from their cupboard. Charlie had brought a bottle of ginger beer for them to share and she licked her lips – it was all the things she liked but had seldom been given either at home or the infirmary. It made up for the hours she'd had to spend on her own.

Charlie smiled at her, looking pleased. 'I've found a place not far away where yer could go while I'm working,' he told her. 'If it's a nice day there are swings and a roundabout to play on – and there's a shelter yer could go under if it got a bit wet. I could lock the door then and keep our things safe.'

Maisie spooned some of her dinner into her mouth. 'Someone tried to get in earlier,' she told him as she swallowed the delicious food. 'Someone else called to him and he ran off.'

'That's probably the tramp I saw hanging around this mornin'. He's looking fer a place to sleep, Maisie, just like us, so it would be best if I lock the door when I leave. Yer can play on the swings while the weather's warm and when it changes – we'll look for somewhere yer can go fer free.'

Maisie nodded. She didn't tell her brother that she'd been scared. Charlie wasn't frightened of anything. 'I'd rather do that than stay here alone.'

'Once I've fetched me packages from Mick's, you could come with me and wait while I deliver them,' Charlie said thoughtfully. 'Mick only needs me a couple of times a week – and I deliver the groceries on Saturdays. I'll earn enough for what we want fer a while anyway.'

'Couldn't I look fer work too?' she asked but Charlie shook his head.

'There's loads of men lookin' fer work, Maisie. I only get the work no one else wants – or because it suits Mick to use me. It's not proper work, see – and there's no work on the docks for a girl.'

'I could pull a trolley!' Maisie pouted, but Charlie just smiled.

'Yeah, yer could – but could yer fend off the lads that try ter take the goods orf me?' He nodded as he thought of something. 'Yeah, that's what I'll tell Mick. I'll say I've got you to hold on to the trolley when I 'ave ter fight the other lads off.'

'Does it happen often?'

'Nah, only once – but Mick won't know that, will he? He might give yer a bob or two fer yourself, Maisie – and I can keep an eye on you and lock our shed up.'

Maisie nodded happily. She would much rather be out playing on the swings or following her brother while he did his jobs than shut up in this shed, which was fusty and hot when the sun shone overhead.

'I'd rather be with you,' she said and smiled as she scraped the last of her pie from her packet.

'Mebbe you could go back to school after the holidays?' Charlie suggested. 'You can tell 'em yer had to go away while Ma was bad. It's the truth and they won't know where yer living.'

'If they want to know too much I'll run away,' Maisie said. It was five weeks or more until school started again and so she didn't need to worry until it happened. For the moment she was enjoying her adventure, especially now that Charlie had said she could go with him when he delivered parcels for his friend.

'We'll go up the municipal swimming baths tomorrow,' Charlie said. 'I saw a notice on the wall where they're lettin' kids in free in the mornings for the summer holidays. We can 'ave a warm shower and wash ourselves and our hair – and then we shan't get fleas.'

Maisie nodded happily. Charlie had taken her to the pool when it was free before. She liked going to the indoor swimming baths, even though she only splashed in the shallow end, and she didn't mind getting under the shower if it meant she could have fun in the water. Last time they'd been on the streets they'd both got nits and Maisie had hated it but this time Charlie had it all worked out. She looked at him admiringly. He filled bottles that had held fizzy drinks with water from the water tap in the square and brought them home so they had water to make cocoa but if Maisie wanted to relieve herself she had to use an old pail, which Charlie took to the toilet block to empty when it was dark; it was the worst thing about living in the hut, but Charlie said they couldn't be seen going to the toilets too often or someone would become curious.

It was like a game of hide and seek, Maisie thought and giggled. Last time she'd been scared, afraid that Ronnie the Greek would find them and wanting her mother all the time, but now she was starting to have fun.

'We're all right, aren't we, Maisie?' her brother asked looking a bit anxious. 'You're not fed up yet, are yer?'

'No, I'm all right,' she said stoutly, forgetting the fear she'd felt when that man had tried to get in earlier. 'As long as I've got you, Charlie, I ain't scared of anythin' . . .'

CHAPTER 27

'Well, Mrs Johnson, Mr Johnson, I am glad to welcome you to our family of carers,' Lady Rosalie said and consulted her notes. 'You've been approved and I see you are willing to take small children up to the age of seven . . .' She nodded as she looked in her book. 'I have quite a few children of about that age – if you could stretch to eight years, I have two little girls. Gillian is six and her sister is just eight. They are good children and I doubt you'll have any trouble with them – but we're always here to help. If you would be prepared to consider the two, I can arrange for you to meet them at two tomorrow afternoon?'

'That would be perfect,' Mrs Johnson said and smiled. She was a pretty woman with fair hair and a slightly nervous look but her husband seemed to be strong-minded and well able to cope. They had asked for one girl but were prepared to take two of the right age. 'We shall be here on the dot.'

'I shall not be here myself,' Lady Rosalie said. 'I have some children coming in from overseas and I must see them allocated to temporary shelters.' She shook hands and then sat down at her desk.

After a few moments of writing up her notes a knock came at the office door and her secretary poked her head round the corner. 'A lady has called without an appointment; will you see her?'

'Is she suitable?' Lady Rosalie frowned. 'Most people make an appointment . . .'

'She says her name is Mrs Gwen Cartwright – and that the Matron of the Rosie told her to come and see you.'

'Ah, I see – yes, I do know about her,' Lady Rosalie said. 'Yes, send her in and then bring in a tray of tea please, Millie. I think this lady might turn out to be very interesting!'

'You look tired, love,' Sarah's mother said when she came into the kitchen that evening. 'I've made a nice shepherd's pie and there's apple crumble to follow with a bit of custard.'

'We had a busy day on the ward,' Sarah said and sighed. 'One of our patients died and then we had some kids brought in – three of them, all brothers, all suffering with rickets, and by the looks of them it will be a while before they're well enough to go home. We've had to put them in the little isolation ward for the moment, we're so busy.'

'It's as well those Howes children aren't taking up beds,' her mother said as she took the pie from the oven and placed it on the table.

'I wish I knew where they were,' Sarah said. 'I really cared about them, Mum, even though I knew they would have to go away.'

'Well, perhaps it needn't be like that,' her mother said and smiled. 'I went to see Matron this morning and she sent me round to Lady Rosalie's office – and she's put me on her list. She said that normally she looks for couples but because you work at the Rosalie and she knows you're reliable she will put me on the list – subject to the usual checks, of course, but she thinks there will be no bother and once the children are found I'll be able to have them here until their aunt is found or until they're old enough to leave school.'

'Oh, that's wonderful, Mum!' Sarah threw her arms about her and hugged her. 'You're sure it isn't too much for you?'

'I wouldn't have gone for the interview if it was,' her mother said. 'I like cooking for people and I like taking care of people – and having kids about will make the house come to life. I miss your father, Sarah, and I always shall, but I'm not the sort to fade into the curtains and spend my life weeping. I thought about going out to work but when you said about the children, I made up my mind it was what I wanted.'

'I'm so pleased,' Sarah said. 'You can start with Charlie and Maisie when they're found – but even if they go to their aunt there will be others. The boys they brought in today look as if they've been half-starved. They will need foster homes unless they send them to the orphanage as soon as they're well enough.'

'There will always be a child in need, Sarah,' her mother said. 'Especially with so many men out of work and all the troubles everywhere. I can't take them all, but I'm looking forward to taking those I can manage and giving them a bit of decent cooking and a good home.'

'They're the lucky ones,' Sarah said. 'Some of the people who offer to take children for fostering aren't the right sort – look what happened to Charlie! Matron was telling me that Lady Rosalie is determined to take only parents she can trust – and that means she really took to you, Mum.'

'I liked her too.' Sarah's mother nodded. 'It was quite a pleasant morning one way and another – and I bought myself a new dress off the market. I got it for five bob and it's a real bargain, nearly new and worth five guineas in the shops.'

'You should buy a new one, Mum,' Sarah said.

'Why, when I can get a dress hardly worn for a fraction of the price? It's good enough for Sundays, Sarah, and I'll keep my money for more important things – like a new outfit for your wedding. I'll be buying new then!' She smiled at her daughter. 'You'll be inviting Ruby to it, love?'

'Oh yes, Julia and Sid too,' Sarah said and then made a face at her. 'That's if Jim ever gets around to arranging it!'

CHAPTER 28

'Sid! Our Julia's gone missing!' Ruby rushed at her husband as he came home from work that evening. She was frantic with worry and he grabbed hold of her, giving her a little shake. 'She went to see a friend, hours ago, and now she's missing!'

'What do yer mean "gone missing"?' he asked. 'Steady on, Ruby love, and tell me slowly so I know what you're saying.'

'Julia said she was goin' down the market and that she would call on a friend of hers on the way back so wouldn't be home until lunch – but she never came back!'

Sid stared at her. Julia was so reliable. She would never dream of worrying her mother.

'Where does this friend live?' he asked, preparing to go straight back out.

'I've already been round,' Ruby told him. 'She hadn't been there and she'd promised Lucy she would.' Her eyes were full of fear. 'Do you think she's had an accident?'

'I don't know . . .' Sid's guts were churning. Ruby

was already beside herself with worry and he didn't want to make her more upset but he had a feeling this was something to do with the police arresting Ronnie the Greek. In Sid's mind the fear that his daughter might have been snatched in retribution was growing. The shadowy men behind the thug that had terrorized shop-keepers and pub owners might think it was Sid who had informed on him and he was being punished. 'I'm goin' ter look for her, love. She might 'ave met someone and be having a cup of tea with another friend some-where near the market.'

Even as he said the words, Ruby was denying them. Sid knew she was right. Julia wasn't the sort to lose track of time and let folk down. She was reliable and kind and intelligent and loving – and it would kill both him and Ruby if anything happened to her.

'I have to look for her,' he said and went out. Ruby was saying something but he didn't listen. Anxiety was gnawing at his guts, making him tremble inside with fear for his beloved daughter. Oh, God, don't let anything happen to her! He didn't care what they did to him, but he couldn't bear it if his daughter was harmed – or killed. She had such a bright future before her and his throat was tight with a mixture of anger and fear. Why had he had to be there when the murder happened – and why the hell had he taken the knife and hidden it? He cursed himself for his stupidity. If anything happened to Julia, he would never forgive himself and Ruby would hate him.

Yet surely, they wouldn't harm her? They wanted the evidence he'd got, because they must fear it would lead to the man who wielded it. Sid wondered why they hadn't just slit his throat when he was walking home at night. He would rather they had done that than his daughter suffer in his stead.

Tears were on Sid's cheeks as he thought of all the things those vicious thugs might have done to his girl. If they'd harmed her, he would kill them – or as many as he could get close to. He made the vow to himself that he would find Julia or die in the attempt.

The market square was empty, deserted apart from a couple of youths sorting through the debris that had been left by the traders. Rotten fruit, outside cabbage leaves and bruised potatoes were sometimes discarded and men who were close to starving would pounce once the traders had packed up and gone – old crates could be used for fires and rotten fruit might be good in parts, discarded leaves could help bulk out a stew. There was little left, because the scavengers had been and gone but youths were collecting bottles and tins which could be sold to the scrapyard for a few pennies. Some of them looked filthy, their hair matted and crawling with lice. These were the children who lived on the streets because they had no homes and no one to care for them; the thought of his Julia living like that made him feel ill.

Sid asked the lads if they'd seen a young girl. He described Julia but they just shook their heads and slouched off, eager for their money so they could head for a shop to spend it on broken biscuits or crisps, a diet that might include a few chips if they earned enough.

A few of the shops still had their lights on and their doors bore the open sign. Sid asked in all of them if anyone had seen Julia. One man knew her by sight.

'Julia? She comes in sometimes to buy sweets with her friends. I reckon I did see her earlier, mate. She was at a stall – and some bloke went up to her. I noticed because she went off with him and looked worried. I thought it was a bit strange, because she didn't look like that sort of girl. Too young for a start.'

'What do yer mean – that sort of girl?' Sid's throat was dry with fear now.

'Cheap – goes with men for money,' the shopkeeper said. 'I've seen that bloke afore and I know he's a pimp. He runs half a dozen girls and I've seen them come down to the market in the evenings with black eyes. Feel sorry for them, I do – they don't know what they're getting into until it's too late.'

'Do you know his name?' Sid's stomach was clenching.

'Might be Jason. I heard one of his girls saying how vicious he was when she didn't do what he told her.' He shook his head. 'I couldn't understand why a decent girl like that would just go off with him – he didn't use force and she seemed eager to go.'

Sid frowned. 'My Julia wouldn't go with anyone like that willingly. She's orf to grammar school in September and wants to be a teacher.'

'Well, I can't help you, mate,' the shopkeeper said and turned away as a customer came in. 'But it sounded like the girl you're looking for.'

Sid strode off feeling angry, but then the anger turned to sickness and he knew what had happened. Mr Penfold had sent one of his thugs to get her. Goodness knows what he'd told Julia to get her to go with him willingly. He must have spun her a pack of lies. If he was a pimp, he'd know how to turn the charm on, because that was how men like that drew the girls into their web, telling lies and promising help.

Sid's instincts turned him towards his home. As he passed the pub where he'd often drunk in the past he was tempted. He needed a drink – but if he went home smelling of beer when he was supposed to be looking for his daughter, Ruby would never forgive him.

His wife was looking out of the window when he got back. She opened the door to him, looking frantic with worry. 'Have you discovered where she went?'

'No one has seen her,' Sid said, because he wouldn't add to his wife's anxiety by telling her what the shop-keeper had said. It might not have been Julia and there was still a chance she would come home and tell them she'd met a friend from school.

'You need to go to the police, Sid,' Ruby said. 'Julia is a good girl. She would never worry us like this – something has happened to her. She's had an accident or – or something bad . . .'

'Shall I go to the hospital?' Sid said. He hadn't thought about anything that simple. 'Yes, I'll go there first – she will either be at the Rosie or the London.'

'Go to the London first,' Ruby said. 'Matron knows our Julia. She would have sent us word if she'd been taken in there.'

'Yes, all right, I'll ask if a young girl of Julia's age has been brought in – and if they say no I'll go down the station . . .'

Sid was hungry and weary by the time he'd visited the hospital and the infirmary and then the police station. The desk sergeant shook his head.

'We can't put her on the missing persons' list for at least a week or more,' he told Sid with a frown. 'I know you say it isn't like your daughter to go off without letting you know – but all the fathers think they know their children until something like this happens. Your wife is worried, of course she is, but your daughter will probably be home by the time you get back, sir.'

Sid nodded; he'd expected something of the sort. Many young girls and boys went off because they'd had a row at home, but that wasn't true of Julia. She was getting everything she'd ever wanted and she'd been as happy as he'd ever seen her. He'd wondered if he should tell the sergeant what the shopkeeper had told him, but decided against it. There was no point – they'd just think it confirmed what they'd suggested, that Julia's absence was of her own choice.

Ruby was sitting in the kitchen staring at the wall when he got in. This time she didn't look up hopefully and he sensed that something had happened.

'What is it?'

Ruby looked at him, despair in her eyes. 'They've got her,' she said in a flat voice. 'Those devils have got our Julia – and they're threatening to kill her unless they get what they want!' She rubbed a tear away angrily. 'What 'ave you *done*, Sid?'

Sid sat down with a bump as all the strength went from his legs. A groan of such despair left him that Ruby looked startled. She'd blamed him but he already blamed himself.

'They must think I went to the cops and told 'em and they blame me for Ronnie the Greek's arrest . . .'

'But that weren't your fault!' Ruby said. 'It was the

lad that run away what turned 'im in because the Greek beat his mother and she died.'

'I know – but they might not . . .' Sid stared at her. 'What do I do, Ruby? If they want the damned knife they can 'ave it – I just want my girl back!'

'It was my fault,' Ruby said. 'If I hadn't put you out that night this wouldn't be happening!' She started to cry noisily, her shoulders heaving.

Sid was stunned, because he'd never seen his Ruby cry like that and he couldn't bear it. He went to put his arm about her, patting her shoulder clumsily.

'Don't give up, love. I'll go and see Mr Penfold, tell him he can 'ave the knife. I ain't split on 'im and I shan't.'

'No, you mustn't. They said they'll be in touch.' Ruby took a crumpled sheet of paper from her pocket. Letters cut from magazines had been stuck to it.

Sid read it out:

'"Your daughter is safe. Keep yer mouth shut and she might stay that way. You grassed and that means you pay. Go to the police and your daughter is dead and you're dead unless we get what we want. We'll be in contact."'

Sid stared at it, vomit in his throat. Julia was young and pretty and the thought of what might happen to her made him want to sick his guts up – but he couldn't tell Ruby his fears for their child. She was already close to collapse and he knew he had to do whatever these men wanted.

'I'll give them whatever they want,' he promised Ruby. 'I don't care if they give me a beating or kill me – as long as we get our girl back unharmed.'

'Oh, Sid, I'm sorry . . .' Ruby brought her head up, fighting her despair. 'You must be starvin' but I couldn't think of anything but Julia and I haven't cooked any food.'

'I'm not sure I could eat anything,' Sid said but his wife had started to fill the kettle. He watched as she cut two thick slices of bread and spread it with strawberry jam.

Sid stared at the food. He didn't want to eat it but forced himself to take a few bites. It tasted like sawdust in his mouth but he knew Ruby needed to be busy so he ate one slice and pushed the second away.

'I could do with a cup of tea,' he said as he saw she was staring at the wall again. 'We mustn't give up, Ruby. I'll wait until they tell me what ter do and I'll do it. She's done them no harm – it's me they want. It's me they'll punish for taking that knife . . .'

Ruby nodded and for a moment she focused on him. 'You should go down the pub,' she said. 'They'll be watching yer – and that's when they'll strike.' A little sob left her lips. 'I don't want ter lose yer, Sid – but . . .' He saw the utter despair in her eyes and nodded.

'I understand, Ruby. It's our girl. She means the world to both of us. I'd rather they slit my throat than touched a hair of her head!'

Ruby bent her head. She was crying silently now and it shocked Sid to the core. His Ruby was strong. Nothing ever bothered her and she gave as good as she got, but this had floored her and Sid knew why. He wanted to scream and shout and cry, but his guilt was too strong for him to give his emotions free rein. It was his fault and if he lived to see his girl once more, he would never let her be hurt again . . .

CHAPTER 29

'Haven't you finished the cleaning, Miss Saunders? It is past eleven – really not good enough!'

Kathy looked at Matron nervously. She seldom had to speak to her, because Ruby was usually there to speak up for them both.

'Ruby didn't come in this morning, Matron,' she said, 'So I've been doin' her work as well as my own . . .'

'Mrs Harding did not come in?' Matron looked surprised, because Ruby had always been reliable. 'Did she send a message? This is most unlike her.'

'No message, Matron,' Kathy said, still nervous because she was in awe of all the nursing staff but particularly Matron. 'I'll catch up as soon as I can.'

'I do not expect that you can manage everything yourself,' Matron said in a softer tone. 'I will speak to Mr Rush – it may be that he has time to help you wash the windows.'

'Oh, thank you!' Kathy blushed.

Bert Rush was always doing little things to help Kathy and she didn't like to think of him being asked to do her work as well as his own, but she couldn't tell Matron that, because she would look down her nose at her and that always made Kathy cringe. It reminded her of her mother when she was annoyed with Kathy, which she so often was these days.

Bert came just as she had started to wash the outside windows at the front of the infirmary. He took the bucket and cloth from her with a smile.

'Sister asked me to take over,' he said. 'You haven't finished inside – and it will be time for you to take the lunches round soon. You've only got one pair of hands, Miss Saunders.'

'Oh, yes, I know,' Kathy said. 'Thank you, Mr Rush. You're so very kind to me. I know you often help me finish jobs and I'm not sure Matron would approve . . .'

'Well, she told me to do this,' he said cheerfully. 'Off you go then and get your trolleys ready. The patients will want their lunches taken up to them.'

'Yes, I know. The kitchen staff don't have time to take them all round so I do the children's ward if Ruby is busy – but she likes seeing the children.'

'It's odd she hasn't come in this morning,' Bert said frowning. 'She's not one to let folk down as a rule.'

'No, Ruby never lets anyone down. When I first started, she was always showing me what to do and finishing off if I got behind.' Kathy looked at him anxiously. 'Perhaps Julia isn't well – Ruby is so proud because her daughter won a scholarship to the grammar school. If Julia was ill, she'd stay home with her but I'm surprised she didn't send her husband to let us know.'

'I'll pop round this evening and ask if everything is all right.'

Kathy smiled. 'That is really kind of you, Mr Rush – I should like to come with you, if that's all right?'

'Of course it is.' His smile lit up his homely features. Bert's hair was a sandy red, his skin pale and freckled and his nose was a bit too long, but he had a generous mouth and his smile made him look very attractive, or so Kathy thought. She really liked him. 'I should be proud to escort you – and see you home afterwards . . .'

'Oh – I couldn't let you do that,' Kathy said awkwardly. If her mother saw him, she would get a lecture on the evils of letting men near her. 'But we could visit Ruby together, of course.'

Bert looked at her oddly. He'd hinted that he would like to take her somewhere nice a couple of times but she always made an excuse. It wasn't that she didn't want to go to the pictures with him; she would have liked it very much, but her mother would be so cross and she would make Kathy's life a misery for days if she dared to do such a thing.

Kathy left Bert to tackle the windows. She set the trolley with the food the kitchen had prepared; corned beef, tomatoes and bread and butter, followed by a dish of stewed plums with a little cold custard. Most of the children would enjoy their lunch today, she thought.

When she started serving the lunches to the children those able to eat started to tuck in immediately. Kathy thought it was a lot better than many of them got at home, where corned beef would be a luxury and they never saw fruit or custard.

Sarah was helping one of the sicker children to swallow a little water. She shook her head when Kathy stopped by the bed.

'Timmy won't want anything today, Kathy. He's feeling very poorly.'

'Poor little love,' Kathy said and moved on to the next bed.

She'd just finished serving when Sarah came up to her. 'I've heard that Ruby isn't in today – do you know why?'

'No, she didn't send a message,' Kathy said and frowned. 'Bert is going to visit her this evening and I'm going with him. It isn't like Ruby not to come to work without she lets us know she's ill or Julia is.'

'Julia was fine when I saw her yesterday,' Sarah said. 'I was on early morning to lunchtime and I saw her on the bus. She got off at the market and waved to me.'

'Well, perhaps it's Sid who isn't well. I'll see what she says this evening.'

Sarah nodded and went back to her patients. Kathy returned the trolley to the kitchen and picked up the lunches for the women's ward. She would collect the dirty dishes and return them to the kitchen when everyone had eaten and then she would finish any other small jobs before she went off for the evening.

Kathy reflected that there weren't really enough cleaning staff. It worked when both she and Ruby were well but if Bert hadn't stepped in, she would not have managed all her chores that day. She thought that two women in the kitchen was hardly enough either but she realized that the infirmary had limited funds to manage on. Sometimes, volunteers came in and helped with the teas and perhaps Matron would call on her volunteers today.

Kathy tidied up downstairs and then collected the

trolleys, cleaning them ready for the next day. Bert came in and looked at her just as she was drying her hands.

'Ready then?' he asked.

Kathy smiled. 'Yes, just about. It's four o'clock. Ruby was on until six tonight but I haven't been asked to stay so Sister must have called in her volunteers.'

'Yes, perhaps,' he agreed and offered his arm. 'Let's go and find out how Ruby is, then.'

'Are you sure this is the house?' Kathy asked. Bert had knocked several times and no one had answered. 'I wonder where she is – do you think she is at the hospital?'

'She may be.' Bert looked concerned. 'Look, I'll leave a note to let Ruby know we called. Perhaps she'll be back tomorrow – or at least she'll let us know what is wrong.'

'Yes, I suppose. Make sure she knows the note is from us.' Kathy watched as he scribbled in his notebook and then tore out the page and put it through the door. 'We'd better go.'

'Yes, no point in waiting, she might be ages,' Bert agreed. 'We'll catch a bus to your house – unless you'd like to go out for a cup of tea and an iced bun?'

Kathy hesitated, then, 'I daren't, Mr Rush. I'm sorry but my mother will wonder where I am and she gets angry if she thinks I've been out with a man . . .'

Bert stared at her thoughtfully. 'I suppose I'm a bit old for you. I shouldn't have asked.'

'Oh no,' Kathy said quickly. 'I like you, Bert – I mean Mr Rush!' She blushed hotly. 'But my mother is funny like that – she was furious with me when I went to a café for a cup of tea with a school friend. She was in my class at school but Mum accused me of being with a man – and she said it as if I'd done something dirty.'

'I'm sorry,' he said sincerely. 'I wouldn't get you into trouble for the world, Kathy – you know I like you . . .?'

'I like you too, Bert.' She blushed again. 'I'd love to come out with you – to the pictures, too, but she wouldn't let me.'

His smile lit up his face. 'Well, no one can stop us being friends, Kathy – even your mum.'

Kathy gave a little giggle. 'No, she can't,' she agreed. 'If we have time at work, we might have a cup of coffee at the café across the road . . .'

'That's a date,' he said. 'Ruby can cover for us when she gets back.'

Kathy smiled and took his arm. Neither of them looked back and saw the upstairs curtain twitching.

CHAPTER 30

Ruby washed her face in cold water. She couldn't seem to stop crying since she'd read that awful letter. Her eyes were red and her face was swollen and blotchy. She hadn't been able to face work that morning, even though Sid had gone in as usual.

'I 'ave to carry on, love,' he said. 'We need the money and I can't let my boss down. Besides, they will come 'ere if I don't show my face. I'd rather they took me off the street than barged their way in 'ere.'

Sid had warned Ruby not to open the door or look out of the window. 'I don't want them roughing you up,' he'd told her. 'It won't be long, you'll see – they will get to me and tell me what I 'ave ter do to get our girl back. You stop in bed,' he said gently. 'Have a rest and try to sleep.'

Neither of them had slept all night, but Sid wanted to carry on as normal. The sooner Penfold's lot nabbed him the better. He knew he was in for a beating and there was no getting out of it; he had to take it and do as he was told or they would hurt his girl. He just prayed that Julia hadn't been harmed so far – and he thought

245

that if she was dead, he would swing for Penfold and whoever had snatched his little girl. They would die even if they took him with them, but he would endure anything to get Julia home.

For Ruby, the day was a long one. She was unable to sleep or rest and, after endless cups of tea, she had a headache and felt worse than if she'd done a day's work. When she saw Kathy and Bert walking away, she felt sorry she hadn't answered the door, but she couldn't until she stopped this silly crying. She made up her mind that she would write a letter to Matron. She would tell her the truth, because she knew the one person in the world who wouldn't let her down was Matron. She'd ask her to keep it to herself and knew it would go no further . . .

Sid knew he was being followed soon after he left work that evening. It was still light but he didn't bother to turn round. He just walked steadily and decided to go to the pub. He would have half a pint, just as he'd done last night, and make it last; when he came out it would be getting dusk and make it easier for his enemies to grab him without being seen, though they hadn't done so the night before.

The landlord asked him where he'd been recently and Sid explained that he'd been working. He was congratulated and the friendly publican insisted on buying him the other half, saying he hoped Sid wouldn't be a stranger again. Forcing a smile, Sid drank the beer and left.

It was that time before dusk and the lamps being lit and he knew exactly where they would nab him, because there was a narrow alley he needed to traverse to get home.

Sure enough, he heard the footsteps and then felt something sharp in his back. He held his breath, refusing to show fear and waited.

'Shout or ask for help and both you and the kid die,' a voice threatened.

'I'm not shouting. What do yer want?'

'You know what yer found. We want that and we want yer fingerprints on it – they're insurance against yer blabbing. Yer shouldn't 'ave gorn to the cops!'

'That wasn't me,' Sid protested and felt something hard jab into his ribs. 'On me life, I never grassed. Yer can 'ave the knife and I'll handle it so me fingerprints are on it – just send my girl back to her mother.'

'Right – now yer goin' ter get a taste of what's comin' ter you and that girl if yer break yer word . . .'

Sid drew a deep breath as he felt the first blow to the back of his neck and then another man came at him from the side and punched him in the face, knocking him to the ground. He tried to rise and a steel-capped boot went into his ribs; he heard them crack and felt the sharp pain, but refused to beg or cry out. This was his punishment and he had to take it like a man. Then the boot connected with his chin and everything went black.

Sid came to when he heard Ruby's voice and felt the touch of her hands bathing his face. He tried to open his eyes but one of them was so swollen that he couldn't. Squinting at her, he saw she'd been crying and he grinned as much as his bruised face would allow.

'It's all right, love,' he muttered, tasting blood on his

lips as he spoke. 'I've told 'em I'll do what they want. I've got ter handle the knife so my prints are on it and then they'll send back our girl.'

'Shush, Sid,' Ruby tried to warn him. 'Sarah is here . . .'

'She won't tell – explain it to her, Ruby.'

Sid's body felt as if he'd been run over by a steam-roller and his head ached. It was hard to keep his one eye open and he didn't think he could manage to sit up.

'You have to swear not to tell!' Ruby said urgently. 'Our Julia has been snatched by villains. Sid saw some-thing he shouldn't 'ave – a murder – and he took the knife and hid it. The coppers arrested one of the rogues involved and they think Sid grassed.'

'Are you talking of Ronnie the Greek?' Sarah's voice asked, horrified. 'He's a murderer and he has to go to prison for it. Oh, Ruby, you must be worried to death. No wonder you didn't come to work today!'

Sid tried to ask who had found him and Ruby bent closer so she could hear his words. 'It was Sarah,' she told him. 'She knew you'd been hurt bad so she fetched some of the men from the pub and they carried yer 'ome.'

'Did anyone call the cops?'

'No,' his wife reassured them. 'They thought it must 'ave been a robbery. You were 'eard to say you 'ad work in the pub and the way things are some blokes would kill for a few bob.'

'Good . . .' Sid drew a sigh of relief. He hurt like hell but he'd taken the beating and given his word that he would deliver the knife with his own prints on it.

He could only pray that Mr Penfold returned his daughter to him unharmed.'

'I'll telephone for a doctor to take a look at you,' Sarah said. 'You've got a broken rib, Mr Harding. It needs a bandage round to hold it or it may do more damage and it will hurt like hell.'

'You could do that, couldn't yer?'

Sarah hesitated. 'Yes, I've got bandage rolls in my nursing bag, but you really should go to the hospital, Sid.'

'I'll mend,' he said. 'It's not the first time I've had a broken rib and all they did was bind me up and tell me to rest fer a while.'

'When they carried you in, I thought you were dead!' Ruby said and he heard the sob in her voice.

'Take more than them to kill me,' Sid said valiantly, even though each breath cost him dear. 'I was told I wasn't needed for two weeks at work. It's holiday time for the gangs and they don't need me while all the brickies are off to paddle in the sea. I'll be right as rain by the time they get back.'

'Oh, Sid!' Ruby gasped as Sarah helped him out of his shirt and she could see the dark bruising on his chest and side. 'That must 'ave 'urt.'

Sid grimaced as Sarah did her work but once she had the bandages pinned in place it felt easier. The pain was still there and his face was so sore he dared not touch it, but none of it mattered.

'You're a good lass,' Sid told the nurse. 'Your Jim is a lucky man. I can't thank yer enough, Sarah – but I must ask yer not to repeat what yer heard here. I was set on and robbed, that's what it was . . .'

Sarah nodded and washed her hands at the sink, drying them on the clean towel Ruby gave her. 'I know better than to talk, Mr Harding,' she said, 'and I think you're a very brave man.'

'Nah, I'm a fool,' he said. 'If I 'adn't got drunk, Ruby wouldn't 'ave thrown me out and I would never 'ave got into this mess.'

'I hope Julia is all right,' Sarah said worriedly. 'How can you be sure you'll get her back?'

'I can't,' Sid replied tight-lipped. 'I have ter put the damned thing back near where I found it. They will be watching me and they said when I leave the knife, Julia will be released.' He made the effort to open his left eye as wide as he could. 'If they've harmed her, I'll do fer all of 'em – or as many as I can get to.'

'Sid, that's wild talk,' Ruby said anxiously. 'How could you kill men like that?'

'If our girl's 'armed I'll have nothin' ter lose,' Sid said and his voice was as cold and hard as iron. 'I don't care if they kill me or I swing fer it, Ruby – I'll get 'im first.'

Sid deliberately held back the name of the man he was determined to kill if Julia had been harmed. The less Sarah knew the better for her own sake. He'd said too much before he realized she was there but he knew she wouldn't talk. His concern was for her and her mother, because the men he'd upset were ruthless and would harm anyone they thought he might have told. Oh, if only he could go back to the night of the murder he would run home as fast as his legs would carry him.

'I'll be in work tomorrow, love,' Ruby said to Sarah. 'Need to try and keep everything normal, like.'

'Just tell Sister that you had a nasty bilious attack,

all of you – something you ate,' Sarah suggested. 'It's something that can come suddenly and be over just as swiftly.'

Ruby nodded. 'Just you remember – tell no one, even your mother.'

Sarah promised again and left. Sid heaved himself to his feet and Ruby stared at him in alarm.

'Where are yer goin'?' she demanded.

'I've got ter get that damned knife and put it back where I found it,' Sid said and stifled a groan of pain. He took a step forward and winced, his head spinning for a moment.

'You can't go tonight!' Ruby was concerned. 'You'll never make it there and back . . .'

'I'm all right,' he grunted even though he felt sick with the effort. 'I have ter do it, Ruby. They won't let Julia go until I've done what they told me – once they have the evidence, they've got insurance. I can't tell because my prints will be on the knife and I would be blamed for the murder.'

His wife nodded grimly. 'It means that devil will be able to blackmail yer fer the rest of yer life, Sid . . .'

'I know,' he sighed. 'But I've no choice, Ruby. Julia means more to me than my own life and whatever it costs me I'll get her 'ome fer yer.'

Ruby nodded but he saw the doubt in her eyes and knew she was wondering if Penfold's men would keep their side of the bargain. Sid had a feeling they would, because once they had a murder weapon with his prints on it, they could force him to work for them. He wasn't sure what they would ask of him – but it didn't bear thinking about and he wouldn't waste his time worrying.

All that mattered was that his girl was sent back to him safe and unharmed. If they'd violated her or she was dead . . . the gorge rose in his throat and he vomited into the kitchen sink. Running the water to rinse it away, he apologized to Ruby.

'I'm sorry, it just came up . . .'

'You're ill,' she said. 'Tell me where the knife is – let me fetch it.'

'No! I don't want you involved any more than you are,' he insisted. 'But if I'm not back in two hours you'd better come looking fer me . . .'

Sid's steps were laboured and he held on to the walls of the buildings he passed. The streets were not well lit and if anyone saw him, they would think he was drunk. He staggered a few steps, rested and then staggered on again until he reached the old building where he'd hidden the knife. It was derelict and due to be pulled down when the money was available. Sid went inside, feeling his way along the wall to reach the loose brick where the knife lay hidden. There was hardly any light but he did not need it; he had been on this journey fifty times in his mind and knew exactly where he'd put the weapon.

His fingers felt the cold of the metal and he sought the handle, making no attempt to prevent his fingerprints being imprinted on both the blade and the handle. Taking it in his hand, he retraced his steps. Once out of the derelict building, he stood under the nearest street light and held the knife aloft so that the man who had followed him could see his fingers around its handle. He walked slowly, deliberately, forcing himself to put

252

one foot in front of the other despite the pain until he reached the quay; then he dropped the weapon on the top step where the barges tied up.

For a moment he lingered and then he turned, holding his hands up to show whoever was watching him that he'd done as they demanded. He thought that at any moment they might bundle him into the river, but nothing happened and then he knew that death was not to be his fate. Penfold and Ronnie the Greek were in the clear for the murder he had implicated himself in, even though he was innocent and he was trapped.

Sid stumbled and lurched home, every part of his aching body screaming with the need to rest. Tears were on his cheeks though he wasn't crying, but he couldn't stop his eyes welling up. A stupid incident, one foolish mistake when he wasn't thinking clearly and his life was ruined.

He couldn't drag his wife and daughter down with him. Sid hardly knew what he was thinking as he stumbled home. All he wanted was to know that his little girl was safe. It didn't matter what happened to him – and yet something inside him was rebelling. He'd always been stubborn and he did not like what he'd been forced to do and what he might be asked to do in the future.

He could see lights all over the house when he got home. What had happened? Sid's fear made him move faster than his body was able and he almost fell into the kitchen as he flung the door open in his panic. Ruby was nowhere to be seen and fear rushed through him. Had they taken *her* now?

'Ruby!' he cried desperately. 'Ruby – where are you?'

She came to the top of the stairs and put her fingers to her lips. 'Shush, Sid,' she said softly. 'Julia is in bed. I gave her an 'ot drink and she went straight off to sleep.'

'Oh, thank God!' Sid sank to his knees, bent his head and wept. The relief was so great that he crumpled into a heap and lay there shaking and crying until Ruby came and put her arms around him, holding him.

'There then, love,' she said softly. 'It's all right. Julia is 'ome and tucked up in her own bed. She was very tired and emotional because she'd been shut up in a dark room and they hadn't given her much to eat or drink – but they didn't touch her. She said one of them threatened her with awful things but his boss told 'im he would stick a knife in 'im if he touched her. She said she was blindfolded the whole time and frightened but they told her if you did what yer were told, she would be brought 'ome – and she said she knew her dad would save her!' Ruby was sitting on the floor with him now and tears were running down her cheeks. She sniffed and then laughed, wiping his tears and then her own with her apron. 'We're a daft pair. She's safe now.'

'And we 'ave ter keep her that way,' Sid said. 'So in the morning you and Julia are leaving. I'll give yer me gran's gold watch and the long guard chain. You can sell it and use the money for yer expenses until yer find work and somewhere ter live. You'll take her down to the sea somewhere and stay in a boarding house until you find somewhere to rent. If there is a grammar school there, they'll take her in a minute when they see the top marks she got in the exams – scholarship marks.

Those devils ain't finished with us yet, Ruby, so you take her away and I'll stay 'ere until I can sort things out.'

'But that watch was fer yer old age – fer emergencies!'

'This *is* an emergency – and far more important. You do what I said, love, and take care of you and Julia.'

Ruby shivered. 'Someone just walked over me grave,' she said and looked worried. 'I don't want ter leave yer on yer own, Sid . . .'

'We ain't got no choice, Ruby love. We ain't safe in London no more. I want you both safe – and then I'll do whatever I 'ave ter do.'

'What are yer goin' ter do?' Ruby said looking frightened. 'Don't do anything daft, Sid.'

'They've got me over a barrel, Ruby love. Penfold can do what he likes with me now – but I don't care. As long as you and my girl are safe, I'll go along wiv 'im. If it comes to the crunch I might 'ave ter kill 'im. I'll know what needs ter be done when the time comes – but you can't be 'ere. They would violate yer and snatch our girl again if I refused, Ruby. Only if you two are safe can I do what I need to.'

Ruby stared at him in horror. 'They could make yer do anythin'!'

'Only if they had you or Julia. If he can't find yer I can do what is right. I might help him do a robbery if I 'ad ter – but I would draw the line at murderin' someone innocent. If they tried to involve me in somethin' like that . . . I'd rather kill Penfold and let them do what they like to me.'

'I never knew you, Sid,' she said bleakly. 'I got on at

yer for 'aving a few too many drinks – but you've got more guts than I ever dreamed.'

'I'm not brave and I did drink too much when I got down,' Sid said. 'It's just they threatened my family – and there's things I can't do. So I need you and Julia safe . . .'

'But my job? Our home?'

'You can find another job and we'll start again, Ruby. I'll sell what I can when I'm ready and you let me know where you are – but send any letter to Sarah's house and she can keep us in touch because I mustn't know where you are, Ruby, 'cos while I would never want to tell them where you are, they're devils, girl, and I don't know how much pain I can take . . . When the coast is clear, Sarah can tell me and I'll come and find yer.'

Ruby glanced around her kitchen. 'It's just a 'ouse but we 'ad friends . . .'

'Yeah,' he sighed. 'I don't like it either, love, but it's the only way. Otherwise they'll snatch her again and next time they won't give her back . . .'

Next morning Ruby and Julia set off as though they were heading for a day out with a bag full of swim things and a picnic. Sid waved them off from the doorstep, certain that Penfold's men would be watching for him and certain they wouldn't follow Julia and Ruby. Before he opened the door, Julia had thrown her arms about him and hugged him hard.

'I wish you were coming too, Dad,' she'd said. 'I love you . . .'

'I'll join you soon,' he said and kissed her. 'When it's safe. Just remember to smile and laugh when you leave the 'ouse so anyone watchin' thinks you're off to have fun with yer mum.'

'I understand, Dad. They were horrible men – and they told me what would happen if you went to the police or didn't do what they wanted.' She hugged him again. 'I knew you would so I wasn't frightened – well, not much. And I know it's better if we go away for your sake too, Dad.'

'You're a brave, clever girl.' Sid smiled at her. 'Your mum will try to find work and when I come, I'll look for work too. My boss will give me a reference and that will make it easier to find a job.'

'I love you,' she whispered. 'Please be careful, Dad. Those men are dangerous.'

'Yes, I know, and I don't trust them,' he said. 'That is why I'm sending you away. I love you, Julia. Take care of your mum . . .'

Julia laughed and looked at her mother. 'Yes, I shall, but I shan't tell her you said so, Dad.'

Sid waved them goodbye, smiling though his heart was aching. His watcher – and he knew there was one – would follow Sid wherever he went so after he'd shut the door he waited for an hour then left the house. He would lead his pursuer a merry dance round London, on and off buses, and finally back home, where he could get back in bed and stay there until some of the pain had eased.

At the moment Sid's head was aching and his legs felt like lead, but he wasn't as unsteady as he had been the previous night. Strength of will was what it had taken to get him to the quayside and back home again, and he needed the same now. Ruby was right when she said she hadn't known how deep he went; he hadn't known it himself. The certainty that he wasn't willing to spend his whole life being jerked about on a string by Mr Penfold was growing in his mind. He would go along with whatever they demanded next, but if pushed too far? Well, Sid was already implicated for one murder. After all, they could only hang him once . . .

CHAPTER 31

Maisie skipped happily along beside her brother as he pulled his trolley. She was enjoying being out in the sunshine and close to Charlie. He bought her food that she enjoyed and took her to the swings, where he'd pushed her for ages. They went to the swimming baths, where they had hot showers to keep themselves clean and Charlie had managed to wash some of their clothes in the shower without anyone noticing. He rolled the wet things up in a raincoat and took them back to the hut. Charlie said they had to let them dry inside and they took ages, but they dared not risk putting them outside in the sun, because it would have made people curious about who was using the hut.

Charlie had bought a couple of hooks which he'd knocked into the wooden struts and he now had a method of locking the door from the inside with his padlock. He'd told Maisie that he was thinking of the colder weather when she might prefer to stay in the shed alone while he worked. Maisie didn't want to think about that; she was having the time of her life; the autumn and winter seemed a long way off, but the sunlit days were going quickly and when the first chill of autumn suddenly struck, Charlie told her that it was only a matter of days before school started.

Maisie looked at him fearfully. She didn't want to go back to school without him but he said he had to keep working. 'I could leave next summer anyway,' he told her. 'I know me sums and I can write. I don't need ter go ter school – but you do, Maisie.'

'I shan't know what ter tell them.' Tears started to her eyes because she wanted her lovely summer to continue. She was afraid of the bullies at school if Charlie wasn't there.

'I'll walk yer ter school fer a start, until yer get used ter it,' Charlie said, 'and I'll be there when you come out at night. I'll buy yer a bun ter take fer yer lunch – but we'll see how much school meals are and if I've got enough money yer can have a proper cooked meal.'

Maisie didn't much want school meals. It was all right if they gave her corned beef and chips or bacon and fried bubble and squeak, but she knew it was more often than not mince and greens with lumpy potatoes.

'I'd rather 'ave a roll wiv cheese from the shop,' Maisie said. Charlie understood his sister's preferences, because he preferred that too, but it was more expensive. He'd thought at first, he might earn enough to save money so that they could find a proper room with a bed and a bathroom they could use. Once the schools started the municipal swimming pool would be closed to the children who had used it over the holidays and that meant they would have to wash in public conveniences and you couldn't strip down in places like that. Charlie knew that once they started to get dirty and the nits plagued them, Maisie would start to be miserable – and the school would want to know why she hadn't washed.

Maisie tried not to cause him any bother, but Charlie was beginning to wonder how long he could manage to evade the authorities. He was pretty certain someone had been sniffing round the hut they were using. It had been abandoned for a long time before they'd moved in but it must belong to someone and one of these days they would bring a crowbar or cutters and cut through his chain and lock – and then the game would be up. Once the police were informed, they would come looking and that meant Charlie had to start searching for another safe place he could take his sister to.

'All right, I'll try goin' ter school and I'll tell them what yer said,' Maisie gave in suddenly and slipped her hand into his. 'I like bein' wiv yer, Charlie – but I know they'll find us one day and then they'll put us in that place Matron said.'

Charlie nodded and held her hand tighter. He knew he wasn't going to let them take them too easily. He wished his ma was still alive but there was no hope of a proper home for them without her. He had to rely on his wits to keep them from starving – and to find somewhere safer and warmer before the worst of the winter was on them. And it needed to be built of brick or stone so that they could light a fire. The picnic stove boiled a kettle but it wouldn't keep them warm in the winter. Where could he take Maisie that would be safe and would not attract the notice of the law?

Suddenly, a thought occurred to him. There were pockets of derelict buildings all over London's East End and he remembered some old cottages not far from the infirmary. He'd explored a couple of them while they'd been living at the Rosie. Three of the four had holes in the roof, but two of them had rooms that were actually dry and both had a fireplace.

The cottages were boarded up at the windows and doors, but Charlie had got in by moving a loose board and notices that the buildings were unsafe kept most folk away. He would take Maisie after Mick had paid him and they would go exploring. If she did not actively dislike the old cottages, he would think about moving there before the winter . . .

For a moment Charlie thought regretfully of the infirmary and the nurse he'd particularly liked. He wondered what Nurse Sarah was thinking about them running off and whether that policeman had found his aunt . . .

'Ah, Nurse Sarah – just the person I wanted to see!'

Sarah turned as she heard the man's voice. She smiled as she saw the police officer. He'd been a regular visitor of late, always with some message or query about the children. 'What can I do for you, Constable Jones? Have you come to tell me that you've found our runaways?'

'No, I'm afraid not,' he said. 'Charlie is a clever youngster. Wherever he's got his sister hidden is a pretty good hideaway, because we've had no reports of anyone seeing two children hanging around. Mind you, the school holidays don't finish until next week. They may be more noticeable then.'

Sarah nodded. 'Yes, when you expect to see children playing you don't take much notice – but when the weather turns and they're looking wet and miserable they will be noticed.'

'I daresay Charlie is already working on that one,' the young police officer said and grinned at her. 'If it's down to a battle of wits I'd back him against most of my colleagues every time!'

She laughed and agreed. 'When Maisie was still here as a patient, he slipped in and out every so often and I'm pretty sure he found himself a few jobs, because he used to buy Maisie sweets and cakes.'

Constable Jones looked thoughtful. 'It would have to be a Saturday job delivering groceries or papers – and perhaps something not quite legal. Yes, that narrows it down a bit . . .'

'Nurse!' Sister Norton's voice made Sarah turn.

'I have to go, Sister needs me.'

Constable Jones placed a hand on her arm, delaying her. 'I came to tell you I have a lead on the children's aunt. I have an address in Cambridgeshire and I'm going down there on my day off to do a bit of investigating.'

Sarah beamed at him. 'Now that is wonderful news. If Charlie knew that his aunt was willing to take them, he would give himself up.'

'Let's hope I can find her . . .' Constable Jones nodded and walked away.

Sarah hurried to help Sister Norton with a dressing. She received a glare from the senior nurse but didn't enlighten her as to the reason for the police officer's visit.

'If your young man wishes to see you, he should wait until you finish work,' Sister said as they finished the dressing and Sarah prepared to take the tray away and clean it.

'The officer was telling me that he thinks they may be able to find Maisie and Charlie's aunt.'

'I see . . .' Sister Norton frowned at her. 'Then he was not your young man?'

'No – Jim works in a bar in the West End.' Sarah sighed, because it was two weeks since Jim had visited and she missed him.

'Very well, in that case we'll say no more about it. Right. It's time you prepared the medicine trolley, nurse. We've wasted enough time in fruitless discussion.'

Sarah took the soiled trolley to the sluice room, discarding the used dressings and washing it down and disinfecting her hands before collecting the medicines she would need for the young patients. Most were in with minor injuries or weak chests and a few were recovering from operations to broken legs or tonsils removal. These cases were isolated for a few days but then brought into the main ward for a couple of days before being allowed home. Very few children stayed more than a week or two, and because Maisie and Charlie had used one of the isolation rooms for some time she'd got to know them so well that she really missed Charlie's cheeky smile and the little girl's air of trust and love when she was given a small gift or something nice to eat.

Sarah was aware that her sense of hurt was more than just missing the runaway pair. For nearly two years she'd been courting a man she loved and fully expected to marry quite soon. She'd dreamed of the home they would have and the children that would come in time – and now she could no longer picture a future with Jim.

He'd promised at the start of his new job that he would come every Sunday and as often as he could in between, but last Sunday he hadn't turned up. She'd waited all day, expecting him to come, and her mother had cooked a big Sunday lunch specially for him. On Monday morning a postcard had come telling her that he wouldn't be able to visit on the previous day.

Sarah had felt left down and her mother had frowned over it but said nothing. Sarah had the beginning of a sick feeling that told her their relationship was drifting apart little by little.

Jim had always been so loving and caring and she had known she could rely on him – but now she wasn't sure. At the start of his new work, his kisses had still carried passion and he'd told her how much he loved her. He'd sent her letters and told her he hated being unable to visit, then suddenly the letters stopped and his visits became more infrequent. She couldn't help wondering why.

Her shift was almost over. Sarah prepared to leave as her replacement came on duty. Nurse Jenny had been on the women's ward for a few days, but after a couple of days off, she was back on the children's ward for the night shift. Sarah stopped to speak to her before leaving for the evening.

'Constable Jones was in earlier,' she told the other nurse. 'He thinks our information may have helped him to discover Charlie and Maisie's aunt's whereabouts.'

'Oh good,' Jenny said. 'Have Charlie and Maisie been found?'

'Not yet – but the school holidays are nearly over. If they go to school the head teacher will let the police know and they will pick them up, I expect. They can't live on the streets in the winter, can they?'

'No – although I'm sure Charlie will have it all planned – and he was working at a grocer's on Saturdays, I think.'

'You don't know where?'

'Not really. I did see him pulling a trolley with boxes on it but that was down near the docks. I'd been to get my shoes mended by the man in the shop at the end of the lane near the docks who does a good job for not much money.'

Sarah nodded. 'Yes, I'm pretty sure I've seen him pulling a trolley near the grocers at the end of Commercial Street. I was on the bus and thought I caught sight of him but I wasn't sure.'

'I'll call in the grocer's in the morning and ask if they have a delivery boy,' Jenny said. 'I don't like the idea of those children being on the streets once the winter starts.'

Sarah shook her head and they parted. If Constable Jones found the children's aunt and she was willing to take them there would be good news for them. Sarah could imagine what they were living on – chips and bread rolls, perhaps with cheese or a bit of ham if Charlie had earned money, but at other times they might have to make do with just bread. Fruit, vegetables and meat would be out of the question, and the children wouldn't think of buying them. Maisie would prefer a sherbet lemon dip to an apple. Such a diet would not harm them for a short time, but after a while it would start to affect them – and she doubted they had the luxury of toothpaste or soap.

Shaking her head, Sarah felt her anxiety for the children gnawing at her. She wished her mother had been given the chance to foster them. Sarah's wage was sufficient to keep the house going and feed an extra pair of mouths if she wasn't saving for a home – and she thought now that putting her money into the Post Office account was stupid. Jim had been the one who insisted that they must have a home of their own but if he'd really wanted to be her husband, he could have taken her mother's offer and moved in with them while they saved. Perhaps it would take longer, because children would stop Sarah working for a few years, but she would have been happy to share a home with her mum. Besides, if Jim really cared for her, he would know that Sarah couldn't desert her mother so soon after her father's death.

She felt a pang of regret. If they'd married, perhaps Jim would have been content to stay round here to work. He'd seemed happy at the local pub and Sarah had enjoyed having him around every day. She decided that she would have it out with him when he visited that weekend – if he did!

CHAPTER 32

Charlie wiggled through the space and held the loose board so that Maisie could get in. He noticed some long nails that looked a bit rusty and warned her to be careful.

'Mind you don't scratch yerself on them,' he said. 'They're sharp and they might give yer an infection.'

Maisie nodded. It was dark inside the building and it smelled dank and musty, because it hadn't been used for years. 'It's not very nice in 'ere,' she whispered. 'Do yer think there are mice and spiders?'

'Nah, I shouldn't think so,' Charlie said, though he knew there probably were – or would be once they started to bring food here. 'The best rooms are upstairs, Maisie. Hang on to me jacket and yer won't get lost . . .'

When they got upstairs, Maisie could see better. The landing window hadn't been boarded up, nor had either of the two-bedroom ones – best of all, there was a chest of drawers, a bed with an old mattress and a cupboard with hooks inside in one.

'We could use this one for sleeping,' Charlie told her. 'The other one will do for living and eating. There is a fireplace there and we might light a fire when it gets cold – we could cook on it then, just soup and maybe bacon for a sandwich.'

If there was one thing Maisie loved above all others it was a hot bacon sandwich, the bread soaked in the fat from the pan. Ma had sometimes made one on a Sunday as a treat, but it was years since they'd had them done the way Ma did. If they bought them, the shop didn't put as much bacon or fat in the bread and, although delicious, it was too expensive to buy often. Two bacon sandwiches would have cost him nearly three shillings, which was more than his slender purse could afford. He could buy a few slices of streaky bacon and a loaf for not much more and make bacon sandwiches every day for nearly a week.

'Won't someone see the smoke and come to look?' Maisie asked and gave a little shiver. She liked the hut better than this derelict house.

'Most won't bother 'cos they're afraid of it falling on top of them,' he said with some truth. 'A copper might come – but there's a secret!'

'A secret?' Maisie stared, her interest aroused.

'The cupboard here,' Charlie said. 'There's a false back. We can get in it and hide in the space between the two rooms and they'll never find us – and if they see our stuff, they'll think a tramp is living 'ere.'

Maisie wanted to see. She giggled when Charlie showed her how the catch worked and how easy it was to hide in between the two rooms.

'Who do you think made the cupboard like that?'

'I should think someone used it to hide pinched goods when the coppers came lookin',' Charlie said. 'I found a packet of fags in there. They'd been there for years and gone mouldy – but they might have been left there when the stuff was moved for the last time. Probably the cottages were condemned and they were forced to move away.'

Maisie nodded. She still didn't much like their new hiding place, but she understood why Charlie wanted to come here.

'We need some sort of light,' she observed. 'It's better up 'ere but it's still dark. I couldn't see anything downstairs.'

'Yeah, I know. I need to get some torches or a candle lantern – something like that.'

'Ma said candles were dangerous.'

'Yeah, I know, but we've used them in the hut when we 'ad to,' Charlie said. The nights had been light and the hut was not far from a streetlight; they hadn't needed a candle often. 'I reckon we could settle 'ere fer a while, Maisie. We can find paraffin lights, like the stove I bought, but the paraffin is expensive . . .'

In the dim light Maisie could see that he looked worried and she knew he was doing his best for them, but she couldn't help saying, 'I wish we could go 'ome to Ma . . .'

'So, do I,' he said and sought her hand, giving it a hard squeeze. 'We'll manage as long as we can, Maisie. Next week, you 'ave ter start school and at least you'll be somewhere safe and warm when it's cold and wet.'

Maisie nodded. She was scared, very scared, but she didn't want to tell Charlie, because he would think she was a silly girl. It had seemed an adventure at the start and she'd enjoyed the summer holidays, tagging in his

271

footsteps and eating the food he bought, but it would be harder now. Maisie remembered the few days when they'd lived on the streets before and been hungry. She didn't want to go back to that, feeling dirty and aching with cold and hunger. It might be better to be in the orphanage than to live like that . . .

CHAPTER 33

Jenny walked to the bus stop the next morning and saw Kathy getting off. She stopped to have a talk, because she didn't often get a chance.

'How are you managing now, Kathy?' she asked. 'Sister Norton says that a new woman is starting Ruby's job this week – have you met her?'

'Yes, I saw her yesterday,' Kathy said. 'Her name is Maggie and she's younger than Ruby – she has two small boys, just started at school. Her husband is out of work so he takes them and fetches them home and she is glad to get the job.'

'I expect you miss working with Ruby?'

'Yes, I do,' Kathy said and made a wry face. 'She had a lot of patience. Maggie is quick to fire up – and she won't do more than her job. Ruby used to do anything, stay on another hour if needed, and she wasn't always paid for it. Maggie says she knows her rights and she never helps me to get finished if I'm behind.'

'Well, I suppose she is entitled to stick to her hours and her job,' Jenny said. 'It's a shame – you got on so well with Ruby.'

'I just wish I knew what happened to make Ruby go off like that.'

'Sarah told me her husband said she'd gone to look after her mother. I think she lives in Bermondsey or somewhere like that.'

'Oh.' Kathy frowned. 'I went round there once and she wouldn't open the door to us . . .'

'Well, perhaps she wasn't there,' Jenny said. 'Sarah said it was all very sudden.'

Jenny nodded and they parted. Jenny got on her bus, glancing out of the window – and saw the figure of a young lad disappearing down an alley. He was pulling a trolley loaded with cardboard boxes and Jenny was almost certain it was Charlie. She was too far from a bus stop to think of getting off, because by the time she walked back he would have disappeared, but she might come into work a little early and see if she could see anywhere in the back streets that she thought he might have made his home.

She was reading her women's magazine, which had a lot of lovely knitting patterns in preparation for the coming winter, when the bus stopped again and she didn't look up until someone sat down next to her. A prickling sensation at her nape made her turn to look at the man sitting beside her and she felt a shock of surprise.

'Chris! I didn't expect to see you. I thought you'd gone abroad.'

'I did but I was recalled,' he said. 'There are some big meetings coming up.'

'I don't want to know,' Jenny told him coldly. 'I'm sorry, Chris – but I'm against all that you stand for and

274

even though I like you very much—' She broke off abruptly and shook her head. 'You shouldn't be sitting here. I told you I couldn't see you again.'

'Did your sister give you my letter?'

'Yes. I told her to burn it but she put it in a drawer instead.'

'And you didn't read it?' His dark eyes were fixed on her. 'No, I can see you didn't. I hoped you would – I hoped you would understand . . .'

The bus had stopped again. Chris stood up, walked down the aisle and got off before she could say anything. Jenny felt a pang of regret and wished she'd given him a chance to say whatever he'd wanted to say, but it was too late. The bus was moving off and she couldn't have gone after him if she'd wanted to.

Foolish tears stung her eyes and she shook her head, mentally reprimanding herself for caring. Jenny had told herself she was getting over Chris. After all, she hadn't known him long. His beliefs were not hers and it could never have worked – yet she still liked him and felt regret as she realized she'd thrown away her chance of making things up with him. She didn't think he would risk another rebuff.

But no, when she thought about it, there had never been any chance for them. Jenny couldn't love a man who worked for those dreadful fascists. She'd read a lot more about Moseley's organization and believed that they were thugs, just as Lily had said. It was ridiculous to hanker after a man she could never trust and so she wouldn't.

Jenny got off at her stop, refusing to weep or feel sorry for herself. Lily had had much worse to put up with when she'd been ill-used and deserted. Jenny was lucky that she'd discovered the truth before things had gone too far . . .

CHAPTER 34

'Shall I cook a big dinner this Sunday?' Sarah's mother asked. 'Or would you rather have chops or a salad?'

'Let's cook the pork chops and have them cold with a jacket potato and some pickle. If Jim comes, he'll have what we have or go without!'

Her mother looked at her hard. 'Be careful, Sarah. You're blaming Jim for his work. We knew it would take up much of his time when he took it – and he wants to make a better life for you both.'

'I'm not sure that's true any more, Mum,' Sarah said and sat down at the kitchen table. She was close to tears and it didn't help that her mother seemed to be on Jim's side. 'Why didn't he come last Sunday? It is his free day. He shouldn't give up his time – *our* time together . . .'

'His card said he was told he had to work and be given double pay – that means he will save more towards a home for you both, love.'

'Supposing I don't want a home up there where Jim is?' Sarah asked. 'Supposing I feel that he no longer cares about me?'

'Have you proof that he's changed towards you?'

'No, but I've sensed something when he comes – which is so seldom and for such a short time, it is hardly worth sitting at home waiting for him!'

'Oh, Sarah . . .' Her mother looked at her sadly. 'Jim has always been the man for you and I think if you don't make the effort to see his point of view, you're laying up trouble for yourself.'

'Why should I always be the one to make sacrifices?' Sarah was stubborn, even though she knew her mother was being sensible. 'If Jim loves me, he would make sure he came at least once a week. He used to be here all the time.'

Mrs Cartwright nodded. 'Yes, I know, love. You miss him and you feel hurt that he doesn't come when you think he should – but perhaps *you* should think about changing *your* job – or finding somewhere closer to where he works to live. Though it would mean you had to travel for work, unless you found a post at one of the central hospitals.'

'That's easier said than done. Everyone is looking for work, Mum. There are lots of nurses who have had to leave London to find work. I was lucky to get my job, even though they don't pay me as much as I might get elsewhere, providing I could find a place.'

'That was in the past,' her mother replied. 'You're a good nurse, Sarah, and I'm sure you could find work nearer Jim's work if you tried.'

Sarah knew her mother was right. If she was honest, she'd seen a position at a prestigious hospital for a children's nurse and knew her qualifications suited her for the job. But it would mean she had either to travel to work or take lodgings on the other side of London. She liked working where she did and knew she would never have considered moving if Jim had got the position as manager of the local pub.

'Perhaps I could,' she admitted. 'I'm not sure I want to, Mum. What I gained in wages I would lose in other ways. You've always refused to take money for my lodgings and I only contribute to the bills. I would have to find money for all kinds of things.'

'Yes, but you might be able to see Jim more.'

Sarah was silent. Was *she* the selfish one? Ought she to look at their situation and try to see it from Jim's point of view? Her mother was deliberately pricking her conscience, making her see the problem from all sides.

'I'll speak to him on Sunday,' she said. 'I'll hear what he has to say.'

Sarah's new reasonable thoughts were severely tested when Jim didn't arrive until three in the afternoon. He came into the kitchen looking a bit wary and for some reason that made her angry.

'I couldn't get away,' he said. 'I'm sorry, Sarah, Mrs Cartwright – I hope you didn't wait lunch for me?'

'We had our dinner at half past twelve same as always,' Sarah said. 'If you're hungry I can make you a cheese sandwich.'

'No, I grabbed a sandwich before I came. Laura makes great sandwiches—' He stopped awkwardly, looking at Sarah. 'Laura is my immediate boss at the pub. She does a lot of food as well as drinks and we open for lunches on Sundays in the summer, because there are a lot of visitors to the city. That's why I've been busy, Sarah. I had to take my turn in the kitchen. Laura asks the barmen and me to help out on Sundays, because the chefs are off. I have to do my share or . . . it's part of my job . . .'

Sarah could see that he was acutely uncomfortable and something told her he was lying. 'Surely she can't force you to work on a Sunday? You work every other day!'

Jim hesitated, then, 'I get Monday afternoons off . . . well, most afternoons after three I please myself, really. And if I help in the kitchen with prep for the evening, I get paid extra hours.'

'So, when I'm on nights you could pop over and see me if you wanted to?' Sarah said slowly. 'You must have at least three hours free.'

'Well, I could,' Jim said hesitantly, 'but I wouldn't be able to stop long and there's a lot of travelling; it isn't really worth—' He stopped when he saw the look in Sarah's eyes. 'I didn't mean it like that! I'm saving as much as I can. Besides, if I'm there I'm asked to do things – like take in extra deliveries of wine and food. And I need to do these things if I want to be a manager. Laura says managers are on call all day and night until closing time – and even then, we're the last off the premises.'

'It sounds as if that place has taken over your life, Jim,' Sarah's mother said before her daughter could answer. 'A job is a job, lad – but a wife you love, a home and children – they need more time. There will come a day when you will have to make a choice. Ambition is fine, but don't let it rule your life.'

Sarah was silent, watching the face of the man she loved, and she saw that he was torn. She kept quiet, allowing him to answer before she spoke, but the silence lengthened and she knew then that he couldn't – or wouldn't – because he didn't like what her mother had said.

'It's all right, Jim,' Sarah said at last. 'You don't have to give up your chance of being a manager for me. In fact, I think you should work all the hours you want and not bother coming here at all.'

She saw her words strike home and knew she had managed to make him think. He wanted to deny her, to tell her she was being stupid and he would come as often as he could, but she knew he wouldn't, because he was caught up in his new life and it was what he wanted – more than he wanted her. Ambition had taken over his life – or was there more?

'How old is this Laura? Is she beautiful?' Sarah asked and saw the guilty colour rise up his neck and into his face, and then she knew for sure. Her mother was wrong. It wasn't just ambition; it was the lure of this successful woman. She had him twisted round her finger and so he would work any hours just to please her.

'Nothing has happened between us – I haven't touched her!' he said defensively.

'No, perhaps not, but that's on your mind and it's what you want: to be with Laura and to work with her.' Sarah nodded. She could imagine a beautiful, successful woman, perhaps a few years older, the manager of a thriving restaurant and pub, and she understood what had happened to Jim. He was bewitched by his new life. 'I understand. It's fine, Jim. I'm just glad I found out before it was too late.'

'Sarah . . .?' There was a pleading note in his voice now, as he began to realize what he'd lost. 'Laura is my boss – I have to do as she asks.'

'Yes, I understand that,' Sarah said. 'I'm releasing you so that you can be with her and please her as much as you like. It is over, Jim. Please leave now and I shan't expect you to come here in future.'

'Sarah . . .' Her mother's voice carried a warning but Sarah was hurting too much to heed it.

'Please leave,' she said. 'Enjoy your life – if you can!'

She turned and walked out of the kitchen, going straight upstairs to her bedroom. She heard Jim call her name and then her mother telling him to leave it.

'She'll come round, if you really want her to,' Mrs Cartwright told him. 'It's your choice, Jim. Sarah thinks you care for this Laura and your job more than her. Prove she's wrong by finding a proper job round here and putting a ring on her finger or accept that it's over. She's been patient for a long time, saving and waiting.'

'Laura is just my boss!' Jim said angrily. 'I admire her and I want to be like her – it doesn't mean I've been to bed with her.'

'Not yet . . .'

Sarah heard no more, because she'd shut her bedroom door. The voices were muffled now and she could no longer hear the words. They went on talking for a while and then there was silence. She lay curled on her bed, hugging her pain to herself for a long time and then her mother knocked at the door.

'Tea's ready. Will you come down and join me, love?'

'Yes, all right, Mum,' she said and got up, smoothing her dress and her hair.

Her mother hadn't waited. She was in the kitchen, making the tea just as normal. Sarah decided to do the same – act normally. After all, it was her decision. She had told Jim not to come again and she must live with what she'd done and not make her mother's life miserable.

'What's for tea, Mum?'

'I've made chicken paste and cucumber sandwiches, and there are some sausage rolls and a sponge cake – you could have some toast and jam if you prefer?'

'No, the sandwiches are fine,' Sarah said and washed her hands under the tap. She sat down at the table and selected a sandwich, eating it even though it tasted of nothing to her. 'I'm on the day shift again tomorrow, Mum.'

'Yes, I know, love.'

Sarah noticed the hesitancy in her voice but didn't say anything. She wasn't ready to open her heart, even to her mother. 'I can call in the shops on the way home if there's anything you want.'

'No, I don't think so. Why don't you go and see a friend or something – you could go to the pictures. It's ages since you did and I think there are some good films on at the moment.'

'We could go together,' Sarah agreed. 'I'll get a paper and we'll see if there's anything we fancy when I get home.'

After tea, Sarah washed up and her mother dried and put the china away. Sarah ran her hands through her hair. It wasn't dirty but washing it would give her something to do.

'Why don't you have a bath and wash your hair?' her mother suggested. 'You can get an early night. I have some knitting to do for Mrs Maine's new baby – and then we can go out tomorrow and relax.'

Sarah smiled and nodded, walking upstairs. They were really lucky to have a nice modern bath. Not all of the houses in the district did, but they had a decent landlord and he kept all his property in good order. The rent was not the cheapest to be found, but Mrs Cartwright said she would rather pay an extra half a crown and not have cockroaches coming out of the walls.

Relaxing in the bath, her hair hanging wetly around her face, Sarah refused to cry. She had loved Jim – she thought she still did love him – but she wasn't going to let him ruin her life . . .

Sarah was feeling tired the next morning as she rode the bus to work. She'd been determined to sleep but even the warm bath and washing her hair had not taken the tension out of her. So, when she first caught sight of the boy pulling a loaded trolley, she didn't immediately recognize him as being Charlie. It was only when they had gone past and she looked back that she saw his sister walking behind him, carrying a bundle of something, and she knew who they were. But even as she jumped to her feet and walked quickly down the aisle, they disappeared from view.

Sarah got off at the first stop and walked hurriedly back to where she'd seen them but there was no sign. Still, they had to be somewhere in the area. Sarah decided that she would call in at the station and ask for Constable Jones.

She was lucky, because he was helping to man the

desk and came to her the second he was free. His smile lit his face and it made her smile in response.

'What can I do for you?' he asked.

'I've just seen them – Charlie and Maisie,' Sarah explained and told him where she'd seen them going. 'I don't know where they've been living but they had quite a few possessions and they didn't look as if they were starving. In fact, they looked like normal kids.'

'I wouldn't have expected anything else with Charlie in charge,' Constable Jones told her with a grin. 'He is a resourceful young man, Nurse Sarah – and I'm quite sure he has every move planned. However, we haven't been idle. If either of them goes to school, we should get a phone call.'

'Good,' Sarah said. 'You don't mind that I came to tell you?'

'No, of course not. We could do with all the help we can get tracking them down.' He grinned at her. 'If we have another war, I'll be recommending they put Charlie in charge of intelligence. I reckon he'd do better than the lot we've got now.'

'Is something wrong?'

Constable Jones glanced over his shoulder. 'Something's brewing. We're expecting trouble on the streets from the fascists – and not just another skirmish. Something much bigger this time. We're supposed to have men on the inside but sometimes I wonder—'

'Constable Jones, I want you to take these men down to the cells.'

Sarah glanced at the desk sergeant. 'I'm keeping you from your duty . . .'

'I'll call round and tell you when we find the children.'

Sarah nodded and smiled and left him as he began to deal with three rowdy youths. She noticed that his manner with the youths was as pleasant as when he dealt with others and he laughed, jollying them along rather than using his fists or his strength, which showed what kind of a man he was, because he was big enough to knock their heads together if he chose.

Sarah glanced at the little silver watch pinned to her uniform. Jim had given it to her as a present when she first started work at the infirmary. It gave her a pang of regret but she refused to let it make her emotional. If she was not careful, she was going to be late for work . . .

CHAPTER 35

'You know what to say if they ask where yer living?'
Charlie said.

He'd been over it with Maisie six times already and
she repeated parrot fashion: 'We're stayin' with our
Aunt Jeanie in Spitalfields and she works so she 'asn't
'ad time to come in and see 'em . . .'

'Yeah, that's right,' Charlie said and grinned. 'Don't
say anything unless they ask – but that's what yer say
if they do.'

'All right.' Maisie looked at him anxiously. 'I wish
yer were comin' too, Charlie. I don't like the bullies in
the playground.'

'If they pick on yer, kick 'em in the shins – or pull their
hair if it's a girl,' Charlie advised. 'You tell the lads yer
big brother will give them a hiding next time they do it.'

'Yeah, all right.' Maisie smiled at him, her nerves
eased for a while. She was pleased to be going to school
in some ways, though she would have liked to stay with
her brother, but she knew he had to find work if he
was going to buy paraffin and food for them. 'I'll
remember what yer said, Charlie.'

He walked her to the end of the street and then saw her tag on after a group of giggling girls about her age. With any luck she would make friends and he would be there to meet her when she came out. In the meantime, he had to find more work.

So far, he'd kept his job delivering groceries and Mick continued to give him jobs two or three times a week. Charlie really wanted to learn carpentry but knew there wasn't much chance of him being taken on as an apprentice in the trade. However, that didn't stop him trying the various yards on the docks two or three times a week. He was thoughtful as he approached one of the yards that morning. Charlie was growing. His jackets showed his wrists now and his trousers were halfway up his calves. Some of the employers he approached still thought he should be in school, but others were inclined to take his word when he said he was fourteen and they hesitated before turning him down. A lot of lads were growing out of their clothes these days – no money to replace them – so it didn't mark him out as different. Charlie approached the wood yard he liked the look of the best, his hopes high as he saw the boss was in the yard and seemed to be hiring men.

'And what do you want, lad?' the boss asked, a smile in his eyes. 'I'm hiring, men not schoolboys.'

'I want ter be a carpenter,' Charlie said, meeting his gaze without flinching. 'I don't mind what I do in the meantime – I'll scrub out the lavvy if need be, but I want ter learn on the tools.'

'You do, do you?' The boss gave a great belly laugh. He was a big man but strong rather than fat and his eyes had a permanent twinkle. 'Well, as it happens, I've got a few mucky jobs the men don't fancy. Show me your worth and mebbe I'll think about hiring you.'

Charlie grinned; he liked his new boss. 'Thanks. I'll do anything, sir.'

'My name is Mr Thorne. I'll just get these men started and then I'll show you what I want you to do . . .'

'Maisie Howes!' A woman's voice made Maisie jump. 'Where have you come from? I heard about your mother. We were all very sorry . . .'

Maisie sniffed but managed not to cry. 'She was hurt bad, miss.' The teacher's name was Miss Hart and she wasn't one of Maisie's favourites. 'I thought this was my classroom?' She looked round in a puzzled way because the children were younger and she didn't know any of them.

'Your classmates have moved on, Maisie. I suppose you did no lessons while you were at the Rosie?'

'I did some sums and puzzles,' Maisie said and the teacher frowned.

'I see – and where are you living now?'

'Wiv me aunt in Spitalfields,' Maisie said and the teacher's frown deepened.

'Then you should have been assigned to a new school there, but since you *are* here you may as well sit down and learn what you can. I shall want to know your aunt's address later so that we can tell her of a more suitable school, something closer to your new home.'

Maisie bit her lip. If she gave Miss Hart a false address she would get caught out. She bent her head over the exercise book on her desk, turning to page one, and took down the questions the teacher wanted them to answer.

All of the girls were younger than Maisie and new to this class. They had all been asked to write down their names, ages, and their addresses. For a moment she puzzled over the address and then wrote down the number and street where she'd lived with her mother. She crossed her fingers beneath the desk as she wrote, because perhaps she would be lucky and the teacher would forget she'd told her Spitalfields . . .

Fortunately for Maisie, Miss Hart had a lot on her mind. A spinster for many years, she had recently received a proposal of marriage from a man she both respected and liked. He was older and a widower and she knew that he needed someone to keep his house and care for his children. It was not a love match, but it was perhaps her one and only chance of marriage and her mind was so occupied that when the time came for her to check the exercise books, she paid little attention to Maisie's address. The girl had not been in her class previously and she had no idea where her mother had lived and so she gave Maisie a C for her work, which was badly spelled and to her mind illiterate and moved on to the next.

Had Maisie known that she wouldn't have worried, but she was anxious to tell Charlie what she'd done when he met her after school.

'Ten to one she won't notice,' he said. 'I had her for my second year and her bark is worse than her bite. Just do what they tell you and we'll get away wiv it, Maisie.'

Maisie nodded, happy to believe him. She'd enjoyed

most of her day. In the playground she'd met old friends and played a game and in class the teacher had set them some sums she'd already done with Nurse Sarah. After the sums they'd sat and listened to a history lesson about some people called the Saxons and Normans. Those people had lived a long time ago and she thought their lives sounded better than hers; she would have liked to tend pigs and geese rather than go to school.

'Did you find a job today?' she asked her brother.

'Yeah, a good one,' Charlie told her with a grin. 'I 'ad ter sweep up a yard and clean the toilets; they ponged a bit but I didn't care – because afterwards Mr Thorne took me in the workshops and let me watch the men turning a lathe. He told me my job will be to sweep up and collect the shavings fer a start, as well as other odd jobs, but if I'm reliable he will take me on as an apprentice joiner!'

'Did he say how much it would cost?'

'Nah. I reckon he won't charge me anythin', Maisie. I think he took a shine ter me – nothin' wrong, just he likes me 'cos I look 'im in the eye.'

She nodded happily, slipping her hand into his as they approached their shabby home. It had been condemned for so long that most folk didn't even notice it. Charlie looked all round, to make sure that no one was close enough to see, and then he held the opening for her to squeeze inside before following.

It was very dark and Maisie pressed close to her brother. This was the bit she didn't like. It would be better upstairs and once Charlie had put the heavy sacks over the windows, they could light their candles. All their belongings were hidden in between the cupboards, because Charlie didn't want to risk a tramp stumbling on their home and helping himself to the bits and pieces they'd accumulated. If that happened, he couldn't afford to buy them all again.

'I've got some bread and a tub of dripping from the butcher,' Charlie told her. 'There are the tomatoes I got yesterday orf the market – so a sandwich now and bread and dripping in the morning.'

Maisie nodded happily. Charlie knew what she liked. Ma had often made tomato sandwiches for her tea and they'd had toast and dripping most mornings. A bag of chips or an egg on toast was a real treat. The food had been more varied at the infirmary but Maisie was used to a sandwich or bread and dripping and it suited her better than minced beef and greens or fish in white sauce, which made her feel sick.

'When I get paid this week, we'll have a slice of ham and some chips,' Charlie said and Maisie clapped her hands.

'You're the best brother in the world and I love yer!'

Charlie pulled a face at her. 'Don't be daft, Maisie. I can't afford much yet but one day I'll be trained and I'll earn enough money for a house and proper food yer can cook. We'll be grown up then, and we can look out fer each other.'

Maisie nodded. She perched on the upturned orange box Charlie had found somewhere and looked at him. In her opinion this was the perfect life and she didn't care if there was no running water and no proper sanitation. There was an outside lavatory in the backyard, which still worked, and a tap that cold water ran from when Charlie turned it on – a big improvement on the watchman's hut.

'If yer cold, get inside yer sleeping bag,' Charlie said. 'I don't want ter light a fire yet because the evenings are still light. When it gets dark folk won't notice so much.'

'I'm not cold,' Maisie declared though, truthfully, she did feel a bit chilly round her back.

'We'll go in the bedroom,' Charlie said, 'and we'll both get into our sleeping bags.'

'All right,' Maisie agreed. She was sleepy after a full day at school but it soon felt nice and warm inside the sleeping bag. They hadn't used the old mattress so far, because Charlie thought it might be damp or have fleas, but Maisie thought it would be more comfortable than the floor. However, she was soon sleeping, her cares forgotten.

Neither of them realized that their time of freedom was close to its end.

The next morning Miss Hart told her headmaster that Maisie Howes had returned to school and the first thing he did was to ring the local station. It happened to be Constable Jones' day off and so the officer sent round to the school knew neither of the children by sight. He was taken to the headmaster's office and then to the year three classroom, where Maisie had her head bent over her books, her tongue peeping out of the corner of her mouth as she concentrated.

Miss Hart pointed her out with a frown when the young constable asked and he nodded, preparing to approach the child.

'What are you going to do, Constable Williams?'

'Just question her, ma'am.'

'It's Miss Hart,' she said, a little irritable now. 'And I think you should wait until after class ends. I don't want you upsetting all the children.'

'I'm just going to ask where she and her brother are living – and to take them in so that they can be properly cared for.'

'Wait until play time . . .'

'I'm sorry, Miss Hart, but I was told to question the child and if her answers were not satisfactory to bring her to the station.'

'She will kick up a fuss, if I know Maisie Howes,' Miss Hart said. 'I can give you her address. She is living with her aunt . . .' She picked up the register, into which she had copied all the names and addresses. 'There she is . . . I thought she said Spitalfields?'

'This is where they came from originally,' the young officer said. 'I'm sorry, Miss Hart, but I'm going to speak to her now – before she gets the chance to run off.'

Maisie had become aware of the long conversation between her teacher and the police officer and the glances they gave her told her that he was here for her. Frightened, she got to her feet and ran out of the classroom before anyone realized what she was doing.

'There – now look what you've done! The whole class is disturbed,' Miss Hart snapped at him.

The other girls were looking at each other. Some were puzzled, others giggled and some looked nervous. What had one of their classmates done that a policeman had come to arrest her?

Maisie was in full flight down the street when the young officer emerged from the school playground. He frowned and started to run after her, because the Sarge would kill him if he lost her. Constable Williams knew they had been looking for Maisie and her brother for a while but wasn't aware of the full story. So to his mind the kid had done something wrong or she wouldn't have run off like that and he was determined to catch her.

Suddenly, Maisie ran on to the docks and disappeared between a moving lorry and a pile of packing cases that had just been unloaded. By the time the police officer had negotiated the lorry, causing the driver to hoot at him as it tried to back towards the packing cases, Maisie had disappeared behind.

'What the hell are you doin'?' an irate foreman demanded. 'You could have been knocked down and then we should've had the whole damned force down here creatin' hell!'

'I'm looking for a child – she came running in here a few moments ago,' the unfortunate young constable said.

'What has she done?'

Constable Williams stared at him, unsure of what to do next. He hadn't been on the force long and this was the first job he'd been sent on alone.

'Nothing – at least, I don't know. I was just sent to fetch her from school. My sergeant says we're looking for two kids, a girl of about nine and an older lad.'

'I haven't seen them hanging around here . . .' The foreman looked at his workers who had gathered to watch and listen. 'Anyone seen a couple of kids on the docks?'

'No, I ain't seen 'em,' said one man.

'Not recently,' another man said. 'I saw a lad a few times and a girl once – they were near the old hut that ain't been used since old George had a heart attack there.'

'Yes, and I didn't see any kids but I saw the 'ut had a padlock on it,' another worker said. 'I thought someone had taken it over . . .'

'Can you show me this hut?' the officer said.

'Get back to your work!' The foreman glared at his workers. 'I'll show you, Constable, but if you hurt that kid my men won't take kindly to it. They've all got nippers of their own . . .'

Maisie had reached the hut but when she tried to go inside, she discovered that it had a new lock on it. Glancing back, she saw that the men had stopped working and were talking to the policeman and she dodged behind a stack of bales, trembling with fear. She watched the foreman and the police constable walk to the hut. They tried the lock but couldn't get in and the police officer tried peering in the window but he couldn't see because of the sacking Charlie had nailed over it. He banged on the door loudly.

'If you're in there, Maisie Howes, come out. I'm here to take you back to the station. You won't be in trouble if you come out now!'

'Damned fool . . .' a voice said softly behind Maisie. She jumped as a big hand gently touched her shoulder. 'Keep quiet, little one, and he'll give up and go away soon. He hasn't got the sense he was born with.'

Maisie almost giggled. She'd been startled, but she wasn't afraid of him. She'd seen this man working on the docks many times and he always smiled at her.

He waited with her until the police officer had gone and then put his hand in his pocket and pulled out a sweet wrapped in paper.

'Do yer like toffees?'

'Yes, please,' Maisie said, accepting it. 'Thank you – you're kind.'

'I've got a boy and a girl not much older than you. Is yer name Maisie Howes?' Maisie nodded as she sucked her toffee. 'I knew yer dad years ago – and yer ma. Pity about what happened . . .' He looked at her speculatively. 'Have yer got somewhere ter go? I thought yer was in foster care?'

'Yeah, I live wiv me aunt,' Maisie lied instinctively. 'I'll go home.'

'I don't know what trouble yer in,' the man said, 'but my missus would give yer a wash and feed yer – she lives just round in the corner in Cardle Lane at number three. Can yer remember that?'

'Yes, I'll remember,' Maisie said, 'but I'm all right. Thank yer fer the toffee.'

'Yer welcome – now get orf quick afore the boss sees yer and calls the cops.' He winked at her conspiratorially and Maisie ran in the direction that he'd shown her, avoiding the men loading the lorry and their foreman.

She made her way to the swings and spent some time playing on them. Maisie knew she couldn't go back to school. She wasn't sure what to do or if Charlie would say they could go somewhere else, and she daren't hang around outside the school for Charlie because someone would see her and tell Miss Hart. All she could think of was to go back to the derelict house and wait until her brother came back.

Charlie waited for half an hour outside the school gates that evening before a boy he knew sidled up to him and told him a copper had come after Maisie.

'Do you know where they took her?' Charlie asked, fear gripping him as he imagined his sister's terror at being taken by the police. Everything had been going so well and now Maisie was lost to him.

'She ran orf and got away from 'im,' the boy said and Charlie felt huge relief; perhaps Maisie wasn't in trouble after all. 'Are yer comin' down the playground to play football?'

'Not tonight,' Charlie said. 'I've got ter find my sister – maybe another time.'

Charlie hadn't got time for playing games these days. He worked down the wood yard until three thirty and then he called on Mick and made some deliveries. He'd collect Maisie from school and buy their food on the way home. He felt like a man doing proper work with a man's responsibilities. Now Maisie had run off and he was in a panic.

Charlie rushed home and went quickly inside the derelict house. He heard Maisie upstairs. She was skipping and singing to herself. He ran up the stairs. She'd found a piece of chalk and drawn the shape of a hopscotch on the floor to amuse herself. He was relieved and cross at the same time.

'What happened? Why did the cops come after yer?'

'I don't know,' Maisie said and tears welled in her eyes. 'I didn't do anythin', Charlie. He came into the classroom and talked to my teacher and they kept looking at me so I ran off before he could get me.'

'Yer did right,' Charlie said. 'Someone must 'ave told 'em yer were at school – and that means yer can't go back.'

Maisie nodded miserably. 'They know about the hut,' she said. 'Do yer think they'll come 'ere?'

'In time, maybe,' Charlie said. 'So we 'ave ter be real careful, Maisie. If they see or hear us, someone will report it to the police – they'll think we're kids doing damage to empty property and tell on us.'

'We can hide, can't we?'

'Yes, for a while,' Charlie agreed. 'But it means we'll have to find somewhere else to go if they start nosing around.'

'He said his missus would give us a wash and somethin' ter eat,' Maisie said and smiled at Charlie.

'Who said?' Charlie questioned. 'What have yer done, Maisie? Yer ain't been messing about, 'ave yer?'

Maisie looked at him, her gaze clear and innocent. 'He give me a toffee and told me ter keep quiet when the copper were lookin' fer me – and he was nice. He told me where his missus lived . . .'

'He didn't touch yer?' Charlie was suspicious now.

'You mean like that horrid Ronnie did Ma?' Maisie shook her head emphatically. 'He smiled with his eyes and he didn't touch me – said he knew Mum and Dad – and he told me where to go if I needed help.'

Charlie nodded. 'That's all right, then. Men ain't all nice, Maisie . . .'

'I know – I remember.' Maisie looked sad. 'I hope they lock that man away and never let him out.'

'He's a murderer. He should hang but he won't . . .'

Maisie looked at him and her tears spilled over. 'What are we goin' ter do, Charlie? We can't live like this forever, can we?'

'No, we can't.' He saw her scratching her head. 'Have yer got nits again?'

'I think so . . .'

Charlie nodded. As yet his own hair was free of the pest but if Maisie had them, he would probably get them. 'When I get paid, I'll buy some of that stuff Ma used and we'll wash our hair.'

'It was better when we 'ad a shower at the bathing pool.'

'Yeah – but it will have to be a Saturday morning and we'll have to pay ter get in; they only do it free in the holidays.'

Maisie nodded. 'I wish I could get a job, Charlie. It ain't right yer 'ave ter work all the time and I don't. I can't even go ter school now.'

Charlie looked at her. 'Would you rather be in the orphanage, Maisie?'

She hesitated and then shook her head. 'No, not yet. I wish . . .' Her words died as she saw the look in his eyes. 'I know. I'll do whatever yer say, Charlie.'

'I'll do my deliveries on Saturday and then we'll go to the baths and wash our hair,' he said. 'I know a bit of writing and sums, Maisie. If I get an exercise book and a pencil, I can show yer things – and set yer some tasks ter do 'ere.'

She nodded, her eyes tearful. 'What we got fer supper?'

'I brought some bread and two slices of corned beef. Yer like that, don't yer?'

'I'd rather have a tomato,' she said. 'There's one left in the cupboard. You have the corned beef. You like that more than me . . .'

It was true but he'd forgotten. He'd seen the corned beef in the shop and asked for two slices without thinking. 'Yer can 'ave some jam. I bought a jar of yer favourite strawberry.'

Maisie's face lit up and Charlie thought she looked a bit like his ma had when she was younger. Maisie was growing up and he knew that this adventure couldn't last much longer. They both needed new clothes and Maisie's shoes pinched. And there was no way he could buy her a dress or a pair of shoes. He felt the weight of her health and happiness descend on him. Charlie was willing to work all the hours he could and spend very little on his own needs, but it would be years before he could look after his sister properly.

The time was coming closer when they might have to give themselves up. Charlie thought he would rather return to the infirmary than go to the police, but until Maisie admitted she'd had enough of hardships he would keep doing his best for her

'I know what yer thinking,' she told him and slipped her hand in his. 'It's not yer fault, Charlie, and I know they'll find us one day but we'll wait for a while, won't we?'

'As long as yer all right, Maisie.'

'Yeah, I'm all right,' she said and sneezed. 'I was cold on the swings but I didn't want ter come back 'ere too soon.'

Charlie nodded, dread filling him. If Maisie picked up a cold or chill, she could get proper ill . . .

CHAPTER 36

Sid felt the touch of a heavy hand on his shoulder and knew the wait was over. He was about to discover just why Mr Penfold had kept him alive. There must be a reason or he would already be dead.

'A friend wants ter talk to yer,' a guttural voice said.

Sid nodded. 'I'm ready.'

'Keep walking. I'll tell yer where to go.'

Sid obeyed blindly. When they turned into a dark alley he was told to stand still and a blindfold was put round his eyes. He felt a hand in his back, pushing him forward, and he stumbled on in the direction he was manoeuvred until told to stop. The blindfold came off and he found he was in a building of some kind. It was large, empty apart from a group of men, and dirty, but there were lights overhead and a man was sitting in an armchair, flanked by half a dozen heavies. It was so incongruous and ridiculous that Sid wanted to laugh, but he knew that one false move would result in a knife at his throat.

'You know who I am?' the man in the armchair asked. Sid thought it absurd that a small, thin man with a pale face and weak eyes should control men with three times his weight and strength. Yet there was power behind the myopic eyes and Sid felt his spine trickle with ice. This man was ruthless, a cold killer and clever too.

'You're Mr Penfold,' Sid said, managing to keep his voice from shaking. 'I know who you are and I know you want something – so get on with it.'

'Watch it!' Sid felt something sharp poke in his back.

'Not yet!' Mr Penfold barked and the hard point dropped away. 'He's not stupid and I like that – we can use him.' He looked at Sid with eyes that looked watery and weak and yet were somehow chilling. 'I have a job for you. Do it well and I might consider keeping you on my payroll – let me down and you're dead. Do you understand me?'

'Yes, I knew why you took my girl. I didn't report Ronnie the Greek and you knew it.'

'I wasn't sure, but I have insurance on that and he's up on a different charge. The stupid fool let his dick lead him astray. He's expendable. I have others capable of doing his work – but the job I have for you will take brains . . .'

Sid wondered if he was supposed to feel flattered. He just stared at the man he hated, giving no indication of whether he agreed or disagreed.

'You know you have no choice – good.' Penfold smiled unpleasantly. 'I need someone putting away for a long time. I could have him killed but it would start a turf war. With Mick the Swede inside I can move into his territory. I have the clubs, restaurants and the girls;

he has the betting shops and the building sites – and I want them.'

'You're asking me to kill this man . . .?'

'I thought you had some intelligence,' Penfold sneered. 'I told you, I don't want a gang war. I want Mick out of the way in prison so I can take over.'

'I've got it.' Sid waited, a chill creeping down his spine. Somehow, he knew what was coming even before Penfold spoke.

'Your boss – the man you thought was so great to give you a chance – he's part of a swindle so big you couldn't comprehend it. Everything he builds, he under-cuts anyone else who tenders and that's why he gets all the work from the government and large firms. I want you to kill him and take the wages – they arrive each Friday in bags of used notes and coins.'

Sid managed not to vomit, though it rose to his throat as he saw the way the vile creature was gloating. 'And how do I do it? If I get caught it won't do you any good.'

Penfold nodded, the gloating expression gone instantly. 'You will use a gun I shall give you. You will wear gloves. You will enter the site office as soon as the money is delivered. You will kill whoever is there and take the money. You will wear a scarf over your face . . . Use your imagination. Make sure to drop the gun as you run.'

'You want the police to find it and blame it on your rival. It's his gun and has his prints on it.' Sid stared into the eyes that seemed to see so little and actually saw so much, except that it was his cold, calculating brain that had worked out the destruction of the man he wanted out of the way. He'd set Sid up once he'd discovered where he lived and taken Julia. He believed Sid was caught in a trap he could not escape.

'Naturally.' Penfold said. 'If you are successful you will be rewarded. I look after my people.'

'And if I fail, I'm dead . . .' Sid looked at him for a long moment and then nodded. 'I don't have much choice, do I? When do I get the gun?'

'It will be delivered to you,' Penfold said. 'Don't think of betraying me. I never forget and I never forgive.'

Sid nodded. 'When can I go?'

'You are free to go. Jigger, take him back where you found him . . .'

Sid allowed himself to be blindfolded again and then he was roughly pushed away towards the door. Out in the cool air, Sid listened for sounds and used his nose to smell what was out there. He could smell tar – and a strong odour that he thought was from a slaughter-house – and he could hear a crane working in the distance. A smile touched his mouth. Sid knew where he was and it amused him that they had gone to so much trouble to hide the location from him. This was just a disused warehouse that they probably used just to intimidate their victims. Sid knew where Penfold had his office – where he was normally to be found in the evenings. He had made it his business to find out.

When the blindfold was taken off, Sid turned and saw the man who had guided him walking away.

The way Sid understood it, he had three choices. He could go to the police, tell them the whole story, and hope they arrested Penfold and his gang. He could carry out the crime and give Penfold what he wanted

– or he could kill the man who had dared to take his girl.

A look of hard determination came into his eyes as he made up his mind which one he would choose. Penfold was giving him a gun, but instead of using it on a man he admired and liked – even if he was mixed up with criminals – he would use it on the man he hated.

He would do this for his family – for Ruby. She was a good woman and he knew she could make a life without him. As long as his wife and his girl were safe, nothing else mattered and maybe Ruby would get her wish and be able to foster a child one day, even if she changed her second name to do it . . .

Mary looked at the letter, recognizing Ruby's large, bold lettering at once, wondering why she'd written. After all, it was several weeks since she'd left her job. For a woman with little schooling Ruby Harding wrote well. Mary opened the letter and read Ruby's message and nodded. I was clear to her that Ruby was hoping she would return one day and that was her reason for getting in touch.

The letter explained everything to her and she understood why her cleaner had not felt able to come in and why she'd chosen to tell only one person. Ruby knew that Mary would not judge. She would keep her secret to herself, even from Lady Rosalie, and she would stick to her promise. If Ruby came to her and told her that her husband was sober and no longer in trouble, she would believe her despite the odds.

Mary knew the folk of the East End and women like

Ruby were like gold dust. She'd known something was very wrong when Ruby just hadn't turned up and she wouldn't blame her for something beyond her control. Instead, she would bide her time and see what happened. Life changed and perhaps one day Ruby's luck would change too . . .

CHAPTER 37

Sarah was making the beds when Constable Jones walked in. She smiled and finished the one she was tidying before walking to join him at her desk.

'Hello. How can I help you?'

'I wanted to tell you that I've found Mrs Marsh – formerly Miss Jeanie Howes!'

'That is really good news,' Sarah said and beamed at him. 'Thank you so much for taking the trouble – will she have the children?'

'She was grateful to me for telling her. She had been anxious about her brother's children, but their mother had refused her help. Apparently, there was resentment between them. As soon as we have them safe, she'll come up and fetch them.'

'That is exactly what I wanted to know,' Sarah said. 'Thank you so much for telling me – I suppose you haven't found them yet?'

'We had a tip-off that the girl was at her school but they sent a young constable, new to the job and who has only been with us a few weeks, and he scared her when he was questioning her teacher. She bolted and he chased her. So, they won't trust us in future . . .'

'Oh dear,' Sarah said. 'It does mean they are living somewhere close by but it could be anywhere.'

'They were probably in a hut on the docks during the summer holidays but they've moved from there. I'm trying to work out where they might have gone but there are so many derelict buildings; they could be hiding in any of them.'

'Yes . . .' Sarah nodded thoughtfully. 'I caught sight of Charlie with his trolley the other day. I was on the bus but he wasn't far from here. And then I saw both of them yesterday morning – but by the time I got off the bus and walked back to where I'd seen them, they'd vanished. When they stayed here, he used to go over the wall quite often. He always came back, usually with a treat for his sister. I think he has a job because the trolley was loaded.'

'I wonder . . .' Constable Jones frowned. 'I might have a lead. A member of the public reported seeing kids on a clearance site – some houses due to be pulled down quite soon.' He hesitated, then, 'Would you come with me? I know it is a lot to ask but if I go alone, they'll run and I would rather not scare them. If you were with me, they might respond better.'

'Yes, especially if I can tell them their aunt is looking forward to having them live with her.'

'She is – very much.' He smiled at her. 'I'm off duty at four today.'

'And I finish at five,' Sarah said.

'Shall we go tonight?' Constable Jones asked. 'Sooner the better, I think, because I doubt Charlie will have them stay anywhere too long. He's a bright lad and he knows that people will see them so they will have to keep moving every few weeks, which makes it hard for him.'

'Yes, he's the one that is keeping them going,' Sarah agreed. 'Maisie would rather be somewhere warm and be looked after. I think she must have heard something bad about orphanages because they frighten her.'

'Some of the tales we hear would frighten *me*,' he said and grimaced. 'An orphanage ought to be a safe place but it isn't always.'

'Yes, I know.' Sarah's smile faded. 'And Charlie had a very bad experience with the people who fostered him. I'll meet you downstairs at five – now I have to get back to work.'

'Yes, I've taken up too much of your time.' He smiled. 'I don't want you to get into trouble because of me.'

'Sister Norton is off today,' Sarah said. 'Sister Ruth Linton is overseeing the wards and she is lovely. Until this evening . . .'

Constable Jones inclined his head and left her and Sarah went back to changing beds. She liked the young police officer because he went that little bit further to help those who needed it. Sarah would be glad to help him find the lost children – after all, she had nothing to do when she got home except help her mother with the chores . . .

'I'd like ter take yer wiv me,' Charlie said when he was ready to leave that morning, 'but I'm working at the yard and they would say you were in the way. Keep indoors, Maisie, and make yourself cups of cocoa to warm yourself. I don't like that cough you started last night.'

Maisie nodded and tried to smother the cough in her throat but it came out louder than ever and she saw the worry in her brother's eyes deepen. 'It's all right, Charlie,' she reassured him. 'I don't feel like doin' much this morning. I think I'll keep in my sleeping bag most of the time an' that'll help.'

'It is beginning to get chilly – I didn't expect the weather to cool down as fast as it 'as,' Charlie said and felt anxious as he saw the flush in her cheeks. He knew that this wasn't suitable accommodation for his sister when she wasn't well. If they could go home, Ma would look after her and give her a spoonful of honey in hot milk, but Ma was dead. 'I'll get some kindling and we'll 'ave a fire tonight. Mick said he won't want me today so I'll be 'ome soon after four.'

Maisie nodded, looking a bit sorry for herself. Charlie didn't blame her. It was horrible feeling ill, especially being in that dark house all alone. He knew it wasn't the best place for them to live, but although he'd been looking whenever he got the time, he hadn't found anywhere better. Most derelict buildings were damp and open to the elements; at least this was dry and if he lit a fire it would be warmer and more cheerful. The only problem was that someone was sure to see the smoke and when they realized where it came from, it wouldn't be long before the coppers knew.

Charlie worried about his sister's future. He was fairly set, because he had a job that would eventually teach him to be a joiner and carpenter and he knew that skilled work was always in demand, even in hard times like these. There were repairs to ship interiors as well as all the houses and schools that needed to be kept right, and the new buildings that were going up. And Mick would always give him a few bob for running errands if he was short.

Charlie had discovered that Mick had business with house builders. He'd thought it was just betting shops and illegal stuff, but he'd overheard Mick talking to a man about a huge government contract coming up that they were hoping to somehow fix. Charlie didn't know what they planned to do, but he'd heard enough to know that Mick was into many things and all of them had a criminal element.

He knew that it would be better if he stopped working for Mick. Charlie didn't dislike him; Mick paid him well and he was friendly, but he was a crook and Charlie suspected that he was far more important than he allowed other people to think. To most he was just Mick the Swede with a warehouse on the docks, who bought and sold like many others, but Charlie had often been tempted to open one of the boxes he delivered for Mick. Something told him the goods inside were not lawful, but he had no idea what they were. However, the talk of fixing contracts, blackmail and bribes that he'd overheard made Charlie shudder.

He'd decided that he would make his next job for Mick his last unless he got desperate. Now that he was working at the wood yard every day, he didn't really need the money except for treats – and Maisie didn't need sweets and puzzles and comics to make her happy; she needed a safe warm home with someone to look after her, and Charlie had begun to realize that she would be better off in an orphanage than living in derelict buildings. It wasn't what she wanted, but she'd be safer – and, as her brother, it was up to him to keep her safe.

He put his worries from his mind. Maisie wasn't ready yet, but he would talk to her when he got home. There must be another way . . .

Charlie worked hard all day and then bought a tin of cocoa, milk and some fresh bread and a jar of chicken paste. He had a small bar of chocolate for his sister and a little pot of fresh honey. Maisie might be feeling better when he got back, but the honey would do her good and ease her throat if it still hurt.

Upstairs was silent when Charlie let himself in by moving back the loose boards. He ran up the stairs anxiously, because it was silent and that wasn't like his sister. When he reached their rooms, he saw that Maisie had made and drunk a mug of cocoa earlier but now she was curled up in her sleeping bag and her eyes were closed. Had she been asleep all day?

'Wake up, Maisie,' he said cheerfully. 'I've got some honey and milk and a bar of chocolate.'

Maisie muttered something but didn't stir. Charlie felt a pang of fear. He remembered Ma saying that his sister was vulnerable when it came to chills and colds and how ill she'd been when they were at the Rosie. If anything happened to Maisie, he would never forgive himself!

He knelt by her side and touched her face. She felt hot and he could see that her cheeks were flushed, her hair damp with sweat. His sister was really ill and Charlie was out of his depth. He wasn't afraid of Ronnie the Greek or the coppers but if Maisie was really bad, he couldn't cope; he just didn't know what to do.

She wasn't truly aware of him. Charlie stood up. He had to get help and there was only one place he knew to go. Taking the stairs two at a time, he left the house and started running in the direction of the infirmary. When he saw Nurse Sarah, he felt a surge of relief and didn't even notice the man with her. Constable Jones was in ordinary clothes and Charlie scarcely looked at him.

'Nurse Sarah!' he said and his voice was hoarse with entreaty. 'It's Maisie. She had a bit of a cough when I went ter work this morning but now she's ill – burning up with a fever.'

'Where is she?' Sarah asked.

'In them houses just round the corner. I thought she'd be all right, 'cos they're dry and all right, but she always did take a chill bad.'

'Don't worry, Charlie, we'll look after her,' Constable Jones said. 'She'll be fine with Nurse Sarah. I'll carry Maisie back to the Rosie.'

'Yes, she will be fine now,' Sarah said and smiled at him. 'You shouldn't blame yourself, Charlie. I know why you ran – because Maisie was frightened of being sent to an orphanage and being separated. Now you won't have to because Constable Jones has found your auntie and she is looking forward to having you both live with her.'

'Truly?' Charlie asked. 'Yer ain't kiddin' me, Constable Jones?'

'Call me Steve,' the police officer said and smiled. 'Your sister is in one of those houses?' He gestured towards the row of derelict buildings.

'Yeah, the second one on the right. Let me show yer

how ter get in . . .' Charlie set off at a run and pulled back the loose board, then squirmed in. Steve looked at it and then tore it off so that he could get in and, more importantly, out, with Maisie in his arms.

'You stop there, Sarah,' he said. 'I'll be down in a jiffy.'

Charlie was at the top of the stairs. Maisie was still lying in the bedroom with her eyes closed. Steve knelt and placed his hand on her forehead. He nodded.

'Good thing you came for us, Charlie. She is really unwell – poor little girl. I know you've looked after her. I can see how you managed it . . .' His gaze took in the sleeping bags and the shopping that Charlie had brought. 'You can come back another time and collect what you need. Our priority is to get Maisie to the infirmary immediately.'

Charlie said nothing, just picked up a few of Maisie's favourite bits. She would want them when she woke up. His throat was tight with tears and it hurt to keep them in. But he had to keep his emotions under a tight rein because otherwise he might have looked daft and he didn't want the copper to see him like that. He'd recognized the police officer now and he knew he was one of the best, but he was still a copper and Charlie was wary.

'Thank you,' he said as Steve picked Maisie up very gently and carried her down the stairs. Sarah was waiting outside and she looked at Maisie, her expression serious.

'Maisie is very unwell, Charlie,' she said. 'I'm sure we can make her better – but I'm glad you came for me. If you'd waited until morning it could have been too late.'

316

Charlie worried at his bottom lip. He felt guilty, because he should have stayed home and looked after her, but he hadn't wanted to lose his work. If his sister died, it would be his fault . . .

Charlie had finally dropped off. He'd stayed by his sister's side most of the night but, in the end, he'd crawled, fully clothed, into the bed he'd been given next to hers and fallen into a deep slumber.

Sarah had sat by Maisie's side, watching over her and tending her through the long night. Her fever had mounted dangerously, but Matron had brought her a medication that had relieved the fever a little and Sarah had constantly bathed her forehead and adjusted her clothes. She'd managed to get Maisie to swallow a spoonful of the honey Charlie had thoughtfully provided and that had seemed to comfort her and she'd mumbled something like, 'Thank you, Ma . . .'

Tears wet Sarah's eyes. She'd asked one of the other nurses going off duty to tell her mother where she was but she refused to leave the children. They needed love and comfort and Sarah was going to make sure they got it for as long as they needed it. When Maisie opened her eyes and smiled at her, the tears finally spilled over.

'Hello,' she said. 'Where's Charlie?'

'He's here,' Sarah told her. 'He fetched help when you were ill and he watched with me for as long as he could.'

Maisie nodded and closed her eyes again, drifting into a gentle sleep.

'And now I suggest *you* get some sleep,' Matron said, putting a gentle hand on Sarah's shoulder. 'Go home

317

and rest. We can take care of the children now and you need rest or you will make mistakes.'

'Yes, Matron . . .' Sarah hesitated. 'Maisie needs to know – when she wakes up – she needs to know her auntie wants to look after her.'

'Yes, I shall tell her. Constable Jones has informed me of the arrangements he has made. The Children's Welfare have agreed it is the best thing for them – and I shall not try to send them to the orphanage again. I give you my word.'

'Thank you, Matron.'

Sarah smiled and yawned. She did need her bed but she couldn't have left while she feared Maisie's life was in danger. Her fever had seemed so much worse than it actually was but that was often the case with children. One minute they seemed at death's door and the next they were up and running around again. One of the pleasures of nursing them was because you got to see the results of your work. Young bodies and minds healed quickly, unless they were damaged beyond repair.

She left the infirmary and walked to her bus. When she got home all she wanted to do was sleep for a week!

CHAPTER 38

Sarah actually slept for five hours and woke feeling a little stiff but otherwise refreshed. She yawned, rose, and went to have a quick bath and then put on her uniform. There were a few hours left of her shift so she would go in and see if she could be of help, even though Matron would have put another nurse on in her place. She wanted to see how Maisie was and have a talk to her.

'Feeling better now, love?' Sarah's mother asked when she went downstairs. 'You were whacked out when you got home this morning.'

'Yes, I'm fine now. I thought I would go in and see how the children are – and if they need me.'

'Yes, that's right,' her mother said, hesitated and then pointed to the table. 'I made you some sandwiches and there is a letter . . .'

'A letter?' Sarah frowned and picked it up, recognizing Jim's handwriting immediately. She hesitated and then slit the envelope before beginning to eat a sandwich. She was on her second one when she threw the letter on to the table. 'I don't believe him!'

'Has he apologized?' her mother asked.

'No, he's told me that he intends to ask Laura to marry him. He wanted to tell me first so that I wouldn't hear it from anyone else.' She felt a surge of anger. 'He's just rubbing my nose in it, Mum.'

'I would never have thought it of him,' Mrs Cartwright said. 'Do you think she put him up to it?'

'I don't know – and what's more I don't care,' Sarah said and then gave a cry of anger. 'How could he, Mum? All those years, he swore he loved me and wanted to give me a better life – and all I wanted was to marry him and have kids, and bring them to see their nan every week!'

'I know, love, I know . . .' Her mother stroked her hair. 'He took me in proper – but I blame that woman. She's turned his head somehow; he's no more than her puppet but maybe he'll see her for what she is in time.'

'I wouldn't have him now if he crawled on his knees!'

'Really?' Her mother smiled. 'Don't cut your nose off to spite your face, love.'

'I shan't,' Sarah said, 'but I waited all that time, Mum. I shan't wait any longer. I'm ready to move on.'

'Good.' Mrs Cartwright smiled. 'If you wanted to give those kids a temporary home, you could bring them here, Sarah.'

'Could I?' Sarah looked at her. 'I should have asked before but my mind was elsewhere. Their auntie is coming for them, but if the infirmary can't keep them, I could bring them home for a few days.'

'Yes, you could,' her mother said and touched her hand. 'Get off now and do your duty, Sarah. You're a nurse and Matron was very good letting you have the time off.'

*

When she reached the ward, Sarah was delighted to see that Maisie was sitting up in bed and looking much better. Charlie wasn't there but Maisie looked relaxed and happy.

'Charlie has gone ter work,' Maisie told her and wiped her running nose with a big white hanky. 'He said I was better and he didn't want ter let his boss down. He's going ter be a carpenter, you know.'

'That's nice,' Sarah said with a smile at the child's innocence. 'Did Matron tell you that you're going to live with your auntie?'

'Yes.' Maisie beamed at her. 'That nice policeman was here earlier. He said she would be here in a week's time. She has to get all the paperwork done, he says, and then she can adopt us and we'll always live with her.'

'That will be lovely for you,' Sarah said. 'And my mum says you can stay with us for a few days – just until your auntie comes. Would you like that, Maisie?'

Maisie nodded shyly. 'Yes, please. Matron is good and Nurse Jenny is nice – but I like you the best, Nurse Sarah. I should like to stay with you and your mum.'

'Then I'll talk to Matron,' Sarah said. 'And Constable Jones too.'

'He said I should call him Steve,' Maisie said. 'He brought me a sherbet dip and a book about animals. There are pictures of a baby deer – and his name is Bambi.'

'Oh, that was nice,' Sarah said. 'He carried you here last night. You were very unwell then.'

Maisie nodded. 'Ma used to give me hot drinks all the time and wrap me up in front of the fire when I felt poorly. It was getting cold in that place and I didn't dare to light a fire unless Charlie was there.'

'No, it might have been dangerous,' Sarah said. 'Are you much better now?'

'I'm still sniffling but I feel better,' Maisie said. 'I miss my mum – but you're kind.' Her eyes held a look of appeal. 'Do yer think Auntie Jeanie will like me?'

'I think she will love you,' Sarah told her. 'You're very easy to love, Maisie. And now I have to see to some other patients!'

CHAPTER 39

'I think Mrs Cartwright will make an excellent foster mother for those children,' Lady Rosalie said when Mary Thurston told her what had been suggested. 'I am quite sure I can make it right for her to have the children until their auntie arrives – and I already had her on our list for possible fostering in the future, Mary. I have been thinking very carefully about this problem and I believe that you are right – we should select more of our foster parents from decent women and men who live in the East End whenever possible.'

'I couldn't agree more,' Matron said. 'These children ran away rather than be separated from the places and people they knew and, if their aunt had not wanted them, I think Mrs Cartwright would have made an excellent carer for them.'

'Then we shall arrange for her to take on some children in the future,' Lady Rosalie said, 'and in the meantime we shall continue to try and find foster parents, first of all amongst the relatives of children in need of care, if possible – but I have circulated details to various GP surgeries and clinics, asking people willing to foster older children to come forward. I need to build up a core list for the future – and to have time to interview them and make sure they are suitable. I do not want to make a mistake like the Robinsons again.' She hesitated, then, 'They have disappeared owing rent to their landlord and the police are looking for them following inquiries into the whereabouts of a missing crippled lad . . .'

'I wouldn't put anything past that pair after what young Charlie told me.'

Lady Rosalie nodded. 'And I think I might have been wrong about Ruby Harding. If she asks again, I will interview her.'

'I'll remember,' Mary replied and kept the fact that Ruby had disappeared to herself. Ruby was a Londoner born and bred and it was likely she would turn up again one day and ask for her job back. If she did, and her husband had stopped drinking, she could recommend her to Lady Rosalie with a clear conscience.

'I think many of these women have good hearts and would provide a good home if given a little help to feed and clothe the children. I personally feel it is the way to go.'

'Very much better than the orphanage, which I think we will resort to only in time of extreme need,' Mary said, smiling. 'This has taught *me* a lesson, I must admit. I was distressed when those two ran away.'

'Yes, of course you were, but thanks to your nurse and a vigilant police officer we got them back before it was too late!' Lady Rosalie sighed. 'I only wish it would happen more often. Two young girls were found living under the bridge only this week and I fear they had been beaten and goodness knows what else – if the

324

doctors save their lives, I dread to think what effect their memories will have on them. And I doubt we shall find foster carers for such damaged little ones. There are some beyond our help, sadly.'

Mary shook her head as she saw the tears on her friend's cheeks. 'I fear it will always be so, my dear – but we do what we can and the more foster parents of the right kind we can find the better.'

Matron was happy for Sarah to take the children home and both of them were delighted to be staying with someone they liked and trusted. When they got to Sarah's house that evening, they discovered that Constable Jones had brought all the stuff they'd left at the derelict house, packed into two large canvas bags, and Sarah's mother had put it in their rooms for them.

'Such a thoughtful young man,' Mrs Cartwright said. 'Not many would have thought about doing that for you, Charlie.'

'Yeah, Steve is all right – that's what he said to call him,' Charlie chirped and grinned. He'd settled in immediately with Sarah's mum as he called her and when she told him to tuck into his tea he did so with gusto. 'I ain't never had such a good tea, Sarah's mum. Thank yer for making all this stuff fer us.'

'You are very welcome,' she said and smiled at him as he munched yet another strawberry jam tart. 'To be honest, Charlie, I get lonely sometimes and I shall enjoy having you to look after for a few days.'

'I'm working proper now,' Charlie said. 'They've took me on at the wood yard and the gaffer says he'll put me on the tools next year, 'cos I'll be fourteen afore the spring term starts so I shan't 'ave ter go back after Christmas. I've got ter watch and learn and do all the odd jobs but I don't mind what I do – and if there's anything you want doin' I'll be happy to chop wood or bring in coal fer the fire.'

'That's kind of you,' Sarah's mother said, smiling confidentially. 'You know, I was lucky with my Sarah but I always wanted a boy as well.'

'If my auntie hadn't wanted us, we could've lived with you,' Charlie said and wrinkled his brow. 'If I wanted to come back to London when I'm a bit older – would yer 'ave me as a lodger?'

Mrs Cartwright looked at him with interest because he was serious. 'Yes, I would, Charlie,' she said. 'I should like that very much.'

'Good. I'll see how I get on wiv me auntie. I'll get her to come down the wood yard wiv me and tell them I'll come back and work for them when I finish school. Gaffer said I should go back to school if I wanted ter be the best – and I do.'

She smiled at him. 'If you've made up your mind to be a carpenter, then that is what you will be, Charlie. I think you are a strong-minded young man and you will always do what you think best.'

'Is that wrong?' he asked. 'I thought it was best to take Maisie away from the Rosie 'cos they were going to send us to the orphanage, but she got ill.'

'And you went for Sarah straight away,' Mrs Cartwright said. 'You trusted my daughter – and I'll let you into a secret, she's a bit like you, Charlie. She won't let anyone push her around!'

'What is she telling you about me?' Sarah asked with

a smile as she collected the empty plates and took them into the scullery.

'That would be tellin',' Charlie said and grinned at her. 'It were only good, Nurse Sarah.'

'I know, and I'm teasing,' she replied. 'Maisie, do you want to bring that dish with you?'

'Can I help you wash up?' Maisie scampered after her happily and was soon heard chattering fifteen to the dozen as she dried the dishes.

'Should I go and help or leave them to it?' Mrs Cartwright asked and Charlie cocked an ear.

'Sounds to me as though they're getting' on all right. Why don't yer sit down and take it easy fer a bit?'

'I was thinking I might make Maisie a new dress for when your auntie comes,' she said. 'I've got a bit of yellow gingham I bought off the market or a red stripe?'

'Maisie looks lovely in yellow,' Charlie said. 'Ma was goin' ter make her a yellow dress fer her birthday but . . .' He stopped and shook his head. 'She's gone and she ain't never comin' back.'

'No, she can't come back in this life,' Mrs Cartwright agreed. 'But she will be in Heaven watching you, Charlie. She will know you're looking out for your sister and she will be happy.'

'Is there really a God and a Heaven?'

'Don't you believe?'

'I ain't sure. I know Ma stopped believing in God, 'cos she said she knew what Hell looked like and she didn't think she would ever see the other place.'

'Your mum had a hard life after your father died, Charlie. She didn't really mean those things. People say stuff like that when they're unhappy.'

'You're a wise lady,' Charlie said. 'I hope my auntie is just like you, Sarah's mum.'

Mrs Cartwright smiled but didn't answer. She hoped their aunt would be a nice, comfortable woman that the children could take to, but wondered why she hadn't bothered to come and see for herself after her brother died.

'I'll take you upstairs when Maisie comes back,' she said. 'You can use the bathroom and then read or play with puzzles for an hour in bed – and then it's lights out so you get some rest.'

Maisie was yawning when she came back and she wiped her nose on her sleeve. Mrs Cartwright gave her a clean hanky but didn't scold. Maisie was doing well but was obviously tired.

'Upstairs and ready for bed,' she told them both. 'You can play or read for an hour, Maisie.'

Maisie nodded and yawned. When Sarah went up to tuck them up an hour later, Maisie was sound asleep and Charlie was in bed, though still awake.

'We're all right,' he said. 'Thank you – you've got a lovely mum.'

'I know,' Sarah said, smiling as she went back downstairs.

'Thank you for the wonderful tea you made for them, Mum. They loved it – both of them.'

'They're great kids,' her mother replied. 'Just the kind I'd like for my grandchildren.'

Sarah nodded. 'I know, Mum. I wish I'd married Jim years ago and we'd got two kids, but we haven't – and it will take a while before I find someone I can love.'

'Oh, I don't know,' Mrs Cartwright said fondly

smiling at her. 'I don't think it will be long before you have other men calling at your door.'

'And what is that supposed to mean?' Sarah demanded, but her mother bent her head over her sewing machine.

'Oh nothing, but a beautiful girl deserves a decent man.' She smiled and changed the subject. 'I think I've still got some of the shoes you had as a girl that may fit Maisie. We shall have to look them out in the morning.'

CHAPTER 40

Ruby had been gone several weeks now and Sid missed her like hell. At the moment he felt numb, as if he were living in a dream. So, when Sid looked at the man he was supposed to kill that afternoon, he felt physically sick. His boss smiled at him and invited him into the office.

'Come to see when I'll need you again?' He nodded as if pleased about something. 'Well, that big contract I mentioned is on the cards. With any luck it will be signed on Monday and then I'll be setting men on again. You come in nice and early and I'll see you first on the list.'

Sid saw the van draw in with the wages and nodded to the man he no longer respected as he once had but still liked. 'I'll be on my way then, sir.'

He left the office and walked away. If he'd been intending to do Mr Penfold's bidding, it would have been easy enough to wait in one of the sheds until the van had gone and then return and shoot his employer and rob him. There was hardly anyone left on site, because they got paid the next day. Penfold hadn't done his homework well enough. He thought the money came from the bank on a Friday, but it was brought on Thursday evening in a van used for carting building gear and that was why it was always waiting in wage packets by Friday lunchtime for the men to collect when they finished.

Sid had known that because he'd been around a few times finishing off all the little jobs other men had left undone and had seen what was delivered. The boss was always alone in the office on Thursday night and anyone still lingering would be told to get off home. Sid knew that he kept a small gun in his desk drawer and considered it protection enough.

Sid walked away, hands in pockets. He was aware of his shadow a few paces behind. Penfold still didn't trust him, even though he'd put up no resistance.

'The gun is in the top of your dustbin,' a voice hissed at his ear. 'It's tomorrow. Make sure you don't let us down!'

Sid inclined his head but didn't turn. He knew that his time was almost up but when he got home, he would have the means to put an end to this farce. He couldn't kill a man for no reason, especially a man who had given him work. So that left only one alternative.

He went straight home, took the parcel wrapped in newspaper from the dustbin and found both a gun and the bullets he would need. Sid had served his time in the first war and he cleaned the barrel thoroughly before loading it. His plan had matured in the days after he'd been forced to that lonely warehouse and told what was expected of him, and he'd been checking on Penfold's movements.

Sid knew that his shadow during the day was replaced by another at night, but the replacement was careless. He watched the back door of Sid's home but seemed to think it was the only way out. Sid had left by the pantry window on four out of five nights since then and he hadn't been followed once. He'd spent some time watching outside Penfold's club and he knew the gang boss often stayed all night, leaving at around four or five in the morning to go home. Sid hadn't bothered to follow him home. His plan was to break the lock on the storeroom door and creep up to Penfold's office when most of the men had either gone home or were locking up. He would shoot the man he despised and then get out quick. If Penfold's men caught him, he would die – but he didn't much care. Once Penfold was dead, he would go to the police and give himself up. He would probably be hung for murder but he was a dead man anyway.

Sid went upstairs, switched his light on and then visited the bathroom, just as he would if everything was normal. After a while, he switched off the lights and lay down. He knew he wouldn't sleep. His brain was going over and over his plan, searching for what could go wrong. He might be seen before he reached Penfold. If that happened, he could make up an excuse and would probably take a beating. Sid shrugged mentally. Ruby and Julia were safe at the sea and the rest was irrelevant. He was already living on borrowed time.

At two in the morning he got up and, already dressed, went downstairs without putting the light on. He'd practised this several times and he counted the steps, knowing that if he fell over something he would make a noise and alert the man watching in the street. It was easy to climb through the pantry window, which faced away from the door. He knew the watcher would be tired at this hour, barely awake and cursing his luck at having to be the one on duty, because it was getting colder now at night.

Sid shivered as he felt the chill of the night air. It was only the start of October but it felt like winter. He turned his coat collar up, walked softly down the lane and away from the house. Walking quickly, he waited for the right moment to glance over his shoulder and smiled as he saw there was no one there. This street was better lit than most and anyone following had nowhere to hide. As before, he'd managed to evade his shadow.

Sid walked briskly. It warmed him up and calmed his nerves. He'd been over and over his plan and he knew it was the only way. Penfold would blackmail him into doing his dirty deeds for the rest of his life, and although the man he'd been instructed to murder was a member of a rival criminal fraternity, Sid knew he couldn't do it. He had a reason to kill Penfold – the same one as he'd had for killing Germans in the war, to protect those he cared for. At one time, he'd been reckoned a crack shot and he only needed one chance. Penfold really didn't know him at all. He'd seen a lame drunk who could be manipulated to do his dirty work, but Sid had his sticking point. He still remembered the terror in the eyes of a boy in soldier's clothes. They'd been taking the Germans' trenches and the boy had his head down, shaking with fear. He'd looked up at Sid with pleading in his eyes. Sid had raised his gun but then lowered it – and the boy had grabbed his rifle and tried to shoot him as he turned away. Another British soldier had shot him through the head, saving Sid's life.

'Bit careless, mate,' he'd said to Sid. 'They're all the same – only ones you can trust are dead 'uns . . .'

Sid had never forgotten the incident and the next time he was one of the first into enemy trenches he went in shooting and he didn't bother to look at how old the men he'd shot were, as long as they were dead.

No, Penfold didn't know him at all. A grim smile touched his mouth as he saw the nightclub up ahead of him. Most of the lights were out, which meant that the punters had been sent home for the night and what staff remained were closing up, checking doors and windows and collecting anything left lying around. He'd come here several nights and now knew exactly what to do to gain entry without being seen immediately.

Sid wasted no time. The lock on the storeroom responded to the knife he'd taken from the kitchen and then he was in. He shut it behind him, put an ear to the inner door and listened. He could hear nothing, no footsteps, and no echoing voices. It looked as if he'd hit it just right, because as he carefully opened the door, he saw a light at the end of the passage and knew that it had to be from Penfold's office.

His heart was racing as he walked softly towards the door. It was dark in the hall and if someone flicked on the light he would be spotted immediately. Outside Penfold's door, he listened. There were sounds coming from inside. Someone was moving around, opening drawers, shutting them – and then the click of a door as it was opened. He took a deep breath and pushed back the door from the hall, revealing Penfold. He was standing in front of the window and, as he turned, Sid saw that he had a pile of banknotes on the desk and a wall safe open nearby to receive the cash. The gangster's eyes widened as he saw who was standing there and he backed towards the window.

'What the hell do you think you're doin' here?' he demanded. 'You won't get out alive!'

'I don't care,' Sid told him. 'I should 'ave died in the war a dozen times. They shot me in the leg and I got shipped 'ome. I knew when they sent me back, they thought I was dying but I fooled 'em all. If I die now it doesn't matter. You'll be dead too!'

'I'll give you money,' Penfold said, and now there was fear in those weak eyes. Sid could see that he was sweating. 'Let me live and I shan't bother you again. You can have all the money in the safe . . .' He turned towards the safe and grabbed something then turned again. Sid saw Penfold was pointing something at him and he just pressed the trigger on the gun he had in his hand.

The sound was deafening. The bullet entered Penfold's chest and, at the same moment, another gunshot sounded. Glass cracked and Sid saw Penfold's body jerk as another bullet hit him in the back. The gang boss's own gun fell from his hand and he slumped to the ground, his blood pumping.

Sid hesitated for a moment, not quite sure what had happened. Then he threw open the office door and walked swiftly back the way he'd come. He heard shouting as he left the club by the back door. Whoever was in the club had taken a few minutes to get to the boss's office, which was tucked well away from the public rooms.

Sid felt the cold air touch his face but he had no emotion or feeling left in him. Penfold was dead – he'd seen the life drain from his eyes. His bullet had gone home. He couldn't have missed from that distance – but the other shot had come through the office window, shattering it. What had happened?

He walked slowly now. His mind was in a fog. He knew what he had to do but he still didn't understand what had happened in there. Had the jerking in Penfold's body been from one bullet or two? In the distance he heard several gunshots, shouting and the sound of running feet. What was going on?

Well, he thought, his mind clearing a little, it didn't matter. Even if someone else had tried to kill Penfold, Sid had killed him – he'd shot with intent to murder and there was only one thing left to do. Turning his steps towards the police station, he decided to leave out the bit about two shots. He'd dropped the gun somewhere. Sid didn't remember it falling from his hand; it must have been when he was still dazed. He'd expected Penfold's men to be there instantly and that he would die by a knife in the guts or a gunshot. He would have rather it had been that way, but at least he would have his day in court. He would tell the world what kind of a man Penfold was and how he'd tried to blackmail him into murdering a man who had helped him. He would still hang, but he was too numbed to care.

He saw the lights of the all-night police station up ahead and walked straight up to it, not hesitating as he went inside and up to the desk. The sergeant on duty looked at him curiously.

'Yes, sir,' he said pleasantly. 'What can I do for you?'

Sid looked him straight in the eyes. 'I just killed a man,' he said. 'His name is Mr Penfold and he runs nightclubs and a protection gang – and he tried to blackmail me into shooting an innocent man. So, I shot him at his own club instead with the gun he gave me to murder and rob.'

'I think you've had one too many, sir,' the sergeant said frowning at him. 'I know of this Mr Penfold and I can't see you getting away with just walking into his club and shooting him!'

'I'm telling the truth,' Sid insisted.

'Go home and sleep it off,' the sergeant insisted just as they heard a siren and the telephone rang. Sid waited while the police officer picked it up and listened. He saw his eyes widen with disbelief as he put it down and stared at Sid. 'It seems that someone walked into the Midnight Angel this morning and shot Mr Penfold!'

Sid held out his wrists. 'You'd better arrest me . . .'

'I don't know how you knew about this but I'm putting you in the cells for the night. When you sober up, we'll have another talk . . .'

Sid sighed but followed the officer round to the door to the cells. He wasn't handcuffed and he knew that the sergeant still thought he was drunk, but by morning they would have changed their minds and would charge him with murder.

'I'm telling you the truth,' he said. 'I haven't even had one drink!'

'I'll be talking to my superiors,' the sergeant said.

'You can spend the night in the cells for wasting police time – but unless you come clean in the morning you might find yourself in serious trouble – you could go to prison for a month for wasting our time . . .'

Sid found himself wanting to laugh except that the reaction had set in now and he was shaking all over.

Slumping down on the bench that served prisoners as a bed, Sid found he was crying, silent tears slipping down his cheeks. His family were safe – but now that he was coming out of the fog that had held him, he wanted to be with them, to gather them in his arms and hug them. Realizing that it was too late, he hunched his knees up to his chest and lay staring into the darkness until the chill and his own misery took him into a kind of restless sleep.

Sid stared hopelessly at the grey stone wall. He'd been given food and one of the young officers had brought him a cup of tea. Sid had drunk his tea and eaten a couple of bites of the sandwich but he wasn't hungry. He'd been expecting the sergeant to come and question him, but he'd only seen the young officer, who had brought him meals three times yesterday and this morning. Sid knew he'd done wrong but he was waiting to be charged and transferred to somewhere to await trial. It felt as if they'd forgotten him.

'Mr Sidney Harding?' Sid turned his head. A man was staring through the bars of his cell. 'I've been appointed as your solicitor – unless there is someone special you would like me to call?'

'I can't afford a lawyer. I committed a crime and I shall plead guilty.'

'We should talk, sir,' the lawyer said and nodded to the police officer, who unlocked the cell door and allowed him to enter. 'As far as the fee is concerned, I don't charge for my services. Everyone is entitled to legal services when being charge with a crime and there is an organisation that pays my fees.'

'So, I'm being charged?' Sid sat up and looked at him properly. 'I thought they were just going to let me stew and then throw me out for wasting their time.'

'That would be the best outcome,' the lawyer said and offered his hand. 'My name is George Bent, sir. And if I have anything to do with it you will walk away scot free.'

'If the law doesn't kill me, Penfold's men will . . .'

'I should like you to tell me the whole story before I give you my opinion – please leave nothing out, however insignificant.'

Sid nodded. He had nothing to hide. There was no point in lying. If the coppers let him out, Penfold's ruffians would kill him soon enough. He described the murder he'd seen, the way he'd hidden the knife, the abduction of his daughter and the way he'd been forced to handle the knife and return it to where he'd found it. He explained that he'd been blackmailed into doing murder and robbery but instead had chosen to kill Penfold and give himself up.

George Bent listened attentively and watched Sid as he told his story. When he'd finished, the lawyer nodded. 'Yes, I believe you – but the police don't know what to make of it all. You see, on the night you chose to shoot your enemy a gang war broke out. Several known villains were killed and some of them have been rounded up and taken to other prisons. Weapons have been found and the murder weapon identified – Mr Penfold was shot through the back from the outside of the club through the window. The bullet entered his heart and killed him. Another bullet was found lodged in a silver cigar case in his breast pocket . . .'

Sid took a long, shaky breath. 'What are you saying? Do you mean that I didn't kill him?'

'I believe that you tried – but had he not been shot in the back, I think you would already be dead, Mr Harding.'

Sid felt cold shivers at his nape. 'So – so it was the second shot that killed him?'

'Yes, that is what the doctors who did the autopsy are saying. The gun that was used belongs to one of the gangs who were involved in the shootings and it was taken from his body after he was shot by one of Penfold's men – and that man is in custody. He shot a police officer who tried to arrest him and he will most certainly hang. The police have their case and they feel that if they charge you for attempted murder, it might result in the true murderers going unpunished.'

'But surely I am guilty of attempting to kill a man.'

'A man who has killed and bullied many others,' George Bent reminded him. 'In many ways, you would have done a good deed had you succeeded – but if you insist on persisting with your story, they will have to charge you and perhaps their case against others may collapse. They have rounded up the whole rotten nest of them and the streets will be safe for a few years if they get what they deserve.'

'So, what do I do?'

'You plead guilty to being drunk and wasting police time and you'll be let off with a caution.'

Sid bent over, feeling slightly dizzy. The sheer relief of knowing that he hadn't actually killed and he was free to go – free to be with his wife and daughter – was overwhelming.

'If that's what suits them . . .'

'Yes, it does.' George Bent smiled and produced a paper from his briefcase. 'I prepared this statement for you to sign; it's to say that you'd had too much to drink and you told the police a story about a shooting but didn't know what you were saying at the time.'

Sid took the pen and signed his name. George Bent smiled and replaced it in his briefcase.

'It was your lucky night, sir. Had the gang war broken out the next night, you would have probably been killed before you could leave London. Now you have a chance to start a new life.'

'I intend to,' Sid said. 'I'm going to join my wife and daughter. We'll find work somewhere and I'll make sure to keep out of trouble in future.'

'I think that is a very good idea,' George Bent told him and shook hands. 'There will be some paperwork but I think you'll be on your way home in an hour or so.'

Sid thanked him. He felt bemused and still couldn't believe what had happened. He knew that it was possible for a cigarette case to stop a bullet, because it had happened during the war and he'd seen a mate's souvenir of a similar lucky escape – and yet at that range? Sid frowned as he thought of the impact the bullet would have had. It might not have penetrated Penfold's heart, but it would have been enough to stun and severely wind and bruise him. The second shot into the back as he stood there in front of the window, staring in horror at Sid, may have been the one that finally killed him, but it was unlikely the assassin in the street would have had such a clear shot if Penfold hadn't been distracted by Sid's shot. He'd played his part in the man's death, no matter what the lawyer said.

The police wanted a clear-cut case against the rival gangs. Between them they must have a list of crimes as long as Regent Street and it was no wonder the police felt as if they had won first prize. The gangs had done to each other what the police were unable to do and the authorities were determined to make the most of the chance to put as many of them as they could away for a very long time.

It seemed a long hour as Sid waited, because he wasn't sure that they would accept the lawyer's solution, but it couldn't have been much longer when the young officer brought him a hot mug of sweet tea and his possessions.

'You can get dressed and leave as soon as you're ready, sir.'

'Thanks!' Sid took him at his word and signed the release chit.

Outside in the cool air, he breathed deeply. The lawyer had said that Sid was in the clear but he hadn't done the job Penfold had wanted and there might be some of the gang still at large. Sid thought things over as he walked home. The house didn't belong to him and the furniture wasn't worth much. He owed three weeks rent and if the landlord sold everything it would just about cover it with a few quid left over. Ruby and Julia had taken all they wanted and it wouldn't take Sid long to throw a few bits and pieces in a bag. He had a bit of money under the floorboards in the bedroom, which he'd been saving for Julia these past weeks since he started work, and he would take that and clear off.

He wished he could have explained to the man who had employed him, but it wasn't possible, especially as he'd been told his boss was part of a rival gang. Sid didn't know if it was that gang who had had the shooting match with Penfold and his thugs. He shrugged. There was only one way and that was forward to the future. Sid could only hope that wherever he and Ruby ended up, he would find the kind of skilled work he enjoyed and not be forced into standing in line waiting for someone to give him a job . . .

CHAPTER 41

'I just thought I would call in and say hello,' Constable Steve Jones said when he saw Sarah in the children's ward. 'How are Charlie and Maisie doing?'

Sarah smiled at him. 'I'm glad you called this morning. I've heard from their auntie and her adoption papers have come through at last, so she is coming to fetch them on Saturday. I thought you might like to visit them at my home this evening?'

'Yes, I'd like that fine,' he said. 'What time would suit you – I'm off at four today?'

'I'll be home at six. If you can arrange to get there about then you can stay for some supper.'

His smile lit up his face and Sarah felt a glow of pleasure. There was no doubting his sincerity or his kindness towards those children. 'Mum will be really pleased to see you again.'

'She's a lovely lady, your mum,' he said. 'Thank you, Sarah. I shall look forward to it.'

'The children will be pleased to see you,' she replied. 'Charlie says for a copper you're not half bad and Maisie thinks you're wonderful.'

He grinned and walked off chuckling to himself. Sarah turned to see Sister Norton looking at her.

'You really must warn your young man that he cannot come here wasting your time while you are working, nurse.'

'Yes, Sister, I will,' Sarah said. 'He was wondering about the children . . .'

'Ah yes, Charlie and Maisie – how are they?'

'Happy – and Maisie is running about again, completely over her fever.'

'I am pleased to hear it,' Sister Norton said and looked thoughtful. 'I do not know if your policeman told you, but the man who killed their mother has been charged with manslaughter for her death. Apparently, he has been giving evidence against other members of the gang he was in and because of that the police are not charging him with murder.'

'A pity,' Sarah said. 'He ought to hang for what he did.'

'Yes, I agree with you,' Sister Norton said. 'However, his evidence has given the police the chance to take quite a few criminals off the street and they believe it is worth the compromise.'

'How do you know?' Sarah asked. 'I haven't seen anything about it in the papers. I know there was some gang warfare and some important criminals were killed in the shootings.'

'I know a lawyer – his name is George Bent and he has been working on the case with the police.' Sister Norton smiled. 'Of course, he cannot tell me everything, but he'd heard about the children and thought I might like to know the man who killed their mother would be going to prison for some years.'

Sarah felt surprised. She'd never heard the senior nurse speak of a male friend before and realized that perhaps there was more to Sister Norton than she'd guessed.

'I'll be sure to tell Charlie when I get home.'

'You do that – and remember what I told you. No visits while you're working – unless it is urgent.'

'Yes, Sister. I'll tell Steve not to do it again.'

'Steve?' Sister Norton nodded. 'Yes, a nice name – and he has a good solid look about him, nurse. You won't go far wrong with a man like that – and now you can fetch the medicine trolley. Doctor will be here in exactly five minutes . . .'

Sister Norton trotted off to scold a patient who had pulled his covers out at the bottom of the bed and tuck them in again. Sarah went for the medicine trolley. On the mornings when the doctor did his rounds, they waited to administer treatment until the duty doctor had given his verdict. Three of their patients were on the mend and Sarah thought that at least one of them would be going home when his mother came to visit that evening.

'They're goin' ter put him in prison for a long time?' Charlie said looking at Sarah intently. 'So, he ain't goin' ter get away wiv it.' He smiled and nodded thoughtfully. 'If I'd 'ad my way he would be hung, but I ain't a judge. Prison for several years is more than I expected he'd get.'

'*You* did that, Charlie – when you dared to go to the police station and tell them what he did to your mum.'

'Shall I have ter go in court, then?' He looked at her curiously.

347

'No, it won't be necessary,' Sarah told him. 'Ronnie has confessed to beating your mum. He pleaded not guilty to murder so they're going to charge him with manslaughter. He's done lots of other things as well but he has given evidence against others and so the police have accepted his plea.'

'I reckon that's as good as we could 'ope fer,' Charlie said with the philosophical acceptance of a much older mind. 'Thanks fer tellin' me, Sarah – did it come from Steve?'

'No – though he might tell you this evening, because he's coming to supper.' She heard the knock at the door and smiled. 'That will be him now . . .'

Steve entered the kitchen bearing a bunch of carnations for Mrs Cartwright, a box of chocolates for Sarah and bags of sweets for Charlie and Maisie.

'You didn't have to do this,' Sarah's mother told him with a smile. 'We're only having sausage meat with onions, fried in the pan with chips and a bit of buttered cabbage.'

'And a strawberry jelly and ice cream fer afters!' Maisie said, running to Steve and throwing her arms about his legs. 'And my auntie is coming tomorrow. She wrote us a lovely letter and said it is all due to you.'

'I just asked her if she knew you were on your own,' Steve said and ruffled her shining hair. 'She couldn't wait to claim you for her own but I told her it was best to get the proper paperwork first so it took a bit of time – but now you'll have a home of your own.'

'I like being with Sarah's mum,' Maisie said, 'but if

my auntie is nice it will be all right; Sarah says I can come and visit sometimes.'

'Of course you can,' Sarah said and smiled at the child's glowing face. 'Charlie wants to know if Ronnie the Greek will get a long sentence.'

'Let's hope so,' Steve said. 'He might get ten years or so, hopefully more, but he won't come after you when he gets out, Charlie. He doesn't know that you told us what he did.'

'Well, I might want ter come back ter London one day,' Charlie said doubtfully. 'I want ter be a carpenter's apprentice.'

'I'm sure it will be perfectly safe for you to return when you're ready,' Steve said. 'Where he's going, he may never see freedom again. The law won't stop him, but there are a lot of angry criminals who have a grudge against Penfold's men and he may not survive.'

'Please stop frightening the children and me,' Mrs Cartwright said, though she smiled as she administered the reproof. 'Your supper is ready so I want you all at the table straight away.'

Charlie and Maisie scrambled for their seats, and Steve waited, choosing the seat next to Sarah. She smiled at him as he sat down and then they all began to eat their meal. The children tucked in eagerly, because such a treat as they were being given was something they'd never experienced until they came to stay with their beloved Sarah's mum.

It was as they were beginning to clear the table after every scrap of jelly and ice cream had been devoured that they heard the knock at the door. Mrs Cartwright went to answer it as Sarah and Steve carried dishes into the scullery. They had volunteered for the washing-up and were laughing when someone appeared in the doorway.

'Sarah, I wanted to talk to you . . .'

Sarah's head came round and the colour drained from her cheeks as she saw who was standing there. 'Jim,' she whispered hoarsely. 'I wasn't expecting you . . .'

'No, obviously not,' he said and there was bitterness in his voice as he looked at Steve. 'I thought you might be interested that my old boss has offered me the job of manager at the pub, because the last one let him down – but it didn't take you long to get over me, did it?'

'Jim . . .' Sarah floundered, struck speechless by the unfairness of the attack. 'Steve is a friend to us all!'

'Really? I can see the way he looks at you, Sarah, and I saw the look in your eyes. I was going to ask you to walk out with me and see if we could patch things up but clearly it would be a waste of time.'

Sarah had begun to recover from the shock and now she was angry. 'You've got completely the wrong idea, Jim. I don't know Steve well and we are just friends, but as far as me being your girlfriend again – the answer is no. I am delighted for you that you have the job you always wanted but I don't want to be dangled on a string again. I waited for years and then you decided you wanted someone else more—'

'Laura was too far above me,' Jim interrupted and didn't seem to understand that his words were insulting to the girl he'd once vowed he loved. 'She was a bright star I could never hope to capture – but *we* could have a good life now that I have the job as manager.'

With those few words Jim shattered any chance he'd

ever had of Sarah taking him back. She knew exactly what had happened. He'd tried it on with Laura and she'd made it clear that she wasn't interested in him as anything more than someone she had at her beck and call. That was why he was happy to return to his old job. Laura had probably told him to leave.

'I'm sorry you didn't get what you wanted,' she said quietly. 'But you have your answer. Please leave, Jim. Just leave . . .'

He shot a venomous look at Steve, glared at her and strode out of the scullery. They heard a door slam as he shut it hard behind him. Sarah felt embarrassed as she saw Steve staring at her, a teacloth in his hand.

'I'm sorry you were subjected to that,' she said. 'He had no right to come here and make foolish accusations.'

'He wasn't far wrong in my case,' Steve said, his eyes never leaving her face. 'You were right when you said we didn't know each other well and that we are just friends – but that doesn't mean I wouldn't like it to be more.'

'You don't have to say anything . . .' She was blushing.

'I've been wanting to for a while,' he said. 'I didn't because I respect you, Sarah, and I thought it was too soon – but I intended to ask if you would like me to take you somewhere – perhaps to a dance?'

Sarah met his steady gaze and relaxed. Jim had made her feel uncomfortable but she saw there was no need. 'I should very much like to go to a dance with you, Steve.'

His smile lit his eyes from inside. 'Great. It's one of the police benefit dos and we all buy a few tickets. I wasn't going to use mine but now I shall.'

'It sounds posh?'

'Oh, a pretty frock will do. I'll wear a suit.'

'I've got a long black velvet skirt and a pretty white blouse.'

'Just right,' he said and put down his teacloth, moving towards her. 'I don't want to rush you – and I realize that you've recently broken up a long-standing relationship. I don't want you on the rebound, Sarah. If you still love Jim, I shall understand.'

'No,' she said firmly. 'I don't love him. But I'm not sure yet how I feel about you, Steve. I like you very much, but we do need to get to know one another much better than we do now, build a relationship.'

'I agree, and I'm looking forward to each stage of it,' he said, his eyes warm and caring. 'I'm going to leave you now, Sarah. I think you need time to think about what just happened – but if it's all right with you, I'll call for you next Saturday evening at seven.'

'Lovely,' she agreed. 'Oh, Sister Norton warned me today that you shouldn't make a habit of visiting the ward, but you can always come to see us here.'

'Thank you, Sarah,' he said and leaned in to kiss her cheek. It was the lightest of kisses and then he was gone. She heard him talking to the children and her mother and then the door opening and closing.

Her mother came into the scullery just as she'd finished wiping the last plate. 'Everything all right, love?'

'Yes, Mum, fine,' she said and hung the cloth up to dry. 'That was a lovely tea you got us – Charlie and Maisie woofed it down.'

'Don't change the subject, Sarah. You know what I mean. What was wrong with Jim?'

'He wanted to take up where he left off – and he got the manager's job he'd been after for years. Apparently, the other chap didn't work out.'

'Yes, I gathered that bit – but what about you? You didn't send him away out of temper, did you?'

'No, Mum, I didn't,' Sarah said. 'I told him I wasn't going to wait around for him any more. I'm over him, I'm moving on . . .'

'If that is how you really feel, I'm glad,' her mother said and smiled. 'Steve is good with kids, isn't he?'

'Yes, he is, Mum. I like him. He has asked me out and I shall go – but as a friend. I'm in no hurry to get into a relationship again. I am over Jim, I promise you, but I'm just not sure where I want to go next.'

'That's fine by me,' her mother said and smiled. 'It means I've got you at home for a bit longer!'

'If I have my way, I'll always be no further than a brisk walk or a short bus ride,' Sarah said. 'This is where I belong, Mum. When I do marry and settle down to have kids, I want their grandmother to be there for them all the time.'

'You know what I said when Jim asked you to move up West. I want you to be happy, Sarah, and I'll never hold you back. I'll be fine as long as I see you sometimes.'

'Well, *I* won't,' Sarah said and put her arms about her mother and hugged her. 'You're the best mum in the world and I love you. The man who *really* loves me will adore you too.'

Her mother shook her head but she was laughing as they went back into the kitchen to find the children poring over Maisie's latest jigsaw puzzle. Sarah had bought her one cheap from the market and, because it had lots of pieces, it was keeping the pair of them busy.

'Another twenty minutes and up to bed,' Sarah's mother said and looked at her daughter.

She knew exactly what her mother was thinking, because she was thinking the same. One day the children piecing together the puzzle would be hers and they would love staying with their granny.

Sarah had arranged to have the afternoon off when Charlie and Maisie's aunt arrived to take them home with her. She wanted to make sure everything went well and that the children were happy to go with their relation.

Sarah's mother had the kettle on and when they saw a plump, middle-aged lady walk up the front path, she started to make a pot of tea.

'Hello,' Sarah said as she answered the knock. 'I'm Sarah Cartwright and the children have been staying with me, because I became fond of them when I was at the infirmary.'

'I'm Jeanie Marsh. My brother was the children's father,' the woman said and smiled. 'How are they? I wanted to come sooner but there was all the paperwork to allow me to foster them and I've been having their rooms decorated and new furniture delivered. I wanted it all to be just right for my brother's children.'

Sarah's first opinion was that she was a genuine, kind woman and it didn't change when she greeted the children and gave both of them a kiss. She'd bought a book about football for Charlie and a book with pictures of small animals for Maisie.

'I thought they might keep you amused on the train,' she told them. 'There are lots of things waiting in your rooms at home, but these were easy to bring.'

'Cor, that's smashing, that is!' Charlie said as he glanced inside his book. 'I've always wanted one of these.'

'Good – I wasn't quite sure what you like or exactly how old you are.'

'I'll be fourteen in December and Maisie is just nine,' Charlie told her. 'I want to be an apprentice at the wood yard on the docks. Will you please come and tell my boss that I will go back to school now because I have to but then I can come back and be apprenticed . . .?'

'Well, I can arrange for you both to attend the school I teach at, but I'm not sure about the apprenticeship.'

'He says he'll take me on for free – you just 'ave ter tell him it's all right.'

'Charlie, let your auntie sit down first before you drag her off!' Sarah said but smiled because he was so eager.

His aunt looked a little taken aback. 'How would you live in London alone, Charlie? Has your future employer offered you a home as well as a job?'

'No, but Sarah's mum has,' Charlie said and grinned. 'She is a smashing cook, Aunt Jeanie. We can stay ter tea if yer like.'

Aunt Jeanie looked at Mrs Cartwright. 'Is Charlie right? Would you be willing to give him a home? I could pay something for his keep . . .'

'I've loved having the pair of them and Charlie is very welcome – but I told him he has to ask you if you mind.'

'I see . . .' Sarah thought their aunt looked a little uncertain, perhaps disappointed as she said, 'What about you, Maisie?'

Maisie looked up at her. 'You look a bit like my dad used to,' she said shyly and inched closer. 'My book is nice. Can I live with you, please?'

'Yes, of course you can, darling,' Jeanie said. 'I thought Charlie would too . . .'

'I shall until I leave school at the end of term,' he told her. 'And I'll come 'ome fer holidays – but I want ter be a carpenter and it ain't easy ter find someone as would take me on without me paying a lot of money – and the gaffer said he would take me on fer nothin'; he likes me 'cos I work 'ard and I want ter learn.'

'Oh, I see . . .' Jeanie's puzzled look cleared as she understood his urgent request. 'Perhaps we could find you an apprenticeship nearer where we live, Charlie – might that be as good?'

'Yeah, it might if we could afford it,' he agreed. 'But I'd like yer ter meet the gaffer . . .'

'Let's do that then,' his aunt said. 'Is it far away? Only the train I thought we'd get is at five this evening and there isn't another until half past seven.'

'We thought you might like to stay overnight and go back in the morning,' Mrs Cartwright said. 'Only if it is convenient, of course.'

'How thoughtful you are,' the children's aunt said and smiled at her. 'I knew you must be, of course, to take the children in until I could fetch them. Well, I think we must speak to Charlie's boss and hear what he thinks – so it may be best to leave in the morning. If you're sure it is no trouble?'

'I enjoy company,' Mrs Cartwright said. 'Sarah is going out this evening with a friend and we'll be able to sit and have a talk – get to know each other. I think if Charlie wants to return to London it would probably suit us all.'

'Yes, it would, because I work every day except Saturday and Sunday and I might not be able to look after both of them as they deserve – though I am happy to try,' Jeannie agreed. 'Thank you, I *will* stay. It will give us time to speak to Charlie's employer.'

'You will have a cup of tea before you go down to the docks?' Mrs Cartwright said. 'Charlie, take that ball into the garden and play with Maisie for a while and then your auntie will be ready to take you to see your boss.'

CHAPTER 42

'I've got good news, Sid,' Ruby said, smiling with relief as she met her husband at the small seaside railway station. He'd sent her a note through Sarah as they'd arranged before she and Julia left London and she'd sent him a card the same way, with a time and place and date. It was best, Sid thought, to be a bit cautious until they could be absolutely certain that none of Penfold's gang were out to get him. 'I didn't tell you before, but I was offered a job as housekeeper looking after an elderly lady. She needs someone to do her garden, too, and there are some jobs need doin' on the house – mending fences and broken windows, locks, and stuff like that. So if yer wanted, yer could take it on while you look fer a proper job or else just do that full-time. And she's given us the cottage at the bottom of her garden. Julia and I moved in a few weeks ago.'

'It sounds a bit of a ramshackle place.' Sid looked doubtful. 'Can she afford to pay us?'

Ruby's face broke into a smile of delight. 'You just wait until yer see the 'ouse, Sid! She's got pots of money but she lives alone, has done since her husband and son were both killed in an accident over forty years ago – the boy was only seventeen – and she's a bit forgetful. Her sister-in-law offered me the job and told me I looked like the sort she could trust. Mrs Lawson needs good people, Sid. There's plenty would take advantage of her, but we shan't.'

'Where is it?' he asked, surprised when she led him towards an old but stylish automobile. 'What are you doin', Ruby?'

'Edward is Mrs Lawson's chauffeur, Sid. He has been with her for years and he is devoted to her, but he couldn't do everything alone so they advertised for a housekeeper and an odd-job man.'

Sid looked at the man behind the wheel of the car. Edward got out and opened the back door for Ruby and then offered his hand to Sid.

'Welcome, Mr Harding. I'm pleased to meet you. Your wife is a treasure and I believe the two of you will be just the ones to look after my lady when I've gone . . .'

'Edward hasn't been too well and he was worried about Mrs Lawson,' Ruby explained as Edward put Sid's bags in the boot of the car.

'I'm pleased to meet you too,' Sid said. 'I don't currently hold a driving licence, I'm afraid, though the Army taught me during the war.'

'I could help you pass a test,' Edward said. 'I shall be around for a bit longer . . .'

Sid looked at Ruby, who nodded and smiled. This was all so unexpected. He'd thought she was living in a village nearby and had sent his card there.

'The postmistress knew I was living at the cottage

now,' she explained. 'It's a bit of luck for us, Sid. Lovely little village and there's a bus into town so Julia can get to her school and we can go in if we want – but we're tucked right out of the way . . .'

Sid knew what Ruby was thinking. If the men who had tried to blackmail Sid came looking, they wouldn't think of looking in such a quiet place – a place where everyone knew everyone else, where a stranger asking questions would be noticed at once.

A quiet country cottage was the last thing that Sid had envisaged when he'd told Ruby to look for work that might suit them both. He'd thought a busy town where he might find plenty of building work going on – but she'd found them a home and a job that sounded pretty easy.

When the car reached the end of a long tree-lined drive, Sid's breath expelled in a gasp of astonishment. It was almost like a stately home at first glance. He realized it wasn't as big as the really important old houses, but it was a strikingly beautiful country house with ivy-clad walls and leaded windows, the thatched roof sloping low like something in a picture book.

'It's lovely,' Sid said, awestruck. 'I ain't never seen anythin' like it – except in a book.'

'I know, but it needs so many little jobs fixing,' Ruby said. 'Edward tries but he isn't much of a handyman.'

'I can fix anything,' Sid said easily. 'Little jobs are never any trouble.'

'My lady will be pleased if you can fix the roof of the conservatory, as it leaks,' Edward said as he held the door for Ruby. 'Mrs Lawson wanted to meet you, sir. I'll take your husband's bags down to the cottage, Ruby.'

'Thank you, Edward. We'll go in and say hello – and I'll have tea for you in the kitchen at half past four as usual . . .'

Sid followed his wife into the beautiful but neglected house. He could see how old it was inside and how wonderful if must have looked when first built. However, so many jobs had been left for longer than they ought that there was a sad air of neglect. Sid realized immediately that a house like this would eat money and time; he could start at one end and work his way through and when he'd finished it would be time to start at the beginning again. It would be a never-ending task . . .

Ruby led the way into what had once been a grand sitting room. These days the colours were muted and the hangings were faded and old – but not as old as the tiny lady sitting in the wing chair by the fire. Her hair was white, her face heavily lined.

Her eyes, however, were bright and knowing as they fixed on Sid's face. For a moment she just stared at him and then she nodded.

'Make up the fire, Harding. Mrs Harding, you may make my tea. I hope you are settled into the cottage?'

Sid poked the fire in the grate and placed two large pieces of coal on it and it began to spark and throw out more heat.

'Yes, thank you, ma'am,' Ruby said. 'Come on, Sid, Mrs Lawson is satisfied.'

Sid felt slightly dazed to be accepted and dismissed so lightly and followed his wife into the kitchen. He sat down at the table as Edward entered and joined him. Ruby set a silver tray with delicate china plates, tiny sandwiches and even tinier cakes, also a pretty cup, saucer, milk jug to match and a silver teapot. Edward lifted it and went off to deliver it to his mistress. He was soon back and Ruby poured them all a cup of tea from a large brown pot. She had tomato sandwiches with chicken paste, which was Sid's favourite at home, and a seed cake. Edward tucked in with evident agreement.

'You're a lovely cook, Ruby,' he said. 'Much better than the last one who came to work here. My lady couldn't eat her food and she wasn't here long!'

Edward chattered for a while and then the bell went and he disappeared towards the sitting room once more.

'Well,' Ruby said looking at him. 'Will it do?'

'Do you like it here, Ruby love?'

'Yes, I do. It's a lot of hours sometimes but it will be easier with you helping me – and it's a nice place for Julia to bring her friends to – she's already made a few good ones at her new school. It meant I didn't 'ave ter sell your grandmother's gold watch and chain. Mrs Lawson doesn't mind if Julia uses the gardens as long as she behaves, and she's allowed to bring a friend – but you've got ter live 'ere as well, Sid, so it's really got to do . . .'

'I reckon it will more than do,' Sid said and smiled. 'Things will cool down back 'ome in time. If they're looking for me now, they'll give up if I'm not around. One day we'll probably go back, and then we'll see about fosterin' that kid yer want – but this is better than I ever hoped for, love.'

'I feel safe and needed here,' Ruby said. 'And this is a place that grows on yer, Sid. You'll see . . .'

Sid nodded, looking about the large kitchen with

approval. It was certainly in need of work and he could improve so much. He'd been noting jobs that needed to be done urgently ever since he arrived and that made him feel better. Sid was a realist. He couldn't go back, at least not for a while, and here he would earn a living and his wife and daughter could be happy and live without fear of abduction. Providing Sid had work to keep him busy he wouldn't be bored and he could always walk down to the village pub of an evening for a pint . . . Just one, mind. That was his limit.

'I reckon we've done all right,' he said and saw Ruby's smile of pleasure. 'This will do us fer a few years, love, and then we'll see . . .'

CHAPTER 43

Jenny was getting ready to go to work when Lily got home. She'd been busy all day and looked tired, but though she acknowledged the tea Jenny poured for her she didn't immediately drink it but went to the radio and switched it on. A man's voice was giving a weather forecast and Lily shook her head.

'We've missed the news,' she told her sister looking serious. 'There was a big riot in Cable Street – well, it has been all over town but the worst violence was there.'

'Was it the fascists?' Jenny asked, sensing something in Lily's voice. 'Were many people hurt?'

'I heard that lorries were overturned, the roads strewn with broken glass and a Jewish tailor was attacked and hurt by the rioters.'

'That's terrible,' Jenny said. 'Did you have anyone brought into the infirmary?'

'Yes, a few with cuts and bruises,' Lily said. 'But many of the injured were taken to the London and that is why I wanted to hear the news.'

'I should have had it on,' Jenny was saying when a sharp knocking at their back door made the sisters look at each other. Instinctively, she knew who it would be before she opened the door and saw him standing there. He was wearing a raincoat over the uniform of the Blackshirts but his face was cut and bruised and she could see his right hand was bleeding. He'd wrapped a handkerchief round it but it looked soaked through with blood.

'Chris – what have you done?'

'I wouldn't blame you if you hated me,' he said. 'I couldn't go to the hospital because they are looking for me and I hoped you might help me.'

'Who is looking for you – the police?'

'Come in,' Lily said. 'He's hurt, Jenny. Let's treat him and we'll ask questions later.'

Jenny pushed him into a chair at the kitchen table and unwound the handkerchief. It was a deep, nasty wound made either by a knife or broken glass. Lily had fetched a bowl of warm water and some clean linen. She washed the blood away and looked at the wound, which was right across his palm; fortunately, there was nothing left in and the cut was clean.

'I'm going to stitch that for you,' she said. 'I can't give you anything for the pain and it will hurt but the alternative is the hospital.'

'I can't go there. If they see me, I'm a dead man.'

'What do you mean? Have you killed someone?' Jenny asked and he looked at her with such reproach that she felt ashamed.

'I saved someone's life – a Jew, as a matter of fact. I got this cut grabbing the knife that was aimed at his stomach.'

Lily nodded. 'Too much for your ideals, was it?'

Chris's gaze went to her. 'Neither of you read my letter. I asked you to believe that I wasn't a fascist, even though I belong to the movement.'

'So, you didn't throw that Jewish man through a glass window or take part in the riots?'

'I tried to stop it happening,' Chris said. 'I've blown my cover now – so you might as well know the whole – or as much as I can tell you. I work for British Intelligence and I infiltrated Mosely's organization to garner information about what they were doing. I couldn't tell you all of it, Jenny – and I still can't – but in my letter, I did tell you that I wasn't what you thought.'

'Yes,' Lily said. 'I thought it might be something like that – but Jenny didn't want to listen and I wasn't sure I was right.'

'Lily! Why didn't you tell me?'

'You were angry the last time you spoke to Chris. You told me he was bad-tempered and a bigot and you didn't want to hear his name again – and I'm not a good judge of men as you know and I might have put you wrong.'

A cry of pain from Chris as she dabbed the cut with antiseptic made her look at him. 'Well, I'm sorry, but I warned you it was going to hurt. I'll put some honey on and that will help it heal; it's an old-fashioned remedy but it works.'

'It's all right, carry on.'

'So, why couldn't you go to the hospital?' Jenny asked.

'Because some of the men I betrayed have been taken there with wounds. If they saw me, I would be high on the list of revenge targets, and, believe me, there are ruthless men in their ranks. However, the tide is turning against them. There was such resistance to their march that even the police were taken by surprise. Some of the harder members are going to be looking to get even because their cause took a beating today and some of that is down to me and the people I work for.'

'Stop there! You've told us more than enough.' Lily placed a clean linen pad over the wound and bound it. 'I can give you an aspirin if you wish, but I doubt it will do much good.'

'I'll put up with it,' Chris said and smiled at her. 'Thank you for being a good nurse and for listening. I'll get out of your way now.'

'Don't be a fool,' Lily said bluntly. 'If my sister was angry with you, you had only yourself to blame. If you want a future with this family, tell her the truth, as much as you can, whatever it is. She can keep a secret – as can I.'

'Lily!' Jenny was blushing. 'Chris came here for help not because there is anything between us.'

'Now, *you're* the fool,' Lily said and her dark hair swirled as she moved her head. 'I should bang your heads together. Don't let pride get in the way, either of you. If you love each other, then listen and learn. I didn't get the chance and I want my sister to have hers.'

'Oh, Lily,' Jenny said in a very different tone. She looked at Chris, a flush in her cheeks. 'I don't have to leave for work, because it is my day off . . .'

'I'll leave you alone for a bit then,' Lily said and smiled as she went out.

CHAPTER 44

'I'm going to walk you home,' Bert said to Kathy as she was leaving the Rosie that evening. 'After all the violence on the streets today there might be some rough types about and I don't want you getting hurt.'

Kathy hesitated and then nodded her head. 'Yes, thank you, Bert. I'll admit that I was feeling nervous. The men who attacked Mosely's lot had been fired up to do it and you don't know what sort of element was in that crowd.' She smiled at him and allowed him to help her on with her jacket as they went out into the cold air.

'I was thinking we might go to the church social next week,' he said as they walked. 'It's just a few refreshments, a tombola, a few stalls and some general fun. Some of the men play dominos and others play cards, and the older children dance and take part in games.'

'You know I'd love to come but I'm not sure my mother will let me.' Kathy looked uncomfortable. 'You'll have to leave me at the end of my lane, because if she sees us . . .'

'Don't you think it is time she knew we are friends?' Bert said. 'You know I would never harm you or do anything that would lead to gossip, Kathy. If I spoke to your mother—'

'No, please, not yet,' Kathy said. 'I should never hear the end of it.'

'She'll have to know sometime,' Bert said and he stopped walking to look at her. 'I care for you, Kathy. Perhaps I'm too old and you may fall in love with a younger man, but if you don't, I shall be here for you . . .'

'Oh, Bert!' Kathy looked at him with glowing eyes. 'I like you very much and I should like to – to be courted, but my mother is so strange about men.'

Bert nodded. 'I'm not going to push it, Kathy. You must make the decisions but I hate to think of you havin' no fun – and being scolded for no good reason.'

'I enjoy my work, even more now that we're friends,' she said and smiled. 'I'm still young, Bert. Perhaps when I'm eighteen Mum will relax her guard a little.'

'I hope so – for your sake as much as mine.'

They walked in silence for a while, taking their time, not wanting this pleasure to be over too soon, but eventually the corner of her lane was reached and Kathy stopped, looking up at him.

'I'll go on alone now, Bert. Thank you so much for seeing me safe home.'

Bert nodded but didn't walk away as she continued down the lane to her house. He was still watching her when the man suddenly lunged at her out of the shadows. Kathy screamed and Bert started running. The ruffian had her up against the wall and he was tugging at her skirts when Bert put an arm about his throat and dragged him off her. The man struck out with his elbows and threw Bert off, then he turned to meet him, striking with his right arm. Bert seized it and they wrestled, the fight veering this way and then the other and he took some hard punches before he managed to knock the rogue down to his knees, but then he lunged at Bert and brought him down.

There were shouts from the neighbours and a woman came up to Kathy, leading her away as the two men fought on the ground. 'I saw what happened – and I saw that other man come to yer rescue, love.'

Kathy refused to go inside, even though her mother had come out to see what was going on. Bert was getting the worst of it but then he managed to land a punch square on her attacker's jaw and he went down again, this time striking his head on the kerb.

'Kathy, what happened?' her mother demanded but she was saved from answering by her next-door neighbour.

'Kathy was attacked by that ruffian – and this brave man saved her!' her neighbour said importantly. 'I witnessed it all.'

'Yes, I saw it too,' one of the local men said and clapped. 'Well done, mate. I reckon he was one of them rioters from earlier – a load of cutthroats and murderers if yer ask me.' He turned to someone behind him. 'Run down to the box and ring for the cops, mate.'

Kathy's mother gave a little shriek. 'Are you hurt, Kathy?'

'No, Mum – Bert saved me. He works at the infirmary and insisted on walking me home for my safety. If he hadn't, I should have been – been violated . . .'

'Oh, my lord!' Mrs Saunders said, her cheeks white. 'Bring him in, Kathy. He's a hero – and we must make sure he is all right – that murderer might attack him again.'

Kathy went quickly to Bert who was shaking his head. She could see blood on his mouth and his hands. 'Mum says you're to come in,' she said. 'She wants to thank you for saving me.'

'Good,' he said gruffly. 'Don't worry, Kathy, it looks worse than it is.'

He followed her into the kitchen, receiving the praise of Kathy's neighbours as he passed through them. Mrs Saunders turned to look at him and he could see that she had once been as pretty as her daughter.

'That was a brave thing you did, sir. I don't know your name?'

'Bert Rush. I work as the caretaker at the Rosie.'

'I can see you've been hurt. Kathy, fetch a bowl of warm water and my first-aid box. The least we can do is to bathe Mr Rush's hurts and offer him a cup of tea.'

Kathy did as her mother bade her, but let her do the bathing and soothing. She made a cup of tea and brought the teapot and her mother's second-best china to the table. Mrs Saunders nodded her approval and managed a thin smile.

'Kathy makes a good cup of tea, Mr Rush – and she's a decent cook. I taught her myself.'

'She makes a good cup of tea at work sometimes.'

Mrs Saunders nodded. 'So, you've known each other since Kathy started working at the infirmary?'

'Yes, Mrs Saunders. We help each other out when we're busy.'

'Mr Rush does most of the helping,' Kathy said and blushed as her mother looked at her and nodded.

'You were lucky he chose to accompany you home this evening, Kathy. I am glad you have a decent friend at work. You must visit for tea on a Sunday, Mr Saunders – unless you have a wife and family to be with?'

'I live alone,' he told her. 'I took care of my mother while she lived. She was an invalid for some years – and then I was injured in the war. I enlisted at the age of fifteen. I was a cadet at first but towards the end I saw some fighting. I have a wound that aches a bit in the wet weather but otherwise I'm fit and I enjoy my work for the Rosie. As I own my cottage, it's a good wage . . .'

Kathy's mother looked at her and the message in her eyes was one of approval. 'You sound like a thoroughly decent young man, Mr Rush. I am grateful you walked my daughter home this evening. Had she been violated by that brute I fear it would have killed me. She is my only child . . .'

'Yes, I understand that,' Bert said and looked her in the eyes. 'My intentions towards your daughter are only good ones, Mrs Saunders.'

'I can see that for myself,' she said and smiled; the first natural smile Kathy had seen for a long time. 'If I know you are looking out for my girl I can stop worrying.'

'She will come to no harm when I'm around,' Bert said and she nodded.

Kathy's mother pressed him to drink his tea, which he did, complimented Kathy on its quality and said he would see her the next day.

'I'll be on my way. By the sound of things I think the police have arrived and they'll want my side of the story. I'll see you tomorrow, Kathy. Goodnight, Mrs Saunders.'

'I shall expect you for tea,' Mrs Saunders said. Bert smiled, glanced at Kathy and left. After he'd gone, she looked at Kathy. 'Now he is the kind of man I hoped you might meet one day. You've been luckier than I was, Kathy.'

'What do you mean?'

Her mother's eyes met hers. 'What almost happened to you this evening happened to me when I was your age – except I wasn't lucky enough to have a man who cared about me watching out for me . . .'

'You were . . .?' Kathy couldn't say the word. 'Did he – am I . . .?'

'The daughter of a rapist?' Mrs Saunders smiled oddly. 'No, you are not. I did have a child – a boy – but my father forced me to have him adopted. They took him from me as soon as he was born. I gave him his first feed and never saw him again.'

'I have a brother?'

'Perhaps . . .' Her mother shrugged. 'I tried to forget that he had ever existed. My parents moved away from the area where my shame was known and when I finally started courting, I pretended that nothing had ever happened and so on my wedding night . . .' She faltered and looked beyond Kathy's shoulder. 'Greg accused me of being a whore. He went out and got drunk every night for a week and then he beat me. I was in hospital for a month. When I came out, he begged my pardon and said it would never happen again . . .'

'Oh, Mum, I never knew!' Kathy was on the verge of tears.

'I didn't want you to know.' Her mother shook her head. 'Greg did one good thing for me before he finally walked out – he gave me you. But he never forgave me and any love he'd had for me died the night he discovered I'd borne a child out of wedlock. In the end we hated each other. I was determined that no man would ever treat you that way . . .'

Kathy was crying now. She didn't know what to say. Her mother's strictness, her nagging, her refusal to let Kathy date had seemed harsh and unfeeling but now she understood.

'Mum, I love you,' she said and ran to her, hugging her. 'Bert is lovely and I might love him – but you're my mum . . .'

Mrs Saunders drew back and looked at her. 'Get to know him well, Kathy. I married hastily because I was grateful a man wanted me after what had happened – but once he knew he used me like a whore. I don't want that for you.'

'Bert is gentle and kind and considerate,' Kathy told her. 'We've talked about his mother and he nursed her for a long time as well as working. I know he would never hurt me.' She looked up. 'He wants to take me to his church social – may I go?'

'Yes, Kathy, you may court your young man – but please do not let me down.'

'I promise I won't,' Kathy said. 'If we want to marry one day, we'll do things properly.'

'That is all I ask,' her mother said, 'and now we'd best have our supper. It's just as well I only prepared cold ham and potato salad – anything else would have spoiled before now.'

Kathy nodded and hurried to set the table. She could hardly believe what had happened that evening – Bert's heroic rescue, her mother's reaction and the subsequent revelation. It meant that everything she'd ever believed was turned on its head. Until now she'd believed her father had died of his war wounds, but now she knew he'd walked out on her mother, leaving her to bring up Kathy alone. It explained the bitterness and the sharp tongue, the demands to come straight home and not talk to strange men. She wished her mother had told her – and yet understood why she had not.

Kathy felt as if a load had lifted from her shoulders. The bitter virago she'd tiptoed round for years had suddenly become someone she could talk to and it made her happy. She was looking forward to going out more with Bert, but even better was the knowledge that she could tell Mum about it when she got home.

CHAPTER 45

'You look happy this evening,' Sarah said as she met Kathy who was just about to leave work two weeks after the incident near her home.

'I am,' Kathy told her. 'Bert is taking me to the church social this evening and my mum has invited him for tea again this Sunday. She likes him!'

'I'm not surprised,' Sarah said. 'Everyone likes Bert. He is always so thoughtful and hard working. Enjoy yourself, Kathy. I'm on nights again this week, but my friend is taking me to a dance next week. We went to one a couple of weeks ago. That was a police benefit but we're going to the Palais this time. Steve is a really good dancer.'

'I've never been to a dance,' Kathy said, 'but Bert says we will at Christmas. It's put on by his church and it's a family thing so Mum will be coming too.'

'Well, that's nice,' Sarah said. 'I need to get on – have a good evening.'

Sarah went upstairs. Kathy had seemed such a quiet little thing when she first came to the infirmary but her friendship with Bert was bringing her out of her shell.

She'd talked of Christmas and Sarah realized that it wasn't so far away now. November was just beginning and it was cold; she thought about Steve walking the beat. He'd told her he didn't feel the cold when he was on duty but she thought he must, even though he wore a warm coat over his uniform. His feet and ears would get chilly, even if his back was warm.

She went up to the children's ward. Nurse Jenny was just finishing her rounds before leaving for the night and she took temperatures and wrote them on her chart. Sarah took the time to read the day nurse's report. They had two new arrivals and three children had gone home that day – always a cause for celebration.

'How are the new patients?' she asked as Jenny approached.

'Cyril has a cracked bone in his ankle and Jonny is recovering from a severe bout of influenza. His doctor was worried about his chest and that's why he asked Matron to take him in for a while because he is subject to bronchitis in the winter. You will need to keep an eye on him, make sure he isn't coughing too much.'

'I suppose Jonny is over the infectious stage?'

'Yes, certainly. He should be up and running around again but he feels poorly.'

'I'll watch him,' Sarah promised and smiled. 'I expect you're tired?'

'Yes, a little. Chris is going to drive me home this evening. We'll have a special supper with Lily and Gran, and then I'll get some sleep. He is taking me out this weekend. I'm off early on Saturday.'

'You get off, then.'

Sarah made her round, as she always did when first

on duty. The two new patients were the only ones still awake. She checked their temperature again just to be sure but neither were abnormal.

'Would you like some cocoa?'

Both children said yes and she left the ward to make the milky drink in the small kitchen. Cyril drank all his and then settled down, his eyes closing. Jonny sipped his slowly and then closed his eyes but she knew he was not yet asleep.

Hearing a noise behind her, Sarah turned to investigate and discovered that Matron had just brought in two young children, a girl of about eleven and a boy of perhaps six. They had clearly been washed and were wearing clothes given to the infirmary by well-wishers.

'This is Millie and Sam,' Matron told her. 'Their mother is very ill and they have been coping on their own for a week. They haven't lived on the streets but Millie did not have any food in the house so she had to beg.'

'I wasn't begging,' Millie said giving the nurse a reproachful look. 'I asked nicely if I could clean the man's shop windows for two sticky buns. Sam was 'ungry.'

'Well, we shall look after you now until your mother gets better.'

'I'm 'ungry,' the little boy wailed. 'My tummy aches!'

'Will you look after them now, nurse?' Matron asked.

'Yes, of course, Matron,' Sarah said and smiled. Then, 'Oh, I wondered how Nurse Anne was getting on . . .'

A smile touched Matron's lips. 'Nurse Anne has taken her exams and will be returning to us in the New Year. We shall be very pleased to have her back with us.'

'Yes, of course,' Sarah said and smiled. 'Come along, Millie, and you too, Sam. We've got a nice little room for you all on your own. When I've got you tucked up in bed, I'll fetch you a chicken paste sandwich, a rock bun, an apple and a cup of cocoa – how will that do?'

'That will be really nice,' Millie said. 'Thank you. My mum is in your sick ward for ladies – will we be able to visit her?'

'When she is a little better,' Sarah said. 'Come on, the sooner you are in bed, the sooner you can have your supper . . .'

Sarah soon had the new children tucked up in the beds Charlie and Maisie had slept in just a few months back. She missed seeing them, even though she knew that they were happy with their auntie. Maisie had written her a few words on the end of Aunt Jeanie's letter to say they were settling in well.

Before they'd all left to catch their train, it had been arranged that Charlie would finish his schooling and then, if he still wished, return to London to take up the apprenticeship he'd been promised. Charlie himself had written to Sarah's mother, a surprisingly neat hand, full of the rooms he and Maisie had and how much he liked his new school. He was a bright lad and she thought he would do well.

'I'll pop in and see your mum in the morning,' she told the new children. 'What is her name, Millie?'

'Mrs Phyllis Green,' the girl told her. 'She was proper bad when the doctor said she had to go into hospital and me dad is in the Navy. He's at sea fer months but he should be home by Christmas.'

Sarah nodded and left them to settle while she went

380

to fetch their supper from the kitchen at the end of the ward. It was only equipped to make sandwiches and drinks and the children would get their first proper meal when the canteen kitchen opened in the morning.

She returned with the supper tray and left the pair to get on with it. When she returned to look at Jonny, he had finally fallen asleep. Thankfully, it looked like being a quiet night . . .

CHAPTER 46

'So, you don't think your new children will need fostering?' Lady Rosalie asked when she telephoned Mary that evening.

'I believe their mother will recover. In this case it is just a couple of weeks before they should be able to go home – and they do have a father who'll be home by Christmas.'

'Oh, that is good,' Lady Rosalie sounded pleased. 'Although I do have two new prospective foster mothers in mind should anything happen. I have vetted them myself and we just have the formalities to consider but then they will be ready – and both are from the East End and live not far from you.'

'That is wonderful.' Mary nodded her satisfaction. 'If your list continues to grow it will be a big help – though I fear there will always be more children in need than good foster parents.'

'Unfortunately so,' Lady Rosalie agreed. 'Well, I must go. I have some influential friends coming to dinner this evening, and I am hoping for some contributions to the fund. I might even get you that new wing for the Rosie you would like!'

Mary smiled as her friend replaced the receiver. Lady Rosalie was a force to be reckoned with and if anyone could make something happen it was her.

The Matron of the Rosie smiled as she prepared to make her evening rounds. Charlie and Maisie were happily settled and that was a blessing, but as fast as one set of orphans was settled, there was another waiting for a home. Not all of them were orphans, of course. Some were street kids, children whose parents had either neglected them so much that they ran away or, in severe cases, simply abandoned them. As a woman who loved children, Mary could never understand how any mother could do such a thing, but they did. Cases of abuse and neglect happened all the time and it was up to her staff to tell her and then she stepped in. Sometimes it was not possible to rescue the child the first time they were abused, but parents who habitually harmed their little ones would be noted and eventually the children would be placed in care.

Long ago Mary had accepted that she couldn't help every woman or man found on the streets, half-starving and often covered in sores. She couldn't make society fairer or eradicate poverty but she could help the elderly sometimes and a few children now and then, and with Lady Rosalie's help, that number would rise. Now they had an established list of foster carers and, as it grew, they would be able to pass the children on to a good home sooner.

A smile touched her lips. Once she'd hoped to marry and have her own children but the war had put paid to that and she'd turned her grief for John into a burning dedication to help those in need, knowing that she would never love again. It was a good life, especially when things went well . . .

CHAPTER 47

Sarah was about to leave the infirmary the next morning when Sister Ruth Linton caught her on her way downstairs.

'Nurse! Can you spare me a moment, please?'

'Yes, of course, Sister – what can I do for you?'

'I have a patient in the chronically sick ward. He has a nasty bout of influenza and with his history we do not expect him to live long.'

'A man?' Sarah was puzzled. 'What do you need for him?'

'He is asking for you – says he wants to see you before he . . .'

Sarah felt a sinking sensation inside. 'You mean Woody, don't you – Woody Jacobs?'

'Yes. He is quite desperate to see you, nurse.'

'Of course, I will come.' Sarah had already visited Millie's mother in her free time and told the children their mother was slowly getting better, but she couldn't refuse a request from Woody. He must be really sick this time if he was in the chronically sick ward.

It was called the chronically sick ward but was actually

a series of rooms with thin, movable partitions that made it possible to isolate infectious cases and influenza was one of those most commonly seen in winter.

Sarah hurried to the main ward and then looked along the partitions until she saw him through the glass window. He was lying with his eyes closed and looked so ill that her heart caught. He was a very sick man and she thought the nurse had been right. Woody was unlikely to live much longer. He'd waited as long as he could before coming in because he did not want to go for the tests that would determine whether or not he had TB.

Sarah stood next to his bed for a moment, looking at him and feeling sad. What a lonely life he must have had. As though he sensed her presence, he opened his eyes and smiled at her.

'You came,' he croaked. 'You're a lovely lass, Nurse Sarah. If I'd been a young man, I'd have given the young 'uns a run for their money . . .'

'I expect you had lots of girls when you were young, Woody?' she teased.

'Only the one. She died – the babe inside her died too – and after that I didn't care . . .' His smile was sad and yet content.

Sarah reached for his hand and held it; her throat tight with compassion. 'You must have loved her very much.'

'I did . . .' A smile touched his mouth. 'There was only my Sarah for me – and I was the only one for her.'

'Her name was Sarah?'

'Like yours – and she was lovely, just like you. That's why I know she would want you to have this . . .'

Woody took something from under the bedcovers and handed it to her. It was a small and rather grubby box. Sarah hesitated, because as a rule they refused gifts from patients. 'Please, take it. I could never have sold it and she would have been pleased for you to have it.'

Sarah took the box and opened it. Inside was a beautiful heavy gold cross on an exquisite chain. It must have cost a lot of money when bought and she knew in that moment that Woody had once been a successful man. He'd lost his wife and whatever he worked for was abandoned, because for him life was empty without those he loved – but he'd kept the necklace to remind him of his Sarah.

'It is beautiful,' she said. 'I shall always treasure it.'

'I hope you'll wear it sometimes in memory of me and my Sarah . . .'

'Yes, I shall,' she said. 'I promise you; I love it.' Her eyes stung with tears.

Woody smiled and closed his eyes. Sarah knew he was sleeping but she doubted that he would wake again. He'd held on for her.

'You should go home now, nurse,' Matron said. 'You can leave him to us. He knew to come back to us when it was time . . .'

'Yes, he did . . .' Sarah felt the tears rolling down her cheeks as she walked away. It was always sad to lose a patient, but Woody had been special to her. She'd wondered about his story and now she understood the only bits of it that mattered. He hadn't always been alone; he'd known love and happiness and he'd kept his memories right to the end.

Steve was waiting for her outside the hospital. She

saw him standing there and she ran to him, the tears still flowing.

'Sarah, my love,' he said and put his arms about her. 'What's wrong?'

'It was a patient I liked . . . he's dying . . .' Sarah rested her head against his broad shoulder. It felt so good and she knew it was where she wanted to be for the rest of her life – in his arms. 'He gave me something – a lovely necklace that had belonged to his wife before she died . . . he'd been on the road for years and his name was Woody.'

'Sarah,' Steve said gently and bent his head to kiss her softly on the mouth. 'I love you so much . . .' He looked down into her eyes. 'I know Woody well. I've moved him on and given him a bob for a cup of tea for years. Most avoided him in fear of his tongue which could cut like a knife. Only you would look at him and see the man inside that scruffy exterior . . .'

Sarah laughed, her sadness leaving her as she looked up at the man she now knew she loved. 'I love you, Steve,' she said. 'Have you got time to come home with me for a cup of tea?'

'Your mum promised me breakfast,' Steve told her with a twinkle in his eye. 'She said if I wanted a hot breakfast after a cold night on the beat, I was to come home. I'm going to take her up on it!'

'Yes,' Sarah said and took his large hand in her own, comforted by the strength of his fingers as they curled about hers. In her heart she knew that this time, she wouldn't be let down. 'Let's go home to Mum . . .'

You can also find out more about Cathy Sharp at www.lindasole.co.uk and you can read on below to find out what inspires her . . .

You've had a long career as a writer, how did it start?
As a child, I was always making up stories in my head about a princess in a castle being rescued by a prince who would carry her off and look after her. A bit of a loner, I wanted the enchantment of being truly loved so I made up my own stories. When I was older and started to put down some of the stories in my head, my first attempts were awful. It took years of trying, rewriting and learning from my mistakes before I had something published, and even then, it was romance rather than the stronger fiction I write now. So I would say writing comes through experience.

What stories inspired you when you were starting out?
I used to read Ethel M Dell and several others of her era, and then I read Mills & Boon Historical stories, and it was these Historical books that made me want to write and brought my first success. I had more than seventy books published with Harlequin Mills & Boon before my sagas really caught fire.

Have you done a lot of research and if so, what is the most surprising thing you have discovered?
I research only what I need to for any particular book, because, if I do masses of it, when I write the book it all comes out like a history lesson and I can lecture my readers

for pages. That isn't what fiction is about. The story and passion behind the idea makes it appeal to readers, and, in my opinion, the research should be woven into the book so lightly that you hardly realise it is there. It's always best if it comes over as news or a conversation, or a thought, I don't enjoy books when someone tries to teach me something or moralises at me so I don't expect my readers to stand for that either.

I think the thing that surprises me most about researching the past is the terrible suffering of people before our modern age. Today, we complain about poverty and sickness, but, at least in Britain, we really don't suffer in the way they did a century or more ago, when so many people went hungry day after day and died of things that the doctors can cure today. Living standards were appalling in the majority of workers' homes. Often, they didn't live to be much more than forty, and in some earlier centuries twenty-nine was a good age, and so many children died in their early years. Our standards are much higher and we don't expect a child to suffer hunger these days, though there are unfortunately still cases where they suffer both hunger and abuse, and we all condemn and hate it when we hear of it.

What does your typical writing day look like?
I get up, have breakfast and have my bath, and then I just sit down in my study in an armchair and write on the laptop until lunchtime. I seldom do much writing in the afternoon, except to read through a few pages. I used to write all day but that is too much for me these days. I work straight on to the computer and I always revise a few pages of the previous day's writing before I start new work. It reminds me of what I was thinking when I left off, always reluctantly – but we have to eat!

Where do you find inspiration for your characters? Are any of them based on real people?

None of my characters is a real person, but little bits of them are. I will notice habits that amuse me and put them into a character, and I remember things people have said that impress me and I use a form of their opinions when making a character come to life. I find that characters mature and grow as I write the book, and I always go back to the start and change the first chapters as my people evolve and I understand that they just would not have said or done something I made them do before I knew them – and in the case of the hero – fell in love with him.

What hobbies do you have in your spare time?

What spare time? :) I read a little in bed and I watch TV in the evenings, but I find there is almost always too much to do in a day.

When on holiday in Spain I enjoy walking on the sea front, swimming and just lying in the sun. I love eating out there – and here – when I find somewhere nice, but apart from holidays there isn't time for many hobbies.

What would be your 'Desert Island' book?

Can I have my kindle instead please? I could take so many more books with me. Of course, it would need to be powered by the sun, but surely they can invent one of those? I've just read all ten of the *Last Kingdom* books by Bernard Cornwell in one go – couldn't put them down. I've read so many lovely books how could I choose one? I suppose, if a gun was put to my head, it would have to be *Gone With the Wind*. It would take me ages to read and I do love it, but then I rather like *War and Peace* and . . . No good, I refuse to be marooned without my kindle – powered by the sun!

Read more about Cathy Sharp's orphans whose compelling stories will tug at your heartstrings.

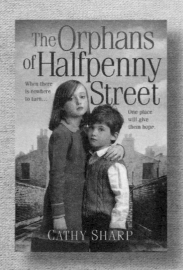

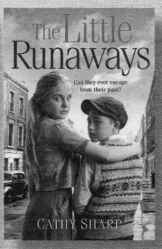

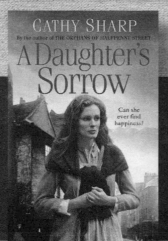

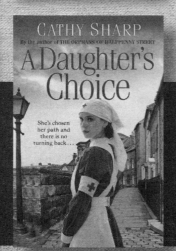

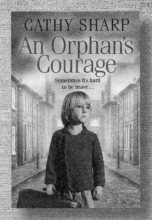

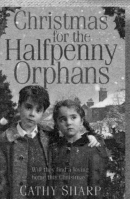
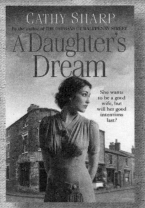
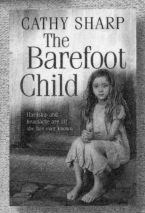